HEX
LIFE

HEX LIFE

WICKED NEW TALES OF WITCHERY

EDITED BY **CHRISTOPHER GOLDEN**
AND **RACHEL AUTUMN DEERING**

TITAN BOOKS

Hex Life

Paperback edition ISBN: 9781789090369
Electronic edition ISBN: 9781789090352

Published by Titan Books
A division of Titan Publishing Group Ltd
144 Southwark Street, London SE1 0UP
www.titanbooks.com

First paperback edition: October 2020
2 4 6 8 10 9 7 5 3 1

This is a work of fiction. Names, places and incidents are either products of the author's imagination or used fictitiously. Any resemblance to actual persons, living or dead (except for satirical purposes), is entirely coincidental.

No part o̶f̶ ̶t̶h̶i̶s̶ ̶p̶u̶b̶l̶i̶c̶a̶t̶i̶o̶n̶ ̶m̶a̶y̶ ̶b̶e̶ ̶r̶e̶p̶r̶o̶d̶u̶c̶e̶d̶,̶ ̶s̶t̶o̶r̶e̶d̶ ̶i̶n̶ ̶a̶ ̶r̶e̶t̶r̶i̶e̶v̶a̶l̶ system, or transmitted̶ ̶ ̶ ̶ ̶ ̶ ̶ ̶ ̶ ̶ ̶ ̶ ̶ ̶ ̶ ̶ ̶t̶h̶e̶ ̶p̶r̶i̶o̶r̶ ̶w̶r̶i̶t̶t̶e̶n̶ ̶ permission of the pu̶ ̶ ̶ ̶ ̶ ̶n̶o̶r̶ ̶b̶e̶ ̶o̶t̶h̶e̶r̶w̶i̶s̶e̶ ̶ ̶ ̶ ̶ ̶f̶o̶r̶m̶ ̶o̶f̶ ̶b̶i̶n̶d̶i̶n̶ or cover other than̶ ̶ ̶ ̶ ̶ ̶ ̶ ̶ ̶ ̶ ̶ ̶ ̶ ̶s̶i̶m̶i̶l̶a̶r̶ ̶ ̶ ̶ ̶ ̶ ̶ion being i̶m̶p̶o̶s̶e̶d̶ ̶o̶n̶ ̶ ̶ ̶ ̶ ̶ ̶ ̶ ̶ ̶p̶u̶r̶c̶h̶a̶s̶e̶r̶

A CIP ̶a̶v̶a̶i̶l̶a̶b̶l̶e̶ ̶f̶r̶o̶m̶ ̶t̶h̶e̶ ̶B̶r̶i̶t̶i̶s̶h̶ library.

TABLE OF CONTENTS

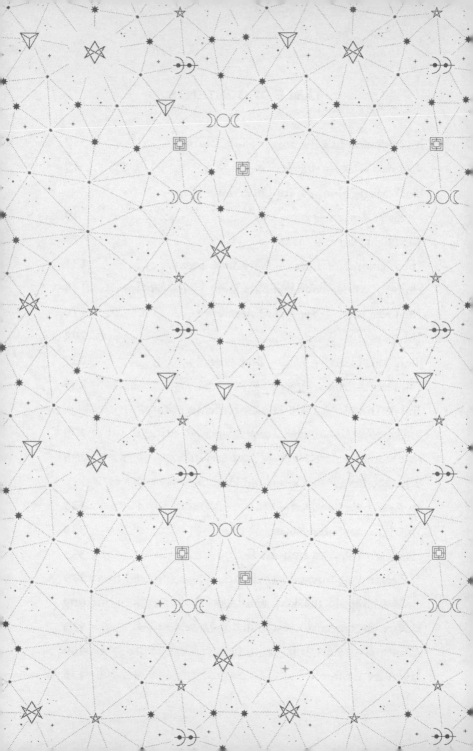

AN INVITATION TO A BURNING
Kat Howard

Merrinvale was a town that needed witches. Most places do—witches, after all, are the ones who make sure the small and large magics work. Things like the rising of bread and the turning of the seasons and safe passage through birth and death, all the work of witches. Some places accept this, and so they welcome their witches the same as they welcome any others and life moves in harmony.

Merrinvale was not one such place.

Merrinvale burned its witches, when it found them.

Most people, if asked, would swear that a witch burning hadn't happened in years, if it ever had at all; that it was only a story told to frighten people into proper behavior. But when the fog came in, evening thick, it smelled of burning wood and worse things besides. The Merrinvale hills echoed with screams. And they called the fog the Witches' Breath.

The fact that Merrinvale did not want its witches, much less accept them, did nothing to change the need of the place for them. And there were, as there always are, those who made sure the necessary things were done. But magic, when ignored, when forbidden, twists upon itself and becomes strange. Witches, when forbidden, seek this strangeness, and wrap themselves in its transformations.

"They burn witches, you know." Ronald spat at the ground near where Sage sat.

"So I've heard," she said, not looking up from the rabbit she was untangling from a poorly cast trap of knotted twine. Her hands did not shake as she did so, and her face didn't tense in fear, and Sage was proud of both things. Ronald was large, and Ronald was always angry, and Sage was not the first woman he had taken against. At least one of the others, Lilah, quiet and lovely, had disappeared, never to be seen again. "It's a good thing I'm not one, then."

"You could be," Ronald said. "And if you did burn, that's what everyone would think. Just another witch, gone and good riddance."

Sage lifted her hands from the ground, and watched as the rabbit, now free, hopped away and out of sight. She curved her fingers into claws. "And if I were a witch, and here you were alone with me, with no matches in sight, what do you think would happen then?"

Ronald spat again, his eyes pinched and mean. But he said nothing else and he stepped back, away from the path where Sage walked.

She kept her back straight and her head up, but the taste of fear, bile and slime, coated her mouth.

Sage found the note on her front porch. Black letters on a thick white card—one she nearly didn't see, as a pile of maple leaves, rust-edged red, had heaped itself against her door overnight. But the corner of the paper showed through, and she set the information written on it to memory.

It was an invitation to a burning.

Sage arrived at the indicated address at precisely the correct time. She couldn't remember ever seeing the house before, which would not have been strange had she not lived in Merrinvale her entire life. Even now, the place looked abandoned, the windows all dark. Her hand went to her pocket, to remind herself that she had brought what was required.

The door whispered open. Sage stepped inside.

The cool violet air of the evening followed her into the house. Inside, the house no longer looked decrepit and empty. Soft candles lit floors of elegantly worn wood. The air smelled of the warm sweetness of beeswax and the sharp green of herbs. And something else, underneath. Something that flared her nostrils and raced her heart.

Smoke.

Nothing stopped her, and so Sage walked farther in.

At the first branch of the hall, a woman draped in veils sat on a stormcloud-grey velvet chair. She held her hands out, gloved palms up, and Sage set hers on top of them. The acrid scent of eucalyptus sliced through the warmth of the air, and Sage gasped, yanking her hands up and away.

The woman in the chair did not speak or move. Sage squared her shoulders, and set her hands upon the woman's again. The hands beneath hers were cold, the deep cold of iron in winter, and her joints ached from the contact. The ache passed into burning. The woman tightened her hands around Sage's and pulled her down, so close her veils whispered against Sage's skin.

"Remember what it is the fire burns. Remember why you've come. Remember what it is to have power."

Her voice was familiar. Not so much that Sage could put a name to it, but enough to know they had said their hellos in passing on the sidewalk, or while picking groceries. It could have been a shock, but it was instead a comfort: here was another, like her, quiet and unseen and powerful all the same.

The other woman let go of Sage's hands, and raised a gloved finger to her lips, silencing any questions. Sage waited a moment, but the woman was so still it was as if she stood next to a statue. Sage continued on.

The house twisted and turned on itself, a labyrinth lined with bookshelves. Sage walked through narrow hallways, warm golden wood sighing under her feet. Through rooms with furniture shrouded in dust cloths, past the sob of an unseen violin. The veiled woman's words beat along with her pulse: Remember, remember, remember.

As she walked, she saw no one. She heard nothing. It was as if she were the only soul in the house.

Then Sage turned a corner, and the hall opened up before her. Kept opening, really—it looked like a ballroom, where the back wall had been removed to let the night and the forest in.

And she was no longer alone.

In the ballroom were women Sage had seen her whole life, those she had waved to and passed by and traded bowls of soup and baskets of cookies with. Women who taught children and ran businesses and made art. They looked different than they did in their everyday lives. Both wilder and more natural, somehow. Flowers bloomed in their hair, and vines twined their arms. A belt of bones chained a waist. As strange as they would have appeared on the streets of Merrinvale, here they looked like they belonged.

Shadows thickened like piled velvet in the room's corners. A spiraling pattern had been drawn in salt on the floor, incomplete sections open like the entrance to a labyrinth. Slowly, the other women in the room made their way toward the center. In singles and in groups, they barricaded themselves inside the boundary of the salt. They sat delicately, skirts pooling about them like puddles. They slumped to the ground as if they were wilting flowers. They tucked their legs to the side, leaned shoulder to shoulder, held hands. Connected.

Sage felt something inside herself pull as they did, a thread that wound her into their pattern, and so she sat, too.

Flames danced, salamander red, on the edges of her peripheral vision, and the smell of the fire grew stronger. But here, in this room, there was no terror in the scent, in the heat and crackle of the flames.

The air snapped, electric, then settled again. The salt

patterns complete, creating a barrier between the women gathered and the world without.

The firelight flickered, shuddered, blinked, and when it settled, a woman with antlers spiking from her head stood in the center of the room. The antlers did not look like a hat—they looked like they had grown, curling up from her skull.

She was shrouded all in tattered tea-colored lace, from her antlers to her feet. Even her face was obscured. A shiver fluttered at the base of Sage's spine, and traveled along the branches of her nerves. The hair on her arms stood up.

"You have come here," the antlered woman said, "to burn your past. To scorch from yourself that which you would leave in the ashes. To cast off your old skins and make yourself new. To claim your power, if you are able.

"Bring what you would burn."

The same words that had been written on the card inviting her here. Sage reached into her pocket. She had hesitated while making it, this small doll that was a copy of herself. She had thought that it might be easier to burn a doll that looked like Ronald, and watch all his hate rise up in smoke. Or an image of Merrinvale, to burn it before it could burn her. And so she took those impulses, the things she disliked in her own self, her fear and panic, and she sewed them into the doll, that the fire would not destroy her, but would clarify her instead.

Salt in the air surrounded the women in the circle like weeping, sticky on skin. The deer woman strode among them, regal. She stopped and brushed a hand over a head, bent to offer a word, a nod. To examine the offerings of those who had come to be witches. She paused before Sage, and the air smelled of the forest, secret and wild. In the woman's eyes behind her veils, Sage saw only reflected flames. The woman bent her head, an acknowledgement of Sage's offering, a blessing upon it.

With each interaction, color crept up the hem of her dress, shadows soaking into the fabric, darkening it. Magic shimmered like heat in the air around her. Sage felt that magic, too. Felt it shake the air and quicken her blood. She felt part of herself reach toward it.

The fire was brighter, the air sticky hot. The deer woman stood in their center, her dress red now, red darker than black, and wet, as if it bled.

"And now, the fire."

Not every woman there was a new witch. Some had already claimed their power, and were there simply in support and community. The new among them brought their offerings to the fire, a private magic between the witch and her gift. Sage felt the flames like a warmth in her core as she tossed in her doll, felt them spark through her body. She felt an unraveling in herself, a calmness, as that which she had given up burned away. Margaretha, who ran the bakery in the center of downtown, held her hands out to Sage: "Welcome."

When they had finished, when the fire had chosen the new witches and they had accepted its gift, the antlered woman brought a bowl into the center of the circle, carrying it like a blessing. Thick and heavy-looking, a pattern carved into tarnished bronze, full of wine, darker than the night. "Now," she said, "we drink."

What they drank didn't taste like wine. Cold and deep, like iced plums, but also the bright sweetness of summer's first strawberries. The warm burn of whiskey in the lone hours of the night, the taste of flame. Sage's head spun.

The room shifted. Sage could feel her heart beat in time with the other women's, see the breath that moved in and out of their lungs. She could live their memories. Here, now, the fire that the fearful would use to take their lives bringing them their power.

The flames stretched into the night, casting their shadows onto the walls, bending and twisting them until the women looked snake-haired, until they were horned and winged. And then it faded, dying down, making their shadows recognizable again. Until they looked like themselves. Until they looked like witches.

The dawn light replaced the fire's light, and the women, witches old and new, looked no different from other women that lived in Merrinvale. The house shed its glamour to appear abandoned and forgotten, and ritual returned to ordinary.

Remember, remember, remember Sage's heart beat, and she did as she walked slowly home. The feeling of connection, of power, of belonging.

And then the feeling of twine, tightening around her feet and ankles, tangling her, as if she were a rabbit.

"Witch." Ronald's voice ugly with certainty.

Light flared from a torch held in his hand and the heat of flame crackled, and Sage stood in perfect stillness. "And if I am?"

"Witches are for burning." The fire thrust closer.

Sage reached inside herself. She remembered the feeling of her fear burning away, the connection with the other women, the witches, their welcome. She remembered her power.

"Are we?"

Fog rose from the ground. Witches' breath. The twine untied itself from where it had bound her, and slithered away, snaking into the quiet darkness of the forest.

"Witch! Stop that!" Ronald shoved his torch at her, the flames licking at her hems, at her hands, at her hair.

None caught.

But fog, choking thick, surrounded the edges of Ronald's clothing, his hands, his hair. The more he forced the fire on her, the thicker the fog grew, until the fire was gone and the fog seemed nearly a solid thing.

Sage sighed out a breath. The fog rolled away, and Sage stood alone.

Merrinvale was a place that needed witches. Most places are, even if the people who live in them don't realize it. And even when hidden in secret, witches still hold power.

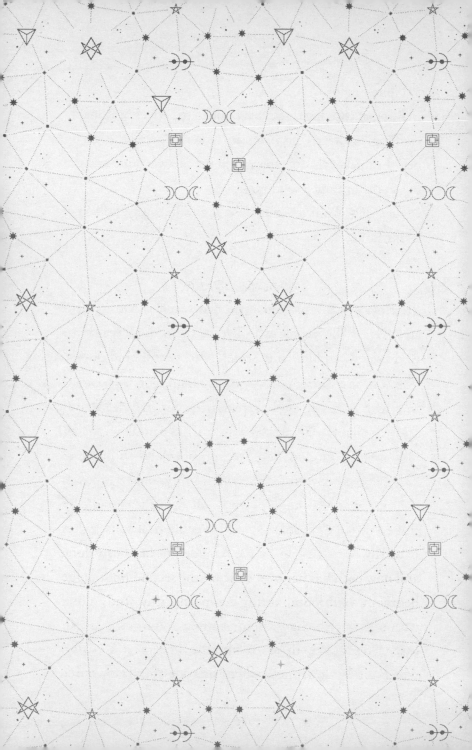

WIDOWS' WALK

Angela Slatter

The house on Carter Lane—Second Empire style, mansard roof with dormers, a tower, patterned shingles, deep eaves and elaborately pedimented windows, all painted in shades of white, cappuccino, and deepest chocolate—is home to four widows between the ages of fifty-nine and eighty-two.

Once only Martha lived there but the others gradually shifted into it as husbands shuffled off mortal coils, either naturally or otherwise. Some remodeling has been done and now each has her own suite on the second floor: large bedroom, bathroom, sitting room and tiny study nook with a desk and chair; there's a guest room, too, just in case. Downstairs, there's a kitchen, library and parlor, where the Widows meet when they've a mind, for meals and discussions of various matters. Every morning the first to rise—invariably Sarah, the oldest, whose bladder won't let her rest past five—taps on the others' doors to make sure no one's died in the dark watches.

Rumor in Mercy's Brook says that this task might well be performed by any of the three cats (only one of which is black) that've taken up residence with the old women, for as all know, both felines and aged females are equally suspect. Although anyone who knows anything about cats also knows they are ultimately self-interested and won't trouble themselves to check on anyone's health unless it's likely to affect their own feeding.

Despite the fact they're far from the coast, there's a widow's walk on the roof—which gives the house its unofficial name—but only Eugenie is inclined to use it. The youngest, she's surest on her feet and she goes up there to smoke, sometimes blue-fumed cheroots, sometimes something sweeter to dull the pain of her arthritic fingers. Virginia prefers to sit inside the tower room and stare out the windows on the days when her inclinations lean that way, overlooking the garden, watching it grow, watching the foxes that visit. Sarah spends her time in the library, mostly, reading and writing down the things she doesn't want lost to the world when she dies. Martha's favorite spot is the garden, actually being in it, digging and planting, growing and cultivating things for use in the kitchen and her apothecary experiments.

They rub along, the Widows, rather better than might be expected given their differing personalities and interests, and Eugenie's tendency to swear mightily at the drop of a hat, which often offends Martha's delicate sensibilities. She's grown adept at pursing her mouth to communicate disapproval, which inevitably brings "Don't you give me fucking lips of string, Martha Foster!" shouted so loudly it can be heard from the street. Yet they'll all admit quite freely that living with each other requires less effort than living with their husbands ever did, and when matters boil over, as they occasionally must, things simply settle back into a comfortable rhythm with no residual resentment or bitterness.

They're all born and bred in Mercy's Brook, the Widows, which isn't such a bad place, and no one actively points fingers and calls "Witch!" when they see the old women doing their groceries or taking tea at Abigail Hobbes' bookstore and café (although those of German extraction occasionally whisper *hexen* behind their cupped palms). No children throw stones at the pristine windows that Martha pays a local lad to clean fortnightly, nor do they run up to ring the bell and bolt away; then again, that might have something to do with a fear that the black-painted gate might somehow lock itself at an inopportune moment. But Virginia has noticed with a certain glee that folk do sometimes cross the road when they walk past; Martha says it's so they can see the glory of the house better, not because they're afraid. Sarah and Eugenie don't bother to contradict her, though they roll their eyes something fierce.

It's early, this morning, just gone half-past five, and the light is barely scraping the sky. The temperature is beginning to dip and soon the leaves will be on the turn from green to orange-flame, as if the trees are burning themselves to stay warm. All the Widows are awake, three in the kitchen: two gathered around the coffee pot, one slicing the bread that's fresh out of the bread-maker. No lights are on, though, not today. Virginia's still upstairs, in the unlit tower room, which is empty but for the armchair she likes, a footstool and a small polished wooden side table where she can rest her teacup in the afternoon.

When she calls, they can hear her voice quite clearly for it carries unnaturally well along the hallway and down the stairs. The place has always had good acoustics, Martha's said before with a shrug.

"Girl's out there again."

Eugenie, Martha and Sarah share a knowing glance and grin. Eugenie takes a sip of her coffee then sets the mug on the counter. She opens the door to the root cellar, making sure to flick on the powerful lights that illuminate the subterranean room like a ship at sea—oh, one of the others will turn it off as soon as she's in place. Then her slipper-clad feet take the path downward.

Chelsea Margaret Bloom, mindful of the warnings she's heard about exits that snap shut at inopportune moments, has propped her bicycle in the gap between gate and fence. It's still quite dark, and although she's done this very same thing five days in a row without consequence, she's not entirely confident.

The streetlight outside Widows' Walk never works, for the Widows find it annoying, and no number of repairmen from the local power company have managed to fix it for any great length of time. Eventually, the neighbors gave up reporting it. The Widows, strong believers in positive reinforcement, sent everyone in Carter Lane boxes of homemade cookies; some were eaten and declared wondrous and almost as good as those served in Abigail Hobbes' café (in fact, they were identical, the Widows being Abi's supplier), but others were sent straight to the bin, for some will always believe that no good gift comes from the hands of witches.

So, Chelsea's at least reassured by the remaining darkness, by the fact she knows she only requires a few moments to do what she needs to, and so is perhaps a little less attentive than she's been on previous occasions. She doesn't notice that the bushes of sneezeweed with their flowers of orange and yellow have been pruned back somewhat, that the tiny basement window level with the garden bed is ajar, or that a shadow moves behind its glass. It's still quite gloomy, after all, and she's paying more attention to the bigger windows for some gleam that will show her the Widows are awake.

There's nothing.

Chelsea does what she's done the better part of the last week: takes a deep breath and begins to tiptoe along the cobbled path in her worn sneakers, and tries not to think about how hungry she is, hopes that her stomach won't betray her by growling (Honestly, how loud could it be?). She tries not to think about the tales they tell at school of boys who've set out to explore Widows' Walk and disappeared, only to be found a few days later, wandering in the woods, with no memory of where they've been— although no one can ever give the names of those boys, and it's not as if Sheriff Taylor has ever been reported as looking for them. Or the stories of the girls who've gone to live in that house and come out changed, moving away from Mercy's Brook afterward, or staying. Chelsea shakes her head, eyes her prize.

Two milk bottles on the top step: full cream with silver-blue caps on top. The milkman has already been, left the daily order. Chelsea only takes one, just one, she's not greedy. Heck, she'd only take half if she could, but it seems kind of rude to leave a half-empty bottle of milk... it's not like folk are going to drink the leftovers, right? Who knows what might have been done to it?

Besides, it tides her over, that whole bottle, so she's only a little hungry by the end of the day, and when she gets home... well, generally, her mother has roused herself to get some groceries, make pancakes, or to bring something home from the café where she gets a few shifts a week because Miz Hobbes is kind. But lately Ellie's been more distracted than usual...

Chelsea creeps closer; hard to believe that this is the easiest house to steal from, but there you go: it's on her route to school, the neighbors aren't too near, and Chelsea's got an idea in her head that old folks sleep more than they actually do. She thinks, for a second, she hears something: a scrape, a creak, a crack, and she freezes. But though she freezes forever—or maybe only fifteen seconds—nothing else stirs. She hears a crow caw, and decides that must have been it, a fat crow on a branch too thin. Chelsea keeps going; she makes it to the top of the path, does what she always does, which is not go up the stairs, lest she be too visible from the glass-paneled doors, but rather step to the side, half-in-half-out of the garden, the sneezeweed brushing her scrawny legs. She shuffles so her stance is solid, then leans forward, and her stick-fingers are reaching for the nearest bottle, slowly, slowly…

…when a hand grabs her ankle, and she almost pees herself.

She certainly lets out a god-awful shriek that conjures a laugh, only a little malicious, from the cellar window, and activity at the front entrance, where two old women swarm down to her, embroidered dressing gowns flapping like cloaks, like wings. When it's sure she's in the crones' custody, the hand around her ankle lets go, the laughter gets softer as its owner moves away from the window, and Chelsea is bodily lifted up the stairs and into the house, astonished, in the beats between her fear, at how strong the Widows are.

"She's too young for coffee, really." Martha fusses with more slices of toast.

"Well, hot chocolate will send her to sleep, then how will the girl fuc– function at school?" Eugenie seems to be mindful of keeping her language under control, given their company.

"You could give her tea?" ventures Virginia. She's quelled by the looks of the other Widows.

"I like coffee just fine," says Chelsea in a small voice. These are certainly the most peculiar witches... unless this is some sort of a Gingerbread House situation and they're trying to fatten her up. She doesn't mind, the bread and jams are the best she's ever had. The first proper breakfast she's had in the longest time.

"Make it weak," says Martha, and when she turns her back Eugenie pours the blackest of brews and lightens it only a little with milk. Chelsea takes it with a grin, not sure she should be so happy.

"So," says Sarah, who has long silver plaits neatly intertwined with blue ribbons that match her eyes, "little thief."

"Little thief," Virginia repeats with a smile. Her hair is iron-grey, short and wavy, and her eyes an indeterminate mix of yellow and brown. "You know, they used to accuse witches of stealing milk straight from the cows, leaving them with empty udders. Did you know?"

Chelsea is silent, but her gaze goes wide.

"Bottles are more convenient," says Eugenie lightly. She's got more color left in her hair than the others, black but with many rivers of white, coarser, thicker than the rest, like serpents with minds of their own.

Martha, ash-blond, green-eyed, just butters more toast, adds lime marmalade without asking if the girl likes it. Chelsea, thievery notwithstanding, has good manners and eats it without complaint—plus, she's starving. Martha says, "Little thief, tell us your tale before we pass judgment."

"I…" Chelsea looks around, takes note of the three cats sitting on the sill of the kitchen window, all watching her attentively as if what she says next is of great importance. She's old enough to understand that her position is one of shame; not because of the theft so much as being a child whose parents cannot feed them adequately. The shame isn't hers, but she still feels it, suffers for it on her mother's behalf. She says lamely, "I leave home too early for breakfast."

And the faces of the Widows are all painted in varied shades of disappointment at the lie. Not much surprise, and a lot of understanding. But still, disappointment. Silence hangs for a long moment.

"Hungry thief, then." Sarah's gentle expression doesn't waver.

"Well, you need to make restitution," says Eugenie sharply. "We need help around the house, especially Martha in that damned garden."

"I'd be happy of a scribe," chimes Virginia. "I'm cataloguing the library."

"Sarah will be bottling jams and preserves soon enough," says Eugenie.

"What do you need me for?" ventures Chelsea.

"I've no need of help." Eugenie looks the girl up and down as if finding her of no use. It's not a mean glance, just frank.

"Then it's settled," Martha announces, and no one gainsays her. "Your penance will be to come here for breakfast before school every weekday. And after school, there will be chores."

"For how long?" asks Chelsea.

"Until your debt is worked off or you're no longer hungry."

The girl nods slowly, then looks at them in turn, as if reluctant to bring up a problem. "My mother…"

"Never fear, my dear, we'll talk to your mother—" Virginia raises a finger to forestall any objections— "but we'll not mention the small matter of dairy larceny."

"Thank you!" Chelsea smiles with relief. "My mother worries, she gets stressed…"

All the Widows hide their lips of string, hearts warmed that the girl is kind enough to defend her parent, but hardened that the child must lie to keep herself protected from the truth.

She looks apologetic now as she adds, "I do need to get to school. If I'm late…"

"Here." Martha hands her a paper bag. "A sandwich and some fruit. Don't throw anything away, Chelsea Margaret Bloom."

Virginia sees her to the door.

It's only when she gets down the stairs, retrieves her bike from the maw of the gate, that Chelsea realizes between her capture and her breakfast she hadn't ever given the Widows her name.

"The mother works at Abi Hobbes' place sometimes," Virginia says as all four of them cluster at the largest window in the parlor (where the Widows have been known to read fortunes for the townsfolk and whisper charms for the lovelorn), and watch Chelsea pedal off down the street toward Mercy's Brook High. Thin legs pump up and down, and flossy blond hair flies behind her like something woven of spider webs. The heel of one sneaker is flapping, her jeans have been washed fragile, and her red t-shirt's faded beneath a coat that's nowhere near warm enough.

"Pretty woman, terrible waitress," adds Eugenie. "Always gets the order wrong."

"Always?" Martha asks.

"Always. It's a talent, if you think about it," Eugenie says with a shrug. "Consistency is rare."

"That's surprisingly generous of you."

Sarah interrupts to cut off the inevitable bickering. "That girl needs new clothes for a start. The problem at home?"

"The boyfriend," says Virginia.

The Widows have been observing Chelsea Margaret Bloom for the better part of a week. Alerted by the cats, they'd watched her from the upper windows the first day she stole a bottle of milk, and every day thereafter. They took in her expression, her general demeanor, the fact she looked half-starved and all scared. They started making enquiries around Mercy's Brook. At Abi Hobbes', Eugenie and Sarah began a discussion about daughters with other women who were there. Everyone chimed in but Ellie Bloom, who showed a striking lack of interest in joining the conversation, which the Widows noted. And they also noted, when Sarah introduced the topic of husbands, boyfriends and lovers, that Ellie was only too anxious to chat about her beau, Teddy Landreneau.

Teddy was a mechanic, employed at Hannigan's Garage; a man with long black hair, dark eyes, and pock-marked skin. He was not Mercy's born, nor was he pretty, but he was big, seemed like he might be protective—which was a mistake several women before Ellie Bloom had made. Others might continue to make it too, if she ever got her head right and gave him the boot. At the moment, however, that seemed unlikely. They'd been seeing each other for four months, living together for two (which was convenient, whispered Abi Hobbes, after he'd been thrown out of his own apartment for fighting and not paying his rent—Sheriff Taylor had had to deliver warnings to him on more than one occasion). And these last two months, rumor had it, coincided with Chelsea Margaret Bloom looking thinner than she was genetically wont to be and terrified to boot. The Widows had seen plenty of girls with that same look, and they recognized it the first day she'd stolen their milk.

Now, while Sarah butters more toast, Martha pours more coffee and asks, "Who should take Mr. Landreneau?"

"Me. I love a bully," says Eugenie.

"Play to one's strengths. I'll try talking to Ellie Bloom, then," says Martha.

"Good luck," says Virginia with an uncharacteristic sneer.

"Now, now. There's always hope," Sarah says gently. "In one form or another."

"You know where I'll be then," Virginia finishes; she goes to one of the cupboards and pulls out a bright blue vial. "I'll have this ready soon."

✳

School had never been enjoyable, but Chelsea kept her head down and didn't draw attention; she didn't yearn for friends or a greater connection, she did her homework assiduously, made sure her marks were good enough to keep her below anyone's worry radar. She loved reading and spent her lunch hours and free periods in the library. Chelsea tried to make herself as small as she could, so no one noticed her and she didn't attract her mother's random tempers; she was doing well at it until Teddy entered Ellie's life and, by unfortunate association, hers as well.

Yet it had been manageable until he moved in with them.

That crossing over, that incursion, caused a bleed in the rest of her life. She became actively miserable and that drew notice to her as surely as a beacon. The mean girls, like tall blond Becky Silverman, suddenly found in her a target for their barbs. Worse, the bully boys, whose eyes had passed over her unseeing for so long, suddenly saw her. Her schoolwork suffered, which meant teachers who'd had no concern for her now talked about her in the staff room as "at risk". It didn't occur to Chelsea that her previous invisibility had been a kind of magic, something she could do without thinking, but also something that could, unfortunately, be easily sent awry by unhappiness because, unaware of it, she wasn't in conscious control of it.

Since the shift in Chelsea's universe, since the veils around her parted, she's been in Becky Silverman's sights, which would have been bad enough on its own. But unfortunately Becky's boyfriend has also noticed Chelsea. It wasn't like he was paying her court or anything nice. But Becky's kind of fucked-up about relationships, and can't tell the difference between what's healthy and what's not, so even though Evan's been making jokes at Chelsea's expense, it's enough to set Becky's jealousy off like a rocket.

So, this afternoon, during English, which is the last class of the day, when Chelsea asks to go to the bathroom, Becky follows. Chelsea can hear the footsteps behind her in the hall, risks a glance over her shoulder and clocks the look on the other girl's pretty face. It's enough to make her break into a run. She knows Becky's faster than her, too, coz she's on the track and field team, but that's no reason not to try to escape.

As Chelsea bangs through the big double doors into the fresh air she trips on the flapping sole of her sneaker. She tumbles down the stairs, grazing elbows; the knees of her jeans tear away to leave the skin of her legs vulnerable to bruises and cuts. As she rolls to a stop, she finds a pair of old suede boots, red in color, very close to her nose. Chelsea cranes her neck to see a pair of black leggings, a burgundy tunic and a thick knitted long black cardigan. Yellow-brown eyes, iron-grey hair, and a kind smile look down at her.

"Trouble brewing?" Virginia asks, just as Becky Silverman skids out.

"Bitch," spits Becky from the top of the stairs. Her features twist, blond curls do too, like snakes. Whatever has drawn this spite out of her, it's Medusa-like in nature. She begins to curse up a blue storm that might even put a blush in Eugenie's cheeks.

"Now, now, girl. If you can't say anything nice, don't say anything at all." Virginia's right hand barely moves, but the fingers curl upward elegantly, and abruptly the stream of profanities coming from Becky's mouth ceases. Not by her will, though, for she keeps trying, and her eyes grow wider with every passing second that she fails to produce a sound. Virginia smiles, and the malign expression looks a little ill-fit on that gentle face.

She reaches a hand down to Chelsea, who takes it with only a small hesitation.

"How long…?" asks the girl as she hurries down the path beside the old woman, whose pace is more leisurely.

"Long enough to teach her a lesson." Virginia smiles again, and it's less frightening. "Come along, we need to get you some new clothes."

"My mother…"

"Oh, darling. We both know your mother won't be looking for you." Then to soften the blow, she adds, "Don't worry, Martha is making arrangements."

Eugenie spends her morning sitting in a café across from Hannigan's Garage, making bad coffee and a stale pastry last. The roller doors are up, so she can see Harper Hannigan and his employees moving back and forth as they work. Eugenie makes a mental note to talk to Harper about his choice in workers; Sookie Delorme is fine, been with him for thirteen years, but Teddy Landreneau was clearly a mistake.

He's muscular, for sure, and Eugenie lets her mind wander a little, but when lunchtime comes and Teddy heads off toward the low-rent diner a ways down the street he goes to every day, she's all business. She leaves money on the table, a generous tip, and a lot of crumbs, then follows Teddy with a stride not her own: it's a hobble, really, an old lady's gait. It distracts people; no one notices harmless little old ladies with limps.

But before he reaches the diner, Teddy takes a detour, nips between the iron gates in the fence around the rambling park. Eugenie puts on a burst of speed now, no sign of the slowness of age or infirmity; she buries her hands in her coat pockets, the right one fidgeting with the item she finds there. The trees are thick around the entrance so she hurries to get the mechanic in sight again, sees his broad back at last, disappearing around another bend.

If she'd given it any thought, which she doesn't because she's concentrating on pursuit, she might realize he's gotten farther away than he should, even on his long legs; that he's run while out of sight. That he's drawing her deeper into the park, farther from the main thoroughfare, farther from the ears and eyes of witnesses, farther from potential aid.

Eugenie's sturdy boots make no sound on the path and that's probably what saves her: Teddy's not quite ready when she rounds the corner, so he's slow in swinging the thick branch, which in turn gives her a little time in which to jump backwards.

He catches her a glancing blow, however, and she's knocked off balance. She totters, is amazed that he caught her where her late unlamented husband Sidney always used to. The pain in her left breast is astonishing, and she remains incredulous that she never developed cancer there, after all the abuse; but it's over her heart, and she knows that's where all the true damage was done.

Still and all, she's grateful: if Teddy'd been prepared he'd probably have taken her head off, or at least given it a damned good rattling. And to her advantage, his miss-swing upset his equilibrium, and so gains her a few seconds. She pulls her hands out of her pockets (Honestly, Eugenie! Hands in pockets, how can you defend yourself that way?), the right one tugs the wooden thing up… and the thing makes a hollow pok pok pok as it hits the ground.

Eugenie scrambles after it, but finds herself hauled back and held aloft. She's surprised, though she knows she shouldn't be, at his automatic unprovoked violence against an old woman. What could possibly cause this? Being followed by an ostensibly harmless relict?

Now she's being dangled. Her toes barely touch the dirt, the tips of her boots making a soft scrape. She feels like a cat held by its scruff.

"Bitch!" Teddy sneers, and breath reeking of cigarettes and old meat hits Eugenie in the face. "What the fuck do you want?"

She manages in her best cowardly quaver, "Why are you hurting me? I was just taking a walk!"

"Bullshit! You've been watching me all morning."

"I was feeding the pigeons!" She injects, she hopes, just the right note of innocent despair. It's the truth, too, she always carries seed in her coat pockets in case she needs a cover; prefers to feed the ravens, but pigeons are more numerous, less noteworthy, more mundane.

He glares at her with eyes so dark that pupil and iris are indistinguishable; whatever he sees in her face seems to convince him. Teddy throws her away.

She lands awkwardly, and feels the little finger of her right hand twist entirely the wrong way. Eugenie lets the cry out even though her natural instinct is to bite down on it. But it will make her seem innocuous. She scoops up what looks like a twig covered in thorns, and feels it puncturing her fingers; it doesn't matter, she's immune after all this time.

Eugenie stands, shuffles over to Teddy Landreneau, who's now regarding her with utter disinterest. She moves past him as if to continue on her way. He doesn't even turn his head to watch her passage, so dismissive is he, and that's when she takes the opportunity to slash the twig down the back of his left hand. It's fast-acting, the poison, digitalis-based, some paralytic in there too so he doesn't even have the moment required to make a fist. Then he's tilting and tipping as surely as a felled tree, landing with much the same shuddering effect on the earth. It'll look like a heart attack; the scratches look quite natural, something he'd incur in the fall.

The Widows are clever and careful.

Eugenie stands tall, looks at her handiwork; the only effect the poison has on her is a slight numbing in her hand, which she welcomes as it means she can't quite feel the pain in her fractured little finger. It'll do until she gets home and Martha can attend to the injury properly.

Virginia has walked Chelsea home, neither saying much, and now they're at the mouth of the dank little street where the girl shares a dank little house with her mother. Virginia stops very firmly beneath the sign that reads "Erebus Drive"; she won't go further. She turns Chelsea to face her so she cannot see the police cruiser parked in the driveway of number 42, then hands over three shopping bags.

"Make sure your mother knows these were a gift."

Chelsea nods. "Thank you, Miss Virginia. I don't—"

Virginia holds up her hand. "Chelsea, your mother's going to be a bit upset. I'm given to understand that something's happened to Teddy." Virginia pretends not to see the look of hope on the girl's face. She pulls a bright blue bottle from her pocket; it's stoppered with a small cork and sealed by red wax. It has no label.

"How do you—"

"Hush. You'll learn that good and bad news travel at the same speed, but via different messengers." Virginia drops the bottle into one of the shopping bags. "This will help her sleep tonight, and tomorrow she'll be a new woman. Five drops, that's all, then bring the bottle back to us when you're done."

Virginia touches the girl's cheek. "Remember that you are welcome with us anytime. Should you need a refuge, our home is yours. The same goes for your mother. She is also welcome."

"Thank you, Miss Virginia." Chelsea smiles, then her face clouds over. "What about—"

"Oh, Becky will be back to normal tomorrow morning and more's the pity. But you'll find her less willing to trouble you, I'll be bound. And, Chelsea?"

The girl says nothing, just waits with bated breath.

"We will teach you how to deal with ones such as her, how to walk in the shadows for your own safety. You need only attract attention when you wish."

And Chelsea thinks this is the most wonderful news she's ever heard, even better than Teddy's accident. She gives Virginia a swift, hard hug that drives the air out of the older woman's lungs, who laughs and hugs back.

Chelsea turns down the street toward her home, which looks bleaker than it ever has; she stumbles a little, seeing the sheriff's car parked outside, then recovers, mindful of Virginia's comment about Teddy. She throws a glance over her shoulder, gives the Widow a wave, and moves on to disappear up the broken path to number 42 Erebus Drive.

Ellie Bloom's been crying for about two hours now. It didn't take long for Teddy Landreneau's body to be discovered by joggers, and it took even less time for Sheriff Taylor to call by and let Ellie know that he was gone from her life. The bruises on Ellie's cheeks and wrists made Sheriff Janey Taylor wonder if it was any loss at all, but that didn't seem to slow the tears. After a while, she then began to wonder where Chelsea was, because surely it was time for the girl to be home from school? Not that she wanted to leave Chelsea alone to deal with her mother, but she couldn't quite figure out what she could do to fix the situation. Janey had had men like Teddy Landreneau in her life when she was young, her own mother had collected them like bad pennies, but when she lost her calm and said "C'mon, Ellie. You know you're better off without him, don't you?" Ellie just howled louder.

Sheriff Taylor is therefore quite relieved to hear the jingle of keys in the front door, and the sound of light footsteps along the short hallway. Janey hurries to meet her before she steps into the sitting room.

"Chelsea!"

"Hello, Sheriff."

"Chelsea, some bad news, I guess. Teddy…"

But Chelsea just nods, and Janey realizes the girl already knows. The Sheriff doesn't think to ask how: Mercy's Brook is small enough that news flies like a winged thing.

"You give me a call if you need anything. I'll drop by tomorrow to check on you, promise."

"Okay, thanks." And Chelsea sees Janey out, takes a deep breath, then goes into the sitting room where her mother weeps on the loveseat.

"Teddy's gone!" Ellie manages through snot and tears.

"I know, Momma. I heard."

"And you don't even sound a bit sorry!" Ellie's tone is sharp as a knife, but Chelsea doesn't deny the accusation.

"Momma, he wasn't good for you."

"He looked after me! Loved me! Treated you like a daughter!"

And that last comment takes Chelsea's breath away. If Teddy's behaviour was paternal, then no wonder the world is so fucked up. Before she can form a response, Ellie starts in again.

"And now you want to leave me! My own daughter! Ungrateful!"

"No, Momma, no! Why would you think that?" But Chelsea's voice trembles, knowing it's true.

"That woman came here! That old bitch! Said they want to teach you. They'll take you, take you away like they did those other girls! Taken from their own good mothers…"

Chelsea thinks about the girls fostered by the Widows, how they finished high school, then went on to college. Sometimes they come back to visit. When they do, Mercy's Brook stops to watch, all the gossips churning internally, whispering and sniping. Some stayed here, made lives, but all their mothers went off on travels when their daughters moved into Widows' Walk and have never returned from their holidays and have not been seen since as she can recall.

Ellie might not have felt quite so attached to her offspring had she not lost Teddy so recently; nor if Martha's visit this morning wasn't so fresh in her mind. All Ellie can think of is the older woman's voice, quite reasonable at first as she proposed Chelsea, Ellie's one and only baby, spend some time being tutored by the Widows. Then, the old bat had finally lost her temper and said, "You know, Ellie Bloom, you're meant to care more about what comes out of your cunt than what goes into it. I'm not quite sure if you'll ever learn that lesson, but I do hope you get the chance at some point."

Ellie couldn't know that half of Martha's high color was from praying Eugenie would never learn of her lapse in manners.

"I'll get you a drink, Momma, to calm your nerves, then we can talk about all this."

In the tiny yellow kitchen Ellie finds a clean red-wine glass and fills it to the brim with white wine from a box in the refrigerator. She's put the three shopping bags on the kitchen table, grateful that Ellie had been too distracted by her grief to ask where they'd come from. She digs the blue vial out of one of the bags, tips five drops in, resisting the urge to tip in more (an act of restraint of which the Widows would approve), then stirs it in with her finger. She needn't have bothered, the fluid is clear as water.

She hands it to her mother, curled on the loveseat by the window, the crocheted blanket wound around her lap. Chelsea goes to sit on a chair opposite. She doesn't say anything, but watches as Ellie guzzles the liquid down with barely a pause.

"Now, Momma…"

"Oh, my, that is strong."

And as Chelsea watches, something strange happens: Ellie's outline begins to change, to soften, her weeping changes to something new, something sharper and higher, a feline plaint.

The wine glass falls to the carpet with a soft thud. Where Ellie Bloom once sat there's a pretty tortoiseshell cat, with long whiskers and a floofy tail, green eyes, and an expression of surprised displeasure.

Chelsea finds a cat carrier in the garage, dusty, with a sprinkling of mice droppings across the top, from back when they'd had a pet. Chelsea packs her few treasures into the shopping bags. There isn't much she wants to keep.

She locks the door behind her and leaves the house on Erebus Drive, makes the shortish walk to Carter Lane. Ellie meows loudly the whole way there; she's heavy too, not just sitting in one spot but prowling the bottom of the cage as much as she can. Chelsea pauses at the fence, staring up at the big house. The closed gate clicks open without her having to touch it, and there's only the smallest hesitation before she steps through.

Tomorrow, Sheriff Taylor will drop over for morning tea and the Widows will let her know that Ellie Bloom's gone for a little holiday, that Chelsea will be staying with them for a while. Sheriff Taylor will look at the pretty new tortoiseshell cat sitting on the window ledge beside the black cat and give both a nod. Janey Taylor knows every inch of this house, having been fostered here herself. She will recall the Widows telling her that the transformation only lasts as long as the mothers remain selfish; the black cat's never changed back into her own mother. She will wonder if Ellie Bloom will one day walk on two legs again. She will smile and pat Chelsea Margaret Bloom on the shoulder before she advises the girl to be careful with her shoes—the cats often register their disapproval in unpleasant ways, at least until they get used to their new living arrangements.

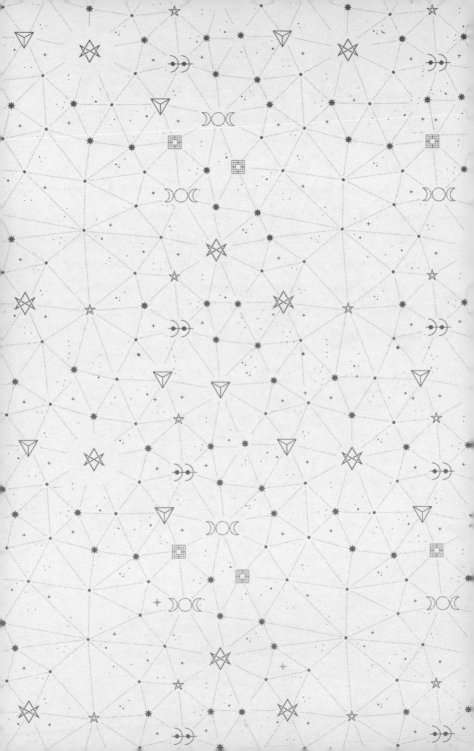

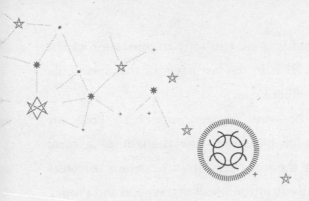

BLACK MAGIC MOMMA:
AN OTHERWORLD STORY

Kelley Armstrong

St. Louis, 1995

As I throw open the refrigerator, I hit the button on my answering machine.

A tentative male voice says, "Eve? Eve Levine?" as if I normally answer the phone by brusquely telling the caller to leave a message.

The voice continues, "I was told this was your number."

A pause. Then a throat-clearing. "My name is Harold Palmer. You don't know me."

I catch the supercilious twist in those last words. *Of course, you won't know me. We don't travel in the same circles, my dear girl. Not at all.*

"I was also told you are currently in possession of the Airelle grimoire. That is, the lost pages of that spellbook. That *sorcerer's* spellbook."

He stresses the word *sorcerer*, unable to keep the indignation out of his voice. The thought of a mere witch possessing the lost pages of an infamous sorcerer's spellbook...? Truly an affront to all that is good and proper.

I snort and crack open a Coke. As I slug it back, Palmer continues, "I don't believe you are aware of what you possess, Miss Levine."

Yep, totally am. But go ahead and explain it to me anyway.

He complies, of course. "That is a rare and valuable book, and yes, I'm sure you understand *that* part. I have heard of your... activities on the black market. But you cannot fully comprehend what you have in those pages."

Dark magic lost for generations. Magic requiring human sacrifice with the promise of healing any illness or infirmity? Nope, I have no idea what that is.

"It is dark magic. The darkest magic. In the wrong hands..." He inhales dramatically, voice hissing on the recording.

In the wrong hands, people will die, my dear child. Die. Do you understand that? These are not spells for turning pigeons into puppies.

Palmer continues, "I understand that you are an independent young woman, raising your child without the support of a Coven or a husband."

I choke on my Coke at that.

"So I am prepared to offer you five hundred dollars to take those pages and dispose of them properly. It is vital that they be destroyed."

And you'll do it for me. Paying me one-tenth what my client is offering.

"How can I resist?" I say aloud and then hit the End button as Palmer rattles off his contact information. On to the next message where yet another sorcerer offers to take the pages off my hands. At least this one doesn't pretend he's going to "destroy" them for the good of the universe. He even offers me a substantial improvement on what my client is paying.

I jot down his information as a potential future customer. I won't be taking him up on this offer, though. I may be a dark witch, but I'm not stupid. With the kinds of items and services I deal in, screwing over a client is a sure way to guarantee that the next time they need a sacrificial victim, I'll be first on their list.

I finish my Coke. Then I check my watch. Time for the most dangerous part of my day: braving rush-hour traffic to pick up the kiddo at school.

*

My daughter, Savannah, attends a private school across town. That's a luxury I can ill afford, but with my transient lifestyle, I need schools that'll take her for one term and not look too closely at her fake ID. As Palmer said, I am indeed raising my child alone. Have been since she was born. Her daddy is a sorcerer, heir to one of the most powerful—and corrupt—Cabals in the supernatural world. If I stop moving, he'll track us down.

And what if he does find us? What will he do? Execute his former lover and half-witch child? Anyone who knows Kristof Nast would think that's exactly what I fear. Nothing could be further from the truth.

I loved Kris. Still do. While I'm not sure he feels the same after nine years, our daughter was indeed conceived in love. Kris is looking for me because he's an amazing dad. As a single dad to two great boys, he wants to play a role in his daughter's life, and it kills me to refuse him that. Yet his father—the Cabal CEO—would literally kill me if he discovered that a dark witch bore his heir's child. Even if Thomas Nast didn't murder Savannah, too, he'd hide her where Kris would never find her.

So I run for Savannah's sake and for Kristof's, too. Better for him to know we're out here, safe and alive, than to be responsible for whatever his father might do to us.

After creeping across the jam-packed city streets, I pull

into the student pickup loop. Other parents are out of their cars, waving so their kids can find them. I stay where I am. There's no way Savannah can fail to see my ten-year-old cherry-red Jeep in this snaking line of silver luxury vehicles.

Do I watch these flawlessly coiffed moms wave manicured hands, reflect on Kris's wealth, and think, *That could be me*? Nope. I cannot even visualize it. I certainly wouldn't want it.

But do I look at their daughters, climbing into those plush leather seats, about to be whisked off to horseback-riding lessons and dance classes, and think, *That could be Savannah*? Yes. I do.

I look at these carefree and privileged girls, knowing that's the life Kris would have given our daughter, and I wish that for her—all the opportunities and all the stability he could have provided. Especially the stability.

I can teach dark magic to suburban witches and earn enough money to send Savannah to private school. I can trade in black-market artifacts and give her those horseback-riding and dance lessons. Yet, at any moment, I may have to say, "Baby, it's time to go," and she knows there's no point crying about the friends she'll leave behind or begging to stay until her dance recital. My heart breaks for that. For the one thing I cannot give her, no matter how many damn grimoires I sell.

I spot Savannah before she sees the Jeep. She's not yet nine, but already her dark head rises above the other girls— and most of the boys. She strides along the walkway, her waist-length hair swaying, with a girl on one side of her, a boy on the other, the three of them chattering the way only eight-year-olds can, all three seeming to talk at once.

Seeing me, Savannah grins, says a quick goodbye to her friends and breaks into a run. She throws open the door and clambers in with, "Hey, Mom."

"Hey, baby."

"Nice truck," a voice says, and Savannah looks over at a blond girl with a sneer that catapults me back to my own school days.

"It is," Savannah calls back as she rolls down the window. "Especially four-by-four'ing in the summer with the top off. So much cooler than—" she points at the girl's chauffeur-driven town car and wrinkles her nose "—whatever that is."

The girl sniffs and turns away.

"Friend of yours?" I say to Savannah.

She rolls her blue eyes, the mirror image of her father's. "That's Tiffany. She's a total bitch."

"Savannah…"

"Sorry, Mom. I should roll the window up before I call her that."

I stifle a snorted laugh, but not very well. Savannah

grins at me and settles into her seat.

"Can we practice spells tonight?" she asks.

"We certainly can."

She fastens her seat belt. "I'd like to learn a fireball."

"So you can use it on Tiffany?"

Savannah's brows shoot up. "That would be wrong. I'm not ready to learn a big fireball, anyway. Just a little teeny-tiny one that might set her hair on fire. Accidentally, of course."

I shake my head and pull from the spot, cutting into the outgoing line of traffic and ignoring the hand gestures of the driver behind me.

It's nearly midnight. I'm in my apartment living room, cross-legged on the floor, meditating, which for me requires more effort than conjuring a fireball big enough to set the entire building ablaze. I just don't have the personality for meditation. That's why I'm doing it—practicing extreme focus in hopes it'll turbo-boost my spell-casting power.

Not that I need the boost. I already get one from my demon blood. Dad is Lord Demon Balaam. When I was a kid, Mom would say he'd tricked and impregnated her, as demons are wont to do. Later, in one of her Valium-induced trances, she admitted she'd conjured him for the sole purpose of that impregnation, to piss off her Coven by bearing a half-demon child. I appreciate the extra powers. I do not appreciate the years of being treated like an unwanted puppy.

Because of my own experience, I'm very careful with what I tell Savannah about her dad. She knows I cared for her father. She knows I wanted her very much. She knows she is the best thing that ever happened to me. When she's eighteen, I'll tell her who her father is and let her decide what she wants to do with that information.

Tonight's meditation is going remarkably well. My mind is clear, and I'm focusing on my reservoir of spell-casting energy, envisioning it as an orb drawing energy from the elements as I feed my demon blood into—

A creak sounds in the front hall. My eyes fly open. I see nothing but darkness—I've turned off the lights and pulled the blinds.

When I blink hard, my night vision kicks in. I get more than a spell-casting boost from dear old Dad. As an Aspicio half-demon, I'm blessed with enhanced distance and night vision. When I look around, though, I still see nothing.

I rise, straining to listen. The apartment is so silent that I catch the inhale and exhale of my own breathing.

Then I realize that's not *my* breathing.

I turn away from the sound, as if still looking and listening. Then I whip around and launch a fireball. A yelp, and a figure stumbles from under a cover spell. She's about my age. Blond hair worn in a wedge cut that makes her look as if she should be passing out orange slices at a peewee softball game.

"Hello, Dora," I say. "What brings you to Saint Louis? I hope you're not a Cardinals fan, because you're in for a big disappointment this season."

"You know why I'm here, Eve, and the sooner you hand over those pages, the sooner I can escape this midwestern hellhole."

"Mmm, better be careful who you say that to."

"Yes, I'm sure the locals wouldn't appreciate me referring to their fair city as a hellhole."

"Nah, that's fine. It's the midwestern part that'll give you trouble. Technically, yes, it's the Midwest, but to some folks, them's fighting words. We're southern, y'all."

"Then give me the pages, y'all," Dora says. "You can see where I'm standing. Between you and your cub. A dangerous place to be…" She conjures a fireball of her own, spinning it on her fingertips. "Unless you're me."

"Did you really think I'd let my daughter stay in the place where I'm keeping those pages? She's at a friend's."

"Nice try, but I can hear the soft but unmistakable sound of a child snoring. You're never nearly as careful as you think you are, Eve. You're too busy being clever."

"Tell Fosse I'll accept half."

"Lyle Fosse?" She snorts. "You think I'm working for that pompous ass? I'm an independent operator."

Now it's my turn to snort. "You don't even book *flights* on your own, Dora. Too much work. I found the pages. I fetched them—at great expense and great personal risk. Then I offered them to Fosse, who is supposed to be meeting me tomorrow to buy them. But he really hates to pay full price, so he hired you to steal them from me. What did he offer you? A grand plus expenses? He's paying me ten."

She hesitates. Then her face hardens. "Bullshit. He told me he's paying you five, and I get half that."

"For sweeping in after I did all the hard work? Whatever happened to sisterhood? Witches stealing from witches to enrich the very sorcerers who've kept us scurrying like mice for centuries. Isn't it time we—?"

"Spare me the girl-power talk, Eve. It's a stalling tactic as you try to figure out how to walk away with a bit of money and a bit of dignity. What you should really be worried about is…" She hooks her finger toward the bedroom. "Hand me those pages, and I'll spare you the humiliation of having your little girl see me kick her momma's ass."

I slam her with a knock-back and go to follow up with a binding spell, but she casts a fog spell, and when I throw the binding, she's no longer where she'd been.

A doorknob squeaks.

"Wait!" I say. "Let's negotiate. I'm sure—"

I throw a fireball through the fog, directly at where I know she'll be standing. She must duck it because she lets out a snarled curse and shoves the bedroom door open.

I tear after her. She's already striding through the darkened room to the bed, following the sound of snoring. I dash in and throw another knock-back. When she stumbles, I race to the bedside, hands raised in surrender.

"You win, okay?" I whisper. "I'll give you the pages for five hundred. That's what I paid to get them. I just… I really need the money. Savannah's school fees are due, and I'm short."

"You should have thought of that before you had a kid, Eve. May I never be so stupid."

She marches around the other side of the bed. I keep pleading, wheedling, asking only for that five hundred, one-fifth of what she'll get. She ignores me, reaches over and yanks off the coverlet.

"Come on, kid. Wakey—"

She stops, staring down at a figure made of rolled-up

towels with a dark wig for hair. The "figure" is still snoring. I pull a handheld recorder from under the pillow.

"Yeah," I say. "That's the problem with not having kids, Dora. You actually did presume I *would* let my kid sleep in the same apartment as those pages. Like I said, Savannah isn't here."

Dora whips a fireball at me. I easily dodge it and run toward the door. She tries to come after me… and stops short. One growl of frustration as she tries—and fails—to take another step. Then she looks down at her feet.

"Binding circle," I say. "So much more effective than a binding spell. Why do you think I herded you over to that side of the bed? You really aren't that bright, are you, Dora?"

She whips another fireball. Then she switches to knock-backs. I duck and weave, avoiding them all until, finally, her fingers fly out in a spell, and nothing happens.

"Burned through all your juice," I say. "That's a shame. Now, let's go talk to Mr. Fosse."

Dora doesn't give up that easily, but she's drained her spell-caster reservoir, and I have not. Plus, I know plenty of tricks she's never learned. The great thing about trading in black-market spells and grimoires is that I get access to all that magic. I write it down before I pass it along to the buyer. Even if it's in a language I don't know, I'll photocopy it in hopes I'll find someone to translate.

Once Dora surrenders—well, the third time she surrenders, the first two being fake-outs, which I expect—I get Fosse's address from her. Then I gag her, which is essential for any spell-casting captive.

Once we're in my car, I casually note that, if she's lied to me, there is a really amazing spell in those lost pages that I'd love to try—I just need a sacrificial victim to do it. Her eye gestures and muffled exclamations suggest she'd misremembered Fosse's address. I lower the gag long enough for her to correct that information.

In the world of supernatural collectors, Lyle Fosse is strictly amateur level. He's like the kid from the Bronx who makes a fortune in illegal casinos and then decides it's time to reinvent himself as a man of culture by building a collection of first-edition books he'll never read. In Lyle's case, he's actually from the suburbs of St. Louis, made his fortune hiring out supernatural rent-a-thugs, and has now decided he wants a collection of rare grimoires.

Fosse is one of the reasons I settled in St. Louis. I love guys like him because, like human collectors, they have no idea what's actually valuable. Ask him to choose between a tattered one-of-a-kind handmade grimoire and a mass-produced old book with a fancy leather cover and pretty pictures, and he'll take option two every time. In my six months here, he's single-handedly financed Savannah's schooling, covered all our living expenses and let me sock away thirty grand.

The only kind of client I like better? One I can actually trust. I can still salvage this relationship, though. I have to. Savannah has two months of school left, and while I'd never promise her a full year, it's my dream to give it to her this time. For that, I'm willing to play nice with Fosse despite his betrayal.

Fosse owns a house in the country, where his wife and kids live, and a condo in the city, where he keeps his mistress. Tonight, though, is business, so he's in his "office"—a body shop hidden in an industrial park.

At this time of night, all the other businesses in his complex are closed, which is both convenient and inconvenient. Convenient in that I don't have to worry about panicking an employee into dialing 911 when he hears shouting next door. Inconvenient in that I can't just pull into Fosse's parking lot without being spotted. I drive to a nearly identical complex beside this one. Then I lead Dora over and leave her between two trucks, binding her legs to keep her from running.

I approach the body shop from the opposite side. A lone

thug guards the entrance. He wears coveralls and smokes a cigarette as if he's just an employee on break. When I hit him with a knock-back, though, his gun comes out. I freeze him in place with a binding spell, pluck the gun from his hand and secure him before I even get a chance to see his supernatural power.

I haul the thug aside. Then I peer through the brickwork. That's another of my powers-from-Dad: minor X-ray vision. I can't see through an entire wall, but I can create a little hole, like an apartment peephole, with an equally crappy view, distorted and unclear. It does the job, though, and I see Fosse at a desk, doing paperwork while another guard in coveralls lounges nearby.

The bodyguard is a beefy behemoth that Fosse must have plucked from his rent-a-thug pool. Good advertising, too—Fosse shows up with him, and new clients think that's the sort of guy they'll be hiring, only to have Fosse pull a bait-and-switch, sending them a regular-sized man like the one I disabled. Fosse hasn't bothered getting the guy custom-made coveralls, though, and he looks like sausage meat stuffed into a too-small skin.

I continue surveying until I'm sure no one's here except Fosse and his bodyguard. Then I slip in the back door under a cover spell. The door's locked, but an unlock spell fixes that. I have a deeper reservoir of power than Dora—that's part of my goal in meditating—but I still use it judiciously, and as soon as I'm in the darkened back rooms, I cut the cover spell and rely on my night vision instead.

I slip through until I can see the front room. Then I recast the cover spell and consider my options for the big guy. A binding spell requires concentration, meaning I can't cast it and then get distracted chatting with Fosse. A knock-back only throws an opponent off-balance. Fireballs and energy bolts are either minor distractions or deadly shots, and I don't want to kill a guy who's just doing his job.

I consider, and then I decide the best offense is no offense at all. Conserve spell-power until I need it. I walk in and say, "Hey, Lyle."

The guard spins, but that's all he does. Wheels and fixes me with a lethal glare that is not actually lethal. There's a ninety-five per cent chance the guy is a half-demon. Most thugs are. A sorcerer would consider such employment beneath his dignity. A necromancer is only useful in a fight if there are corpses to raise. The thing about half-demon powers is that most don't work remotely. You have to get up close and personal. I have a spell ready, should this guy charge, but he doesn't.

I walk to Fosse, who's made no move to attack, either. Fosse is not the attacking type. The guy looks as if he belongs at that desk, a nebbish office worker who'll never rise above assistant manager.

"Eve." His voice crackles, as if trying to conceal his dismay.

"So, Dora paid me a visit," I say. "I offered tea, and she tried to take my kid instead. So much for witchy hospitality. She's currently chilling in an undisclosed location, where she'll slowly die of dehydration unless we come to an agreement. The pages are still yours, at the agreed-upon price, but it'll cost a grand more to get Dora back."

When he speaks, his voice is higher than I remember, which was already shrill enough to summon dogs. "And why would I *want* her back?"

"Because she isn't stupid. She'll have told someone what she's doing tonight, and if she disappears, word will get out, and you won't be hiring anyone except thugs dumb enough to think you won't do the same to them."

The thug-in-residence scowls, but there's uncertainty there, not sure whether he's been insulted.

Fosse laughs, and it's definitely higher than I remember. My hackles rise, not just from the pitch but from the edge in it. Nervous laughter. Not what I expect. Fosse might look like he'd run from his own shadow, but that's an illusion—he'd never have amassed his fortune otherwise. I hear that laugh and notice sweat trickling down his narrow face despite the fact I'm wishing I brought a sweater.

I don't glance at the mountainous thug, but I remember his too-tight coveralls. Coveralls meant for a smaller man.

"Screw this," I say. "When you're ready to pay, you have my number. I'll expect cash. Dora will expect freedom. She'll get the latter when I have the former."

I turn to walk out, and the thug charges. I expect that and hit him with a knock-back. I'm ready to follow it up with something stronger when fingers grab my arm. I spin, a spell at the ready, but my attacker's other hand claps over my mouth, his fingers searing hot, and I yelp in spite of myself. It's the guy I secured outside—apparently he burned his way free. The half-demon only clamps down harder. I grit my teeth against the pain as I kick, punch, and bite.

The bite has the half-demon pulling back enough for me to cast a binding spell, but then the mega-thug grabs me from behind, and I curse myself for holding back and not hitting him with something truly dangerous, even deadly if necessary. Hell, I have a damn gun in my waistband. The problem is that I don't know how to use it, and I'd probably shoot myself instead.

As the two thugs subdue me with a gag and cuffs, another man walks in. He's older, bordering on elderly, a silver-haired man with a cane. He walks up to me and, without a word, points at the gun hidden under my untucked shirt. One of the thugs pulls it out. The old man takes it and walks toward Fosse.

"Mr. G-Glennon," Fosse stammers. "I wasn't going to let her leave. I have everything under control."

The old man lifts one gloved hand and shoots Fosse between the eyes. I don't even realize what's happened until Fosse collapses against the wall, a red hole blossoming on his forehead. His shooter pockets the gun, turns to me and smiles.

Harry Glennon. A collector who's been trying to buy from me for years, and I've ducked contact, knowing even to speak to him and refuse, however politely, could put me right in Lyle Fosse's current position.

"Eve Levine," he says, and something in his voice… I've never met him before, but that voice…

"You didn't return my call this afternoon," he says. "That was most impolite."

The message on my answering machine. The one offering to buy and "destroy" the grimoire pages. Not "Harold Palmer." Harry Glennon.

"I'll take those pages now," Glennon says, "at half the price Mr. Fosse was offering, but I believe you'll agree that's very generous of me, considering I don't need to pay anything at all."

He orders his two goons to pat me down. They find only my car keys. As they hold them up, Glennon studies me with reptilian-cold eyes. Then he reaches into my shirt. His bony fingers are as icy as his eyes, but I don't flinch. I can see by his expression he's not doing what he might seem to be. He reaches into my bra and pulls out a key engraved with a number.

Glennon sighs. "Please don't tell me the pages are in a train-station locker."

"Bus depot," I say when one thug ungags me. "The number is on the side of the key. The address is—"

"Do you really think I'm going to fall for that, my dear? The locker is empty. Or it contains a trap spell that will trigger when I open it."

I start to object, but he cuts me off with, "We're taking a trip, Miss Levine. And if those grimoire pages are not there, I have other ones requiring human sacrifice."

"And you'll use me for them," I say.

"You?" He smiles, all too-white teeth. "No, Miss Levine. I have spells that require something much more difficult to come by. The life of a child. I believe you have one of those."

I wrench away, casting under my breath, but the thug slaps the gag over my mouth and drags me from the body shop.

✳

We're in the bus depot. Fluorescent lights buzz overhead but do little to illuminate the gloom in this corner. While they ungagged me in the car, the mega-thug has his arm firmly around my waist, fingers biting in. Glennon left the half-demon at the body shop, presumably to torch the scene. His type are very good at that.

Glennon finds the locker and hands me the key. They stand back as I swing open the door, taking a bit of malicious pleasure as they both jump when the hinges squeal. I reach inside, pull out the papers and hand them over.

"No trap," I say.

Glennon leafs through the pages. "An honest thief. I'm shocked."

"I'm not a thief. I came by those pages semi-honestly."

He laughs. "I like your style. I believe we'll work very well together."

I try not to tense and say, as politely as I can, "My plate is full right now, but I'd definitely like to exchange contact information. If I come by something you might want in the future, I can let you know."

"That wasn't an offer of employment. I shot Mr. Fosse with a gun you'd handled, one bearing your prints. And my employee stayed behind to ensure Mr. Fosse's security tapes show only you arriving, incapacitating his employee and then entering through the back. My man is now waiting for my call. If he gets it within the next twenty minutes, he'll take the tape and gun as he leaves. You may work to buy those from me. If he does not receive my call, he'll phone the police."

"What? No. We had a deal—"

"You had a deal with Mr. Fosse. My terms, as you'll discover, are very different."

He motions for the thug to take me. The man wraps one meaty arm around my waist. I dig in my heels, but after a glare, I go along with it. I hold off until we're in the waiting area, where a couple of people sleep on the benches. Behind the counter, a middle-aged, heavyset woman watches us.

I meet the clerk's gaze, my eyes going wide, conveying a story every woman recognizes. Her gaze shunts to the mountain with his arm around my waist. I mouth, "Help me," and she lumbers to her feet, barking, "You there!"

A security guard appears from a side hall, cardboard coffee-cup in hand. His gaze goes to us.

"Hey! I'm talking to you," the woman says as Glennon and his thug keep walking. "I know you, girl. You stiffed the fare last week. Get your ass over here."

The security guard approaches. My captor looks at Glennon, who says, smoothly, "There must be some mistake. My granddaughter—"

"—is a hustler," the woman says from her cage. "You don't exactly blend into a crowd, girl. What are you? Six feet tall? Get your skyscraping ass over here."

"If my granddaughter forgot to pay her fare," Glennon begins, "I'll gladly reimburse—"

I hit Glennon with a knock-back. He falls, and I'm about to wrench from my captor, but the guy sees his elderly employer go down, and he goes to his aid, releasing me. I still give him a shove... nicking the car keys from his pocket as I do. Then I freeze Glennon in a binding spell, and I run.

The security guard gives chase, but the woman shouts, "Let her go! It's these two who are the problem. I've already hit the alarm. Police are on their way."

I glance back once to see the thug helping his employer up, ignoring me because the old man isn't giving him any orders to do otherwise. He can't.

The binding spell snaps soon after I get out the door, and I hear Glennon's enraged shout even through the bus depot walls. But by the time the thug comes after me, I'm in the car, and the police are whipping into the lot. I back out as quietly as I can and then slip through the rear exit.

✳

I reach the body shop no more than fifteen minutes after leaving the bus depot, but it's too late. Police cherries cut through the night, and an ambulance whips past. I park in the next-door lot, near my own car. Then I jog to a building across the way and watch the scene, my heart hammering.

My prints aren't in the system. I'm relatively sure of that. But someone is bound to recognize the photo if the police go wide with it, which they will. Glennon will probably call Crime Stoppers and ID me himself.

Get Savannah and run. That's all I can do. Run faster and farther than I ever have before.

When footsteps sound behind me, I wheel, binding spell at the ready. Dora lifts her hands. "Don't cast. I come in peace."

I snort and turn away.

"So you *did* leave that razor blade for me," she says as she walks over. "I thought it was too convenient, lying six inches away under a rock. Why'd you do that?"

I don't answer. The truth is that part of me will always be a Coven witch, believing that we are more together than we are separate. The Coven institution wasn't for me, but the concept still resonates. I didn't trust that Fosse would let Dora go, so I'd hidden that blade for her to cut herself loose if she had the initiative to find it.

"You might want this." She holds up the tape. My gaze goes to the burn around her wrists. "Yep, the tape didn't come easily. But I know a few tricks and convinced the guy to talk. I even called the police for him... after I knocked him out, wiped down the gun, put his prints on it and stuck it in his waistband. There was also a small fire." She nods to the fire engine pulling in. "His fault. Mostly."

"Thank you." I pocket the videotape and put out my hand. "The money, please."

"What money?"

I give her a look. I know Fosse would have brought the money there to pay her, and she wouldn't have walked away without it.

Dora sighs and takes a wad of cash from her bra, and I have to chuckle at her choice of hiding place. She hands it over. I count off a thousand and give it back to her.

"You know," Dora says as she bra-pockets the money. "We make a pretty good team."

I shake my head. "I work alone, thanks. But I'm not your enemy."

"Just my competition."

I shrug. "Maybe. Maybe not. Plenty of other competitors out there. Plenty of jobs, too."

"Don't step on your turf, and you won't step on mine?"

"Something like that."

Dora invites me for a drink, but I decline. Savannah is at the home of a suburban witch I've been teaching. I need to pick her up. And then I need to tell her that we're running. Again.

She won't complain. She never complains. This is just a fact of her life, and I hate that. I hate that my kid won't beg and plead to finish her term, won't rage and threaten if I don't let her, because nothing in her life has taught her that such a thing is a possibility.

My hand moves to the money in my pocket. Between this and what I've saved, I don't need to work for a while. I will, though. We'll move to a new city, and I'll work my ass off until fall, when we'll move again, and she can start school, and I won't take any jobs until spring. That'll keep her safe.

Safe as long as Kristof doesn't find us.

Safe as long as Glennon doesn't come after us.

Safe as long as no other lowlife I've crossed paths or locked horns with or just plain pissed off doesn't decide to track us down.

There is no "safe" for my daughter. Not unless she's at my side, ready to run at a moment's notice. That's how it has to be, how it always has to be.

I climb in the car and prepare to pick up my daughter

and flee in the dead of night. Again.

I just hope someday she'll understand.

I hope someday she'll forgive me.

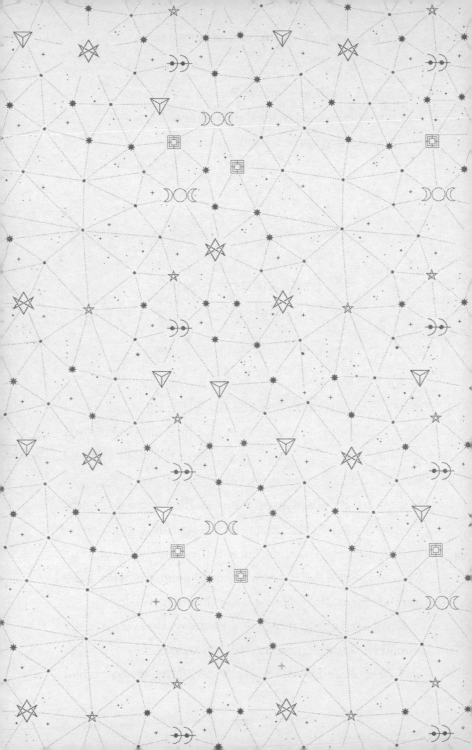

THE NIGHT NURSE

Sarah Langan

Before

When the night nurse first told Esme that she was a witch, Esme did not believe it. Or at least, she hadn't envisioned the dark arts. She'd pictured a group of Waldorf School mothers sitting in a circle, knitting boiled-wool dolls and talking about their menstrual cycles. They had trust funds, smelled like patchouli, and they were gentle as pillows.

Esme first met the night nurse at the Brooklyn Children's Museum. She'd been seven months pregnant with baby number three. *Baby one too many*, in other words.

It had been one of those school holidays that wasn't really a holiday: *White Hegemony Day* or *Teachers Hate Their Jobs and Need Four-Day-Work-Weeks Day*. The museum had been a mob scene of kids with no place else to go, their moms and babysitters punch-drunk with anxiety. She'd lost five-year-old Lucy as soon as they got there. The kid ran straight past the ticket line and into a black-hole-dense crowd of humans. Ten minutes later, Esme assumed the worst: a sex-crazed pervert had stolen her child. Right now, he was speeding across the Lincoln Tunnel, her lovely daughter hogtied in the back of a van.

"LUCY!" she'd screamed while carrying Spencer, who'd been too heavy to carry but had walked too slowly to keep up. Two-year-olds, constitutionally, are passive-aggressive. It's literally a hallmark of their personalities.

She found Lucy in the *Tots* section, dressed in Native American garb and reading *Babar Goes to Paris* to a rapt three-year-old, the picture of maternal sweetness. At this, Esme cried with relief while trying not to cry, because when moms cry it's very upsetting for their children. To an outsider it had looked like hiccoughs, or else those shivers you get when you suddenly have to pee.

The trip ended at the gift shop, where both children conspired against her, begging for an ant farm colony because it was educational. They promised that they would name and love these ants like pets. She'd been blanking out, adrift in a mental vacation along the Amalfi Coast, when the old lady at the register had taken her by the elbow with a plump, callused hand.

Wendy, her nametag read, and Esme had been reminded of the last scene of *Peter Pan*, Wendy all grown-up and shriveled.

"You're goina need some help," Wendy had said in a thick, southern accent. She was about six feet tall and strong-looking, her face wrinkled and her eyes bright blue. Her hair was shocking white, like someone had scared the hell out of her thirty years ago, and she was still getting over it.

"Help?"

Wendy'd reached lower, and pressed her hand flat against Esme's belly. It felt awkward and inappropriate, the hand radiating a damp ick. But Esme didn't mind. It's nice, sometimes, just to be noticed.

"I can help. I'm a night nurse. Trained and licensed."

"Oh, I'm sorry. I'm broke," Esme had answered.

Wendy'd reached into the pocket of her green corduroy dress and produced a soft and wrinkled business card that smelled like lilacs. "We can work somethin' out. I'll bill your insurance for ya." Then Wendy waved and smiled wide at the kids. Her too-cheerful manner reminded Esme of all her still-single friends who liked kids only in theory. In reality, they preferred something that stuck to a script. A Japanese hug robot, for instance. Or a boyfriend that didn't live with you.

The kids, sensing Wendy's phoniness, had looked away.

"I should warn you. I'm a witch," Wendy had said. "Some mothers don't like that."

"Like, a feminist?"

"No. A real witch." She had this glimmer in her eyes. Delight or something deeper, an emotion that hewed to her bones.

Creepy!

Esme bought the stupid ant colony, then put Spencer in the stroller and Lucy on the kickboard and they took the handicap ramp heading out. "Thanks, anyway!" she called behind her shoulder.

She got a text from Mike that night, saying he had to work late. After she put the kids to bed, she discovered the lilac-scented card in her back pocket and Googled *Wendy Broadchurch, Night Nurse*. The website showed pictures of the woman from the museum, tall and strong, holding tiny babies with loving skill. Under these were testimonials about how she'd saved families by allowing frazzled parents to sleep, helped babies bond and latch, worked miracles.

WENDY BROADCHURCH, NIGHT NURSE
SHE'S MAGIC!

Literally, every testimonial said she was magic. Her fee was on a sliding scale. New moms, and she dealt only with new birth mothers, could pay whatever price they were able to afford.

Weeks passed. Esme thought about Wendy when she woke early to do her exercises, which included labor-prep squatting and shoving her legs up a wall to drain the swelling from her sad, sick cankles. She thought about her while getting the kids ready for school. She thought about her while cooking dinner, and she thought about her when collapsing onto the couch at night, too tired to make it to the bed. The woman had smelled rich as a pine forest, and the touch of her hand had been so soothing. She hadn't really been creepy. It's a special skill to be good with infants, and that skill doesn't often translate to being good with kids or even adults. The woman's words haunted her: *You're gonna need help...* Even a stranger could see it: this third child was going to sink her.

Esme rubbed her thumb along the wrinkled card as she dialed the number. "Just let me know when you're home from the hospital," Wendy told her. "I'll be right there."

"I'm worried my husband won't be happy about the money. Can he meet you?" Esme asked, and partly this was true, but she also wanted to interview this woman who'd be holding her infant half the night, alert in her home full of sleeping loved ones. But she didn't know how to come out and say that. She was out of practice negotiating with adults.

"I don't deal with husbands," Wendy said, then hung up.

Month One

Esme felt a cool hand on her forehead. Callused yet strong. She rolled to her side and pulled down her soft, cotton nightshirt. A suckle. It hurt the way it always hurts when newborns first start nursing. The way no one ever tells you, just like they don't tell you that delivering a baby feels like smashing a basketball through a buttonhole.

The baby bit too hard, latching more with skin than nipple. Esme's eyes popped open, and there was Wendy, the white-haired night nurse, her head bent low, holding baby Nicky in place. When she saw Esme's pain smirk, she slipped her thick index finger inside the baby's mouth, un-suctioning the latch and then refitting it.

Before kids, Esme would have been appalled by such intimacies between strangers. But your body's less precious once someone else has lived inside it. A man on the subway might squeeze your ass while you're too busy wheeling the stroller to fight back. Everybody you ever meet might feel obliged to comment on the size of your boobs, your baby weight, how much of it you've lost. You feel you belong to the world, and so it's especially wonderful when someone notices you in particular.

"Thanks," Esme whispered, her voice all gratitude as she drifted back to sleep, and the baby suckled. And along the blue sheet, milk and blood.

Wendy was gone when Esme woke. Her shift lasted from eight at night until five in the morning. At five-thirty, Nicky started mewing and Esme nursed him, then occupied Spencer in the den of their parlor-floor apartment, trying to keep them all quiet so Lucy and Mike could get a full rest. Around seven, she put Nicky on the kitchen floor in his boppy, held Spencer to her hip, made toast breakfast, then packed Spencer's snack and Lucy's lunch.

Mike left for work at seven-thirty, which gave her forty-five minutes to brush Lucy's hair and get everybody ready for the day. This involved a lot of running around and then running back to get the thing that had been forgotten, and then socks, always socks! No one could ever find, match, or put on their own socks! And then securing the double stroller, and Lucy would have to walk even though she didn't want to, and somehow, even though Esme had promised she wouldn't yell she was literally screaming and the children became frightened and cried, and then baby Nicky was crying, and they all sat on the couch and wept while Esme explained that *mommy's very sorry*, and then it was off to school.

Getting the kids to school was probably the worst part of Esme's day, in part because she was still tired from the night before, and, having drunk three coffees to make up for it, was now irritable and likely to pee her pants, which happened from time to time.

Also frustrating for Esme was the group of perfectly coiffed moms who materialized at drop-off before heading out to jobs like television producer and advertising copy writer and office manager. These occupations, which had once seemed mundane, were now like the tips of sailboats floating away from the horizon, Esme standing on the shore.

The other group at drop-off was the home-maker wives, who wore Lululemon and complained about money, but spent the time their kids were at school in group yoga classes, training for half-marathons, or having Friday lunches with unlimited mimosas. They tended to have nice figures and their children tended to be the smartest and best adjusted. They supported each other, too, doling hugs and laughs when this child-rearing gig got *just too darn hard!* Some of them even watched each others' kids and shared cooking obligations. Esme had tried to befriend these women, but they happened to be the same kinds of women who read *Eat, Pray, Love*, and considered *Love, Actually* the best movie of all time. They were lovely women who would raise lovely children and Esme had nothing in common with them.

Also, now that she had three children she'd broken an unwritten rule of Brooklyn parenting. Everybody kept saying, "I don't know how you do it! Are you moving to the suburbs?" Unspoken and more to the point, it's hard to arrange playdates with a mom who has three kids. Nobody wants that many people in their tiny apartments.

So, drop-off. First at PS11, then the preschool, and then home with baby Nicky, a two-mile walk round trip. By the time it was done, the cold had taken its bite. Though the baby was well wrapped, Esme's hands were frozen too much to flex. But you can't drive in Brooklyn, particularly not with three kids (you can double park, sure, but if you leave anybody in the car some asshole calls child services), so walking it had to be. This was also the problem with alternate-side-parking-street-cleaning days. Don't even ask!

Drinking more coffee, she tried to type while the baby slept. She was working on a story she thought was good, about the prison system in Riker's Island. She thought maybe someone would publish it, like they used to publish her work back when she'd been able to make deadlines. As a favor, her old friend who now worked at the Huffington Post asked for a first look when she finished. But she didn't finish that day, because Nicky started crying. And she knew she was supposed to go help him. All the baby books demanded this. If you did not help a baby when he cried, he didn't properly attach, which led to personality disorders like narcissism and borderline and even psychosis. Yes, you had to answer babies when they cried or you were a BAD MOTHER.

So she got up and held the baby. Offered her breast, which the baby bit, tearing up the scab that had just healed. "I don't want you," she cooed sweetly, because babies don't know English.

Pick-up happened two hours later. Nicky was napping so she had to wake him, because Spencer threw fits when she was late, which it turns out is normal for a two-year-old, but somehow unacceptable at a preschool for two-year-olds.

She was in such a rush that she forgot her gloves, or maybe there just wasn't time, but at least she'd remembered that tenth cup of coffee. Off they went, carrier and empty stroller, walking fast as waddling ducks.

The preschool on Prospect Avenue had this cheesy awning of happy stick-figure kids. A bunch of moms were waiting outside—the happy moms who'd all gone out for coffee and talked about their feelings during the last two hours. They smiled when they saw Esme and she tried to smile back but she was sweating at her core and ice-cold on the outside. Like a cherry pie à la mode.

The doors opened and Esme felt the familiar thrill. Her beloved, returned. Toddlers ran out from a large playroom with its indoor slide and bounce animals. They rushed for their mothers and that one overwhelmed, lonely dad. Playdates were arranged for the post-nap dead zone. The room emptied.

Esme felt a hand on her shoulder. It was the director. A sixty-year-old woman named Meredith who taught the children about hatching chicken eggs and self-esteem. "He's in the office," she explained. The lagging-behind mothers heard this, and offered looks of schadenfreude wrapped in sympathy. She followed Meredith into the office where Spencer sat on one of the small training potties instead of an adult chair, which would have been too big. His put-upon teacher Natalie stood beside him, seeming concerned.

It was always concern. Never anger, frustration, or annoyance. Just concern.

"He ran out of the classroom. We have a stop sign so that doesn't happen. We teach them to read that sign on day one. For safety. But he ran out into the big playroom anyway."

"Oh," Esme said. Spencer came to her. Leaned in. Nicky yawned with closed eyes.

"We planned a field trip for next week. Spencer will have to stay home with you. It's not safe."

Esme felt all kinds of ashamed, which she always felt when this kind of thing happened, but also all kinds of confused. Because Spencer surely knew the difference between a classroom and a busy street full of cars.

"Well, if that's what you think," she said.

"It is. We're so sorry. Maybe you could work with him at home."

She felt she should defend her kid, but she was so tired that she was afraid she'd start crying. "Okay. We'll work on following rules more. Except it's hard because he's two years old."

"That might be the problem."

"Hm?"

Meredith, the big gun, stepped in. "Have you been spending enough time with him? I think it might have to do with the new baby. He's acting out." She said this in front of Spencer, like he wasn't just willful, but retarded.

"Oh. Should I cram this baby I'm holding back into my vagina?" she asked.

Everybody got all quiet and uncomfortable. Even Esme, who was not the kind of person to use the word *vagina* out loud.

"Okay! Sorry about the stop sign," she said, took Spencer's hand, and walked out.

*

They got home with two hours to spare before kindergarten pick-up. Her fingers weren't numb this time, just really cold. She fed everybody and then napped everybody and then they had a half-hour. She drank another coffee and somehow peed her panties and jeans, and promised herself to stop having coffee, because she was a grown woman capable of impulse control. Right?

Then she remembered the thing she kept forgetting, which was the ointment Wendy had brought to heal her sun damage. So kind! Because Esme was black, almost nobody ever noticed her sun damage. Her rich, drunk mom used to send her outside all summer long back in East Hampton. She'd felt this was good for Esme, as it had afforded them both more freedom. Esme was less sure. But now Esme's face had all kinds of weird freckles and parts of her nose were scarred little spiderweb calluses from blisters over blisters over blisters, summer upon summer.

She couldn't remember where she'd put the ointment, and then she remembered Wendy saying to her really slowly, "I'll put it in your med'cin cabinet 'cause it's strong magic. I don't want the children messing with it."

So, in her bathroom. She rubbed it on her face. It was a small jar, its contents reeking of frankincense and bergamot. The secret ingredient, Wendy had told her, was the blood and milk she'd collected from Esme's nipples, which may or may not have been a joke.

Her skin tingled in a good way. The ointment pressed through her pores and went deep. She could even feel her bones. She worried briefly that Wendy had actually given her a whitener, since hillbillies from Kentucky probably thought blackness was a thing that needed curing. But then she looked into the mirror, and yeah, she could even see it. Her spots softened, the pigment turning uniformly dark. The scars on her nose looked smaller. She glowed.

"I'm still pretty," she whispered with total surprise.

It felt so good she put it on her hands. The cracks merged together to heal. Heat sank deep, into her bones. The chapped red softened into muted brown. She was about to put it on her raw nipples when she looked at the clock. Time to go!

They went out again, this time straight to PS11. Lucy and her best friend Ritah came whizzing out the side, kindergarten exit. Ritah's mom was this angry twenty-something from Massachusetts who was training to be a doula. She was always asking Esme to look after Ritah, which was actually pretty easy because Ritah was an easy kid, but it also kind of sucked. Today both moms took all the kids to the park. Lucy and Ritah played on monkey bars and sang their best-friend song and practiced their best-friend handshake. Ritah's mom complained about how hard her life was because her ex-husband had a trashy girlfriend, and then something about how she wished she had some OxyContin. As Esme surveyed the situation, nodding politely at this woman's litany of mistreatment, Nicky and Spencer stuck to her like extra appendages, Esme decided that private school would have been a better bet. They'd have met a higher class of family, whose kids used more normal cuss words. For example: what the heck is a douche-slut? Does she cheat on one douche with another? Do they even make douches anymore?

Esme, Lucy, Spencer, and Nicky got home at four in the afternoon. Everybody collapsed on the couch. Lucy cried because she missed Ritah and Spencer cried because two-year-olds cry in the afternoons, sometimes for as long as an hour, and Nicky cried because he heard other humans crying and wanted to be in on the fun, so then Esme cried, and then the kids all got really upset because mom was crying, so Esme turned the television to *Animaniacs*, which they streamed for an hour while she ordered groceries from Amazon, thank god for earth-scorching, minimum-wage-slavery Amazon, because no way she was getting these kids out of the house one more fucking time, just for Hamburger Helper.

She got the text from Mike that he'd be coming home late. He had this pattern since they'd started having kids. He stayed away until they were sleep-trained. Over the years, she had vocally protested and threatened and at last begged for his help, but her pleas had fallen on deaf ears.

She was not a moron—she'd done the math. But divorced people had to do stupid things, like splitting the kids between apartments three days a week. This sounded fantastic (three nights on her own, her husband stuck taking the kids! A fantasia! She'd brush her teeth and take baths and get real writing done!), but then you consider the practicalities. The kids were attached to their home, which they'd have to leave for something cheaper. Mike would certainly not take care of the kids. He'd have his mom do it. His mom was competent and loving but also a bully, which explained Mike, who never met a confrontation he didn't avoid by either working the longest hours possible or just drinking his feelings into itches. You know how people with hammers are always looking for nails? His mom was an iron, always looking for something to flatten.

The stuff you have to manage—playdates and emotional well-being and simply asking the kids about their lives—this would not happen unless they were with Esme, nor would the doctor appointments and sick days. While she'd not been able to work for years, Mike was finally earning real coin. If she put a wrench in those gears, then they'd all be struggling. And while this situation wasn't working for her—this was, in fact, terrible—she indeed loved these people. Even Mike.

She'd planned to revisit the notion of divorce, or at least couples' therapy, once Spencer started kindergarten. Two kids in school full time, she'd have been able to work and make decisions with a clear head. But then she got pregnant again. The pill that was supposed to solve the problem didn't take. And then the second pill didn't take, either. She never got around to making an appointment for an abortion. She'd known it was specious thinking, but with the kid having survived so much, she'd gotten the idea that he'd had more of a right to her body than she did.

When Wendy arrived that night, she wore this red cloak with a black underside and she hugged Esme, hard, like she could guess just by looking how tough the day had been. Esme cried. She wished her mom, or even her husband's mom, had done this after any one of the babies had been born. Just once. She would have cherished it.

Spencer and Nicky were already sleeping. Lucy wasn't keen on Wendy. She thought she smelled bad and was weird, which Esme couldn't actually refute. So it was Esme who put her to bed, this time with three chapters of *Junie B Jones* and a back scratch. When she came back out to say goodnight to

Wendy, the woman was waiting at the kitchen table.

"Sit," Wendy said.

It felt weird, another woman at her kitchen table, telling her what to do. Even if the woman in question happened to be her savior. "Why?"

"Trust me."

Esme sat. Wendy put Nicky in the bassinet, then pulled a boar bristle brush and a spray bottle from her mammoth, old-lady sack of a purse.

"My hair's tricky," Esme said.

"No, it's not." She sprayed something oil-based along Esme's scalp. It smelled like a field of spearmint, and it felt much better that that. Her scalp tingled, drinking thirstily. She felt this wave of freshness wash over her, all the way inside her ears and sinuses and even her bones. Then came Wendy's hands, sure through every snarl. She didn't braid. She let it loose.

Wendy showed her what she looked like in a mirror. Her skin was dewy. Her hair soft and full. She'd never pulled this look off before, always afraid it would appear like a failed afro. But this was something different. Something just her own.

"My mom could never get this right," she whispered.

Wendy handed her the oil. A blue bottle, small. She opened and saw that the contents were clotted white marbled with red. She was too grateful to ask the obvious question: *is this my blood?*

Wendy leaned in, her breath like bergamot, and kissed her on the cheek. This wasn't the first time this had happened. More like the third.

Mike walked in, mid-cheek kiss. He stopped where he was standing, like he'd just caught them fucking a double-ended dildo while smoking crystal meth. "Who's got the baby?" he asked.

Esme looked away, ashamed.

"Is he lost? We thought you had him," Wendy answered. Then she said to Esme, "Go to bed. You're exhausted. And put that ointment on your nipples and vagina. It'll help."

Blushing at the words *nipples* and *vagina*, Esme got up fast and went to her room. From there, she turned on the monitor, where she heard Wendy and Mike talking low so as not to wake the kids. This was new. He didn't usually talk to Wendy. Just came in super late and walked past her, collapsing next to Esme on the bed.

"Did we ever get a résumé or references from you?"

Esme died a little bit. Not literally. Or maybe literally. The part of her that loved her husband died a little bit.

"Do you need them?" Wendy asked.

"You know, now that you bring it up, that'd be great!" Mike said.

"I'll give them to your wife," Wendy answered, just as cheerful.

"I can take them," he said, and he said this curtly, like it meant nothing. He was doing her a favor. She recognized the tone. But she heard it with new ears, now that he was employing it on someone else. It occurred to her that Mike, so cowed by conflict, so meek toward the outside world, might also, like his mother, be a bully.

"Actually, I'm so sorry!" Wendy said, with the same tone a person might use when explaining that all the gum in the pack is gone. *There's no more Doublemint! I'm so sorry!* "You can't have my references because you're not my employer."

"You can bet I'll be the one paying you," he said, and now he'd switched from charming to paternal, like he was clearing something up for poor, confused Wendy, the sixty-five-year-old hillbilly whose day job was selling ant colonies at the Children's Museum. Which, you know, they'd never ordered the ants for. The ants had involved an online code from the inside of the box. So all they had was an empty ant house in the middle of the living room.

"I'll waive my fee, maybe," she answered.

Nicky started crying, which stopped the conversation. Esme heard shuffling, and then, "Oh, don't be such a piggy," Wendy whispered. "Let your momma relax." Then a beer can cracked open, which would be Mike.

In the dark, Esme rubbed the ointment on her nipples and then her vagina. These, too, went deep. She felt the ointment all through her, vibrant and healing and startlingly alive. The healing felt like a window opening. A mountain moving, just slightly, proving that such things were possible.

It wasn't so surprising, then, when Mike came in an hour later, and kissed her neck and felt between her legs, that she went along with it, and even came, her sore body throbbing with confused joy.

Around midnight, Esme was woken by a callused caress. She rolled halfway. Fed Nicky. He made suckling, animal sounds but her nipples didn't mind as much and there wasn't any blood.

Wendy smiled at the baby and she smiled more at Esme, like she mattered. Like she was a person who could be seen. "Cunt's all cleaned up now, isn't it, lucky girl?" she whispered. "It's like you never had them at all."

Month Two

The next day Mike slept in because it was Saturday and he was tired. She and the kids padded around the creaky, two-bedroom, brownstone floor-through until nine and then went for a walk in Brower Park and then to the Children's Museum. She was hoping to see Wendy, whom she wanted to talk to about the whole *cunt* thing. She didn't exactly know how to articulate it. She thought she'd say something like, *chill out on the language*. Or, *can we not talk about sex while I'm nursing a four-week-old?* But maybe she'd say nothing. Just smile and pretend everything was fine. Just reassure herself that Wendy was a functional person with a day job and a place in the world and friends. But none of this happened, because they were told she didn't work there anymore. In fact, no one there could remember her *ever* having worked there.

Back home, she put both Nicky and Spencer down for a nap and played Uno with Lucy, but kind of fell asleep during a discard, at which point Lucy climbed on top of her and started humping her face, which—little known fact—most children do until you say, "Get the hell off! Stop humping my face!" and then they stop.

That night, Marlene the date-night sitter showed up. She was from Trinidad and the kids loved her rice and beans. They greeted her with utter joy, unlike the way they greeted Wendy, whom they viewed as some kind of smelly penny that kept turning up at their door. Wendy would not return until Monday. She had weekends off.

While Nicky cried in his boppy, Esme took a shower and then used the new spray on her hair so that it shone pretty. Her bones felt different now, from regular ointment use. Stronger and reknit somehow, into a slightly different configuration from the woman she'd once been.

She let her hair hang loose, the best it had ever looked. Her dress was this blue tiger print number that she'd gotten online and she looked great. Mike wore jeans and a suit jacket. They took Nicky with them and headed for the restaurant, where they were meeting the rest of Mike's team along with their spouses.

The restaurant was on Vanderbilt Avenue. Mike walked ahead of her and Nicky that last block because they were late. The table had two spaces left, far away from each other. She was happy for this, which felt a little like betrayal. But only a little.

The food got served family style. She had a glass of wine and fed the baby from milk she'd pumped, so she felt dizzy and cheerful a half-hour in. The man next to her was from Scotland. He told her he liked black people. "I do, too!" she said. He thought she was funny. "Mike, your wife's funny!" he said.

Mike nodded, kept talking to the guy next to him, the big boss, with whom he wanted to start a new division. She turned to the woman on her left, who was married to the man on her right. The woman on her left was from a town outside Chicago called Berwyn. She said she loved babies and could not wait to have some. She got tears in her eyes when she said this, like babies were something that came from a bank, and there was a run on them. "Have my baby!" Esme said.

Then she heard Mike say a crazy word. A word she'd never have guessed he knew, let alone repeat. It sounded like *Wigger*.

"What?" she called across the long table. Mike kept talking. The four people around him were laughing hard. "What did you just say?" Esme shouted, loud now and a little angry. They stopped laughing.

"I was just telling them about our hillbilly night nurse," Mike said. Mike was from Florida. The state where people smoked bath salts, then ate each other's faces. Esme was a Presbyterian from Westchester who'd gone to boarding school until college, and who'd have inherited a ton if not for some jerk hedge-fund manager's Ponzi scheme. Her people had been professionals for generations, long before the Civil War. His people had come over during the Potato Famine. This is for background. For the establishment of who gets to call whom a low class.

"What about her?"

Mike grinned. It was his phony work grin because sometime between meeting her and the first baby, he'd lost his real grin. "All those potions," he laughed. "She thinks she's a witch or something. The two of you smell like potheads."

"Did you say *wigger*?" she asked. The men and women around him averted their eyes, sheepish.

He looked at her like she was crazy. "Of course not."

Nicky and his fucking timing. He started crying.

"I think Dan's on board," Mike said on the ride home. "This is really big."

She broke pace and walked in front of him on the way back to the apartment. "Did you say wigger? Be honest," she called behind.

Mike looked at her blankly.

"When you were telling some mean story about Wendy. Did you call her a wigger?"

"Honey, I'm so drunk. I don't even remember talking about her," he said.

Inside the house, she paid Marlene, and then Marlene asked to speak to her privately, outside the apartment.

"Are you using voodoo?" Marlene asked as they shivered on the cold front stoop. She looked upset. Shaking and close to tears.

"Oh! You mean the night nurse?" Esme answered. "She's into organic. She makes all these great ointments. They're really helping me."

"It's voodoo," Marlene whispered. "I can smell it on the children. You're marked."

This sank inside Esme, sidling across her bones. "I don't believe in magic."

Marlene shook her head. "Please."

"Please, what?" Esme answered.

Marlene started down the steps. From the cramped, dim vestibule, Esme watched her turn around the corner, lost to the sideways horizon.

She put sleeping Nicky down in his bassinet. He'd sleep until his next scheduled feeding at two in the morning. "Can you feed him? I left a bottle," she asked Mike.

Mike popped a last beer, and answered like he'd only vaguely heard. "Sure."

She'd been through this before. *Sure* meant *absolutely not*, but she decided to let it play out.

Like clockwork, Nicky's insistent hunger cries started at exactly two in the morning. She shoved Mike but couldn't wake him, and she knew that if she let Nicky keep going, he'd wake Spencer and Lucy in the next bedroom, and then everybody would be crying messes all day long. Plus, there's that whole attachment parenting thing, about how if you don't hold them when they cry they become psychopaths. Plus, the milk was practically exploding from her nipples. She got up and warmed the bottle and then figured that one glass of wine six hours before wouldn't kill him, and went ahead and nursed.

He looked up at her with soft, small eyes, and she loved him like you might love the first sight of a new and beautiful planet populated by Muppets. "I'm so unhappy," she told him.

She couldn't sleep after that. Too angry. Her first thought was to open Mike's whiskey and get soused. But then she saw how Wendy had cleaned up the tiny corner of her kitchen that was her workspace, arranging pencils next to the laptop. When had that happened? Yesterday? A week ago? When was the last time she'd tried to write?

She sat down there, and saw the note Wendy had written, "You go, girl!" It made her smile, and then chuckle (*You go, girl?*), and then start typing.

The problem with Riker's Island was that there wasn't enough room for the inmates, so they floated around on barges. If they refused to plea bargain, they had to wait for at least a year, trapped, before they could stand trial. They're stuck there, all these women. On fucking barges.

She finished a draft two and a half hours later, then made herself an exhaustion snack of torn crust from sliced bread smeared directly into a bar of butter—her favorite, secret late-night snack, which maybe explained the stubbornness of the baby weight. But God, it was good. Especially if you sprinkled a little salt on the top.

Nicky woke up. She took him out of the bassinet and brought him into the bedroom with the bottle. Held him next to Mike until he opened his eyes. "Your turn," she said. He stayed like that for a ten count, then took the baby and the bottle and got out of bed. By the time Esme woke again it was after ten in the morning. Lucy had turned on the television and was watching it with Spencer. Nicky was just starting to coo. Mike had stuck a note to the fridge:

Putting in a few extra hours at the office. Have a great day!

Month Three

The next few weeks were uneventful, but also very eventful. Esme kept yelling; Nicky kept eating and sleeping; the weather stayed cold; Spencer kept getting in trouble; and Lucy kept playing with the kid who shouted weird cuss-words at PS11. Esme's sun damage totally reversed. Her skin could have been mistaken for belonging to a twenty-five-year-old. True to Wendy's word, so could her cunt.

It happened one Friday, that Esme woke to find Wendy still in the house. She'd made pancakes. These were thicker and more cake-like than normal pancakes, and they smelled like lavender. Everybody except Esme took three bites to be polite. Esme drowned them in syrup and butter and then they were fine.

"Thought I'd stick around, help out," Wendy explained.

The kids stayed especially quiet because Wendy freaked them out. No panic attacks about mean teachers or bullying friends. No shouting about how she loved one of them more than the others, or that everything was totally unfair. It gave Esme's nervous system time to breathe.

Wendy waited inside the car with the remaining kids when they stopped at PS11 and then the preschool, too. They were done quickly, and with significantly less physical tax. Nicky wasn't upset because his nose wasn't cold, and Esme didn't pee her panties even a little.

"Turn left," Wendy commanded, so Esme did. Instead of going home, she directed her to the old armory in East New York, about two miles down Atlantic Avenue. Wendy told her to pull over. She did. *Do you work here, now?* Esme wanted to ask. *I heard you're not at the Children's Museum. You gave that up… Why couldn't they remember you?*

Wendy smiled at Esme with real warmth, or what passed for it. Her eyes squinted into a grin and her voice got soft, like she was reminding herself that gentle people whisper. "It happens in a blink," she whispered. "And there's so much power in it."

"I know what you mean," Esme said. "It's so nice to have you, Wendy. I can't tell you how grateful I am, to have someone in our house who cares. These first months are so hard. I'm counting down the seconds, wishing they'd pass faster, but I know it'll be over in a snap. It all happens so fast and I love them so much… Saints and poets."

Wendy looked at her with confusion. "Oh. Right." Then she got out of the car.

Always before this, Esme had seen mammoth Wendy behind a register, or crouched by the side of a bed, or sitting at her kitchen table. But now Wendy stood tall. The outdoor expanse was finally wide enough to showcase her girth. She loped up the walk, her body in graceless disjoint, then pushed through an ornate wooden door and disappeared inside.

Esme watched the closed door, the giant turrets above, the pretty red brick faded to the color of city-soot and rust. She had questions. So many.

"What do you think?" she asked Nicky. Nicky cooed, because he liked Esme's voice. All her kids were like that: they loved her more than anybody else in the world. It's a kind of love so momentous that you can't let yourself think about it or you'll be like that guy, Narcissus, drowning in his own reflection.

She took Nicky out of his car seat and headed for the armory, which she realized looked a lot like a church. She climbed the steps. A funny feeling ate at the pit of her stomach.

A piece of red poster paper that looked like it had come from her house read:

No Men Allowed!

She opened the heavy door, and then another heavy door. She entered a giant atrium with an altar at the center. The room was empty. Dust motes filled the air. It stank of patchouli. She headed for the altar, where she found a pile of ashes and amidst this, a knot of black, human hair.

She turned and started out. The door squeaked loudly. She pressed her lips to the top of Nicky's head and, panting, ran out. Up in the window, a top turret, a white-haired face peered down.

✳

She meant to confront Wendy after that. To say: *Uh, what was that place? Who are you?* But when she got home there were tasks to accomplish, and she was afraid to tell Mike, because once she did that it would be out of her hands. He'd fire Wendy and she'd be alone in this apartment. So she decided to soothe her nerves with the ointment. It calmed her. Ran through her, placid and healing. After that, she ate the kids' and Mike's leftover pancakes, too.

She'd been paranoid. Wendy was a helpful person. She'd taken the morning just to give Esme a hand. She already knew from neighborhood meetings that the armory was a homeless shelter. Wendy surely volunteered. How could Esme possibly respond to her night nurse's kindness with ungracious questions?

Besides, Wendy's work was coming to a close. Nicky would be sleeping through the night any day now. A week at the most. Why end the relationship on a sour note?

On a Monday, Wendy ran Esme a bath full of clay while chanting softly. Tuesday, she caressed Esme's cheek until she started crying and couldn't stop. While Nicky fed, Wendy held her. Strong, callused hands. At one point, she wiped away a tear and ate it.

"What do you want?" Wendy asked. "If you imagine it,

then the spirits give it to you. They divine it."

Wendy thought about her Riker's Island article, and about her friend from the Huffington Post whom she'd sent it to weeks ago, but who still hadn't read it. She thought about this cramped apartment, and the shitty preschool which she wished they could afford full-time, and she thought about the person she shared her bed with, who made her feel so invisible, and mostly she thought about sleep, and how much she missed it.

"I want my mom," Esme said.

Wendy climbed into the bed. Spooned her like her mom had never done, but she'd always wished for. It felt awkward, and then weird, and finally bad. Esme got up, pretending to need to use the bathroom, and didn't come out again until Nicky started crying.

Wednesday, at exactly twelve weeks, Nicky slept through the night.

Esme's breasts woke her up. They were too full. It was nine a.m. The kids would be late for school! "Lucy! Spencer!" she called. Nobody answered, and she had this irrational fear that Wendy had stolen them. That was the price. And now the loves of her life were gone forever.

She raced into the kitchen, where the dishes were

washed and the counters cleaned and Wendy was standing at sweet attention.

"I dropped them off," she said.

"You did? How? What about their lunch sacks? It's such a walk!"

"I took the car. I made their lunches. It was fine."

"Oh."

Esme tried to smile, but she was afraid. Something had changed. Something was wrong. Also, not cool to take a car without permission. "I guess we should talk about your fee. I think you should stop coming."

"See you tonight," Wendy said.

Wendy didn't show up Thursday night. So Esme put the kids to bed, finishing up another *Junie B Jones*, and snuggling Nicky until his breath got deep. It felt like the end of something momentous, the beginning of another chapter, too.

Around midnight, she jackknifed awake, sneaked out of the bedroom where Mike was sleeping, and found Wendy sitting at her kitchen table. The apartment felt different. Everything rearranged and of different hue. Was this what happened at night? Did the house switch loyalties, locating a new master?

"Sorry I'm late," Wendy said.

"Oh, it's fine," Esme answered. "But I should pay you. I think we're not in the market for night nurses anymore."

Wendy opened her giant old-lady purse and pulled out a deck of Tarot cards—the cheap, Walmart kind. "I made dandelion tea," she said, sipping from and then passing the full mug in Esme's direction. "It'll help dry you out. I'll leave the bottle."

"So, the fee?"

Wendy laid down the cards. The light was low. She was too big for the chair. Twice Mike's size. Probably twice as powerful, Esme suddenly realized.

"Can I read for you?"

"I'm so tired. Can it wait?"

Wendy shook her head. "I've already started." She flipped a bunch of cards. To be polite, to get her on her way, Esme sat and listened. Something about cusps. Something about choices and rebirth and gobble-de-gook that you nod and smile at, because this person had held her defenseless infant all night for three months, and given her love and affection when she'd needed it most, and maybe she was crazy but who else would do such a thing? And then she nodded off, because when she woke up, Wendy was looking at her with this obscene smile on her face; gaudy, wild, and insane.

"Yeah?" Esme asked.

"So you're about to make a big decision," she said. "This is the turning point of your entire life."

Esme stared at the card, which was marked death. She looked back at smiling Wendy. And the cup, she looked inside. Was it really dandelion tea? Because it had curdled to thick, custardy pink.

"You need to think the name. While you sleep, you'll think the name, and in the morning they'll be gone," Wendy said.

"I don't understand," Esme answered.

"Of course you do," Wendy answered. "It's my fee."

"Why don't I just pay you in money from a bank?"

Still with that disquieting, bone-deep psychotic grin, she packed her Tarot cards into her giant canvas purse and left.

Esme did not go back to sleep. She stayed up all night and drank a lot of coffee and fed Nicky and got the kids ready for school. Before heading out the door, Mike hugged her hard and told her he loved her, which made her wonder if maybe she'd turned psychotic, and none of this life she was living was reality.

Then she dropped Lucy off. Lucy kissed her hand like they were in love, then waved this sweet, adorable wave before disappearing into mammoth PS11. "I'd love you even if you were a stranger," Esme called out, to her own surprise.

Meredith and Natalie were waiting at the preschool. They ushered Esme and Spencer into the office for another talk, Spencer sitting on the training-toilet.

"Could you get my kid a real chair, please?" Esme asked. Meredith immediately complied, unhooking it from the stack in a closet just behind her desk. Then Natalie suggested a psychological interview, as she was worried Spencer might have oppositional defiant disorder, a rare condition that demanded immediate attention. It came from poor infant attachment and physical abuse. To this, Esme replied, "How much am I paying you? Just... Fucking keep him alive for two hours. Can you do that?"

Nicky strapped to her chest in a bright orange Moby Wrap, she left without Spencer (she forgot him!), then returned and took his hand. "I trust you'll give me my money back. A false accusation of child abuse is a big deal. I can't imagine you'll keep your accreditation if I sue."

Back at home, they watched television. Not even *Sesame Street. Ozark*, followed by *BoJack Horseman*. It was unclear to her whether she was repudiating or following in her shitty mother's footsteps.

Five hours later, they picked up Lucy. Ritah's mom asked Esme to babysit. "You realize I'm drowning and you've never once offered to watch Lucy, right?" she asked, and then she kept walking, her face red with shocked blush.

Once home, she got an e-mail from the Huffington Post that her story had been accepted and would run front page. This was her first real publication since Lucy, and she was delighted. To celebrate, she brought out her mom's Baccarat and everybody drank orange juice out of $200 crystal. The bedtime routine lasted two hours. Mike caught the tail end. He held Nicky, who shared his small ears with joined earlobes. Soon, even Mike was snoring but Esme wasn't, because what had Wendy meant about a fee? About thinking a name before sleep, and when she woke, the person with that name would be gone?

She Googled *Wendy Broadchurch* again, but the website about the night nurse was gone. What she found instead, not even buried, but on the first page, was a newspaper article from the *Washington Post*, about a woman in Whitesburg, Kentucky, who'd stabbed her husband and three children to death. A self-declared witch, she'd then engaged in ritual sacrifice, peeling the skin from their bodies and hanging it on the backyard trees.

Wrong woman, had to be. Except, there was the photo of a young Wendy, her crazy eyes just the same. Esme used her account at LexisNexis that the *New York Times* had never revoked when they'd fired her for getting pregnant, but had pretended it wasn't because she was pregnant. A downsize upon a downsize upon a downsize of a collapsing industry.

After murdering her family, Wendy served twenty years in a psychiatric hospital in Lexington. She didn't seem to have a handle in chat sites, but her name showed up a lot. Mothers talked about her like she was a ghost. They called her a savior. They called her a monster. They said she'd been their night nurse. They'd met her in dime stores and coffee shops and libraries. She'd earned their trust. And then she'd stolen their children. But no one believed. No one remembered the children, at all.

Esme was shaking when she finished. She still hadn't slept. She didn't sleep. Two nights in a row. That morning, Mike hugged her hard, and kissed her goodbye, because husbands always know when they've pushed you too far. They always come back, because the last thing they want is for you to break.

She got Lucy, Spencer, and Nicky dressed and cleaned for the day, but at the last minute turned back from the front door and had everyone take off their coats. Because it was Saturday. No school day, after all.

While the kids watched television, she went on another Wendy Broadchurch deep dive. There were three mentions of Wendy Broadchurch in the Park Slope Parents Listserve, dating back to 2004, when Wendy first moved to New

York. All named her as the nanny they'd employed when their families fell apart.

Esme called one of these women, having located her name in an online directory, and paying the five dollars to get her cell-phone number. The woman answered on the first ring. "Hi, my name's Esme Hunter, and I'm writing an article about the Park Slope Parents. I was wondering if I could speak with you?"

Esme explained that her article was about the usefulness of web groups for women over the last twenty years. "Did you find your nanny on a website?"

The woman's voice got soft. "Yeah."

"Right. And she was named Wendy Broadchurch?"

A long pause. Can you feel rage through a phone?

"Is it you?" the woman asked.

"I… what do you mean? My name's Esme Hunter?"

"Give me back my fucking baby!" the woman screamed. "Give her back. Give her back. Give her back, you sick fucking cunt. When I find you I—"

Esme hung up. The phone starting ringing from that same number. She silenced it, her heart beating so fast it felt like all the vessels had burst, and blood was everywhere inside, drowning her.

She went to the children and held them one by one, and then altogether. They smelled like patchouli and bergamot and frankincense. The whole apartment reeked of it. She found the dandelion tea, which stank of blood and milk. She found the hair oil and the skin salve. She put them in a Ziplock bag and threw them in the garbage outside the house.

Late afternoon, Esme called Wendy on the phone. "I'd like to pay you your fee. I can sell my family's Baccarat crystal or I can give it to you. It's worth about five thousand dollars."

Wendy's voice was cold. The deep-down voice. The bone voice. "Sleep, honey. Stop avoiding it."

"This is crazy. You're crazy. I know about you. I changed the locks," Esme answered.

Esme heard faraway laughter on the other line. She had to strain her ears. Then Wendy hung up.

After that, she really did have the locks changed, and then she texted Mike and asked him to come home. Something was wrong. She needed to explain. He called back right away and she told him everything. "I'm afraid to fall asleep. What if everything changes? Do you believe me?" she asked.

"I believe that you believe," he answered. He said he'd be home as soon as his new department finished its meeting.

At last, she joined the kids on the couch. Her eyes kept closing. *Mister Rogers* played. The soft light of the setting winter sun pushed through the parlor window. Her mind skipped stones.

Wendy. How had they met?

The Children's Museum, where no one remembered her.

Had Mike ever met her? She'd heard them talking through the baby monitor, but what if she'd imagined all that? What if half the interactions she'd had with Wendy were imagined? A wish fulfillment, becuase it's hard to be a mom when you've never had one. It's hard to run a family when your job commands no respect.

…Was Wendy real?

This calmed her down a little. Actually, a lot. She was post-partum nuts. Nobody was trying to take away her kids. It was just a weird, sleep-deprived, hormone-induced psychosis. Baby blues to the power of fifty.

She put Nicky down for his afternoon nap, and then went to her bedroom to get some rest while Lucy and Spencer started a *Teen Titans* marathon. As she dozed, she wondered which child she might have picked. Nicky, of course. Because she loved him, but he'd been a setback. She could do without Nicky, and all the better, if no one had to know.

But she'd never do that.

Lucy and Spencer? No. They were a part of her, sewn

in tighter than her stomach.

Mike? In magical fairy land, she could do without Mike, but not in the real world, where cash was exchanged for goods and services. Then again, he did have a life insurance policy.

No, not Mike. He was the father of her children. Not Mike.

In her dream, her skin tingled. Her bones broke and reknit with the architecture of briar-patch vines. These vines filled the room and the apartment. They covered the children and then broke the children apart. Everything stank of blood and sour milk.

Not anyone. Of course, not anyone. She chose no one.

And then she thought: *Esme. Esme would love to disappear*.

"Dad!" Esme heard as she awoke in her bed. "There's a lady!"

She stood, and it was Lucy, dressed in a fancy frock adorned with purple hydrangeas, her hair a ragged mess like it had been combed by white people. Then Spencer was toddling beside her, wearing a polo pullover instead of a t-shirt, shorts belted. When he saw Esme, he screamed.

Esme came to them, but they started running. She followed them into the kitchen. Which was different. Her office was gone. It was refinished like she'd always wanted, in sparkling marble. Mike's mom was cooking supper. She wore this frown on her face even before she saw Esme. The frown was the same one the kids wore. A light had gone out inside of them.

Mike's mom lifted the cast-iron frying pan as a weapon, but it was hot and burned her hand. She yelped as she dropped it. Esme turned out to the living room. There was Mike, holding baby Nicky. He was about forty pounds heavier, his light gone, too.

"It's a lady!" Lucy screamed again.

"Get out of this house," Mike's mom said, because underneath all that bullying, she'd always been a nervous wreck.

Esme was at the door. Somehow her shoes were on her feet, and her coat on her back. The furniture, she now saw, was different. Crate and Barrel instead of the stuff she'd inherited from her mom. No Baccarat for Lucy to inherit, either.

She was in the doorway, and she wanted to explain, but they were all so upset. And then Mike came closer, baby Nicky in his arms. Nicky wailed at her like he couldn't stand her stench, but something in Mike showed recognition. Something deep remembered. Because he looked at her with the most perfect expression of hatred.

Then he shut the door.

THE MEMORIES OF TREES

Mary SanGiovanni

The Faithful intended to hang the child at dusk.

She was a ward of the old woman of the glen, the reclusive widow who put her faith in the ancient religions instead of the new. The old woman, one Martha Weede, had been arrested the week prior, and after extensive questioning, had been found guilty of witchcraft. It was the mind of the village elders that both Weede and her young ward, Ellena, be hanged together.

Ellena was a sweet young girl of about thirteen, round and pink of face with soft blue eyes and pretty red lips. The old woman would not promise her as a wife to any young man in the village of New Ipswich despite the Third Law, which was to propagate the human race with strong, eligible specimens as soon as they were of the age to conceive. Ellena certainly seemed to be able to bear children; she had already developed breasts and Cora Rawlins had once reported seeing the girl rinsing blood from her undergarments in a nearby stream.

It was not the Weede woman's violation of the Third Law, though, which made her and her adopted daughter the targets of the townspeople's disdain. Few of the proud families, particularly those whose elders had survived the wars and plagues of the early Twenty-First Century, would have sought the lovely Ellena as a wife for their sons. They wanted no part of a young godless harlot who wore only a shift when prancing about the woods alone and unchaperoned. Instead of binding up her long blond hair, she let it stream freely behind her as she danced and ran. She and old Mother Martha never attended the New Church in town, either. Their monuments of worship were made of wood and stone, out in the forest. They did not believe in the New Church teachings or the God of technology. Their gods did not care about the electronic debris scattered across the land, nor did they demand it be gathered and repurposed. Their gods were ancient, older than the gods of the extinct religions of the Christians and Muslims and Jews. Their gods were old when the world was new, or at least when those fumbling first steps of human technology were fire and spears and the wheel.

It was said Martha and the girl gathered herbs and plants from the woods to make potions to poison cattle and cause babies to abort themselves from their mothers' wombs, and that they talked to forest devils and spirits and cavorted naked with them at night by moon- and firelight. It was said they could conjure the forest spirits to protect them and to exact revenge on those who had wronged them.

Of course, those were just stories, so much swirling smoke from fires stoked by fear and jealousy. Science and technology had seen to erasing any silly, childish notions of the existence of magick long ago. If the women were conducting any kind of sorcery, it was of a manipulative, imaginative, and psychological kind.

Nevertheless, those stories made the people of the village uneasy. To them, the feral world before the Final War of 2021 was the stuff of terrifying and sinful myth, and Ellena and Martha were haunting phantoms of that myth.

The village schools did not teach about the world before the Final War, beyond a few pivotal turning points in its history. They were instructed—or perhaps, catechized—regarding the Digital Deadzone Plague, when the New God was angry at the wanton ways of the world and sent balls of fire and electromagnetic pulses from the sun to render dead and useless the technology that He had bestowed upon them. Every aspect of society had been connected like a great spiderweb—banks, businesses, defense systems, electricity, plumbing, even the production of food. All was leveled by God's pulses of wrath, and it was only a matter of time before the Faithful understood that their Lord wanted to wipe the slate clean, just like an old god of myth had once wiped out the earth with a flood. Thus, the creation of the First Law of the Faithful: all technology developed or recovered should be put into the service of worshipping God.

The children were also taught about the Culture Battles, the dissention between the Faithful and the Heathens, which led to a Final War to claim the world that was left and its scant resources. The history books—they'd had to go back to books once the iPad textbooks lost their charge—said the Plague of Invisible Mouths was actually a flesh-eating virus, a weaponized biological agent that halved the population and then halved it eight times more.

It is not only history that is written by the winners of war but also the future. The Plague of Invisible Mouths was the hand of the New God, devouring the flesh and brain tissue of the enemies of the Faithful and scattering the surviving Heathens and their ancient beliefs to the wind they honored so much. So the wind blew the Heathens to the forest, where the trees have long memories. The trees are patient.

Mother Martha remembered the time before the Final War and knew all the stories not told in schools. She had been a girl then, a child much smaller than Ellena, but she had a memory like the trees. Martha would recount those stories to her daughter and the other children, forbidden fairy tales that they passed on to each other behind small, cupped hands, the myth and history of the Heathens. The village children liked the old woman's tales about the ancient gods and the world before the Final War. They liked that she had a memory like the trees.

To the village elders, Martha and her stories were a poison, sinister and downright evil. Since evil had once dismantled the world, it had to be rooted out and destroyed before it could take hold again.

In the dank cage of cold metal and hard edges, Ellena did as Mother Martha suggested. She closed her eyes, relaxed her body from the top of her head to the tips of her toes, and imagined a great altar in her mind's eye. Then she swept all the fear off that altar, all extraneous thoughts, all distractions, like so much collected dust and cobwebs. She tuned out the heavy, labored breathing of Mother Martha and of the abused women and men all around her. In the silent darkness that engulfed her inside and out, she smelled the stone of the prison and felt the soft breath of the wind as it tried to reach her through the tiny barred transom above her. She heard the rustling of leaves from the nearby trees and in it, heard their words of comfort, of promise.

She and Mother were not alone. It would be all right.

I'm scared, the girl thought.

Fear is natural… but unnecessary, the trees' rustling told her.

They mean to kill us. The girl felt a heavy panic try to settle in her chest and she swept it away.

The trees replied, *We will protect you…*

The girl wiped at the unspilled tears in her eyes and added, *Their weapons are of iron.*

Our weapons are older, stronger, the trees responded. *We will not let you fall, little one.*

Not all were unsympathetic to the suffering of Martha and Ellena. Jonah Harwood, whose family once lobbied against developing rainforests before repenting and turning to the New Church, went to visit the women in their jail cell. He brought biscuits and a jug of water in a small basket. He felt it was his religious duty to tend to the sick, imprisoned, and suffering, though many whispered that was a holdover from his family's old Christian roots.

The jail was a large holding cell once called "the Tank" in the crumbling remains of an old municipal building in the center of New Ipswich. It stank like stale sweat and urine, rotting food and rotting sores, and other less pleasant things. It had grown jagged from rust and age, its metal flaking and splintering, but it was nevertheless a formidable barrier to the outside world. As it was in the basement of the old building, it was exceedingly dark and damp. The tank held a grave and weighty sense of timeless suffering unlike anywhere else in New Ipswich. It was as if decades of people's miseries had bled from their bodies into the ground, cooled, and grown hard, layer after layer, forming the very prison that continued to leech others dry.

Harwood picked his way over bodies either unconscious or dead and found the women in a far, cobwebbed corner of the cell. Both had been stripped down to their shifts and had their hair crudely and unevenly lopped off close to the scalp. The girl looked scared and pale, but otherwise unmarked. Harwood was glad for that; some of the jailers had a tendency to avail themselves of the bodies of pretty young things, particularly those accused of witchcraft, since none of those women was ever set free. To the jailers, the pity of a conviction was often a waste of good flesh.

The old woman was in a far worse condition. Having been further accused of the corruption of an innocent soul through teachings of witchcraft and nature magick, she had been beaten, and possibly worse. The village of New Ipswich had managed to repair an old generator, and put its ability to power brief electrical sparks through metal prongs into the service of cleansing souls. Mother Martha bore the burn marks of such a cleansing. Further, her left eye was nearly swollen shut and three of her fingers looked broken. Her dry lips were split in two places and her bare arms and legs wore patches of bruises. A remaining strand of her long, silvery hair fell against a bruised cheek.

She cradled the scared girl and was singing a lovely, soft song in a strange language when Harwood approached.

"Miss Weede? Miss Ellena?" he asked.

The old woman stopped singing and looked up at him. The abject coldness in that one good eye chilled him. In it he saw a steel will, an authority and power born of dignity, and for a moment, he both admired and feared her.

"Yes?"

"I brought food. Water. For you and the girl."

The old woman looked skeptically from Harwood to the basket and back again. "Why?"

"I… I think you're innocent of the charges against you."

Those lips, still full, still somehow beautiful, smiled painfully. "I assure you, I am not."

Harwood blinked. He wasn't sure what to say, and while his mouth worked open and closed in attempting an answer, she continued.

"However, your kindness is appreciated, Mr.

Harwood. It will not be forgotten."

Flustered, he said, "Please, take the basket. Innocent or not, you need water. The girl—she needs to eat."

Ellena looked up at him. Unlike her adoptive mother's, her eyes were soulful and scared, an endless blue like sky and water and the blended place where they met. Perhaps Mother Martha was guilty of witchcraft, but surely the girl—

"The trees remember. The wind remembers. The water and land and sky remember. And I, too, will remember, when those who came before come again, to save us."

Perhaps the old woman was crazy. She let the girl take the basket, though, and smiled fondly down at her little blond head as Ellena devoured a biscuit and drank from the waterskin.

He left quickly. Martha had begun to hum, and Harwood could have sworn he'd heard a low humming in reply, carried by the wind through the rustling leaves of trees.

On the morning of their execution, the sun rose with reluctance, taking its time to fire up its glow; the waiting dawn was a bleak fog of chill and colorless countryside. The oaks and pines and maples surrounding New Ipswich stood back and waited, patient but seething, a gray-green army gathered on the hillside.

The place where the elders of the village had been executing condemned Heathens lay just beyond their fields and farms but before the edge of the forest. It was a barren spot where neither shrub nor grass would grow; it was said that the blood and rotting bodies of the condemned had soured the ground, and in that hard spattering of dirt, they had erected a gallows.

"Mother, I'm scared," Ellena whispered as they bumped along over the rocky path. The dust from the road kept getting into her nose and throat and mixing with the tears on her cheeks. She and her mother had been bound and put in the back seat of a convertible 2021 Volkswagen which Joseph Abbott and Creedence Burnell had found out on the old toll road one day. It had wheels but no engine, and that was right in the eyes of the New God, as it was to be a ceremonial vehicle pulled by their mules.

"No fear," Mother Martha whispered back through her cracked lips. "You'll see; all will be as it should. You remember the words, in case you need them?"

The girl nodded. "Are you sure they'll come?"

Her mother didn't answer. They had crested the hill and now the gallows were in full view. The villagers had found pictures in old books from the ruins of the library, and they had cobbled together a serviceable set-up from scraps of old telephone poles. Frayed wires served as a noose.

Ellena saw that and could take in little else. She imagined what it would feel like, having those wires tighten around her little throat, imagining her air cut off and the bones in her neck snapping and—

The mules brought the car to a sudden stop, rocking the passengers within.

Rough hands grabbed and pinched and yanked them from the car. Ellena recognized two of the men to whom the hands belonged: Liberty Baker's father, Obedience, and Prudence Pickering's uncle, Jeremiah. The men shoved her toward the gallows and her stomach wrenched itself into a knot. Her mother, whose ankle had been broken with a hammer when she refused to elaborate on Ellena's involvement in magick rituals, was dragged toward the gallow steps by Cotton Pratt, whose wife once came to the glen to buy a poultice for the bruise he had given her. When Martha fell, they kicked her and dragged her to her feet again.

It hurt Ellena's heart more to see how they treated her mother than to suffer any personal indignities at their hands. Her mother's moon was waning from abuse at the hands of monsters, and it wasn't fair! Ellena hated them. She hated them! And her hate was strong because she was strong, because *her* moon was waxing. If they did manage to string her up, it would take a long time to kill her, and she was scared that it would hurt for all that time, but she wouldn't cry because her anger wouldn't let her.

The wind blew and the trees rustled. *We won't let them hurt you. It is our promise. We won't let you fall.*

On the stage of the gallows, Ellena was shoved to the ground near the prostrate form of her mother. The other villagers had gathered before them to watch. Ellena clutched her hands into little fists. They were judging her and her mother—there, Chastity Parke, who had come for a potion to stop the baby growing inside her, and there, Zebede Ratcliffe, who had once come, hat in hand, to beg Mother Martha to remove a curse on his land and put it instead on his neighbor's. Perhaps they felt guilty; more likely, they were afraid of being called out. They shouted to drown out whatever they felt, and their cruel words were sharp slivers of metal in her ears.

"Now, Mother? Will you say the words?" she whispered.

"Not yet," Martha replied.

The trees rustled impatiently.

"Why? Why not now?"

"Silence!" Elder Barrow said from a pulpit built near the gallows. "Your sin has bound you thus, and your magick has no power here."

"Soon," Martha whispered as Obedience Baker and Jeremiah Pickering yanked her to her feet.

Ellena looked up at her, confusion holding her tongue.

"I am speaking!" Elder Barrow roared, and Ellena couldn't help flinching. "You will respect the law."

"Your law has no bearing on us," Martha said. Despite her injuries, her voice was loud and clear and silenced the shouting of the crowd.

Elder Barrow glared at her, his face red. "Martha Weede, you stand accused of witchcraft and corruption of another's soul. You have been tried and found guilty, and now you are condemned to death according to the Eighth Law. Have you anything to say for yourself or your ward?"

Martha stared silently above the heads of the villagers to the line of mountains, hazy in the distance. Ellena knew she was clearing the altar in her mind.

"By the power vested in the court of New Ipswich, your sentence shall be carried out this twentieth day of MidSummer beneath the gaze of our New God."

Mother Martha finally began to speak the words, and the dawn sky grew dark again. The stone-colored clouds elongated into sharp blades across the sky. The villagers of New Ipswich looked up and muttered anxiously to each other. The Elders looked worried, too, but their uneasy gazes were fixed on the villagers, not Martha and Ellena.

"I said, your magick has no power here!" Elder Barrow shouted, his red face turning berry-purple. To the men holding Martha up, he added, "Cut out her tongue."

It was the first time Ellena had seen her mother look afraid since she had been arrested. She struggled against the iron grasp of her captors as another man she did not know approached her mother. He punched the old woman in the face and then squeezed her throat until she opened her mouth to gasp for air.

"Stop!" the girl cried out, terrified for her mother. "Don't do this, please! Stop this!"

Elder Barrow's expression didn't waver, except to allow a tiny, almost imperceptible smile. He would not be moved. If anything, he would enjoy the pain and suffering of helpless women on his stage of paraded sins, and her anger swelled.

Ellena rose to her feet but before she could do anything to help her mother, Zebede Ratcliffe had jumped the gallows stage and taken hold of her. His grip was strong; it hurt her ribs. She turned her head to other faces she knew in the crowd, the ones who looked just as surprised and horrified as her mother. "Please, somebody—help her!"

No one moved or spoke as the man used a pair of pliers to take hold of the old woman's tongue. Once he had a good grip on it and had pulled it over her lips, he let go of her throat and drew a knife from his belt. Then he cut Martha's tongue out at the root.

The old woman screamed, but the sound was drowned by a gurgle as blood spilled from her mouth and over her chin, splattering the metal tools. The lump of bloody muscle was tossed aside, and all three men stepped away from Martha, letting her sink to the ground beside Ellena. The old woman did not cry, but her eyes were wet and shining and large with pain. She extended a hand to her daughter and the girl took it and held it.

The old woman tried to speak, but managed only to send fresh waves of blood over her chin and neck.

All around them, the trees rustled angrily. *Now,* they whispered. *Say the words… say them now…*

"Now?" the girl echoed, and her mother nodded. Martha had only a moment to squeeze her daughter's hand before Elder Barrow was barking orders and the men were on her again, dragging her toward the wire noose.

Ellena turned her head. She didn't want to see. She had to concentrate, and her time was running out; once they were finished with Mother Martha, they would turn their hate on her.

She began to speak, softly at first while they were distracted with hanging her mother, then louder as the angry fire in her bellowed outward.

"*Rí agus Banríon na Foraoise páirt a ghlacadh linn inár n-am gá! Cuimhnigh dúinn le linn na bhflaitheas agus cuirimid naimhde a mharú!*"

✳

And so we came. Though it was not our custom to get involved in the affairs of mortal men, we had grown fond of our little Martha and her girl-child. They had long been good to us and protected our trees from axes and fire. They had looked after the Little Ones and fed them when the forest buried itself beneath the snow. Further, we had grown tired of the village's endless persecution of those they called Heathens, those who sought the old ways and invited us back into the world we had once ruled.

We are endless like the water, and immortal. We move with the wind. Our memories are longer than those of the trees or rocks.

And we keep our promises.

So I led my people, the people of the woods, made of elements and stars and ancient magick, into the village of New Ipswich. My soldiers called blue fire up from the places outside the earth to burn their homes and fences of dead wood. They froze their monuments until rust engulfed the metal and devoured it, like the Plague of Invisible Mouths, and razed them to the earth.

As the wind carried us along the streets, I spread my fists and the earth opened. Thick roots of the nearby trees sprang from deep within the ground, wrapping around

Joseph Abbott, Chastity Parke, Cora Rawlins and other fleeing forms and yanking them back into the hole. The displaced dirt rushed back in to bury many of the villagers alive. We watched as their clawing, scrabbling forms sank beneath the dirt. Cora's mouth gaped open and then filled with dirt and she was pulled under.

The roots, however, had laid claim to Joseph and Chastity. The dirt, hard now like stone, held both at the waists while the roots tightened around their necks and ribs and crushed their bodies. They dangled limply toward the earth like starving plants, and the roots, with a taste now for blood, sought more villagers to ensnare.

I commanded thorny vines to loose their hold on the woods and snake through the village, spearing eyes and lungs and hearts. Some, glowing pale green and blue with rage, took hold of villagers' limbs and tore bodies apart.

Blood washed the dirt streets and the moans and wails and screams of Mother Martha's enemies mixed with the howl of our savage winds. We spared the children, who ran away into the woods. Little Ellena had asked for that, and we obliged. The men and women of the village, able-bodied farmers and strong-backed workers—the breeders of the new human race—we slaughtered and left where they fell.

We made our way to the gallows.

Creedence Burnell, Obedience Baker, and Jeremiah

Pickering huddled on their stage, watching with frozen, horrified faces the carnage swirling around their village. The limp, mangled body of our little Martha hung from their gallows pole like a broken branch from a dead tree. I cut Martha's wire-rope with a gesture and she fell, a lump of rags and beaten flesh. Then I sent others to sweep around Ellena in whirling dervishes of wind and protect her. She stood very still among them and covered her eyes with her hands.

Those three men of the village cowering before us were not like the men of old, who in facing our wrath stood firm and stoic with their weapons drawn, ready to greet death. These wept and begged, and then they fell like kindling when we caused their gallows to splinter and spear their eyes and throats.

The village elders had fled to their New Church. Decades ago, they had built it from sheets of tin and metal and iron, from old shipping containers and scraps of ships and cars and trucks. Electronic circuitry, long dry, formed an arch over the doorway. Cell phones lined the windows like frames of blind eyes. Braided electrical cables had been furnished as architectural embellishments. Taking in so much of the technology of the New God, I couldn't help but remember the fear that had once driven us into the ground and the deepest shadows of the forest.

And then I remembered the anger.

My army at my back, we burst through the doors.

The village elders we found huddled near the altar, clutching each other behind the 72-inch flatscreen television which formed its front face. Some prayed to their New God. Others looked ready to fight.

Ellena was right; they brandished iron. They had also fashioned crude weapons from remnants of steel and tin and other alloys of metal. They had charged up their generator, and the metal prongs of their soul-cleansing device sparked almost like magick.

"W-What are you, woman?" Elder Barrow asked in a voice part bluster and part terror. "What manner of Heathen devil are you?"

We did not answer. Instead, we swept toward the altar.

They swung their weapons and the prongs of metal vibrated and sizzled with electrical sparks, but we were practiced in avoiding their machines. Zebede Ratcliff thrust at us with his iron spear. I gestured with my fingers and his head turned all the way around, snapping his neck. Cotton Pratt, who beat Martha worse than he had ever beaten his wife and daughter, swung at me with an iron axe. I flew out of its way, and with a nod, raised him above the ground and dashed him against the stone floor. We crushed them, broke their bones. We used the old magick, the substance of our souls from the dimensions we in ancient times called home. The secrets of that substance were many, perhaps too many for most whose bodies and minds had so short a memory.

Elder Barrow fell to his knees. "Oh, ancient goddesses and gods, forgive me! Please forgive me! I didn't understand before, but now—now I see!"

"You will never see again," I said, and a fog overtook his eyes. He cried out, clutching at his face, whimpering that he was blind. I considered slitting his throat. Instead, I caused his right hand and arm to shrivel and curl up to the elbow, as well as his left foot to the ankle and his testicles.

He might not have the memory of trees, but I would make sure he remembered who he had angered that day.

When the bodies of the Heathens' enemies lay in a bloody heap on the altar like the sacrifices of old, their remnants of technology scattered about them like a halo, we looked around. One man was left, cowering in a corner. When he saw us, he didn't beg. He didn't fight.

He simply looked up at us, nodded, then closed his eyes and said, "Please be merciful and make it quick, Ancient Ones."

"Jonah Harwood," I replied. "You will let the girl return to the house in the glen and live as she has lived, and you will protect her. You will allow no harm to come to her as it did to her mother. Do this, and we will let you live."

Harwood opened his eyes. They shone with relief and surprise. "Yes, yes, of course. Of course I will. I will protect her until my dying day."

"Then we will remember you," I said, and at that, we returned to the trees.

Ellena tells that story to her children, and her children's children. Sometimes, Grandpa Jonah tells it, though his eyes don't sparkle quite the same way when he does. Sometimes, when he finishes, he stares out the window of the little house in the glen and worries that the cities of the Faithful will hear about the little village where the Heathens won, that they will come out and try to make things return to the way they were.

More often than not, when he looks out that window, he sees us, and the anxious lines in his face soften a little, and he turns back to the children and smokes his pipe and tells them about the rainforests his family once tried to save.

He has no need to worry, because we are still here, among the trees, watching. We still sing the songs in the old language and speak through the rustling of the leaves. We have memories that go on, longer than that little house in the glen will stand, longer than bones will hold up those who live in it. We remember.

And we keep our promises.

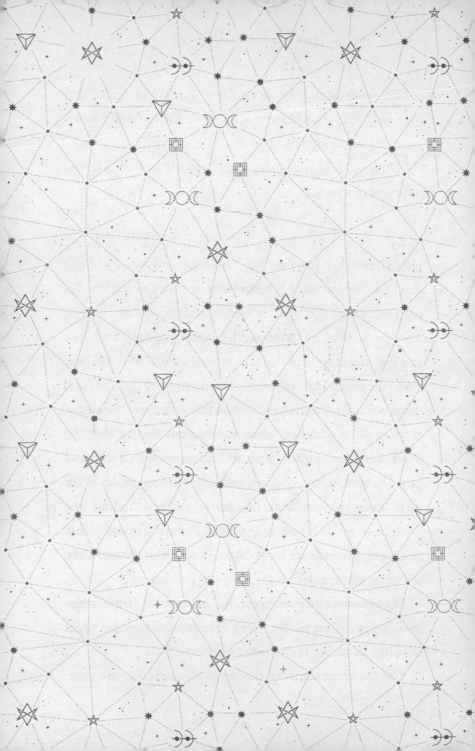

HOME:
A MORGANVILLE VAMPIRES STORY

Rachel Caine

"Oh, shit, no they didn't," Shane Collins said. "Tell me that's not a coffee shop going in across the street."

The banner had just gone up in the window: a standard graphic of a coffee cup with steam coming off it. What wasn't normal was that the steam formed a skull and crossbones. Not a bad image for a Morganville shop, but as he snapped a quick cell-phone picture of it, Shane knew it meant real trouble.

"Yep, it's definitely a coffee shop," his wife Claire confirmed as she sipped her mocha from Common Grounds, which sat directly on the opposite side of the street.

They were sitting near the window. Outside, an awning

stretched over the sidewalk to block out the blazing noon sunlight; heat shimmered off the road between the two stores, and it had the effect of animating the skull and crossbones. Weird and *not* okay. None of this was okay, Shane thought.

"Who are the owners? Do you know?" asked Claire.

"Nope," he said. "But I'd better find out fast. Picking a spot like that is just asking for a fight. I guess my next stop is City Hall. Somebody has to have something, right?"

"I'll check with Oliver, if you like."

"Check about what?" asked an antique English accent, and Oliver was suddenly standing right there at their table, staring out the window as he wiped down a freshly washed mug with a hand towel.

He broke the mug by squeezing it too hard. From this angle, Shane couldn't tell if the vampire's eyes had gone blood-red, but he didn't doubt it. Oliver was old, for a vamp, both in years and in general appearance; he'd been frozen in late middle age, sharp features and graying hair, and he didn't suffer fools. He never suffered anything, really. He just transferred that to somebody else, usually the person standing next to him.

He knew better than to try it with Shane or Claire. That was some comfort.

"Way to waste your blood donations," Shane said, and nodded at the cuts that had opened up in Oliver's hand.

Thick, dark-red blood was dripping from the palm: darker than regular human blood, and slower to trickle out. Oliver cursed under his breath and wrapped the towel around his hand, then went back to glaring at the competition. The competition did not burst into flames or run in terror. It didn't seem to notice. Oliver wasn't used to that.

From the counter, Eve Rosser (she'd kept her last name after marriage, to which Claire had given a big thumbs up) said, "Boss, I'm not cleaning that blood up. Just so you know." She was a tall, gorgeous lady, and lately she'd been working out and building muscle on those arms; it looked good on her. "What the hell is going on? Trouble?"

Oliver made a low sound in his throat, like a purr that built to a growl. Kind of confusing, that sound. Claire met Shane's eyes and raised her brows. Took another sip.

Oliver's temper wasn't unusual. But that weird sound definitely was.

Eve came over and handed Oliver another mug. This one was full of blood. "Drink," she said. "You sound hungry."

"I sound angry," he shot back, but he took the mug and downed it in two gulps. Thrust it back at her. "I have to go."

"Go where? It's the middle of the day," Eve said. Vampires like Oliver—even as old as Oliver was—didn't generally go out for noon strolls... but that question was already moot, because Oliver had yanked open the door of Common

Grounds and was striding across the street, in full sun, without even a hat. "Jesus. Somebody better go after him. But not me because I *deeply* don't want to lose this job."

Oliver's skin started crisping and smoking halfway across the street, but he didn't speed up or slow down. There was something relentless about his pace. And Shane sighed and got up.

"Fine," he said. "Guess this is my problem now." He put on his white Stetson. It was a good one, fitted to his head, but the gold police emblem on it made it heavier than he liked.

Claire stood up too, watching Oliver, and gave him a quick kiss. "Be careful."

"Always."

He bent to give their baby girl—asleep in her carrier—a kiss on her chubby little cheek, drew in the clean, sweet smell of her skin, and kept that with him as a talisman as he walked after Oliver across the street. It was a baking hell of a day, typical for summer in this part of Texas; humidity close to zero, but temps that threatened to flatten you in minutes anyway. *But it's a dry heat,* he told himself with the proper degree of sarcasm.

Being chief of police in this isolated, insular town was bad enough without the vampires; it was still a dead-end town for humans, even though things were better now than they'd ever been. The vamps lived in their own enclaves for the most part, and though they'd given up some of the businesses in town to human ownership, they certainly hadn't ceded all of them. Two hundred vamps, twelve hundred human souls, and most of the wealth still concentrated among the undead.

One of those human souls belonged to his precious infant daughter, and that had shifted Shane's perspective quite a bit. He'd never been a fan of vamps; he'd just learned to live with them. Now, it was different. He had a family to protect, not just from the random hunger pangs of some nightstalker, but from the things even the vampires feared.

Having some pop-up coffee store across from Common Grounds? That was a clear, obvious challenge to the powers-that-be of this town. The Founder, Amelie. Oliver, her lieutenant and enforcer, especially. Having the balls to do that meant someone had come to town who was either desperately stupid... or had serious power. Neither was good.

Oliver had already opened the door to the shop on the far side of the street. Shane lengthened his stride—long legs for the win—and got there just a few steps behind.

Coming out of the fierce sun felt like walking face-first into a black velvet curtain, and he blinked fast and hard to try to adjust his eyes. The smell hit him next. What was that? *Cookies?* His mouth started to water. Oliver's shop never smelled this good.

"Hey there, my very first customers," said a cheerful voice. Not a Texas accent, not even East Texas; more of a Deep South thing. Georgia, maybe, mint juleps and sweet tea from syrup. "Welcome, both of you, to Dark Brews. Sorry about the lights. Can I fix you something, boys?"

Her voice was bigger than she was. The woman was even smaller than Claire, though lush in her curves. Shane's first thought was that she was about thirty, but then sunlight from the window hit her a different way and he revised the estimate up to fifty. Long blond hair worn straight. Clear blue eyes. Skin the color of gold dust that she *must* have gotten out of a pretty expensive tanning bed.

Oliver stopped halfway to the counter. The woman stood on the other side. It didn't protect her a bit, but she didn't seem to even notice his stillness or the threat that came with it. She smiled and set out Texas-sized cookies on plates, and if she realized who Oliver was she damn sure didn't show it.

"I don't want whatever swill you think to serve here," Oliver said. "I want you gone, Jane."

Jane? Shane drew in a breath, then let it out without speaking. The hope that all this was some kind of innocent mistake was gone. Jane, whoever she was, intended to be here, across from Oliver's shop. And she wasn't here to make cookies.

"Oh, stop," Jane said, and smiled. It was an objectively adorable smile, with dimples, and almost flirty. Was that a *wink*? Shane couldn't be sure. "You old sweet talker, you. Sit yourself down. What's your poison these days, Oliver? AB? Or are you off the red stuff now?"

"Jane." Oliver's tone was a stone wall, a locked gate, and a moat on fire. "You aren't welcome here. You need to leave Morganville. Now."

"Well, I can't do that, now can I? I just got this place open! Why, I haven't even made my first sale yet. Would you like to be the first?" She stood there, hands on her hips. She looked utterly unthreatening, open, and friendly. She turned to Shane. "How about you, sweet thing? You can have you a nice cup of coffee, not that nasty old stuff they serve across the street, *and* take a pastry to go. On the house."

He wasn't sure what was going on here, and he certainly didn't like being stuck in the middle of it. "Sorry?"

"He's not quick, is he?" Jane asked Oliver.

"Leave him alone. He's not meat for your table."

She stopped smiling, and everything changed. Oh, she was still little and rounded and dressed in hot pink and frills; she still had big blue eyes and the same skin. But she looked *old*. And incredibly dangerous.

Shane put a hand on the butt of his gun.

"If you draw that stupid thing, I'm going to have to refuse service," Jane said. "And cook that arm for my dinner. Oh, who am I kidding, I'll feed it to the cat."

"Who the hell is she?" Shane asked Oliver. "Jane *who*?"

"You wouldn't know her," Oliver said. "She's nothing. No one."

"Unlike you," Jane said, and crossed her arms. "You continue being *someone*, don't you, old man? You always end up on your feet, never your knees."

"You're a vampire," Shane said. It was the only thing that made sense to him.

"Oh *lordy* no. Can't stand the sight of blood." She nodded slowly at Oliver. "Go on. Tell him who I am."

"What do you want from me, Jane?"

Her accent shifted effortlessly from honeyed Southern USA to something rougher, older, and... English. Like Oliver's. "What I always wanted. Justice."

"Jane. Stop this."

"You remember me now? Well, I'm surprised. I was so insignificant that you didn't even write down my name when you ordered my death."

Oliver went very quiet again. Shane forced himself to walk up all the way to the counter. He leaned on the wood and looked at the very small woman with the very old eyes. She didn't blink. "Look, I get it," he said. "Oliver's a son of a bitch. But the thing is, he's *our* son of a bitch. I don't know you, lady. So why don't you tell me why you're here?"

"Revenge," she said. "Toil. Trouble. Dire and murderous things. And to teach this town how to make a *really* good cup of coffee." She popped that smile again, and years melted away from her. "Here, sugar. You take it black, I suppose? Most cops do."

Shane looked down to find a huge, chunky mug sitting on the counter between them filled with what looked and smelled like fresh coffee. Best coffee he'd ever smelled, if he was honest. And one of those cookies sat next to it.

"Go on," Jane said. "Free. I always support our brave officers."

Oliver said, "Shane. Don't." There was real urgency in his voice. And Shane intended to follow that advice. But there was something about that *smell*, that delicious, incredible smell that made his fingers wrap around the handle and lift it and take one sip. Just one.

The taste was foul, but only for a flash of an instant, and then it was the best damn thing he'd ever tasted. It exploded in spirals through his whole body, a kiss of earth and bliss, and he was drinking more before he could stop himself.

It only got better.

Then the cup was empty, and he felt sick and shaky. He set it down with a rattle on the counter and realized he was breathing too fast. He braced himself on the wood and looked up.

Jane smiled. Perfect, even teeth. "Why, Officer, you'd think you saw the devil himself," that sweet Southern voice said. "Another round?"

The worst thing was that he wanted to say *yes*. His brain was screaming at him that he'd just done something stupid, incredibly stupid, but it was also telling him that it wasn't his fault. And that felt wrong, and also very, very familiar. He'd been here before. A vampire had scrambled his brains and led him around as her pet for a while, and this felt horribly the same.

Shane stumbled backward, and felt a strong pair of hands grip and hold him upright when his knees threatened to buckle. "Jane, leave the boy," Oliver said. "What *do you want*?"

"You," she replied. "I want *blood*. I will have justice before the sun rises, or this town will burn."

Shane didn't remember leaving. His head didn't seem right anymore, not until he was back across the street and Claire was pressing a wet cloth to his forehead. "What just happened?" he asked her. She looked grim.

"Feel like going to a meeting?" she asked. "Because I think we'd better find out."

Eve, who was standing next to his chair, rolled her eyes. It was such a familiar gesture that he felt instantly better.

"God, you'd think he'd be less faint-y after growing up in this town," she said. "Hey, Shane? Don't you dare die on me." She paused. "Uh... how good was their coffee? Asking for a friend."

He sighed. "Honestly? It was great."

"Shit."

The meeting, not surprisingly, was held in the vampire stronghold, in Amelie's meeting room, and it was a war council. Amelie sat at the head of the table, looking as cool as ever; she was an elegant woman, agelessly beautiful, with soft blond hair swept into a gravity-defying style from the 1960s. Her pale gray silk suit matched her eyes. At her right hand sat Oliver, who'd changed from his tie-dyed Common Grounds t-shirt and jeans into a pair of black trousers, severe white shirt, and black velvet coat. The only touch of color to him was a flare of red in the jacket lining.

Claire held baby Carrie in her arms on Amelie's left hand, and Shane had claimed the chair beside them even if it wasn't technically his spot. Mayor Hannah Moses sat next to him; she hadn't dressed up for the occasion, but somehow her simple jeans and worn denim shirt looked like battle armor to him.

Michael arrived a minute later. Michael Glass, Shane's

best friend. Vampire, after a brief shift back to human that hadn't quite lasted. He liked being a vampire. He was comfortable with it.

And he was by himself. "Where's Eve?" Shane asked. Michael looked the same as he had at eighteen, which was becoming a little weird; Shane, twenty-five, could feel the difference. Eve had aged along with the rest of them, thank God. She'd backed off the Goth makeup lately, though she still liked dramatic eye treatments and dyed-black hair.

Michael slid into the seat beside Oliver, probably because he was one of the few Oliver wouldn't backhand for taking the liberty. Amelie made a point of checking her watch and raising her eyebrows; it would have shattered most people, but Michael just raised his brows back and said, "Eve closed up and went home to look after the kid. Seemed like a good day to be off the streets."

Amelie didn't *quite* roll her eyes, but she came damn close. "Excellent. One child at the table is quite enough."

"Hey, Carrie's being good," Claire said, without the slightest bit of defensiveness. "Besides, you know she likes you."

The baby did love Amelie. She was fascinated right now, staring at the vampire's ageless face, the sparkling diamond necklace at her throat. Amelie stared at the kid like she was viewing an odd specimen, then smiled. It was an unexpectedly sweet expression, and Carrie burbled and kicked and smiled back. *Don't do that,* Shane wanted to tell his daughter. *Don't think they're your friends.* He felt his hands ache with the urge to grab Carrie and take her out of here, somewhere safe.

"Oliver," Amelie said, still smiling. "I'm waiting to hear why this meeting is necessary."

"Aren't we still waiting for the idiot to arrive?" Oliver asked sourly. Amelie kept smiling with her attention on the baby.

"The idiot's here," said a voice from the door, as it opened and slammed shut. Myrnin stepped in with a dramatic flair, and twirled. He was wearing some eighteenth-century frock coat in stained, tattered silk over fleece pajamas with fluffy sheep on them. Shane couldn't see his feet over the table, but he guessed Myrnin would have found himself a new pair of fluffy vampire bunny slippers. They were his favorites. "Did you miss me, dear Ollie?"

"Shut up," Oliver said. "Sit down."

"I can't," Myrnin said. "I made a vow to an Elder God that I'll never sit down again and—"

"Sit," Amelie said, and Myrnin instantly took a chair, put folded hands on the table, and looked attentive. She gave him a tiny shake of her head, but she never lost her smile. It was getting unsettling. "Go on, Oliver."

"Jane Penwell's come to town," he said. "She's come for me."

Amelie stood up. It was an instant thing, not a motion—the way vampires moved when they were startled. One blink she was relaxed and smiling at Carrie; the next she was on her feet, rigid and cold, staring at Oliver. Shane couldn't remember the last time he'd seen her do that. She'd relaxed quite a bit over the past few years.

But she damn sure wasn't complacent. "How can that be?"

"I don't know," he said.

"Who turned her?"

"No one," Oliver said. "She isn't one of us. She's… different."

"The witch can't be *alive*. How did you not know of this the instant she came to town?"

"Ask him," Oliver said, and gestured toward Myrnin. Amelie transferred her pale, sharp gaze to Morganville's resident mad scientist vampire, who seemed not to really notice. He was bending over and staring at the wood of the table.

"Myrnin," Amelie snapped.

"There's a ghost in there," he said, as if that made any damn sense, and straightened up. "Sorry, what's the question?"

"There's a witch running a new coffee shop across the street from Common Grounds, and we don't know how she got there," Michael said. "Keep up, man."

"But… none of the usual alarms went off," Myrnin said.

"My my my. Perhaps there's a problem with the…" He didn't finish the thought. He bent over and sniffed the table instead. "Definitely a ghost. I thought you should know, dear lady. You might want to have an exorcist in. Or a carpenter. Whichever."

"*Myrnin.*"

"You're quite sure the woman's a witch?" Myrnin asked. "Well, I suppose you are. You being the expert on such things, I mean. Didn't you burn quite a few of them in your day? Understandable, it's so cold in Scotland in the winter…"

"Generally they were strangled," Oliver said coolly. "Do get it right."

"And you made her acquaintance while you were gadding about slaying clansmen and enforcing your particular brand of puritan zeal all over the bodies of suspected witches."

"If I'd found you *gadding about*, I'd have burned you on the spot, Myrnin." Shane felt a chill, because Oliver's voice was no longer cool. It was vicious, and completely serious. "No one is more of a witch than you."

"Oh, I'm quite completely a vampire. But this Jane Penwell of yours is interesting. I really must stop in and find out her secrets."

Oliver started to reply, but Amelie's voice sliced through like a guillotine blade. "The point is, Jane Penwell is an impossibility. She should not be here if she isn't one of us; Oliver, you did see her die?"

"Yes," he said. "In 1648."

"And burned?" Amelie asked. She raised her eyebrows. "*Please* tell me her body was burned, and we are not dealing with a witch you failed to stop when you had the chance."

Shane looked at Claire, then at Michael. They were feeling the same weirdness.

"Wait," Claire said. "You-you sound like you *actually believe in witches*. Real ones."

"Of course," Oliver said. "Try not to be idiots. True witches were rare, but they were quite powerful."

"Hedge magic," Myrnin sniffed. "Hardly *scientific*."

"Says the man who thinks conducting an experiment is only valid if you do it at the right stage of the moon," Claire shot back.

"There is a perfectly reasonable explanation for—"

"Guys," Shane said. "Okay, so… witches are real, got it, but why exactly are *vampires* scared of them?"

"Because they are an abomination of the natural order," Amelie said.

"Pot, kettle…" Shane murmured, and she at least pretended not to hear, which was good, because he liked his internal organs on the inside.

"And they can kill us, of course," Myrnin said. He sounded

gleeful about it. "Very, very dead indeed. Or as close to it as makes no difference. It would be a useful question to answer, whether dead vampires ever stop actually *thinking* inside those decomposing, inert shells, wouldn't it? Not that I'm looking forward to discovering the truth personally."

"Kill you how, exactly?" Hannah Moses asked. She'd been listening intently, quietly, and she managed to make the question sound like a concern, not an opportunity. Something Shane knew he couldn't have pulled off, given his history with the vamps. "How much of a danger does she pose to the vampire population of this town? And does she also threaten humans?"

"She can kill vampires with a single touch," Myrnin said, and was suddenly at her side, gently poking a finger into her shoulder. "They are venomous to us by nature. They can take our life force from us and use it to refresh their own. Witches are predators, dear Mayor. And if we try to kill them, we must do so at a distance, using human weapons in order to…"

That was weird, Shane thought. Not about whatever weirdness Myrnin was spouting, that was *normal*. No, what was strange was that he had pushed his chair back and he was standing up, every movement calm and natural even though he hadn't *intended* to stand up at all, and he felt his hand on the gun that hung heavy on his belt and the safety snap coming off and he thought *what the hell…*

She's got me, he thought, and tried to fight it. He couldn't.

And then he drew his sidearm and fired three shots into Myrnin's chest.

The next instant, he was free again, *himself,* and Myrnin was staggering backward, mouth open in shock as he stared down at the neat holes punched in a triangle over his heart. The vampire's eyes rolled back in his head, and he stumbled and fell.

Claire screamed. The baby screamed too, equal parts distress and shock from the noise. Shane wanted to yell, too, because something was *very very wrong here* and then Amelie's ice-cold hand was around his throat and he was bent backward over the heavy wooden table.

"Take his weapon," she ordered someone. Maybe Michael, Shane couldn't see. It was wrenched out of his hand, and he heard the metal clatter across the table. Someone else had it now. *Good.*

"Don't hurt him!" Claire shouted. She was on her feet now, with the screaming baby cuddled to her.

"Take the child outside," Amelie said. "Leave."

"No!"

"Now!" There was real tension in the vampire's voice, and Shane realized that she wasn't trying to kill him; she wouldn't have to *try.* She was only holding him down. "It isn't Shane's fault. I won't damage him."

"I'm not *going*."

God, his brave, stupid wife. He wanted her to go, but the hand around his throat choked the words off, and deep down he was *glad* she was here, that he could see her and sweet Carrie one last time and *damn* that was selfish, he wasn't the one who was going to have to live with whatever happened next.

Because whatever Amelie might say now, she wasn't about to let him walk out of this room alive. He just put three bullets into her friend, and speaking of that, *was he dead*? No, of course he wasn't. Vampires weren't that easy to put down, especially not with lead. He saw Hannah rise up from near the floor, and with her came Myrnin—leaning on her, actually spitting chunks of metal, but definitely still undead and kicking. "I am *very* upset with you, Shane," Myrnin said, and coughed up the third bullet. "And someone owes me new pajamas."

"Quiet," Amelie said. She stared into Shane's eyes. "Are you listening, Jane Penwell?"

"Yes," Shane said. Not *him*, exactly. But something inside him, *oh Jesus*, there was somebody talking through him and no matter how much he tried to stop, he couldn't. "Do you like my new familiar? I thought he'd be useful. Oliver seemed concerned for his safety. Unusual. He normally doesn't care about the mayflies."

"Is that what you call them now?" Oliver said. "Out of the boy, Jane. *Now.*"

Shane felt himself laugh. She had him locked up in the back of his brain, and he wasn't even remotely able to bust himself out. He couldn't even tap a pinky finger.

Oliver was right. That coffee was a bad idea.

The coffee. Shane could feel it inside him, like a thick, oily weight in his stomach. It hadn't gone anywhere. Maybe it couldn't. *It isn't coffee, idiot.*

"Let the boy go!" Oliver leaned over, shouting in Shane's face. Maybe, despite everything, Jane Penwell was just a *little* wary of him, because for just a second Shane felt her recede, shrink away... and in that instant he knew what he had to do. He had just enough space to control his hand. His arm.

He jammed fingers into his mouth, deep into the back of his throat, and triggered his gag reflex.

Amelie cursed in some language he didn't recognize, a violent burst of syllables, as he threw up a thick, sludgy black on his face, his chin, her hand... She pulled away, wiping the mess off on his shirt, and Shane rolled on his side to keep vomiting the stuff out. There was a lot of it, but with every drop that emerged he felt more himself. Less *invaded.*

Claire handed Carrie to Myrnin, who looked surprised and cautious, as if the kid might explode. Carrie stopped crying and opened her eyes wide at him.

"Great," Shane said, or tried to say; between the convulsive vomiting and the choking, he sounded like a rusty hinge. "Vampire babysitter."

"Perish the thought," Myrnin barked, but he settled the baby comfortably into his arms. "You drank a potion, I see."

"Guess so."

"Coffee-based, was it?"

Shane just nodded. He'd run out of words and energy. *What if I'd shot Claire? The baby?* If he'd had anything left in his stomach, it would have come up at the thought. He was supposed to protect and defend. Not harm. Myrnin could shrug it off. But those bullets might have gone into someone else just as easily.

Claire pulled him off the table and into a chair, and used a wet wipe on his face. Baby fresh, he thought, and almost managed a laugh. He felt weak and empty and now he was shaking like he'd come off a three-day bender.

The stuff he'd drunk this morning sat on the table in a wet, glistening puddle.

"Hmm," Myrnin said. "Well then. That might not be quite as harmless as it looks right now." He flashed around the table, a flicker and then suddenly still, and gave the baby to... Oliver. That was not okay with anyone, including Oliver and Carrie, who took up her restless wail again. Oliver looked tight-lipped and awkward, but at least he didn't drop her. "Do support her head, Oliver, there's a good lad, while I…" Myrnin dug around in the huge pockets of his ragged coat. "Ah!" He came out with a stoppered bottle. Shane expected liquid to come out, but instead, when Myrnin opened it and tipped it over the black puddle, what came out was a thick, greenish fog that spread and clung to the liquid beneath.

The liquid shuddered like a living thing. It tried to crawl away.

"Jesus," Hannah whispered, and pointed the gun at it, as if that would do any good at all. The puddle didn't get far. It let off a foul smell, then bubbled, and then it turned dry, brittle, and apparently dead.

Myrnin dashed over to the corner, retrieved a trash can, and used a fold of fabric over his hand to nudge the stuff off the table. It landed in the can with a resounding *boom*. Myrnin stripped off his coat and tossed it in after. "Burn that," he told Amelie. She nodded. "And now Shane also owes me a new coat. Right. She's opened her store to serve to our locals her particular potion and make them, ah, minions, is that the correct term?"

"More or less," Claire said. She rounded the table and took Carrie out of Oliver's arms. The vampire looked tremendously relieved. He also retreated to stand next to

Amelie. *Oliver's scared of babies.* Shane was too tired to laugh. "We need to stop her. Now."

"Already done," Amelie said. "Oliver warned me before this meeting that Shane might have been… compromised. We've been monitoring who's come in and out; she's only served two others, both humans. We have them in custody. I suppose a brisk course of emetics would be in order."

"Burn her out," Oliver said.

"And accidentally set half our town ablaze? No." She turned on him. "What does she *want*, Oliver?"

"My death. Obviously."

"She could have accomplished that with a brush of her hand across your skin. It seems she wants something more."

A new voice. "Oliver knows what I want."

Oh shit.

Jane Penwell was standing in the corner. She shouldn't have been there. She *couldn't* have been there… but she was. Amelie and Oliver reacted instantly, but not the way they normally would, to attack; they retreated to the closed outer door, but when Amelie tried with all her strength to open it, the knob didn't turn. She snapped it off. Oliver tried to punch through the door, but his fist bounced off the wood as if it were made of vampire-proof steel. He kept punching, his fist a blur, until Amelie caught his arm in an iron grip.

Then he turned and stepped between Amelie and the

witch standing in the other corner. "You want an apology," he said. "For your execution? No. You were a witch. *Are* a witch. And you deserved it."

"Yes, of course I did," Jane said. "And I know you will never apologize for doing what you think was your duty then, or now. You've always been a fanatic." She crossed her arms and leaned against the wall. The only one of them at ease right now, Shane thought. Hannah was pointing a gun at her, but Jane spectacularly ignored that; Myrnin hadn't retreated, but he hadn't gone for her, either, which for Myrnin was pretty amazing restraint.

"Then what do you demand, Mistress Penwell?" Amelie asked. She stepped out, away from Oliver but no nearer to the witch facing them.

"To right a wrong."

"What wrong?" Michael asked that in the silence, and Jane glanced at him with a strange kind of pity.

"Child," she said, "have you never heard of the witch trials? Countless thousands of us rounded up, put to the question, burned or drowned or strangled or hanged, all for the selfish security of vampires. Ask Amelie. Who began the witch trials? Who wrote the *Malleus Maleficarum*?" Amelie, silent, just watched with eyes so bright and silver they might as well have glowed. "The oldest of them knew what danger a real witch posed. And they decided that we had to die, for their safety. Hundreds of thousands of innocents slaughtered to find a handful of genuine threats. Isn't that right, *sugar*?"

"Yes," Amelie said quietly. "But that began before my time, or Oliver's."

"You took the cause up happily enough."

"It's what we were taught," Oliver said. "Is that what you need to hear? An apology for *that*?"

"Oh no, sweetie. I'm not here for your regret. I'm here for your blood."

Shane could have sworn he saw Oliver *flinch*. "You'll not have it. Kill me, and it's useless. I'll never hand it over willingly."

"You'll get nothing for your spells from us, witch. *Leave our town.*" Amelie sounded angry now. That was very, very dangerous.

"I think I'll stay," Jane said. "You've made it so hospitable."

"We'll burn you out," Oliver replied, and it was a promise. "Witches and fire. Never a good combination."

"I've had a long time to find charms against such things. You think I didn't come here prepared for all your nonsense? I leave when I get what I want. Not before." Jane straightened up and stepped away from the wall and toward the rest of them—a tiny woman, but it felt like a real threat. Michael hadn't moved back with the others. He was in range.

"Mike," Shane said quietly. Michael shook his head. He had that *look*, the one Shane had known all his life—stubborn. Blindly determined. Sometimes that was a great thing, but it wasn't right now. "*Mike*. Dude, watch yourself." It wasn't easy, but he got to his feet. He didn't try to get his gun back from Hannah; she was a better shot anyway, and had been a cop longer than he had.

"I'm okay," Michael said. He walked *toward* the witch. She just watched him, but her eyebrows rose a little. "They're scared of you. I'm not. I don't have history with you. Why are you doing this?" Michael had charm, looks, and the gift of humility; the entire time Shane had known him that had never changed. But sometimes, he relied on that charm a little too much.

"Poor thing. You're so new at this you don't even understand what it is you're dealing with. I'll tell you this: I'm going to let you and your human friends turn around and walk right out of here. I promise to leave you out of this."

"We're not going," Claire said before Shane had the chance to. "This is our town too."

"Well, it *was*," Jane agreed. "My town now, until Oliver gives me what I want."

"He just said he won't," Michael said. He took another step closer, and Shane remembered what the vamps said…

witches could kill with a touch. Didn't Mike get that? "How about my blood instead?"

"Michael!" Amelie's voice snapped like a whip. "No!"

"She's not really my boss," Michael said to Jane, and deployed his killer smile. Shane didn't think it had much effect. "And I'm not afraid of you."

No, Michael, no, you definitely should be. Shane saw the warning flash in the witch's eyes.

"Back away from me, boy."

"Or what?" He took another step toward her. All she had to do now was casually reach out and brush her fingers over his skin. Shane saw Hannah's body bracing to fire the gun she held, and he quickly reached out and pushed the barrel down. Pissing the witch off wouldn't help. If it would have done damage, Oliver would have been roaring for them to shoot the hell out of her in the first place.

"I have no quarrel with you." Jane's voice had changed now, dropped out of its affected Southern accent and gone back overseas into something much rougher and older. "Don't offer up your blood for him."

"I'm not. I'm offering it up for this town. There are a lot of innocents here. You talked about how many were killed to get to you, right? I'd like to avoid that here. You said you need vampire blood. Any of us will do, right?"

"She wants us all dead," Oliver said. "Give her what

she wants and we're all doomed."

"Death is the last thing I want from you." Jane's voice reminded Shane of freezing waves on barren shores. Cold and lonely. "Tell your friends how I died, Oliver."

"The times were different," he said. Shane turned to look at him. Oliver looked... haunted.

"The gibbets were thick with witches. But you didn't do me the favor of hanging me."

Oliver didn't speak. Myrnin did. "Did you burn her?" He sounded sober, and unexpectedly sharp.

For a long few seconds, Shane was pretty sure Oliver wouldn't answer, but then he finally said, "We pricked her for the Devil's Mark, and found it on her body. I wasn't wrong; she was a genuine witch. She demanded the water test."

Even Amelie seemed surprised by that. "You drowned her?"

"No," he said. "She floated. The witch *floated*."

"The whole story, Oliver," Jane said. "Everything. Now. Or I will take the boy, then Myrnin, then your mistress. I'll save you for last. I will hunt every vampire you've given shelter, and then burn this foul town to ashes. *You owe me the truth*."

"Jesus, Michael, back the hell up," Shane said. Michael shook his head. He was probably thinking something dumb and brave, like being an obstacle between her and Oliver.

Oliver must have thought that, too, because he did what Jane wanted. He said, "She wasn't accused alone. Her husband John stood with her. A pair of witches together."

"And so you tied us together," Jane said. "Bound us face to face, body to body. And when I floated, I could not save him. *I watched him drown.* He was an innocent, never a witch, and you wouldn't even give him the decency of a Christian burial!"

"I'm sorry, Jane," Michael said. Shane thought he even meant it. "I really am. But this is a long time back. History."

"Not to me," Jane said. "But I'm not here for vengeance. Only for justice. *I want my love back.*"

"We can't bring back the dead," Amelie said.

Jane laughed and made a wide gesture at the vampires in the room. "Really? You're going to tell me that? But I'm not asking *you* to bring me back my dead as what *you* are. I'm asking for a drop of the blood of a vampire. Only a single drop, given willingly." Jane looked at Michael. "Will you do it?"

"Michael, no!" There was a whole chorus saying it, Shane included, but it was already too late. Michael's fangs slid down, sharp and dangerous. He'd nicked his finger before she could even finish her sentence, and held it out. One drop hit the floor between them.

Then Jane held out her palm, and the second drop hit her skin. She closed the hand into a fist, and for a second she looked like that ancient old woman again. Then like a very young girl, fresh-faced and innocent. Then back to her current—false—form. "Thank you," she said.

"What have you *done,* boy?" Oliver shouted, but it was too late; Jane wasn't there anymore. Gone, in a whisper of shadows. "Witches are liars! And she's no different!"

"Burn that store down," Amelie said. Her face had gone stark white. "Burn her out. Do it *now.*"

Shane got to the storefront just as the first flames took hold.

Amelie stood under the shadow of the Common Grounds awning with Oliver.

"Shit," Shane said, and took out his cell phone. Dialed the fire department. As slow as they were, it probably wouldn't do any good, but he had to try, at least.

"Shane," Claire said. She was still holding Carrie, who'd gone to sleep again, and she shielded the baby's head instinctively as she watched the place burning. "My God, is she inside?"

"I hope to heaven she is," Amelie said. "The last thing we need is a vengeful witch in Morganville, empowered by the freely given blood of a vampire. She could do *anything.* Raise the dead from their graves. Set demons loose on our streets. Curse every one of us with a vile plague—" Her voice died out, and Shane turned to look where she was staring.

Jane Penwell walked out of the fire. She was on fire, but an impatient brush of her hands down her tight pink dress put that out in a wisp of smoke, and she paused in the middle of the street. She had one of those giant coffee mugs in her hand.

"I could do all that," she agreed, as if she'd heard the whole thing. "And any town that gladly welcomes leeches like you no doubt ought to suffer. But I'm not here for vengeance, I told you that. I'm here for this."

She poured the cup into the street. A thick, black stream of liquid that even from twenty feet away smelled like coffee, but wasn't. It hit the street in thick, splattering drops... and then it drew together into a puddle.

Then it *grew*.

"Claire," Shane said, "maybe you'd better go."

She backed off a couple of steps, but his lady never really ran, not from a fight. Not even when she had a child to protect. Maybe especially not then.

The puddle spread out in an oily, shimmering circle, and then it suddenly began to retract.

It built itself up in black ropes like vines that whipped around each other, taller and taller. Knee-high, then waist-high. Then up to Shane's shoulders.

A rough human shape, black and iridescent on its surface.

Then it turned gray and stiff, like an unfinished statue.

Jane whispered, "Malleus," and cracks formed across the surface. They spread out in webs, and then the creature took a step forward toward her, and the gray stony surface broke apart and showered in dust to the street.

A naked man fell into Jane's arms, and she held him tight. She whispered another word, and clothes formed around him—black pants, a black jacket.

He looked like Michael. A perfect copy of him, in fact.

"Jesus," Shane breathed. "What the hell did you do?"

"It's only an initial form. He'll look different soon enough," Jane said. "I thank you, Master Michael Glass, for the loan of your blood. Jonathan will find his own face, and we'll trouble you no more."

Michael's doppelgänger turned and looked at him… but those weren't Mike's eyes. Not at all. They were black, not blue, and they were *really* unsettling, sitting in a friend's face.

"What is this place?" Not Michael's voice, either.

"Insignificant," Jane said. "Except it brought you back to me."

John—at least, that's what Shane assumed—fitted his hands around Jane's face. "*You* brought me back. You and I, love. Finally."

"Finally," she said, and smiled. "After all this time. I'm sorry it had to be this way. But I could never bring back an innocent human soul. You understand."

174

"I do now." His face was changing. Not so much Michael now; it was a squarer face with a sharper chin, clever dark eyes. Hair turning brown and thick and growing long. "Leave the vampires to their dust and desperation. We can be more. We can own the world, if you like."

"My love, I only wanted *you*. Not the world entire. Never that."

"And you have me," he said, and kissed her. "Forever."

He was still changing, Shane realized. Not a man at all now. His skin reddened. He grew horns. And leathery wings that rustled like autumn leaves. Shane's mouth went dry, and he wanted to *not know this*. Desperately. Because when the devil looked at him, its eyes were human.

"He's a demon," Amelie said. "*You called a demon.*"

"It was the only way to bring Jonathan back to me. He's my demon," Jane said. "Not yours. And we won't trouble you again." She sighed and stepped into the demon's arms. Put her head against its chest. "Better to reign in hell than serve in heaven. Take us home, my love."

That's when the fire raging through Dark Brews exploded upward into a whirling tornado, rushed out into the street, and whipped the two of them into the center of it. It only lasted a few seconds, and then it just... died.

All that was left was drifting ash and a pile of charred bone. Silence. The Dark Brew storefront was a blackened, burned-out shell. The desert wind stirred the ashes and blew them into Shane's face, and he coughed and tried to spit out the bitterness.

"Good riddance," Oliver said, and turned and went back into Common Grounds. Turned the sign from CLOSED to OPEN.

"What just happened here?" Shane asked his wife. Claire shook her head. "Did… did we just see that?"

"Witch summoning her dead husband, who turned into a demon and took her to Hell?"

"Yeah. That?"

"Probably not?"

"Okay." He felt tired. Exhausted, in fact. "Just another damn day in Morganville."

"Even for Morganville, that was weird." She linked arms with him and looked up into his face. He kissed her. It was impulsive, and her lips tasted like cool, sweet water. A refuge in the madness, always. "Need some coffee?"

He shuddered. "I'm off caffeine. Probably forever."

"That'll last until the morning." She gave him a good, long look. "Take me home, Shane."

As the hot desert wind stirred bones and ashes, and the fire department finally arrived to clean up, they walked back to the house they shared with Michael and Eve.

Home.

As Shane lay awake that night, remembering the sick feeling of being possessed by Jane Penwell, he also remembered what *she* felt. She'd left some of that with him. Regret. Loss. Sadness. Rage.

He hoped that it would go away. But somehow, he thought it was always going to be part of him now.

"Hope you found your home," he whispered to her in the dark.

He was very happy that the dark didn't answer back.

THE DEER WIFE

Jennifer McMahon

Loves me
Loves me not
Loves me

Pulling the petals off a black-eyed Susan—one of the last of the season, a flower that has somehow survived the first frost—I play the game. A game I played in the schoolyard years ago with a bunch of other girls to see if little Jamie Coughlan whose daddy owned the Buick dealership might really love me, might want to one day make me his wife, have little babies with me that we'd drive around in the backseat of a big old Park Avenue sedan.

Only this time, I'm a grown woman and it's not Jamie Coughlan I'm longing for.

This time, it's not a game.

It's a spell. A conjuring.

If I do it right, she may come.

I get to the last petal: *Loves me.*

I smile and blush, actually blush, as I bury the stem under leaves and dirt, a small offering.

There are other things I do, of course. Other ways I can call her.

I scatter dried corn on the ground in a circle around me. I whisper, "I come in peace, I come with good intentions, I come of my own free will."

I pull my little wooden pipe with the long stem from the basket I've brought, pack it full of mugwort, mullein, willow bark, wormwood and lavender.

I sit on a rock in the clearing, the clearing where I first saw her; the place I've come to think of as ours. I light the pipe and begin to puff gently, imagining the smoke drawing her in.

She won't stay long. Not this late in the season. In the fall, our visits are fewer, shorter, but they burn with a white-hot intensity that comes from knowing that soon it will end. She will be gone for the winter and I won't see her again until spring. That's how it is. How it has been for these past four years. I don't know where she goes or what she does. I don't know how or where she passes the winter.

Some things are not for me to know. Not yet. Maybe not ever.

I close my eyes, wishing, willing, summoning her with my whole self. The smoke drifts out in circles around me. Smoke from the herbs she blended, the pipe she gave me as a gift on the summer solstice. The smoke is supposed to calm my mind. To make me more open to the possibilities the world around me holds.

She's taught me everything I know about magic: how to cast a circle, to call out to the elements and spirits, to channel all the powers around us. She's taught me to use herbs, make charms, to cast runes and read cards. She tells me I have a gift for visions; that I am more powerful than I know.

I hear soft footsteps. Twigs breaking. I feel her near me but don't dare open my eyes. Not just yet.

Her coming always brings an intoxicating mix of desire and fear. My heart hammers, my legs start to tremble.

Run, the logical part of my brain is telling me.

But it's too late.

I feel her breath on my neck.

Only when she wraps her arms around my waist, nibbles on my ear, do I know what form she's taken this time.

"Hello," I whisper, my body relaxing, melting into hers.

I keep my eyes shut tight, afraid that if I open them, she just might disappear.

She's unpredictable. Here one minute, gone the next.

Sometimes I wonder if I've dreamed her to life; if she's even real at all.

"I wasn't sure you'd come," she says to me now, voice teasing and raspy, like wind scattering dry leaves. She knows I can't stay away. I've tried. I've sworn off her a hundred times, promised myself I was done with the whole impossible situation, but again and again I return to this clearing. To her.

"There is nowhere else I'd rather be," I say. It's the only truth I know right now as she gently pulls me from the rock, lays me down on the forest floor, unbuttoning my coat and blouse. Her fingers search, go right for the mark—the tiny dot she inked into the skin just beneath my left breast. She used a sewing needle and tattoo ink she'd made herself: a potion of vodka, herbs and ashes. The mark isn't anything anyone would even notice—it blends in, looks like a dark freckle. But she put it there. She put it there, she says, so she would always be a part of me.

I know what she is, of course. I know what she's capable of.

I've always known. I've known and I've given myself to her entirely anyway. Given myself over to her not in spite of what she is, but because of it.

I'd heard the stories in town for years before I met her, the warnings not to go into the woods alone because you might meet the witch.

They say she lives in a cave deep in the heart of the forest. No one has ever found it. They say for a bottle of bourbon or a basket of food, she can hex a man or woman for you, a sure way to get rid of your enemies. Leave her a gift in the forest and a note with your request (*heal my sick father, make the girl love me, bring my business back from the brink of bankruptcy*) and if the gift is good enough, she'll do your bidding.

They say you can't hear her coming. She moves like the wind. She can read minds. Can see the future when she casts her runes, looks into her scrying bowl.

She rarely leaves the woods; hasn't been to a store in years.

If things go missing around town, it's the witch who took them.

A prize pumpkin, a shirt hanging on a clothesline, a cooler of beer, a pair of boots.

She never takes much, just the things she needs. And you can always tell she's been because for each thing she takes, she leaves a small gift in its place: a little stick figure, a doll bound up, wrapped in cloth and tied up with string, stuffed full of herbs. A good luck charm.

Some people say she's old and ugly.

Some say she's more beautiful than any mortal woman should be.

Some say she's impossible to see—she can cast a spell of invisibility. *Be careful*, they warn, looking around nervously, *she could be watching us right now*.

They say she has always been here; that she's a part of the forest. The oldest men in town, the ones who gather for coffee each morning on the porch of the general store—they remember hearing about her when they were little boys. They remember their own fathers warning them to stay out of the woods or the witch would eat them up, build herself a bed with their bones.

She has killed those who cross her.

She has scared men to death.

If you're out in the woods at night and you hear her song, it'll be the last sound you ever know.

But the stories, they're all half-truths.

For instance, she does live deep in the woods, but not in a damp cave.

She has a cabin, a place she has led me to, a place I've never been able to find on my own, though I've often tried. It's perfectly hidden in a thick clump of trees. The outside is sheathed with the rounded slabs of rough cut logs, the roof is shingled with tree bark, with moss and lichen growing on top. It blends into the forest perfectly, as if it's always been there, grown right up alongside the trees. She says she's cast a circle of protection around the place; an enchantment to make it impossible to see or find unless she's brought you.

Inside it's warm and cozy and smells like herbs and woodsmoke with something else underneath it; her smell—an earthy scent with hints of warm fur and damp clay, bitter roots, the lake after a rainstorm. There's a cast-iron stove she uses for heat and cooking, a bed, a table with one chair, some hooks on the wall for her clothes. She doesn't own much (and most of what she owns, she's taken from other people's houses and camps—another piece of truth from the rumors). She has a frying pan, a saucepan, a good knife, a single bowl and plate, one fork and spoon. When we eat together, we share the same bowl, the same spoon. We feed each other, using the spoon, and our hands. Her exquisite fingers brush against my lips, drop berries on my tongue; she kisses the juice as it dribbles down my chin.

She gets her water from the stream, says it's perfectly safe to drink. She has an outhouse behind her cabin that's tidier than the bathrooms in most people's homes. It's got a skylight and a painting of the full moon on the inside of the door.

There are shelves in her kitchen lined with glass jars full of roots, herbs, berries—things she's gathered in the woods. There are other things too—metal tins of tea, coffee and tobacco, a bottle of brandy, dried beans, cornmeal and flour.

Things she's taken or gifts people have left for her.

I've seen the desperate, pleading notes people leave here and there in the forest.

Please, Witch, please, Aunt Sally's got cancer real bad again and she's the only one who can take care of Gram and Joey so please make her well. She's a good person and doesn't deserve this and we all love her and need her. Here's a pie, a bottle of gin, my grandpa's old silver cigarette lighter and some fresh flints and fuel for it. I hope it's enough.

She enjoys the gifts. Some people she helps. Some, she laughs at with a cruelty that makes me go cold.

Sometimes, she gets a request that she can do nothing with.

There are things, she explains, that are outside of her control.

I ask her if I'm under her control.

"Don't be silly," she says with a wry smile. "You come of your own free will."

"Can you turn me?" I ask. We're back at her cabin and she's at the old wooden table, mixing up the special potion she uses to change: an ointment made from animal fat, deer fur, her own hair, wolfsbane, hemlock, jimson weed, fly agaric mushroom. I've watched her make it many times.

I've seen her make the change, know the words she uses, that ancient incantation.

"Turn you?"

"Can you change me? Like you change yourself."

She looks at me, her irises such a dark shade of brown that they nearly blend with her pupils.

"No," she says.

"Why not?"

"Because once I do it, there's no going back. It's a sort of splitting. The human world… it won't be the same to you after."

"What if I've had enough of the human world?"

She frowns, her face folding into sadness for just a split second. Then she shakes her head and looks away from me. "You have things holding you there. You have your son."

Where were you today?" Levi asks, accusing and suspicious. He has just come in the door of our tiny house, a cold evening breeze following him in. "I came home for lunch and you weren't here."

My back is to him. I am at the kitchen table chopping potatoes, the freshly sharpened knife moving through the pale yellow flesh with ease, the cutting board slick with starchy juice.

"I was in the woods gathering mushrooms," I tell him. "Look at these lovely chanterelles." I turn, show him my basket with a thin smile. "And look, wild onions as well. From down by the river. I'm going to make a soup."

He grunts, dismissing my explanation. He studies my face, trying to catch me in a lie.

I turn up my smile but can't tell if he's buying it.

He's difficult to read. A hard knot of a boy. He's like his father this way.

He's got his father's build, too—tall and lanky, square shoulders and jaw. I watch as he shrugs his way out of his father's old plaid wool hunting coat, hangs it on a peg by the door.

I tell myself, for what must be the thousandth time, that I will stop going to the woods. I will stop this thing between her and me. It's too dangerous. Levi is suspicious. Suspicious as his father was once suspicious.

Levi goes to the refrigerator, takes out the milk, drinks right from the carton.

I've asked him not to do this, but he does it anyway, right in front of me. It's a test, I know. He's pushing, hoping I'll say something. He's always ready for a fight. Quiet fury ripples like a muscle under his skin.

But not tonight. I'm in no mood for arguing tonight. I want to hold onto the glow of my afternoon in the woods for just a little bit longer.

The last time, I promise myself.

It was the last time.

No more.

Milk dribbles down Levi's chin. He wipes it away with the back of his hand, gives me a smirk as he shoves the carton back into the fridge.

Levi blames me for what happened to his father.

We go round and round sometimes, each of us trying to make sense of it in our way.

"Your father made a terrible decision when he got in his truck to drive that night," I've told him.

The last time we had this discussion, Levi scowled at me, his face so like his father's. "The only reason Dad ever drank was because you made him," he said. "Because nothing was ever easy or normal with you two and it was how he coped."

Levi is young and full of anger, but sometimes his insight stuns me, actually takes my breath away.

"I loved your father very much," I said. This is no lie—I did love Neil. But it wasn't enough. It was never enough. The man always wanted more; wanted things I never knew how to give him. And he would get so angry. Levi never saw that side of his father (thank god); only saw that things weren't working between us, and like his father, he blamed me. I was a walking disappointment to them both.

Neil and I were eighteen when we met, both of us just out of high school, working our first shit jobs at the mill. We were married at nineteen, him in a borrowed coat, me in my mama's old dress that I had to take in because I was just a waif of a thing. Neil and I were both so young, both still living at home, eager to move out, to start our own lives, get our own little place; thinking something magic might happen when we did.

How can you possibly truly know a person, or even yourself, when you're so young? How can you help but imagine bright, impossible things for the future?

Levi turned nineteen this past summer. I look at him and see he's just a little boy in a man's body. Like his father was on our wedding day.

"How was your day?" I ask him now.

He gives another non-committal grunt, as hard to read as ever.

Then he goes into the living room, reaches for his wooden box full of knives and wood and sharpening stones. He sits in his father's old chair, takes up a knife and resumes work on the barred owl he's been carving from a piece of maple for a week now. The wood has a burl in it, making it difficult to carve, but giving it a beautiful swirling pattern that looks like the eye of a storm. Levi works carefully, layering in the delicate feathers, his body calm, relaxed. He works with total focus.

Most boys his age, boys he grew up with, are off in college, or out drinking pilfered beer, playing video games, watching funny videos and porn on the internet maybe. But Levi, he goes to work each day at the mill, just as his father did, and when he comes home, he carves. Our house is full of his creations: rabbits, muskrats, beavers, a fox, two ducks, a loon, but mostly what he loves to carve are birds of prey: eagles, hawks, falcons, and owls.

Sometimes his girlfriend, Sophie, comes over and watches him work. They talk quietly by the fire, whispering, smiling. It's always so good to see him smile. Sophie loves our house, his carved animals. Last year for Christmas, Levi made her a carving of her dog, Stewy, who'd died the month before. Levi had gotten every detail perfect. Sophie cried when he gave it to her, said it was the best gift she'd ever received.

"Sophie coming tonight?" I ask him as I start in on slicing the mushrooms. "She's welcome to join us for dinner."

"Nah," he says. "She's got a thing with a friend."

After dinner, Levi puts on his father's coat, grabs a flashlight and the old Winchester. "I'm gonna go check the traps," he says. Sometimes he brings back a rabbit and skins it, prepares the meat and I'll make a stew with it the next day. Sometimes, he'll get a fox, a weasel, a marten. Often, it's raccoons he traps. Once, he got a bobcat. He skins each animal, processes the pelts. Some, he saves. Some, he sells.

I hear a gunshot ten minutes later. I'm waiting in the dooryard when he comes back, dragging something across the dried brown grass.

"What is it?" I call out.

"A coyote," he says, coming into the light now. I see gray-brown fur, the fluffy tail as he drags it by its hind legs.

And I turn away, not wanting to see its face, to think of how it suffered, its leg caught in that steel trap until my son put the creature out of its misery.

I wake up in the middle of the night and know she was just here in my room. I can smell her, taste her in the air. She does this sometimes; sneaks in and watches me while I sleep. Each night, Levi latches the door and windows before bed, just as his father did, but somehow, she finds a way inside. Locks mean nothing to her.

I get up, creep quietly down the stairs, open the front door and step out into the dark yard, hoping I might be quick enough to catch her. My bare feet are cold on the frost-covered grass. The skin under my thin nightgown is covered in goosebumps. The autumn wind whispers through the bare tree branches, seems to call my name. I see only the faint reflective glow of eyeshine from the treeline. "Hello?" I call. "Is that you?" I take a step toward the trees, hear a rustling sound. The hairs on the back of my neck stand up.

"Who are you talking to, Mom?" Levi has come up behind me. He's standing in the open doorway in his rumpled pajamas.

"No one," I say.

"Come back inside," he tells me. "It's freezing. You'll catch your death out here."

I wish I could say I met her after Neil died. That things started between us then. But that would be a lie.

The truth is, I met her a full year before Neil's accident.

She says our meeting in the woods that first day wasn't chance. She says I called her to me. I can't help thinking it was the other way around.

"Why have you wandered so far into these woods?" she'd asked. She'd come from nowhere, made no sound as she moved through the trees. But there she was: a woman about my age with long brown hair, a worn leather coat and boots, a necklace made from a piece of deer antler and rawhide, a large hunting knife strapped to her belt.

Her hands and wrists had faded black tattoos—lines and symbols I didn't recognize.

I took a staggering step backward, suddenly off balance, startled by her presence. I held up my basket stupidly. "I was looking for blueberries," I said as if I needed an excuse, an explanation for being in the woods I had every right to be in.

She gave a mischievous smile; her eyes narrowed, seemed to turn to slits. Surely it was my imagination. "Weren't you warned?" she asked. "Didn't you hear in town that you should be careful? Shouldn't roam far on your own, shouldn't venture off the path?"

"Why is that?" I asked, as if I did not know.

She laughed a wicked little laugh. "Aren't you afraid of the Witch of the Woods?"

"No," I told her. But it was a lie.

She took a step closer. "Maybe you should be. Maybe you should just turn yourself around and go back where you came from."

I shook my head, held my ground. "Not without my blueberries. It's my son's birthday and I've promised him a pie."

She looked at me a long time. "So you'll take your chances with me?"

I nodded. "Yes," I said.

"Come on then," she said, walking away. "Follow me.

I'll take you to the sweetest blueberries you've ever tasted."

I left the woods that day with a basket not only full of blueberries, but mushrooms and blackberries. More than that, I left with a desire—no, not a desire, but a *need*, a strong yearning, to return. To see her again.

Maybe, I told myself, she'd cast a spell on me.

Or maybe it was all me. Maybe it was just that there was something missing, something I'd been longing for without even realizing it until I met her that day.

And so I went back. Again and again. Sometimes she showed herself to me. Sometimes she didn't. But I always felt her there, watching. And always, some part of me was a little afraid.

Neil noticed a change in me.

"You're spending a lot of time in the woods," he said.

"Foraging," I told him. And I'd show him my basket full of treasures: wild lowbush blueberries, crab apples, sorrel, hickory nuts. She had shown me where to find them. She had taught me the names of the mushrooms, told me which were poison and which were safe to eat.

I would come home with my basket full and name each mushroom for Neil: chanterelle, morel, oyster, Dryad's saddle, chicken of the woods, lion's mane. Each one beautiful and delicate and full of strange earthy pleasure.

"Have you ever seen anyone out in the woods when you're off foraging?" Neil asked once.

I took in a breath. "No," I said. "Who would I see way back there?"

His jaw tensed and in that split second, I was sure he knew. He knew who I was meeting. What we were doing. He knew I was devoted to her, addicted to her, had given myself to her in a way I never would to him. "Just be careful, Jules," he said, his eyes dark and brooding.

There were skid marks in the road, at the bend on old Route 4, where Neil had his accident. He'd locked up the brakes and left a burned-rubber trail all the way across the road, hitting the guard rail on the other side and going over it.

Maybe he swerved and was trying to correct himself.

Or maybe he saw something.

Something in the road.

An animal maybe.

That's what the police have hypothesized. And all the alcohol in his system, it didn't exactly give him the sharpest reflexes. His blood alcohol concentration was .16—twice the legal limit.

✳

I didn't tell the police about what made Neil get in his truck that night.

How I'd come home and found him there, already drunk in the kitchen.

"Where's Levi?" I asked.

"I sent him to Ben's for the night."

"Why?" I asked.

"We need to talk," he said. The veins on his neck stood out, pulsating. His whole body thrummed with bourbon-fueled anger.

"I went into the woods," he said. "I went into the woods and saw you."

I swallowed.

"What is it you saw?"

He shook his head, took a staggering step toward me. "I'm not going to say it out loud. I can't. Because it disgusts me. *You* disgust me. How could you, Jules?" He reached for me; at first, I thought it was to caress me, to touch my face and beg me to stop, to stay out of the woods, to love only him.

And would I? Would I have tried? Would I have done that for him? For us?

But he didn't beg me to stop or ask if I still loved him.

Instead, his fingers found their way to my neck, tightened their grip.

And the thing is, I let him.

I didn't fight. Didn't try to get away.

Part of me wanted the whole thing to be over. Done with once and for all.

Then, I looked out the kitchen window and saw her. She was in the yard, watching, not ten feet away from the house.

"What the hell is that?" Neil said, releasing his grip, moving to the window.

I don't know what he saw. I'll never know what she showed him; what form she took, what vision she gave him. His face turned ashen, his body rigid. He made a small sound, a sort of breathless silent scream, then turned and ran out of the house and straight to his truck. He flew out of the driveway, truck tires spitting gravel, not even slowing when he ran over the mailbox.

I should have stopped him. Or at least tried.

But I didn't. Instead, I went into the yard to look for her. To call to her.

But she was gone.

"I'm wondering something," I asked her once, not long after his accident. "About Neil."

We were down by the river gathering willow bark.

"About what happened to Neil that night," I added, not looking her in the eye.

She straightened, touched the sharp edge of the knife she'd been using. "What happened to Neil was an accident. You said so yourself."

I shook my head. "How many times have you told me that there are no accidents? No coincidences?"

She was quiet a minute, running her fingers over the blade.

"What is it, exactly, that you're asking me?" she said, eyes locked on mine. "What is it you really want to know?"

And in that moment I knew (hadn't I always known?) but suddenly didn't want either of us to say it out loud. Not ever.

"Nothing," I told her.

Levi leaves for work. I straighten the house. Do the dishes. Clean out the garden and put it to bed for the coming winter, pulling up the spent tomato plants, the dead vines that were once loaded with beans and sugar snap peas. I try to busy myself. To push her out of my mind. I tell myself I won't see her.

Then, somehow, like a sleepwalker, I'm on my way back into the woods. Even as I'm walking, I do my best to convince myself I should turn back. Go home. Read a book. Clean the chimney. Bake a spice cake to surprise Levi with.

But I can't. I just can't stay away.

When I get to the clearing, she's there, but not in her human form.

She's watching, studying me from the trees. Her white tail flicking, her moist black nostrils twitching slightly, the rest of her body holding statue-still. She's so perfect—the sun hitting her brown coat, making it sparkle and glisten. I have never seen anything so beautiful, so wild.

She comes to me, her hoofed feet gently touching down on the pine-needle carpet.

She puts her head against me and I wrap my arms around her neck, nuzzling her, rubbing my whole face against her warm fur, breathing her in.

I can almost hear her say the words: *I wasn't sure you'd come.*

"There is nowhere else I'd rather be," I say.

It's hours later when I wake. I am naked beside her, my arm draped over her shoulder, the fur soft and warm. Her body is tensed, alert. She's lifted her head and is watching something there, at the edge of the clearing. I follow her gaze, heart dropping down like a lead weight into my stomach.

"Levi?" I call.

My boy, my angry boy, is standing there, fists clenched, eyes as blank and glassy as a doll's.

I cover myself, sit up, but he's gone, running off through the woods, back toward home.

I dress quickly, turn to say something to her, to explain the gravity of us having been seen. But she is gone.

I run home, tearing through the trees, my body knowing the way by heart because I've traveled it so many times, always careful not to leave any evidence, not to break twigs, leave footprints in soft earth, or make any sign of a path.

He's not home when I get there. His truck is in the driveway but there's no sign of him in the house.

"Levi?" I call, standing in the open door, looking out at the yard, listening carefully, but hearing only silence.

I go back into the woods, calling, begging him to come talk to me. I walk for hours, searching the woods until it's starting to get dark, which happens earlier and earlier this time of year, sunset always catching me off guard.

My wool sweater isn't enough to ward off the chill of the evening. The wind picks up. My hands are raw and red with cold. The trees take on terrible shapes around me; the branches turn to claws. A group of crows chatters from a nearby maple, seeming to ask *How could you, How could you, How could you?*

I am far into the woods, almost down by the lake, when I hear distant gunfire. One shot, then two more in rapid succession, coming from the north, toward home. I run all the way, not sticking to the path, but taking shortcuts through thick brush that rips at my face and hands. I trip on tree roots and rocks, turn my ankle stumbling into a hole. On I go, as fast as my body can take me, half limping now as I see the house come into view, the front lights blazing, so bright they hurt my eyes.

Sophie's car is in the driveway and she's there on the front steps to greet me as I stumble into the yard. She's got my apron on and looks so at home there, like it's her house she's just stepped out of.

I feel like a ghost; a figure lost between two worlds, belonging to neither.

"Oh my god, Julie, are you alright?" she asks, rushing to me. I am limping, my face scratched and bleeding. I must look a sight.

"I heard gunshots," I say.

I look down and see great smears of blood in the grass. I can smell the rich metallic scent of it.

She nods. "Levi got a deer," she says. "A beautiful doe."

"No," I say, staggering forward, following the trail of blood, the path he left when dragging the body.

"I know it's not legal, not in season, and that you're only

supposed to take bucks with two points, but he says the deer are such a menace."

I'm not listening to this girl. She keeps talking, saying something about Levi, something about the deer, something about biscuits and gravy she's made, but I don't hear her. Her voice is just static, a low buzz I don't register. I've come around the side of the house and see the doe strung up by her back legs, hanging from the low branch of the maple in the backyard.

All the air leaves my body.

I'm lightheaded, swaying like the hung-up deer.

He's field dressed her: cut her open from her tail to her sternum, opened her up and taken out her insides. Gone are her entrails and organs, all that was once tucked neatly inside her. The only thing he's saved is the heart, which he has in his hand as he turns to me, his face grim but triumphant, his hands sticky with her blood.

Then, he smiles as he holds her heart out to me, showing off his trophy.

I look from the heart to her face, tongue protruding from her mouth, eyes glassy in the way that only dead creatures become.

"Isn't she a beauty?" Sophie asks from someplace close behind me.

Isn't she?

Isn't she?

"Yes," I say, forcing the word out, surprised by my own voice; surprised that I can speak at all.

But there is a reason I can open my mouth and say the word.

It's not her.

This deer is too small, too young.

I back away slowly, eyes down, shuffling along the trail of fresh blood. I turn and walk past the open front door of my house, the place I've called home for twenty-five years now. I leave all my useless belongings behind: the clothes in the closet, pans in the kitchen, hairbrush and toothbrush and the framed wedding photo on the mantel.

"I'm ready," I tell her when I show up at her door.

It's the first time I've ever been able to find her cabin on my own. I can't say how I did it, how I found my way through the dark and tangled forest; only that something guided me, pulled me along. A little voice (her voice?) said, *This way, come this way.* Told me that it was time.

She does not question, does not say a word.

She just holds the door open, inviting me inside where a fire crackles, candles are lit.

She knew I was coming. She's been waiting. There,

on the table, is the ointment. The tea we must drink. And next to it, a necklace matching hers with a piece of antler strung up on rawhide. Candles flicker as she places it around my neck, passes me the cup of tea, begins to chant the words as she undresses me, anoints my body, then her own, with the ointment.

Together, hand in hand, we leave the cabin and slip into the woods and soon, her hand is no longer in mine but I feel her beside me, walking, moving. The forest is alive around us. I hear every sound: leaves falling, a mouse scurrying. I see perfectly in the dark, in front and to the sides, the whole landscape vivid and clear, seeming almost to glow. And the smells! The rich smells of the loamy forest, the lake, a distant fire.

I follow her, at first slowly, then we break into a run following a trail that takes us out past the lake, over a distant hill, through a field.

We move so quickly, so perfectly together.

We are lithe and supple and full of grace.

We do not make a sound.

There is nowhere else I'd rather be.

THE DANCER

Kristin Dearborn

Pink and white cherry blossoms carpeted the long dirt road that led to the Weavers' farm.

As Paul Baker passed in his dusty old Volvo, the dirty, faded petals swirled in intricate patterns before dropping back to the road. The unseasonably warm spring was the driest on record. The land ached for rain.

Baker crossed an adorable covered bridge, beneath which a weak trickle of water flowed. Cherry trees lined Weaver Way, and perhaps a month ago they would have been beautiful. Now the new leaves drooped yellow instead of green, craving hydration, but no rain was forecast. Only sunny skies and warm temperatures. Baker rounded a corner and caught sight of the Weavers' house. Once upon a time it had been a Morgan horse farm, but now it had been converted to a private residence. Too big and too expensive for locals to maintain, it was just the sort of home that people from away would love. Mr. Weaver commuted to New York City for work. Three days in Vermont, four days in the city. Rinse, repeat. More landowners who wouldn't get involved in local politics or step off their land to become a part of the community.

Baker parked his Volvo behind a spotless black Mercedes SUV. The driveway terminated in a well-maintained loop with a struggling brown flower garden in the middle. Smudges of dried color lay dead against the soil, and dust hung in the air. A picturesque red barn hunkered off to one side, and the pastures lay empty. Baker wondered if the family had plans to purchase and raise horses. If not for the drought and everything brown, the tableau would have belonged on the cover of a magazine.

He stepped out of the car, straightened his jacket, and ensured the cookie he'd eaten on the way hadn't left any crumbs.

Mrs. Weaver opened the door before his feet hit the first step. A tidy mat bade him welcome, and stated the names of all the occupants. The Weavers: Bruce, Terry, Zach and Ani. Ani. The reason he was here.

The drawn expression on Mrs. Weaver's face contrasted with the cheery mat.

"Are you Paul?"

"I am Mr. Baker." He hated when people he didn't know used his first name.

"Please, call me Terry."

"A pleasure to meet you." Baker would call her Mrs. Weaver.

The house smelled of flowers. Baker glanced around and saw them: in vases on an end table. Roses that rested in a low, open bowl. Flowers everywhere.

She led him into the living room. The space featured cathedral ceilings, with a wall of huge windows showcasing dry yellow pasture and a forest where the pines were starting to go orange. A stone fireplace dominated the room, nearly big enough to stand in. Baker wondered what it cost to heat the place in the winter. Inside, a bank of houseplants flourished, a bright, sharp green.

Mrs. Weaver gestured for Baker to sit on a white sofa that didn't seem intended for casual use. Certainly one would not enjoy red wine on that furniture. Baker wondered if there was another living room where the family would watch TV and let its guard down.

"Ani will be down in a moment, she was just stepping

out of the shower," Mrs. Weaver said. "Can I get you something to drink?"

A sudden sound might startle her into hysterics, Baker feared.

"No, thank you."

Mrs. Weaver lowered herself into an uncomfortable-looking chair and let her hands rest on her knees. She kept her ankles and her knees together, and sat with perfect posture. They didn't have long to wait.

Ani descended the stairs into the living room. She was seventeen and wore a lightweight pink sweater over black leggings. Her hair was wet, and she wore no make-up to conceal the circles under her eyes. Ani was a ballerina. Band-Aids and deep purple bruises covered her bare feet, and she looked too thin. She had no breasts to speak of. Her movements were graceful and lovely. She chose to stand.

Baker smiled at her. "A pleasure to meet you. Now why don't you start at the beginning? Your mother has emailed me, and I'd like to hear your side of things."

Her eyebrows, immaculately and severely plucked, furrowed. Baker could see lines on her forehead, and she looked, in that moment, much older than seventeen. "They blame me," she said.

"Darling, it's only—"

Baker raised a hand to silence Mrs. Weaver.

Mr. Weaver appeared and parked himself in a doorway, scowling and gesturing that they continue.

Ani turned back to Baker. "We moved into a haunted house, and somehow it's all my fault."

"That's not true, pet," Mrs. Weaver said.

"When did you move?" Baker asked.

"November 25th." Mr. Weaver was fast to answer. "The place was a steal. Look at all this land. Look at that view."

Baker wondered what the steal was… 1.2 million? Only a million?

"What made you decide to leave New York and come to Vermont?"

Ani's jaw tightened.

"Our daughter was having trouble at school. Eating trouble. We needed her in a place where she could get healthy and build up her strength again." Mr. Weaver locked eyes with Baker. Challenged him to argue.

"I was fine," Ani whispered. "I'd never danced better. And you took me here." She seemed to steady herself. "I hate it here."

"We all hate it here." A new face, a new voice in the conversation. Zach. The fifteen-year-old son. "It's haunted. Let's go back to New York."

"We are not going back to New York," Mrs. Weaver said. "We've always dreamed of a house in Vermont."

"*You* have. What do I want with a place where the grocery store's, like, an hour away? We're being homeschooled. We haven't met anyone yet. It's boring here."

"They don't mean it." Mrs. Weaver smiled at Baker, *you know how children exaggerate*. No, he didn't. He cared to listen to them, to actually hear them.

"Tell me about the haunting." Baker pulled the conversation back on topic.

The family got quiet for a moment. They exchanged conspiratorial glances. No one spoke.

"It's why we brought him here," Mrs. Weaver finally said. "How can he help us if we don't tell him?"

"It all started when Ani went on the rag again after being off it for so long because she starves herself," Zach said.

"Paranormal activity is often tied to menstruation—" Baker started, trying to be helpful.

"Zach!" Mrs. Weaver spoke over him. "Watch your mouth. Go to your room!"

"Make me."

Mr. Weaver took a step toward his son. "Upstairs. Now."

When Mr. Weaver spoke, Zach listened. Father herded son up the stairs. A door closed, a quiet click.

"I'm so sorry…" Mrs. Weaver's voice trailed off, and Baker wondered what life was like if that was the worst she'd seen from her children.

"Don't worry about it. Ani, please go on." Baker favored her with a warm smile. She twisted a long strand of auburn hair around her thin fingers. The nails were gnawed to the quick.

"Like a week after we got here, I had this dream."

"Oh, you don't need to tell this part," Mrs. Weaver said, staring at her shoes.

"Whatever you think will help, Ani."

"I dreamed I was flying. Soaring. It was fantastic, the best dream I can ever remember. Like dancing in midair, and everyone was applauding and applauding, a standing ovation. For me." She dropped her gaze from Baker's face and stared at her hands.

"Then I woke up. I sleep with a nightlight—" Baker made a note of this. People who sleep with lights on can't create melatonin properly. "—so I could see something was moving. I thought it was a shadow, like from a waving tree outside, but then I saw it was my toe shoes. They were floating. I screamed, Zach came in." Ani blushed. "He noticed I'd started my period. Like, a lot."

"Did he see the shoes?"

Ani nodded. "He saw the blood, then the shoes. He cursed really loud, and the shoes dropped. Then I had the most horrid cramps of my life."

"The shoes were floating. You and your brother both saw it."

"Not floating, that isn't right. They were dancing." She turned her gaze out the window. "It was the wedding from *La Sylphide*."

"You can't possibly know that," Mrs. Weaver said.

"I know the piece. I danced it myself."

Baker studied Ani. Too thin, but because the girl starved herself for her craft. She looked like an average, self-destructive teenage ballerina.

"May I see your room? The shoes?"

Ani tensed. "Sure," she mumbled. "Follow me." Baker lifted himself off the couch and ascended the hardwood staircase. He could hear father and son talking behind a closed door, the bathroom, he suspected.

Ani's room was designed to please a very small girl. Pink everywhere, glitter, pictures of ballerinas—but not of specific, real ballerinas, engaged in challenging, technical work—they were cartoons on the wall. The carpet was a rich, plush pink. Baker imagined it felt good under her toes. Around her messy desk, patches of the carpet were burned and singed. To one side, a closet door hung open. To the other, a door opened to Zach's room. Baker didn't see a lock. Curious, but sometimes with old houses they didn't include them on all the doors. Ani's windows overlooked the driveway and the bank of dying flowers, a flagpole where an American flag drooped in the heat.

"Get them to send me back to New York," she whispered. "Please, I can't stand it here."

Baker heard a heavy footfall in the hallway outside. "Tell me about the next incident."

Mr. Weaver filled the doorway.

"The fire," Ani pointed.

"She stared setting fires because we made her eat."

"I didn't... they just started."

If the girl was a liar, she was brilliant. Her expression begged her father to believe her.

"Fires don't start themselves."

"You saw the things floating... flying."

Mr. Weaver made a gruff sound of disapproval.

"You *saw* them."

"I don't know what I saw."

"Why don't you believe me? About *anything*?"

Mr. Weaver turned away. "Tell the man your *story* about the fires."

Ani told him about a fight with her family—at first against her mother, then her mother and father, then Zach joined in the fray against her. She stormed to her room, threw herself on the bed weeping, then discovered her trash can on fire.

To Baker, this was all cut and dried. The girl had latent telekinetic—and, it seemed, pyrokinetic—abilities. The distress of leaving her home in New York, leaving her passion, had brought it out in her. He let her finish speaking.

The details lined up. "Your daughter is under stress, and is reacting to it. Remove the stress and the problems should stop."

"The stress of this fantastic farm? This view? The wind in the trees?"

Baker remembered Ani's plea. "Find her a boarding school. An arts school. She needs an outlet for her energy. Like dance."

"Thank you."

He hadn't done anything, just pointed out the obvious.

Mr. Weaver bubbled with rage. "As you've solved the problem so neatly, I suspect we won't be needing your services again. I'll show you out."

"Good luck," Baker said to Ani.

The Weavers called him nine days later. An emergency. Could he come right away? They needed his help. They'd pay, and they'd pay well.

It was the last bit that convinced him. Baker needed the money. So he folded himself into his ancient white Volvo and repeated the two-hour ride south.

He cranked the windows down as he drove. At least that way the hot air blew over him, cooling his sweat a bit. There was relief in sight. Thunderstorms and rain were in the day's forecast, about a week too late to save most of the early spring crops. It would be a bad growing season for Vermont.

Sad brown leaves decked the once-handsome cherry trees flanking Weaver Way. Like autumn, but without festive colors. Under the covered bridge, the stream-bed baked in the sun. The flower garden in the driveway was reduced to a jumble of brown, wilted stocks.

Zach stood outside, waiting for him. Dark clouds loomed in the distance.

"Go back. We don't need you." Zach's eyes were cold.

"Get in the goddamn house." Mr. Weaver didn't have to raise his voice. His tone sent Zach scuttling away like a timid cub.

"Come in, please." Mr. Weaver pronounced *please* as an expletive. Mrs. Weaver hovered behind him.

The vast array of windows in the living room showcased a bank of angry purple clouds.

"It's Ani. She attacked Zach. And me, when I tried to help him," Mr. Weaver said.

Mrs. Weaver nodded in agreement.

"Where is she?"

"Her room."

They ascended the stairs.

Ani lay tied to her bed with straps that seemed made for

the purpose. Did the parents have a fetish? Baker didn't allow himself to think past that. He noticed the door to Zach's room standing open, and nudged it closed before going to Ani's side. They'd used a bandana as a gag.

"I will not work with you or your family until she is untied."

"She'll get you if you—"

"*Get the hell out of here*," Mr. Weaver thundered at Zach. The boy melted out into the hall. Mrs. Weaver pulled the bandana from Ani's mouth, and undid the Velcro strap on her left hand.

"You have to save me!" Ani's voice was a rasp. Ribs jutted beneath a black lycra shirt—even thinner than the last time he'd seen her.

"What is going on here?" Baker asked.

"She attacked him," Mr. Weaver said. He sounded ashamed. Good. He should be. "She made things fly at him. Books, heavy things."

The girl's room seemed in order.

"If she did that with her mind, what good would tying her up do? Have you taken my advice? Made any plans to send her away?"

"They won't let me go…"

"We are a family, Mr. Baker. We're going to live as one."

Untied now, Ani curled into a ball on her bed, knees drawn to her chest.

"What happened?" Baker asked Ani, his voice gentle.

"I'm not doing it on purpose."

"I can teach you some exercises to learn how to control it."

"I don't want to control it, I want to go home. To New York. I want to dance!"

Mr. Weaver boomed at him. "Control it? *Stop* it. Tell me straight, Baker. Can you stop this?"

Baker spoke past a tight throat. "This would stop if you weren't holding the girl a prisoner. Quite literally, it seems. I am a mandated reporter. I need to report this. Ani, if you come with me, I will bring you to Burlington and find a place for you for the night."

He would not be around these people another moment. How often did they tie up their children?

A crash of thunder rent the afternoon, followed by a brilliant flash of lightning and a drumming on the roof as it began to rain. The heavens opened, as though the past month of rain had been waiting for the perfect moment to fall on southern Vermont. The red barn, not a hundred feet from the house, disappeared in the grey wash of falling water.

Baker cursed to himself. If the storm stayed heavy like this, it might be unsafe to drive. He no longer cared if the Weavers paid him, he wanted to get the girl out of here, to safety. Nothing sat right: the blame, the open doors, the restraints.

"You're not taking her anywhere," Mr. Weaver said.

"I am," Baker replied. Though he didn't care for physical contact, he put a hand on Ani's shoulder. Terrified heat radiated through her shirt.

"That's my daughter you've got your hand on." Mr. Weaver started toward them.

Baker raised his hand and moved his wrist ever so slightly, sending a firm wall of air against Mr. Weaver. A warning shot, a gentle shove to say, "stay away."

Ani's eyes went wide. "You can, too?"

Baker nodded. No time for this. Outside, the rain kept falling.

Mrs. Weaver clutched the table, seeming to will the encounter to end. Mr. Weaver's eyes bulged, unable to comprehend what Baker had done.

"You can't just take her." He didn't sound as fierce now.

"I can," said Baker.

"That's kidnapping," Mr. Weaver said, with little conviction. "She's a minor." Baker didn't think it was the time or place to reiterate he was a mandated reporter, that he had a responsibility not to leave children in an unsafe situation.

Baker made a *ladies first* gesture to Ani. She paused, and he said "Don't worry. It's safe." She walked towards the door, moving like a beaten dog.

The repercussions of taking Ani wouldn't be slight, but

Baker had a good lawyer, and he wasn't afraid. This wasn't the first time.

Zach stood before them in the doorway. "You can't take her."

"Are you safe here?" Baker asked.

"No!" Ani shrieked. "He's one of them." She paused, hands flying to her temples.

One of who? Baker wondered. He had to get her out of here. The stress took its toll on her before his eyes. Then Zach lost his footing and fell, landing on his behind. He seemed fine; he stood immediately, and lunged at his sister. Baker raised his wall. Zach's eyes were black with hate and he called his sister a slut and a witch and a handful of other names. Baker led Ani to the car.

Outside, she slipped in the mud, pitching forward and landing on her hands and knees with the rain falling around her. Baker waited a beat for her to get up, and when she didn't he took her by the elbow and hauled her to her feet as gently as he was able.

"You're all right now," he raised his voice over the rain, then opened the car door for her.

"My lawyer will call you," he shouted back toward the house, but the rain took his words.

Inside the car, Baker looked at Ani. They were both soaked. Panicked sobs shook her rail-thin form.

"You're safe now," he said. "You won't have to go back there."

"Nothing to go back to," she replied, her face pale as realization set in.

"What happened today?"

She shook her head. "I can't say. I can never say."

If she didn't say, she might have to go back after all. Once he got onto Route 4 and found a gas station, he'd call the attorney.

Baker inched the Volvo down Weaver Way. The windshield wipers beat frenetic time, trying vainly to keep the water at bay. The headlights barely cut through the sheets of rain. Ani sat, quiet and pale. He needed to get food into her, fluids. She looked sick.

The covered bridge wasn't there. The dry streambed had transformed into a churning rapid of brown water and white foam. The ground had baked for weeks and couldn't possibly absorb the rain. Pieces of the bridge remained, splintered wood where it attached to the driveway.

"We have to walk!" Ani raised her voice over the roar of the water. Some of the color was coming back to her cheeks.

Baker racked his mind. His talents weren't so great he could pause the flow of the water, or get them safely across. It was miles after the bridge to anything, even the nearest gas.

"We've got to go back. See if the phones are working."

"Use your cell." She teetered on the brink of tears. Panic.

"I can't. They don't work around me. Magnetic energy. We have to use the house phone."

"No!" Ani cried. "We can't. We have to go, now."

"You have a house phone, though, yes?" He had to be sure. No point in going back if they all only had mobiles.

The rain cast odd, ever-changing shadows on her face as she clutched the arm rest and nodded. "Please. We can walk."

"I can't walk that far," Baker said.

"Someone will pick us up."

He kept his voice calm; he was essentially talking to a panicked animal. "In this weather? They'll be more likely to hit us."

"We'll *make* someone stop."

"No."

"You can, though, can't you? Make them?"

"No." Whether he could or could not was irrelevant.

Ani frowned and drew into herself, crossing her arms over her chest. She grew paler, and her breath gave a little hiccup. Baker could see the red marks on her wrists. As the rain fell, the creek rose. As they watched it grew higher. Baker put the car in reverse, and tried to execute a k-turn. The passenger back wheel lodged itself in the mud and spun.

Ani started to weep into her hands.

"Stay here. I'll be back in…" Fifteen minutes? Half an hour? "I'll be back soon."

"You can't leave me!"

"I'll be right back."

"You can't go back to the house!"

"I won't let them hurt me."

"They can't hurt you," she mumbled.

His strengths weren't all that impressive. The pushing he'd done earlier combined with the walk to the house and back would lay him up for a week. Now he ran on adrenaline… when it subsided, there'd be hell to pay.

He stepped out of the car. At least the rain was warm. He began to walk.

By the time he got to the house, it didn't feel so warm. It soaked him to the skin, his teeth chattering, and his legs, lower back, and lungs ached. The lights were on in the house, a good sign, the power was still on.

He tried not to limp across the driveway. Before he knocked he took a moment to catch his breath. Baker waited, pulling himself into the door to get out of the rain, listening so he could pull back when he heard them coming.

He knocked again. He wished the rain would subside so he could hear. After one more loud set of knocking, Baker tried the door. Unlocked. It swung inward.

Though he'd only been gone a half-hour, the house had

an uninhabited feel. A light glowed in the kitchen, and the rest of the rooms lay shadowy and dark.

"Hello?" No answer. "This is Paul Baker. I need to use your phone."

He took a few steps inside, wondering where they kept the phone. Kitchen? That seemed most likely. Yes, there it was. Lightning brightened everything and left his eyes aching. The thunder that followed sounded a little farther away. The storm was moving east. He hurried to the phone, the muscles in his thighs and back screaming. He picked it up, a dial tone.

Something caught his eye, pale in the dim light. If it had rested only on white carpet he wouldn't have noticed, but it jutted out over a checkered floor tile. A woman's hand, the fingernails painted an impersonal crimson.

He tried to blink it away. Common sense told him to make the call, get out of the house, and go back to the car.

Instead, he lowered the phone to the cradle. He could protect himself.

An outstretched hand rested on the floor between the kitchen and another dark room. It lay on the lip where thick carpet became sleek black and white linoleum. Red-painted fingernails, black in the unearthly storm light. Mrs. Weaver.

Baker reached for a light switch. The room was a study, and Mrs. Weaver lay prone on the floor, blood pooled around her head. Baker couldn't see a wound. The blood seemed to come from her mouth, her ears, her eyes, and her nose. It soaked her blonde hair. Around her temples he noticed her roots were growing in brown, streaked with grey.

Baker backed away.

"Mr. Weaver? Zach?"

He glanced at the phone. He should call 911. Instead he headed up the stairs, calling their names.

He knew this type of injury. He tabulated his reactions to the Weavers, his anger and his escape... he'd spent decades controlling his talents; he couldn't have killed a woman without realizing it.

Mr. Weaver lay in the hall in front of Ani's door. The floors here were hardwood, and the blood pooled in the cracks.

The rain let up a bit, reducing to a gentle drumming on the roof. Thunder rumbled in the distance.

They were all dead here. Baker didn't need a third body to prove it. Yet something pulled him, drew him to find Zach.

The second child lay in the bathroom. He'd been standing at the sink when he died, and his body slumped back into the tub. He left a great bloody streak on the wall as he fell. One eye was pushed out of the socket from the pressure.

Was he *sure* he hadn't done this?

He took inventory of his aches and pains, of every thought he'd had upon finding Ani tied to the bed. No. He was certain.

Something caught his eye, though, as he headed for the stairs. In Zach's room, papered in posters of half-clad women and fast cars, a door connected the two bedrooms. On Zach's side, a lock.

Baker moved down the stairs toward the phone as thunder rumbled in the distance. He didn't call 911 after all. Instead, he placed his call to the lawyer. He thought of himself at Ani's age. There was still help for a girl like her.

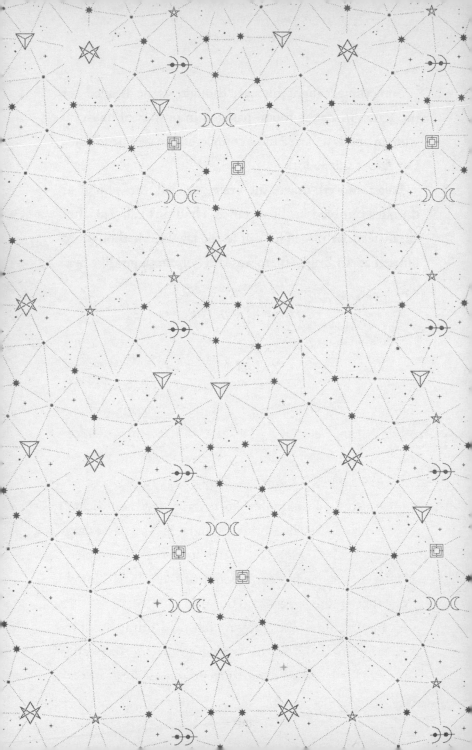

BLESS YOUR HEART

Hillary Monahan

Pamela "Pammy" Washington asked specifically for Audrey's seven-layer bars for the PTO meeting with a whispered aside that if Audrey didn't make them, Janice Motts would, and Janice's bars tasted like hot baked garbage. Pammy wouldn't tell Janice that on account of the bad crazy—admittedly Janice was a few sandwiches shy of a picnic, even by Audrey's standards—but if Audrey would be *so* kind, Janice could stick to something simpler.

"Like chocolate chip cookies out of the tube," Pammy said. "That's more her speed. Poor thing."

Audrey'd come real close to telling Pammy to shit in her Stetson. She wasn't wrong about the hellscape that was Janice's kitchen; Audrey'd damn near lost a tooth biting into Janice's shingle-like peanut brittle at the Christmas social. It was just that Pammy's boy was Colton, and Colton was a little bastard.

Or, not so little anymore at six feet tall and two hundred pounds, with all that thick football muscle. The bastard part remained the same, though.

He should shit in his mama's Stetson, too.

Audrey poured melted butter over her graham crackers so she could fashion the crust, bypassing spoons because working with her hands was more effective. She squished and kneaded, turning it over again and again so it'd get good and flat in the bottom of the baking pan. It was sticky work, but cathartic; she was pummeling it to shit and back again thinking about Colton's chiseled jaw, black hair, and blue, blue eyes.

His outsides were pretty as pie supper.

His insides were so ugly, the tide wouldn't take them out.

Son of a bitch. You'll get yours, just you watch.

It'd all started when her son, Tucker, was seven years old. Tuck was always a little different than other kids. He was short and slight, with dusty gold hair and Coke-bottle glasses over big eyes. He preferred Barbies to GI Joes, and crafts to sports. His favorite color was purple and he watched *Queer Eye* reruns so much, he could quote most of Carson's lines right down to the inflection. All you needed was two minutes alone with the kid to know the big gay writing was on the big gay wall. She'd birthed a boy queer as a three-dollar bill. She was fine with it, but others? Well?

Others could be real mean.

The last thing she figured she'd hear out of his mouth was that he wanted to join Cub Scouts, but he dropped that on her one night over red beans and rice. She'd been happy to oblige—Tuck's best friends were Netflix and his cousin Samantha who lived an hour and a half away—but she had her hesitations, too. When your kid sticks out like a sore thumb, you know other folks are going to notice, and where they lived was big on Jesus, small on kindness. It was a strange juxtaposition. She'd been raised Christian, been raised to see Jesus as love incarnate, but somewhere along the line someone fucked it all up and they were preaching that Jesus only loved *certain* types of folks, and her little boy with his freckles and baby face probably wouldn't grow into that type.

It was shit. She knew it was shit, told others it was shit, but people didn't listen. They kept passing out those pamphlets for conversion camps whenever "the gays" came up during sermon. For the bargain price of two thousand dollars and two weeks' time, you could torture your kid straight, *satisfaction guar-an-teeeed*. It was the end of church for her. It would have been the end of the entire town if she could have swung it, but being a single mom with no support and bills to pay, Podunk it was and Podunk it would have to remain until she could afford a big time move. Montrose, best case. Houston if she was careful with the neighborhood.

Until then, her job was to keep her baby safe and happy, and he insisted Scouts would make him at least happy, so she'd signed him up with a wing and a prayer. At first, it was good. Better than good, even—Tucker came home from meetings sparkling. Pack leader Jason was a real Marlboro Man minus the terminal cancer, and Tuck took to him like a fish to water. He'd made a friend, too, a kid named Alex who lived one town over. He was a short, round black kid who loved comic books and got Tuck into them, too—especially Miles Morales, who she was pretty sure was Tuck's first kid crush.

For months it was right as rain. The boys were inseparable, hanging out every Saturday poring over issues of *Spider-Man* and *The Avengers*, sometimes at her house, sometimes at Alex's apartment, depending on if Alex's father had the car that day.

'Til the fishing trip.

Audrey'd dropped Tuck off as per usual so they could go to the lake and work on their camping merit badge. They weren't supposed to be back 'til suppertime, but at four that afternoon, Pack leader Jason called her at the office to let her know there'd been "an incident."

Audrey straightened up behind her desk, the hairs on the back of her neck bristling.

"What kind of incident?"

"Well, you know how kids can be—" he started.

"Is he alright?"

"Not a hair out of place, promise." Jason sighed. "He wouldn't thread the worm. Got all upset that he'd have to run the hook through the worm so the other kids—well, you know how they are. I told them to knock it off, that it wasn't Scout-like, but Tuck's real upset. I think maybe you should come get him. He won't calm down."

"Knock what off? You still haven't told me what's happened to my son."

The pause on the other end of the line was pregnant with rotten.

"They chased him 'round. Called him a faggot and threw worms at him. I'll talk to their parents later, but—"

"Who?" she demanded. "Who would do that to my boy?"

"Eh, a few of them were involved," Jason hedged.

"I want names. Who's the ringleader? There's always a ringleader."

The Scout leader let loose with another long, defeated sigh, like asking him to tell her all the truth and not just what was convenient for him was beyond the pale. "A kid named Colton. He's not all bad. Just a little too big for his britches. I talked to him. Made him apologize, but Tuck's... like I said, he's real upset."

So Audrey'd climbed into her car and driven a half-hour out to the lake to retrieve her traumatized kid. It hadn't been good—Tuck refused ever to set foot in Cub Scouts again, and when he'd asked her through tear-swollen eyes what "faggot" meant, she had to explain it in a way that wouldn't destroy him forever. She wasn't sure she succeeded. He'd looked so solemn in the listening, like an old man trapped in a tiny, seven-year-old body. She could practically see a layer of his childlike sweetness stripped away as Tuck grappled with concepts far bigger than him.

It'd been a disaster, but at least Alex and the comic books stuck around. They were the silver lining to Colton's first big, nasty fart cloud.

Audrey's fingers were greasy thanks to all the melted butter. She paused to eye her crust. It was perfectly uniform, like something you bought at the store. Satisfied, she reached up to swipe at her sopping brow. September heat had taken its toll while she'd worked; droplets of sweat curled down her hand and curved around her thumb. She shook them off onto the crust, watching them settle on the pale brown paste before being absorbing into it.

Under any other circumstance, it'd be an abominable thing. Not this one. Not for *Pammy Washington.*

Audrey reached into the cabinet to gather the chocolate and butterscotch chips she'd need next. Her mama always told her folks like them shouldn't bake mad unless they were willing to carry that burden later, but Mama hadn't lived long enough to meet Tuck. To know his sweet smile. To hear him singing musicals in the shower or while he took out the garbage. He'd have tickled her pink, and Audrey liked to think Mama would have *helped* Audrey make the angriest damned seven-layer bars in all of Texas were she still around.

Heck, knowing Mama, they'd have been even better than Audrey's.

By some backwoods swamp witch standard of better, anyway.

She measured out the chocolate chips in her Pyrex cup, muttering all the while. *Colton, Colton, Colton.* His name polluted her mouth like the dollar-fifty taco she got from the Grab and Go that one time. Tuck should have been done with him after Scouts, but no, they weren't that lucky. When Tuck moved from elementary school to middle school, Colton was there, too, and Lord, he remembered Tuck and the worms. He made sure every other kid knew about the worms, too. Recess became a time for kids to dig up worms and torture Tuck with them, throwing them at him, putting them into his books. It got to the point the poor kid had to take his recesses inside alone, supervised by a teacher.

Audrey'd shouted to the heavens above that it should have been the worm flingers inside, denied sunshine and freedom, but there were many of them and only one Tuck, so the school'd done some bullpucky "kindness counselling" thing and kept Tuck under lock and key. Which they continued to do into junior high school, when the worms were replaced by horrible notes left in Tuck's locker, spit in his food, and him being tripped so often, she replaced his glasses four times in one year.

He survived it intact, but barely. And now it was high school, where the kids were smarter and more grown-up. They hunted her short, scrawny queer kid like pack animals, weeding him out from the safety of the herd and pouncing. Week after week, he came home with bruises and cuts he was too scared to explain, with ripped clothing she had to mend because they were too broke to replace it. Salt cut through bloodstains real well, she'd come to find out.

Audrey begged, pleaded with him to tell her who was at him, but no amount of mama cajoling would crack her terrorized child. He just shrank and shrank, leaving the house as little as he could. Even getting him to see Alex became a struggle and a half, Tuck preferring the safety of his room and the peace of the internet to the threat of going outside. She was fairly sure Alex wasn't going to ditch him for going through a rough patch, but it wasn't doing a whole lot for her nerves, neither.

Isolating a gay kid in a red county… she knew how that went. He'd end up broken, running off, or dead.

And I ain't losing my boy.

Chocolate chips, then butterscotch chips, spread over the crust before the pecan layer. She hadn't realized she was crying 'til the tears splashed down, but that was fine, as fine as the sweat had been, and just as fine as the blood when she cut her thumb on the sharp edge of the condensed milk can after she opened it. Two fat, red droplets, right into the mix, as she poured the milk all over. As she poured her anger, helplessness, and fear all over, too.

Witching wasn't a good resort, it was a last one. She'd offered to do pick-ups from school every day, but Tuck wouldn't let her. Said he was too afraid she'd get in trouble with her job for sneaking out. She then told him he could homeschool, but he insisted it was just a little while more, he could make it 'til then. Colleges preferred the "real" transcript, he said, and he wanted to get into an art school up north if he could, or maybe out in Miami.

She hated everything about the situation, but she abided, right up until he came home with a black eye and a lip twice as big as it ought to be. Still, he wouldn't talk.

Everything was escalating, had been since he was seven, so she did what she always did in these situations, which was climb into her car and drive up to the school to demand to know what they were doing to protect her son.

The principal, a balding man with bird bones and a skinny tie, blinked at her over the rims of his glasses. "Without evidence, there's not much I can do," he'd said. "If Tuck won't tell us what happened…" His hands spread, palms pointed up at the ceiling.

"Why would he? Y'ain't done diddly-squat to keep him safe! Y'all keep acting like him getting beat happens like rain happens—'cause God said so. But this ain't God. This is Colton Washington and we both know it."

She'd stared at the principal, he'd stared back. His lip flattened in a mutinous line. As per usual, he was as useful as titties on a bull. Audrey was all sorts of done. If he couldn't find a way to keep Tucker from getting killed, she'd plead her case to the PTO—implore the local parents for action. Surely, someone had to understand what it was like to fear losing your baby. They couldn't all be peckerweasels, could they?

Clad in her prettiest dress, notes in hand, she'd marched right on in to the bi-weekly PTO meeting the next week. And promptly shat a brick on the library floor. The PTO president was Pammy *Fucking* Washington in her stupid black Stetson, bottle-job blond hair, and pink t-shirt stretched taut over boobies her husband Ron bought for her fortieth. Normally, Audrey had better things to do than to judge other women for their looks, but Pammy brought out the petty in her something fierce, and Audrey's petty said Pammy looked like Aging Texas Barbie.

No big surprise she birthed an asshole kid.

Tuck used to flat out say it was Colton harassing him. Through junior high school, Colton's name came up over and over again. It'd landed Audrey and Tuck in mediation meetings with Pammy and Colton and school counsellors three times. Pammy was always polite, but she always made excuses, even going so far as to suggest "both" boys needed to examine their actions so it didn't happen again. Audrey'd lost her temper on that one, asking how Colton shoving Tuck's head in a toilet and flushing it was a "both boy" scenario. Pammy had offered that wan, pink-painted smile of hers.

"Well, that *was* rude, wasn't it?" she'd said before prompting Colton to apologize. Which he did, but he never saw even a single day of detention for it. Not then, and not into high school, mostly 'cause as Tuck stayed little, Colton got big, and Tuck got too afraid to out him, figuring the here and there beatings were better than whatever would happen if Colton saw an actual consequence.

But Audrey knew who was responsible. Sure as shit, she knew, and despite Pammy being on the PTO, she figured the other parents were still her best bet, so she kept going back, week after week, waiting for her time to talk. Without fail, Pammy would pull her into every conversation except the one Audrey wanted to have.

"The agenda is too full today, but let's talk about what we can do to challenge some new titles in the school library."

"Would maybe next week work, Audrey? Oh, and what did you think about the mandatory prayer at the flag post?"

"We covered the bullying policy *right* before you started coming out. We'll circle back, promise, but we need to look at raising funds to replace the baseball team's jerseys. The girls' softball team can wait another year."

And, finally:

"I promise we'll get there, doll. In the meanwhile, it's your turn on snack rotation, and I was wondering if you'd bring your seven-layer bars? If you don't, Janice Motts will and that girl shouldn't go near a kitchen. Can't say that— she's got too many cobwebs in the attic, if you know what I mean—but if I tell her you're doing the bars, I can maybe get her to do something simpler. Like cookies from a tube. It's more her speed, the poor thing."

Pammy wanted bars? Fine. Pammy would get bars— an Audrey special she'd never forget. Audrey sprinkled the shredded coconut all over the dessert and shoved it into the oven. Three hundred and fifty for twenty-three minutes exact would give her just enough time to rinse her sweaty body and change.

And then?

Well.

Then it was time to get heard.

She's not even a real Texan.

There it was, Audrey's pettiness being as pleasant as a chainsaw enema again. Her hands clamped on the steering wheel, knuckles white, the seven-layer bars piping hot on the passenger seat beside her. She, herself, wasn't Texas born, but petty didn't care about that. All petty cared about was shitting on a Kentucky transplant who presented like a caricature of any real Texan Audrey'd ever known.

Or been, really. Yeah, she was Texan. Thirty-four years of living in the state said she could call herself that. Mama'd relocated them from the Louisiana bayou to drier Texas air after doctors told her temperate weather would be better on her lungs. Audrey'd been six then, and she'd never been back to where she'd come from. Never had a reason to, neither; Mama said she had no family she'd want near her kid. Audrey'd been her one and only and stayed that way right up until the day asthma took her home to Jesus eighteen years later.

It was strange to think about Mama as she pulled into the library parking lot at quarter 'til seven. Or, maybe it wasn't. Mama was the one who told Audrey a long time ago *no one* should cook mad, but especially not Winslow women because Winslow women had a shine about them. Anyone could catch the evil eye if their cook was riled enough, but from a Winslow woman? You could catch dead, especially if she knew what she was doing.

That's where all those talks about responsibility had come in.

"Texas ain't known for its tolerance, darlin'. They figure out what we can do, we'll be run off, and that's the best-case scenario. Your great-granny got run into the swamp and et by alligators cause she swamp witched too hard. If you use that shine of yours, make sure you're ready for it."

Fine, Mama, I'm ready. Pammy and Colton probably aren't, but I sure am.

She patted her hair into place, snatched the bars, and walked toward the library, her kitten heels clicking on pavement that'd go soft with much more sun. The skirt of her sundress whipped around her knees. Her hair danced inside its clip. She hadn't bothered with much makeup, but there was a smear of red on her lips—a dash of confidence in a tube so some outside part of her matched the rage lava burning in the pit of her belly.

Through the front doors, past the desk and children's section, down by the periodicals to the media room in the back. She could hear Pammy's voice from thirty feet away, greeting every newcomer like she hadn't seen them in sixty years.

"Sarah! Darlin', you are glowing. Baby due in June?"

"Daaaaaale. Gimme a high five, Sugar. Atta boy!"

It went on. And on. And on.

She was holding court at the back of the room, near the podium. The hair was big, the hat was on, the cowboy boots were new with their turquoise stone studs. She walked down a line of parents, shaking their hands like she wasn't the president of the PTO but the president of the damned world. Audrey took her place, holding her squares and hoping her hands didn't tremble. When Pammy finally stood in front of her, all beaming watt-capped smile, her eyes sparkling, Audrey tried to return it.

She probably looked like she had gas, but what the hell else was she supposed to do? Biting her on the face was a felony.

"Oh, look at this red-lipped siren right here!" Pammy leaned in to air kiss next to Audrey's cheek, her perfume stench ripped straight from a French whorehouse. Audrey's insides roiled. A hundred and fifty some-odd pounds of condensed evil had just invaded her personal space, but she didn't flinch, not when Pammy put her hands on her shoulders, not when she gave her a saucy li'l wink.

"You brought your squares, too! Dang. Too bad I'm doing the keto. Gotta get ridda some of my rump." She dropped her voice to a conspirator's whisper. "Though the husband like a little jiggle to my wiggle, if you know what I mean."

Keto? No!

The notion of brewing up a curse only to have it go uneaten was far more upsetting than Pammy's tended—or unattended—ass parts. Audrey notched up her not-smile, even going so far as to show a line of straight, white teeth.

"You got horns holding up that halo," she managed. "But a bite can't hurt, right? You did ask me to make them special for you." Audrey pulled back the foil on the pan to reveal the pre-cut squares with their gooey chocolate, coconut layers, and *little bit extra*. Pammy peered at them a moment, her tongue tip resting on her lower lip as she mulled.

"Alright, alright. A little piece, but that's it." Again she whispered, "Mostly 'cause they ain't Janice's. She bought a cake from the grocer, poor thing."

Yes, poor thing. Whatever. Eat the square, Pammy.

Audrey's satisfaction at seeing Pammy's acrylic talons reach in to pluck a square, turn it this way and that, before nibbling on the corner in such a way as not to disturb her lip gloss was practically orgasmic. When Pammy took a second bite, declaring the first "near-on godly" Audrey's knees quaked. Pammy nodded at her with another wink and headed on down the line to greet her subjects, not just giving the square a sample, but devouring it whole.

So much for keto, bitchbag.

Audrey brought the pan over to the table. Flies buzzed 'round Janice's pity cake, tiny vultures waiting to dive on a confectionary kill. One swooped in toward the squares almost immediately. Audrey swiped at it and, upon catching it in her palm, crushed it before peeling the rest of the foil away from the pan. Bug bits plummeted to join the layered treats, the melted chocolate swallowing a wing, some torso, a few legs. She paid no mind. The curse would only hurt Pammy 'cause that's how the evil eye worked, but for the rest of 'em? Well, what was a little extra protein when she'd already thrown so much of her own in there?

She wiped her hands on a paper napkin before walking around to the back of the room. She sat at the end of her row, crossing her legs and waiting. The other parents settled, as did the PTO board at the folding tables along the front. Pammy slipped in behind the podium, a queen ascended to her throne.

She cleared her throat. It was about to *begin.*

All that rot in Audrey's guts turned to anticipation as her

magic swelled. She couldn't sit still. Her foot tapped. Her nipples went hard. Mama never said witching felt so good, but damn if Audrey didn't feel like she could tapdance on the moon itself if she put her mind to it. Her pulse raced. Her fingers rubbed the thin cotton fabric of her dress between them until they hissed. Pammy blathered on through her agenda, but Audrey didn't hear a word of it. She was too busy squirming like a worm on a hotplate because her witch was awake and Lord, it was hungry.

Twenty minutes later it was the question and answer portion of the evening. Audrey practically vibrated as she raised her hand. The magic inside her was so swollen, she felt like an overfilled balloon, like her skin wasn't big enough to contain the mammoth surging inside her. It was eager. It demanded release, and she would let 'er loose if Pammy didn't give Audrey her due.

Which she didn't, of course, because she knew Audrey's question and didn't want to deal with it. She pointedly picked every other raised hand in the room, and after taking a vote on whether or not girls should actually be allowed on the football team, declared them past time. She even swung a little gavel down on her podium like that slam meant jackall at a PTO meeting.

Polite clapping.

Rustling as people stood from their seats.

"Pammy," Audrey called out over the noise.

Pammy pretended she couldn't hear.

Audrey pulled on that thing frenzying inside of her, that swamp witch presence, calling out Pammy's name so sharply, the room chatter quieted, every head turned. Dozens of eyes fell upon her, questioning, waiting, and Audrey rose from her seat, her fingers clasping onto the back of the chair in the row before her, nails biting into fake leather.

"Yes, Audrey?" Pammy asked, voice dulcet, smile cemented in place, but something undermined the facade. The twitch below her eye. The too-swift flutter of her false lashes against her cheeks. The set of her jaw, maybe.

"I'd like to talk about Tuck tonight. It's early yet, and you did promise we'd get to it this week."

Audrey waited for an answer that wasn't forthcoming. Pammy turned her face to go right on back to conversing with Donna Charlotte, the secretary of the PTO, like she hadn't heard a word. Audrey's monster didn't like that, screeching and washing Audrey's body hot in spite of the frigid air conditioning.

Alright. Go on, then. Start slow.

Pammy's cheek twitched again. Then again. The first time, it was irritation. The second and third time? Well, it was hard to say what was what. The one disadvantage to being in the back row of the PTO Shitfest was Audrey couldn't see the tiny shapes running along the inside of Pammy's skin. She just saw Pammy swat at her face, and Donna Charlotte's eyes grow big.

"Girl, you got something… yeah, right there." Donna Charlotte pointed.

"What in Red Hell? Why'm I so itchy? Something bite me?" Pammy lifted her fingers, rubbing them furiously over her face, the tips of her nails scouring over the surface to leave pink tracks in their wake.

Donna Charlotte's head whipped back and forth, her limp, red hair whacking her cheeks. "It's like you got something— maybe a worm? It's runnin' along under your skin—like. That's… you need a doctor, Pamela. That ain't right."

"WHAT DO YOU MEAN I GOT A WORM?"

There went the smile, finally, right as the first fly flew out from her left nostril. Pammy honked like an irate goose and tried to crush it with the gavel in her hand.

Is this how it's presenting itself? Flies, like what's in the rest of the pan?

Alright.

Well, in for a penny, in for a pound.

"Pammy," Audrey called out. "I'd like to talk about Tucker. Most specifically what Colton's been doing to him. He's beating him raw, you know. Sending him home bloody. That's why I need you to listen. Ain't letting your son kill mine anytime this life."

Pammy whipped her head around to stare at her.

"Not the time, Audrey! Not the damned time, alright?"

"It's moving all over." Donna Charlotte pointed at another shape wriggling under Pammy's skin. "Like, you got another one up by your temple. Oh, Lord. You're a mess." One of the men on the committee looked like he'd step in to help, but Donna Charlotte herded him away, a squat border collie with too-rouged cheeks and a green dress. "I think we best all take a step back? She's got *something* going on. Might be contagious. I'm going to call the nine eleven. Hold on, Pamela. Just hold on, okay? I'm right here. Well, no, I'm not. I'm moving back, but I'm still in the room, alright?"

Donna Charlotte frenzy-dialed.

Audrey's smile remained placid.

"Pammy. I think it's time we talked about Colton and Tucker."

Pammy wailed, her lips parting before she broke out into a dry cough that ended on a second insect erupting from her mouth to buzz around her head. Worst part was how tenacious the little buggers were, the flies swirling around like Pammy was a big, peach-colored pile of dog shit.

Which, let's be real honest ...

Pammy collapsed into a squat, her fingers plunging into

her hair and knocking the Stetson aside. She shredded her perfect coif, the locks coiling around her in a halo of weird, twisted corkscrews that jutted out at all angles. When she drew blood, and that's what was going to happen with those Freddy Krueger nails of hers, it was along her brow. The skin split wide and a stream of viscous blood flowed, coursing over her lashes to drip down her nose and onto her t-shirt.

Took Audrey a few seconds to realize the blood was lumpy, and that the lumps were *moving*. Didn't take long for the new flies to shake off their li'l wings and join their less sanguinated brethren circling Pammy's head.

Oh, that's nasty.

The other parents scampered outside with terrified yelps. Donna Charlotte held out an arm near the door to keep as many folks back as she could. Some poor emergency operator had to listen to her squawking that Pamela Washington had flies busting out of her face and could they get out there lickety split? Three times she had to repeat herself, finally ending on, "Yes, I'm serious. There are flies. Coming. From. Her. Face. Holes. Take the cotton out of your ears and listen to me!"

The thing inside Audrey purred like a big, satisfied cat. It liked the hell it was raising. It wanted *more*. It took all of Audrey's composure not to let it loose to claw its way through Pammy and anyone else stupid enough to stick close. They thought they were fine twenty feet back? They needed miles, at least, and even then, that wasn't a guarantee.

It was big, it was powerful, and it was mean.

Run. Run little flies. Run.

Audrey abandoned her back-row seat to approach the bloody, terrified woman swinging her miniature gavel at the dozen or so flies buzzing around her head. Every few seconds another crawled its way out of the wound, stretching the ragged edges of her cut so they flayed open *just* a bit wider.

She crouched in front of her and kept her voice real low. "I want to talk about Tuck and Colton, Pammy."

Pammy looked incredulous. "Right now? You're serious?"

"Tuck's waited long enough and you know it."

Pammy's enraged shriek could have busted ears. She brought the gavel around, aiming for Audrey's head to give her a thwack. Audrey couldn't tell if it was fury at Audrey's audacious timing, or if she'd figured out that Audrey had witched her good. No matter either way. Audrey caught her wrist easy enough and held it, peering at her a long while. Tiny shapes ran all over Pammy's face beneath the skin, skittering around in a frenzy as they searched for the nearest exit.

The widening forehead cut. The ear. The nostrils. The corner of her mouth.

"It's gotta stop," Audrey said, her voice low. "If Colton touches him again, that's it. You hear me? *That's it.*"

Pammy looked like she was working herself up into a fine bellow, but then her eye pulsed. She froze, blinking fast over and over and letting loose with a low, animalistic groan. A tiny shape worked its way up under her cheek. It skittered along the bone before dashing toward the finely carved line of her plastic nose. The tiny space between her socket and eyeball widened. Another fly wriggled its way out, presenting to the world with a rude splash of tears and blood.

"N-no. Nooooo," she whimpered, whipping her head back and forth. The flies scattered only until she stilled, descending once again to their rightful place. They were the buzzing, carapaced crown for the queen of the PTO.

"It's gotta stop. Now." Audrey squeezed Pammy's wrist to punctuate it. "Stop and I'll never bother you again. Your peace is my peace. You hear?"

Pammy shook so hard she couldn't talk, but she managed a nod, as desperate and scared and frustrated as Audrey was every time Tuck bled. Audrey's free hand cupped Pammy's chin. She forced her to look up, so they were nose to nose. Seeing all the bad Audrey sank into those squares looking back at her, seeing the pain and terror there, the thing inside Audrey quieted. It was still there, still ready if she needed it, but it was sated, too.

It seemed a beast born in fear only knew how to gorge on fear.

"You'll end it?" Audrey demanded.

Pammy swallowed hard, coughing again and spitting out yet another fly. "Yeah. Yeah, I'll end it."

"I got your word?"

"You do. My word. Colton'll leave off. Promise."

Audrey didn't know if she meant it. She could hope she did, but only time would tell. At least she had what she needed, for now. She leaned in to press a soft kiss to Pammy's forehead, right above the cut bubbling with blood and flies. "Alright. I'll be watching. Don't let me down, y'hear?"

"I won't," Pammy croaked.

Audrey grinned as Pammy's halo of flies scattered to library parts unknown. "Bless your heart, Pammy Washington. *Bless your damned heart.*"

THE DEBT

Ania Ahlborn

The earth was soft; lush with a blanket of moss so verdant, Karolin had never before set eyes on green so fresh and alive. The color was the first thing to stand out among the features of the forest. It didn't matter that the sky was overcast. Even without sunshine, that green was electric, almost glowing of its own accord. But the way the ground gave beneath her feet was what surprised her the most.

It feels as though I could sink, she thought, *sink through the ground and into the deep below.*

The forest smelled of soil and that morning's rain. She'd been woken only an hour before by a hand upon her shoulder, her father standing above a bed that wasn't hers in a house she'd never visited before. Karolin found it strange that the house had been empty when they arrived, nothing but old furniture and the scent of mothballs. Two layovers, an international flight, and an additional three hours of driving toward the border of Belarus, and somehow it hadn't been enough of an effort for her grandmother Sylvia to be home when they had finally pulled up to her dad's childhood home. But her father, Greg, had never spoken much about his mother, and this was Karolin's first visit to Poland. She was only eleven, but she was smart enough to know that the relationship between her dad and grandma was complicated; complicated like the relationships on all of those Lifetime TV specials Karolin's mother had once liked so much.

The dewy forest floor invited sterling-colored worms to wriggle their fat bodies across moss and dirt. Perhaps, had Karolin been a year or two older and only *slightly* less averse to all things girlie, she would have been disgusted by those slithery invertebrates. But she was *still a kid*, as her mom had reminded her on the eve of her most recent birthday, and had anyone asked Karolin to name her top three annoyances, they would have been (in no particular order): the color pink, Disney princesses, and anything that didn't involve her red Converse All Stars—a gift she'd received from her father; a little inside joke just between them. As a matter of fact, Karolin had only worn a dress once in her relatively short life. She'd put it on so that her mom could finally see just how pretty she looked in it. Having dragged the ill-fitting thing out of her closet, she'd pulled it over her head in a fit of tears. But her effort had been in vain, because when Karolin leaned over her mother's casket, Mama hadn't opened her eyes. She had simply lain there, a waxen cadaver.

Everyone remembered the day their mother died, but Karolin's recollection would always be extra vivid. Because, just hours before the accident, a room full of friends had sung Happy Birthday over a cake Mom had made herself—a semi-lopsided astronomy-themed confection covered in icing so dark it had stained everyone's mouths a deep, zombie blue. That afternoon, Karolin and her parents had gone to the nature preserve, where she had put her new binoculars to the test and spotted a red-footed falcon—one of the rarest birds in her home state of Massachusetts. And that evening, just before sitting down to watch *Fantastic Beasts and Where to Find Them*—a movie Karolin had been asking for since it had come out in theaters and had *finally* received as one of her birthday gifts—Mom had realized they were out of ice cream. When asked what flavor she wanted, Karolin had replied *rocky road* without so much as a beat of hesitation. But now, nearly a year after the accident, she had spent hours thinking about what could have been had she decided that ice cream hadn't been necessary. She hadn't eaten ice cream, let alone rocky road, since. And she wasn't the only one who had changed. Almost a whole year without Mom, and Dad had gotten weirder with each passing day.

Stepping onto a mossy patch of ground, Karolin's foot dipped down into the earth. She crouched and pulled the moss away, and it came up like an old shag rug. If one had the time, Karolin bet you could roll up the entire forest floor like a giant carpet. And there, beneath the moss at the base of an old oak, were what she and her father were pursuing. Beautiful, golden, fluted chanterelles; like drops of sunshine hidden underground. Chanterelles for Grandma, despite her absence; despite the fact she hadn't greeted them hello.

But why didn't she come home last night? Karolin had asked her father as they had driven a tiny Fiat toward their destination that morning. *Isn't she excited to see us?* Dad hadn't responded to Karolin's inquiry. Not surprising, since her father had been less talkative as the days had gone by. The man who had once been charming and funny and had taken every opportunity to make his only child laugh, was now a distant shell of who he'd once been. And while Karolin understood that he was hurting after Mom died, it still hurt *her* to be treated like a stranger; like a burden he had to deal with because he was obligated, not because he wanted to.

But Karolin was trying to put those hurts behind her,

hopeful that the reason her dad had suddenly been so eager to take her to the country of his birth was because he wanted to rekindle the warmth they had lost. After Dad had told her about their upcoming trip, she'd spent weeks Googling random facts and trivia about a country she'd only vaguely heard about while growing up.

Did you know, she had asked during their flight from New York City to Warsaw, *that Poland is home to the largest castle in the world? Did you know, Dad, that the forest outside Grandma's town is the last place European bison live?*

That town was Hajnówka, and the primeval Białowieża Forest was where Karolin stood now, with moss pulled up and an outcropping of bright yellow mushrooms smiling up at her from their emerald home.

"Dad!" Karolin looked up from where she was crouched, the old wicker basket her father had pulled from a random closet set next to her dirty sneakers. That basket was mostly empty, nothing but a small paring knife resting at its bottom. But when she pulled her gaze away from the ground to look around her, her dad was nowhere to be seen.

The spike of adrenaline was immediate. It zipped through her veins, and within what felt like a nanosecond, Karolin's heart pounded hard against her ribs. *Ba-dum,* like a mallet hitting a bass drum. She shot upward from her crouch despite feeling weak in the knees.

"Dad?!" She spun around, seeking out her father, suddenly face to face with the reality of where she was. Deep in the forest of her father's youth, a place she had visited hundreds of times through a single, dark fairy tale. It was a story about a boy and a witch and a house perched atop impossibly tall, crooked stilts.

That tale had been good fun when it had been told in the comfort and safety of Karolin's bedroom, especially since the protagonist had always been a boy, not a girl like her. But now, as she stood there, pivoting upon the soles of her sneakers like a music-box ballerina, one detail washed over her in a rush, a detail that had been nothing but a joke until now. She was wearing the shoes her father had given her as a gift—red All Stars; a wink to the dark story that had bonded them together. Back then, Karolin had laughed as she had pulled the sneakers onto her feet, imagining that they were the same shoes the boy had worn while running as fast as he could over fallen logs and snarled roots. But now, the sight of them made her want to vomit. What had once been a comforting gift suddenly felt downright ominous. But it wasn't just the shoes. It was everything. Especially those mushrooms. Especially those.

Karolin knew a little about a lot of different things— some common, some far more niche. She knew how to build a fire out of wet wood, how to build a shelter out of branches she found on the ground, and what foraged items could be consumed. Her father had taught her all those things, determined to teach her how to survive out on her own, as though he knew it would come to this. As though he'd foreseen this very moment—his daughter lost in the woods. And Karolin had never minded the lessons. Rather than resisting her dad's teachings, she eagerly absorbed the information. It was why she knew about moss and berries and the fact that most insects were safe to eat, or how to make a tea from spruce needles and bark. But one lesson stood out in her mind as she stared at the chanterelles next to her feet.

If you didn't bury the dead deep enough, they'd sprout mushrooms called corpse finders. Those once sunny-looking chanterelles now struck her as well-disguised harbingers; the Grim Reaper trading in his black robe for a brightly colored three-piece suit.

There are bodies out here, she thought. *In these woods, dead girls feed the trees.*

The thought of it turned her stomach, turned it just as she was turning now, round and round until she stopped mid-spin.

"Oh, no," she whispered, her eyes growing wide as realization dawned. Because she'd just broken her father's first two cardinal rules of wilderness survival.

One: *Keep your head on, don't panic.*

And two: *Whatever you do, do* not *lose track of the direction you came from. It's the direction you need to find your way back.*

"Oh, no!" The forest went watercolor wavy from behind her tears. "Dad!" She just about screamed it. Surely, he couldn't have gone far. They had ventured out in different directions, sure, but had always stayed within visual range, and most certainly within earshot. Karolin had seen him only minutes before. He'd been standing there, motionless, looking into the trees with a strange expression pulled taut across his face, as though he was considering something. Or perhaps he was simply remembering. *Maybe*, Karolin had thought, *it's like déjà vu. He used to come here by himself, and now he's here with me.*

But there was no response to her yelling. No, he was gone. And Karolin stood alone among the trees, her breath hitching in her throat, tears streaming down her face. Her dad would be angry that she'd lost her cool. Heck, this might be a test. She wouldn't put it past him, the survival expert that he was.

She squeezed her eyes shut and tried to think. "The rules," she hissed between her teeth. "Remember the rules, stupid. Think, think, *think!*"

She took a deep breath and let her eyes open. Her gaze traveled across ancient trees and branches that had been downed for decades, maybe even centuries. Trying to pinpoint some clue as to which direction she'd come from, she stared at her basket at the foot of the oak. The moss she'd pulled was resting dirt-side up next to where her foot had sunk into the ground. Had she been traveling north? She hadn't bothered to check. Not that it would have mattered. The moss was so thick it grew around an entire half of the trees' trunks, and she and her father had meandered, not walked in a straight line.

It was only then that that particular detail struck her as odd. *Always walk in a straight line,* he had instructed. And yet, here she was, not knowing where they had come from because of what he had done.

She felt another wave of panic creep over her but managed to push it down to the pit of her stomach. The worst thing she could do was waste daylight by freaking out. If it was still light out, she had a decent chance. But if night fell…

No, don't think like that.

She grabbed the wicker basket by its handle and palmed the paring knife. It was still morning. She had plenty of time to figure this out. But if she was going to try to get out of here, she had to do it carefully. One of her father's rules had been to always mark her trail. Karolin stepped up to the closest tree and used the knife to carve a crooked 'K' into its mossy bark. That way, if she got turned around again, she'd know where she'd been, at least up until this point.

"Dad?"

It was hard to believe he couldn't hear her. The forest was deathly quiet. Her yelling should have been audible for miles. Not like the time she'd gotten lost at Fenway Park during a Boston daytrip to watch the Red Sox play. There, the crowd had been made up of a million blank faces, none of them either realizing or caring that she was in the throes of an anxiety attack. Her, just a seven-year-old kid, convinced that she'd die in front of a hot-dog cart without ever seeing her parents again. Here, that crowd was made up of trees rather than people—nobody to ask, not even a blank and uncaring pair of eyes to plead with. Just Karolin, an eleven-year-old girl convinced that she'd die in the Polish woods miles outside of her grandmother's town, just like the boy in her father's stories had.

In those stories, the boy had yelled, too, but his screams had been swallowed by air that had gone thick with electricity. He'd yelled until he started to choke on a stench that wrapped itself around him like a shroud. *It smelled like a dank old root cellar. Like mold and overturned earth.*

Suddenly, Karolin could smell the very scent her father had described. Stupid, really. She knew the stench wasn't there. It was just her fear manifesting as she spiraled into another bout of hysterics. She began to cry at the thought of that boy, regardless of whether he only existed in some spooky folktale her father embellished every time he told it. She wept as she wandered up to a second tree and carved a 'K' into its bark, then took a rough swipe at her eyes with a dirty palm.

No matter how often her dad changed the details of that story, the boy never found his way out of the woods. Not once in the hundreds of times her father had relayed the tale did that kid escape a grim and terrible fate. Back then, that had been okay. Heck, it had been one of the reasons Karolin had loved the story so much. She had always hated clichéd happy endings. And yet, at that very moment, she wished that the boy had found his way to safety, if only once. She longed for him to never have met that terrible, crooked-spined woman—the one that lived in a house perched upon tree-branch stilts. She wanted to have never heard that awful story at all; the story of the boy who had gone for a walk in the woods only to find himself face to face with a pitiless Baba Yaga, the witch of the woods.

"There's no such thing," Karolin whispered, her breath hitching on her sobs. "It's just a story." But with every new golden mushroom cap she spotted, the more she convinced herself that they were reapers of the dead. Chanterelles would sprout from the remnants of her body, and one day, a girl just like her would venture into these woods with her family for a day of mushroom picking. She'd use a small paring knife, just like the one in Karolin's hand, to cut the mushrooms that sprouted from Karolin's decaying chest.

"Dad!" She tried again, screaming the name as loud as she could.

She wasn't stupid. If he hadn't heard her before, he certainly wouldn't hear her now. And yet, the moment that yell passed her lips, she spotted movement behind an ancient oak as knobby and twisted as a hundred-year-old hand. Karolin's heart sputtered to a stop as she saw a boy run out from the shadow of that tree.

"Wait!" she called, but he was quick, the hood of his sweatshirt bouncing between his shoulder blades as he bolted through the branches and moss.

"Please, wait!" Karolin yelled, her own sneakers carrying her over treacherously soft earth, her grandmother's wicker basket clutched in one hand, the knife in the other.

In the back of her mind, she knew she was only making things worse. Chasing after some random stranger rather than continuing to seek out her father was insane. There was no telling where this kid was going, or whether Karolin would ever be able to find her way back to where she'd started. Yet she blew past tree after tree, none of them scored with a 'K' to mark her path. *It's him,* she thought as she pursued her target. *It's got to be.* Because, while any kid could have been wearing jeans and a black sweatshirt, he had something that Karolin had, too. In every telling, no matter how elaborate, her dad had included that minute detail: the red sneakers. They were the kid's calling card. They were why her father had given her a pair just like the ones in the story.

But who is he? she had once asked. *The boy, what's his name?*

I don't know, was all her dad was willing to say. As if the story hadn't been creepy enough. *Could be you, or me, or anybody. It's impossible to know.*

"Hello?!" Karolin gasped out the word as she continued to run. The wicker basket slipped from her fingers and tumbled to the ground. Perhaps someone would find it one day—the same girl that collected the corpse finders that sprouted from Karolin's shallow grave.

The boy was weaving in and out of the pines, though Karolin couldn't tell whether he was running serpentine to lose her or to make sure that she'd get even more lost than she already was. Not that it mattered. By the time she stopped running to catch her breath, all hope of finding her way back to the spot she'd started from was gone. Her wicker basket, her father, and the few trees she'd marked with a 'K' were but a memory now, completely forgotten.

Because there, in the not-too-far-off distance, was a house in the trees.

There, held up by the thick and twisted trunks of a

few primitive oaks, was a wooden cabin with a roof so impossibly sloped, it looked like a sharpened fingernail pointing toward the sky.

The place reminded Karolin of old teeth—jagged and off-kilter. An entire side of the house was covered in moss. *North*, she thought, though what help north would be now, she hadn't a clue. There was a light on, shining through one of the crooked windows. It glowed jack-o-lantern orange in the shadows of the trees. And just above it, a stack of stones that made up a lopsided chimney billowed a plume of smoke.

Karolin took a backward step, her gaze frozen upon the raven that was perched at the cabin's highest peak. When she moved backward, she bumped against something that hadn't been there before. Spinning around, she stumbled at the sight of a picket fence, or at least something that resembled one. Though this fence wasn't made of wood. No, this fence—the thing that hadn't been there seconds before—was made of something else. With hundreds of brown-capped mushrooms lining the slats like a ribbon of silk, she dared to lean in to get a better view. It was built out of something that resembled polished stone or ivory; something that looked like the stuff she'd found on junior archeological digs.

Bone. The word rang out in Karolin's brain clear as a bell. And those mushrooms...

The panic she had managed to shake off gripped her

again, refusing to abate. She struggled for air, her mouth opening and closing in soundless gasps. Her fingers twisted tightly around the handle of the small knife in her right hand, as though whoever lived in that terrible-looking house could be warded off with the likes of a tiny blade.

It was then that she heard it. That crow emitted a throaty caw from atop its perch, the sound growing louder from behind her as the bird swooped to the ground with the flapping of wings. Then, a rustle of fabric. The soft crunch of leaves underfoot. Karolin froze, the sensation of no longer being alone suddenly so overwhelming that her entire body began to shake. It had been the same at Fenway Park. She hadn't been able to catch her breath. She'd fallen into an uncontrollable tremble. By the time her parents had found her, the hot-dog vendor had dialed 911.

Now there was no one to pull Karolin from beneath the weight of her own terror. There was only the presence behind her, bringing with it the smells of melted candle wax, heady incense, and freshly overturned soil. It smelled of ancient cemeteries and mausoleums. *It smelled like a dank old root cellar.* And then, as if summoning her to turn, the rustle of fabric and leaves was replaced by something far more ominous. A creak, like the sound of a rusty hinge. Except, this was no old door. *This* sound was being made deep inside a human throat.

Karolin squeezed her eyes shut, but the tears continued to flow. Somehow, she brought herself to turn away from the fence she was sure was made of human bones and come face to face with a woman draped head to toe in what looked to be thick oil-cloth. Her hair was obscured by the oversized hood that hung over her eyes. All that was visible of her features was a pointed chin and an impossibly long nose, flat as a shovel until it abruptly bent concave toward the ground.

Karolin tried to produce a scream but found herself breathless and mute, standing there slack-jawed, her face hot with tears, gasping for air. As if amused by the terror she was causing, the ominous rasping emanating out of the crone's throat slid into an even more nefarious laugh. But rather than taking a forward step toward the child before her, she turned away.

It was an opportunity. Every brain cell in Karolin's skull cried out for her to get a grip, keep it together and *run*. It didn't matter in what direction as long as it was away, far and fast. She wasn't sure how she managed to get her legs to work again, but before she knew what she was doing, she was beelining away from the woman, keeping that terrible fence to her right. She was almost at a bank of massive spruce trees when her foot sank hard into a divot hidden by moss. She felt something snap just above her ankle, and it was then that a scream finally escaped her throat, not of terror, but of pain.

Her cry was, however, short-lived. She found herself facing someone familiar, someone she hadn't expected to see.

The boy looked older than Karolin by a good five years. She imagined him reflecting her own expression back at her—horror at the fact a place such as this could exist. That a woman such as the one looming behind Karolin could truly come to be. Karolin blinked away from him and looked over her shoulder, afraid to keep her eyes off the old hag for more than a few seconds. Inexplicably, the woman stood less than a few feet away from them now, having transported herself just as quickly and effortlessly as she'd made that awful fence appear.

"So..." The witch let the word escape her in an almost pleasurable hiss. "You've finally come back, Gzegorz."

Gzegorz. Hearing that name felt like lightning spiking Karolin's heart. Because she'd heard that name before. It was Polish for Gregory, the long-form of Greg. Her eyes snapped back to where the boy had stood, but he was gone. And in his place, her father stood.

"Dad?!" She wanted to yell it, wanted to force herself to her feet despite her broken ankle. She wanted to throw herself into his arms and believe that she'd find safety there. But the name only left her in a weak whisper, because she *knew* who she had followed. It had been the boy from all the stories, the ones in which he had attempted to barter for his life. He promised the witch anything she wanted. Gold. Jewelry. But the witch had wanted nothing except what the boy already had: youth. In each telling, he was seized by the back of the neck and dragged into a crooked house. At least, that was how the story had gone. But now, as Karolin's fingers curled into the moss under her palms, she began to understand.

The boy's fate had been one of her father's many embellishments.

The boy had, in fact, been allowed to go free.

"A promise is a promise," the crone spoke again, her gaze roving over Karolin's slumped form. "Late by over a year," the woman grumbled, then looked to Karolin's dad.

Over a year. Karolin couldn't help but look back at her father. Was that true? Had there been some sort of missed deadline? Had Mom—

"Leave us," the witch said, her voice suddenly forceful, as if annoyed that Karolin's dad was there at all. "This settles your debt."

Karolin's mouth went dry. *What?* She wanted to scream the word into the woods around her, but no sound escaped her throat. She wanted to run again, but that was impossible now. She wasn't even able to stumble backward as the witch closed the distance between them. The scent of overturned soil and candle wax was now accompanied by a new smell—an overwhelming sickly-sweet stench, like fruit that had long gone bad. It was only when the woman reached for her that Karolin was able to draw in a sharp intake of breath, gasping at the sight of bony fingers twice as long as any human hand should have possessed. They were tipped with thick yellow nails sharpened to jagged points; skin thin as tissue paper, wrinkled and pressed over her hands like a terrible attempt at papier-mâché.

With wide, imploring eyes, she dared to look away from the woman and back to her father. Was he really going to leave her here? Was this why he'd taught her those survival skills? Was it why he'd told her the same terrible story a thousand times over? Had he changed the ending from what had happened to him to reflect his own daughter's grim and inescapable fate?

She didn't want to believe it, but the shoes were proof. He'd imagined her here, in this very spot. He'd missed the witch's due date. Mom had died. And that's when he had changed, when he had given her the All Stars, when he'd pulled into himself despite planning an international trip. She'd naïvely believed that this was a vacation, just the two of them healing their hurts together. But she now understood that it was nothing like that at all. As her father took a few backward steps into the darkness afforded by those spruce trees, his intention became clear.

ANIA AHLBORN

Karolin yelped when she felt bony fingers wrap around her arm.

"Come," the woman wheezed, but it wasn't a request. Reflexively, Karolin attempted to pull away, but the grip that seized her arm was as tight as a vise.

"Dad?!" She tried to twist away as she looked back to her father through a veil of tears, but the shadow beneath that massive spruce was now vacant.

"Come," the witch repeated, and Karolin was pushed forward, limping on her bad ankle toward the cabin in the woods. And when she pulled her free hand back and stabbed at the woman's arm, the witch didn't flinch, as though she didn't feel the blade at all. Rather than reacting, she continued to shove Karolin toward the crooked house nested up in the trees, and it was then that Karolin caught sight of something that simply shouldn't have been. There, poking out from beneath the sleeve of her own shirt, was a small outcropping of mushrooms. Not chanterelles, but real corpse finders. They had begun sprouting from her flesh even before the witch took what she was rightfully owed.

TOIL & TROUBLE:
A DARK-HUNTER HELLCHASER STORY

Sherrilyn Kenyon & Madaug Kenyon

The eleventh bell rang out across the dismal shadows of Carrion Hill where three rigid, gray shapes practiced a dark, forbidden art. Yet it was one oft sought by those like the regal man standing before them, who'd shaken off his shackles of organized faith to beseech their wisdom and implore their sinister aid in his cause.

"Oh great Fates, with wisdom of old. Over your cauldron, where you toil. I beseech you now, for your gifted sight. To carry me forward through this night. What will come, good or foul? This I must know, before dawn's first prowl."

He held himself with the familiar arrogance the witches didn't need their single eye to see. Rich robes fashioned from hues of red, orange, and purple which had been woven by the hands of those he deemed unworthy, and trimmed with gold thread until those same poor women had gone blind from their imposed labors.

Now he, the feared master, came to them as a loyal servant to offer minted gold and jewels to the witches three to whom he bowed in utmost respect. And well he should. For they were the shapers of destiny. Older than time and more callous than any king.

Dieno, the sister who had the ability to see every tragedy lurking within a single lifetime. That was her gift.

It was also her curse.

Enyo's visions showed the battles that awaited their querent. Small and large. Every skirmish, every death match. She could tell this king exactly who was plotting against him.

Last was their petite sister, Persis, whom others cruelly mocked as "the destroyer", for she knew the steps one could take to avoid ones fate...

Or cause it. Her words about the future were the ones that mattered most. They were the guidance that could make or break a single life. The irony was that everyone knew it and yet failed to listen time and again. But that was because these Stygian witches were missing their fourth sister, Pemphredo. She'd been the one who could show their querent the way through the prophesies. The one who could guide them to safety and unravel their verse.

Without her…

Humans were screwed.

Since time immemorial the witches of Carrion Hill had foretold and guided the destiny of lord and pauper alike. King and peasant. In their hands lay the power to destroy nations—to shatter dynasties…

Or save souls.

'Twas this power that made them the sole arbiters of truth in a time and land dominated by chaos.

"Listen!"

"Hear!"

"See!"

The witches spoke out, one by one. As they'd rehearsed a thousand times before, the sisters cackled and howled, and prepared their boiling cauldron. They threw in the usual, expected ingredients as they didn't want to disappoint their customer—eye of newt, wing of bat, and the withered tongue of a liar… all humanely gathered, naturally, as the sisters were ever conscious and respectful of such concerns. The last thing they'd ever want was to insult anyone's sensibilities, as that had nefarious endings for their kind, such as causing them to end up tied to stakes and set afire.

Or thrown into ovens by ungrateful, bratling children they'd taken in after their parents had thoughtlessly lost them in the woods.

People were ever vicious that way. And every year more and more of their sisters were lost to such cruelty. Soon it would be just them and Uzarah left to guard the gates, if things didn't change. Then mankind would know why witches had been necessary in this world.

Not to practice magic or foretell silly fortunes for those too weak to make their own.

They were here to cast back into darkness the mistakes the gods had made. To shield mortals from their own stupidity and incessant need to fabricate their destruction. But they, like humanity, were growing old and tired. And with every sniveling request such as this, the sisters three really didn't see a need to salvage this world, or the ones who wasted their time with such trivialities as their own fortunes when the entire universe sat poised on the verge of annihilation.

As the ingredients simmered, they stirred the pot three times, one for each of them, and muttered their time-honored chants.

"Double, double. Toil and trouble.

"Fire burn, and cauldron bubble.

"For a charm of powerful trouble,

"Like a hell-broth boil and bubble.

"Come and see. Come what may.

"Things we want and things to delay."

Now came the fun part… Magic was more art than science and while Dieno could see the trouble that lurked ahead and Enyo hear the battles to come, it would be up to Persis to give him the words he needed to avoid those catastrophes.

Not that it would matter. Mortals never listened. They were ever bent on their own destruction.

Dieno scooped up her Stygian eye from the cauldron in order to look into the prophecy taking form. There, she could see the king's fate in motion while her gray sisters could hear it— a vicious cycle that would continue for a hundred generations. One that was older than the icy hand of time… a foolish family would cast out their own. Despondent and angry, he'd take his revenge upon them in a brutal series of murders, only to be brutally murdered by his own children in turn.

Round and round, the hatred grows.

Killing all kindness everywhere it goes.

Where it stops…

Well, we know.

And they could tell him, but what was the fun in that?

Enyo pursed her lips. "Not the most original of prophecies, is it?" she whispered.

Persis sighed as she grabbed the eye for her own look. "Nay. Seems as if patricide be the crime of the hour. How very gauche."

"Can't they ever come up with something more original? Like pinning cheese to their balls?" Deino retook the eye, trying to find a better outcome.

Same old, same old.

In spite of their steadfast denials, people were seldom original.

After a lifetime of predicting brutal tragedies that ended with such karmic deaths any perpetrator with half a brain should have guessed would happen, the witches had grown so very bored with it all. How many ways could they say the same thing?

Don't be an idiot. Nay, really, stop being stupid. Don't… you will hurt yourself.

Still, they persisted. It was as if humanity wanted to bleed. Worse, they wanted to whine.

Case in point. Such a simple prophecy. One that could be easily avoided by giving the child a loving home. If only the father would do so. But as with Oedipus, he wouldn't listen to their wisdom.

How many times would they waste their collective breaths? Why did he even bother to come here when he had no intention of hearing them?

"Double, double. Toil and trouble.

"Fire burn, and cauldron bubble.

"Humans come and humans die.

"'Me life's unfair,' they always cry."

The sisters took a moment to discuss what they would tell this wretched king.

"No need to speak the truth," Enyo whispered.

"Shall we make a bet?"

Dieno liked where Persis went. "Aye!" She cracked a rare smile as they began to think in verse.

The rules of their species forbade them from ever giving their sight outright.

Clearing her throat, Dieno lifted the eye so that she stared out at the arrogant king in all his finery. "Here your future for to see,

"Clad in darkness, he brings misery.

"A hundred swords light a hundred fires deep,

"And at the knees of each soldier doth a maiden weep.

"Over and over, a kingdom is lost.

"Such a horrid, dreadful cost.

"For in the end, the answer's clear...

"Be careful of the evil you hold so dear."

The king scowled at their prophecy as if he were baffled by it.

Dieno stifled her smile. She could tell he was frightened

by his bleak future. And well he should be. Even so, he mustered a polite bow and thanked them for their time, then paid them well.

"Good riddance." Enyo lowered the hood from her cloak and extinguished the fire. They were done for the night.

"Was it right? What you did?"

They paused at the sound of their apprentice. Eeri was a little snipe of a thing who constantly stuck her nose where it didn't belong. She pretended to have the good of others in her heart, but even blind, Dieno could see through the little blond's treachery.

"Clean out the cauldron."

Eeri watched as the three witches hobbled off to sleep and glared at their departing backs. How she loathed them. They were the worst.

She should know. Her own parents had sold her off to them for nothing more than a bag of grain when she'd been a child. And she'd hated them every moment since. Imagine, being worth nothing more than a sack of seed.

"Bitches' brew," she snarled at their fetid concoction before she spat into it. The bubbling liquid hissed, then a green cloud shot up toward the sky.

Her eyes widened in terror as she feared they might see what she'd done and harm her for it. They could be incredibly cruel over such things. Best not to try her luck with them!

Swallowing hard, she quickly set about cleaning up. After all, she had a big day ahead of her tomorrow. The last thing she wanted was to be sleepy or tired.

The next morning, Eeri made her monthly trek to town to purchase supplies for her witch mistresses. These were the days she loved best of all, as they gave her a break from the three Stygian bitches and their sing-songy lies. She didn't believe in anything they said. How could she? It was always vague nonsense that could apply to anyone.

Screwing her face up, she mocked their prophecy from the night before. "Here your future for to see,

"Clad in darkness, he brings misery.

"A hundred swords light a hundred fires deep,

"And at the knees of each soldier doth a maiden weep.

"Over and over, a kingdom is lost.

"Such a horrid, dreadful cost.

"For in the end, the answer's clear…

"Be careful of the evil you hold so dear." She scoffed, then snorted. "Utter rubbish, I say. Me farts hold more prophecy than that… smell better too than that shite them witches brew."

Letting out a tired breath, she stared up at the bright blue sky. "I'd give aught to be done with the lot of them!"

All she'd ever wanted was to belong to someone. Belong to something like this quaint little village, celebrating the vernal equinox—a time for new beginnings. How she wished she could be one of them. Cheery and friendly, and free of the Stygian three.

Depressed, she walked past bright colors that shot out from open doorways while the townspeople excitedly drank and danced in their revelry. All around, laughter came at her, yet she felt none of it.

Not that it mattered. This was a good atmosphere for fortune-telling. Just as she'd known it'd be. Those around her would make good prey... er, practice for her future trade.

Her spirits perking up at the thought, Eeri pulled out the small crystal ball she'd packed and looked about for a place to set up a makeshift stand. Not too dark or drab. Inviting and promising.

Unlike the bitches in the woods.

They were pathetic and old. And since the day she'd been bought, it'd been her dream that someday, with enough money, she could purchase her freedom from those old heifers. That was all she wanted. A life apart from creatures like them.

Sadly, she had to deal with them. So she made sure to gather their ingredients first, lest she become part of their apothecary. Then, she found a nice corner in the marketplace to set up a makeshift table for her ball.

Within minutes a couple came by and sat across from her. Finally!

"Tell me about my future." The man smiled and handed off a dirty coin.

Eeri could smell the alcohol on him, but he seemed pleasant enough.

The girl at his side gave her a sheepish grin. "I know he doesn't look his best right now, but it's a festival, you know? Anyway, are we meant to be?"

Eeri suppressed a shiver. God save her from that fate. Yet who was she to cast dispersions on the woman's ambitions?

One woman's rose, another's asshole.

With a deep breath, Eeri moved her hands around the ball, calling on the powers of beings from beyond to show her the weave of the universe. If their life forces were entwined. She saw the man before her drinking heavily as burly men looted his home.

The woman by his side wasn't happy. Rather she sat with dejected, dead eyes as the men raided her meager possessions.

A stout man hefted a heavy axe over his shoulder. "This be why you don't go a' gambling, worm. The Lord giveth and we taketh." He cut off the man's hand.

She grimaced at the nightmare, then met their eager gazes. A horrible future easily corrected without verse or the boiling of oats or toads. "Beware your gambling and heavy drinking in the future, if you want to remain together and whole."

The woman let out a gleeful cheer as she shot to her feet. Quickly, she pulled him up and dragged him away. As they vanished into the crowd, Eeri could hear her letting him have it about his drunken tendencies.

She spent the rest of the day dispensing similar fortunes. They were all simple people with simple lives, but she would have it no other way.

Yet all too soon, the sun set and the night grew cold. A chilly breeze sought to drive her from the village, back into the woods and up the hill. Even so, she'd made a pretty penny and it was time to retire for the night and bring her ingredients home.

As she was packing her ball, she felt a peculiar presence near that caused the hair on her arms to stand on end. Until then, she hadn't noticed that the night had become unbearably quiet. No sound could be heard. Not even the barking of a dog.

Only her heartbeat in her ears. Until the sound was overtaken by the heavy footfall of a stranger. The sound grew louder with every step as he came closer and closer still. A figure wrapped in utter darkness, walking straight toward her.

She wanted to run. Needed to run. But fear had paralyzed

every muscle in her young body until the stranger was upon her.

Tall and muscular, he had the swagger of a warrior and the confidence of a king. This man was legendary. Without breaking stride, he took a seat at her makeshift fortune-teller's table. Still wrapped in silence, he pulled out a bloodstained invitation and dropped it beside her hand.

She gulped audibly. What he held was rare indeed. A favor card given by the witches to someone who'd once gone out of his or her way to pay them a kindness. It meant that the bitches now owed him a favor in turn.

Those they hoarded more closely than gold as they never wanted to be beholden to anyone.

Who was this man? She was desperate to know. Yet she could see no trace of any feature. It was as if all light avoided him. As if it cringed from him. All she could make out was a subtle sneer in his dark visage.

He tapped his card three times and her senses returned. As frightening as the man was, he must be close friends with the witches on the Hill. Only one of those rare breeds would have such a card. So she dug out her crystal ball to tell one last fortune for the night.

Cradling it like a babe, she moved her hands over the ball. She saw the man standing proudly next to a flaming pile of dead witches.

A lot of dead witches.

"Witchkiller," Eeri breathed.

With a cruel smile, he leaned closer like a predator before the kill.

Her heart pounding, she yelped and knocked the table over. She heard her prized ball shatter against the cobblestone road as she sent the witches' supplies scattering. Nothing mattered to her at the moment, except saving her own life.

He was evil! Terrified, she ran as fast as she could, and dared not look back in fear that the man would catch her.

I have to warn the others! She might hate them, but no one deserved the deaths she saw.

By the time she reached the small cottage, she was shaking and weak. No one had caught her. Thank the old gods! Relief poured through her.

Until she heard the laughter from inside.

She peered through a window and saw Enyo sat before the fire, playing a game of chess with Dieno. Safe and warm, the sisters were recounting tales of the kingdoms they'd seen crumble in their prophecies.

Life's not fair. Righteous anger filled her. Why should they have a family when she had no one? She'd never harmed anyone and yet here she was, alone, in the dark, being threatened, while they laughed and carried on.

Let them die!

They deserved it. It would serve them right. After all, she'd been gone for hours and they weren't even looking for her. For all they knew, she was dead, like the others. And did they care?

Not a bit.

So, why should she warn them?

Let him have them and you're free.

What she had always wanted. Who would know? Licking her lips, she glanced about. It was true. She knew where Enyo had money hid. It would be enough to see her through.

Aye, this was her chance…

Stealthily, she crept away from the cottage and back into the woods.

"I will find you, money mine.

"And we'll be together for all time."

After all, that was the only thing she really needed. Her money had been lost in the village. She'd been so startled by the man that she'd left it behind. So it was only right and fair that she take from the sisters.

They deserved it.

"Help! Help! I'm caught in a trap."

Eeri froze at the masculine voice. No one should be in the woods tonight. But there was no mistaking the man. She wanted to ignore him, but the bastard was in her way. There would be no way to leave without his seeing her.

And she remembered the card.

A favor for a favor. Mayhap if she saved him, he'd help her escape the Witchkiller. She didn't know how to fight, but this man might.

So she followed his calls until she found him hidden in a small copse of trees. A handsome, beautiful man in the prime of his life with dark-blond hair and glowing green eyes. Caught in a bear trap, he hissed and snarled as he tried to get himself loose.

"Hello?"

He righted himself at her voice and turned to face her.

Startled, she realized that he was dressed just as the man she'd seen earlier. Same black clothes and lethal aura. Yet not quite as bloodthirsty.

His peculiar gaze swept over her body, making her instantly aware of how unappealing she appeared. Covered in dirt and grime, she dripped with enough sweat that he could probably smell her from his distance. Her long hair had come loose of its braid to tumble around her thin shoulders and she was certain he must think her hideous.

But instead of cringing, he laughed. "I'm glad to see someone is faring worse than I." His laughter ended in a hiss of pain.

"Hold still." She went to bend down next to him.

Ugh! The trap was so tightly clamped around his leg

that she couldn't budge it. All she did was hurt him more.

After the third time of her clamping it more tightly to his ankle, she wrinkled her nose at his pain-filled grimace. "I'll go get help."

But she didn't. As soon as she was clear, her common sense returned and she remembered that he wore the same suit as the man who was out to kill everyone like her. He was her enemy.

Do unto others before they do unto you!

Aye, better he should die than should she.

And so she ran away from the village and the Carrion Hill. Just as hard and fast as she could.

Or so she thought.

Confused, Eeri came upon a village that looked strangely familiar. Nay, it was familiar! And it was crowded with others dressed just like the man from her table and the one she'd left to die. Men holding swords...

She started to turn away, but something wouldn't let her. An unseen force kept her there, then suddenly, it felt like her soul had been ripped from her body.

What is happening?

The man in black appeared in the crowd. They parted so that he could walk through them and climb to a small platform and speak for the first time. "I stand before you, not above.

"Never plotting against those you love.

"Speak no evil, not in life.

"Never tarry and cause no strife.

"Yet they stand above us mortal men.

"Plotting against us at their whim.

"We are helpless against their guile.

"Until we're choking on our bile.

"But no more sway will they hold.

"And no more lies will be told.

"Brothers, sisters, is this not what I promised you?

"That there are those who will get their due?

"Savage ends for savage beasts.

"Come tonight, we shall feast!

"Fetch your torches, sword and all.

"A hundred witches tonight will fall!"

Gasping, Eeri turned and almost ran straight into the man she'd left in the woods.

He tsked at her. "With Ate by his side come hot from hell. Shall in these confines with a monarch's voice cry 'Havoc!' and let slip the dogs of war, that this foul deed shall smell above the earth."

"Beg pardon?"

He laughed at her question. "You can beg all you want, little one. But you judged your sisters for your crimes and for that you are damned."

"I don't understand."

Thorn stepped back so that she could see her table, toppled and littered with the sisters' supplies. And there lay her body. "You didn't escape the Carrion beast. Nor did you pass my test." Shaking his head, he looked to the hill, now ablaze from the horde. "Come, Misery. I have a place where you belong."

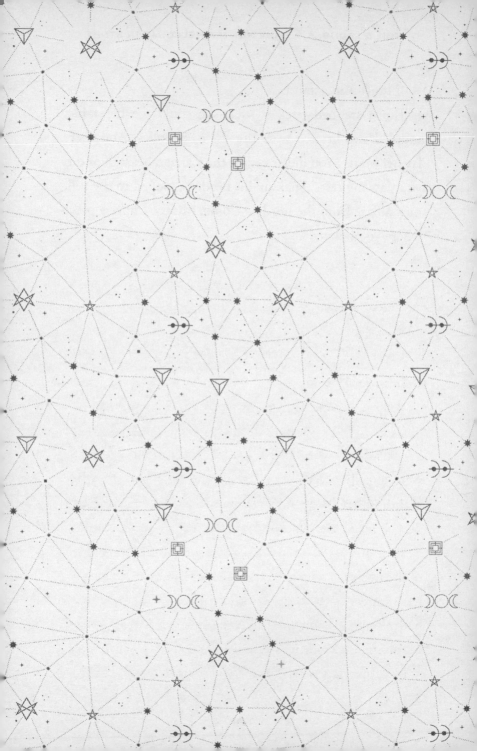

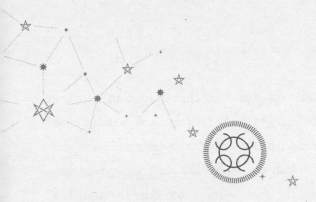

LAST STOP ON ROUTE NINE

Tananarive Due

Gracetown, Florida

"I thought you said you wouldn't get lost," Kai said.

Charlotte's teeth tightened to match the pressure of her hands on the rented Toyota's steering wheel. They were already a half-hour late to the luncheon after her grandmother's funeral in Tallahassee, a drive her navigator said should have taken an hour and five minutes heading west on the I-10. She'd been doing fine until they got off of the freeway and passed the collection of quaint shops on Main Street in the throwback town, but the last few turns had plunged them more deeply into the swampy woods bordering each side of a two-lane road.

No other cars were in sight. No houses. No anything.

"We're not lost," she said.

Kai glared.

Thin pines and oaks with branches draped in hanging moss choked the road, which the clay soil had ground red, as much dirt as asphalt. Mud from earlier rainfall was slick enough to splash the tires. The air conditioner was on full blast, but the sun burned her skin through her sleeveless black funeral dress. The burr of insects around them was loud enough to penetrate the closed windows. Her car sped past a derelict shack wrapped in weeds, its wooden walls gaping from missing planks. The rusted tin roof made Charlotte wonder if it had been a sharecropper's shack. Or a relic from slavery.

Charlotte's twelve-year-old cousin could have joined his parents and aunts in the limousine after the burial, but since Charlotte had to drive anyway because the "stretch" wasn't as big as they'd expected, she'd asked Kai to ride with her to escape the limousine's sadness, and he'd happily agreed. ("I only met her a couple times," he'd shrugged to Charlotte privately.) Until now, he'd been bobbing his head to his ear buds, his face stoic beneath limp braids, his tie loosened with the knot at mid-chest. Like a noose, she couldn't help thinking.

Charlotte hated the South. Her mother had fled Florida at her first chance, never coming back to Gracetown after she'd gone to UCLA as a freshman, just like Kai's dad, her Uncle Harry, who had joined the Army the day he graduated from high school. Uncle Harry loathed the town. He had spent six months in Gracetown's notorious Reformatory when he was Kai's age, and he had blamed his parents for his imprisonment.

It wasn't surprising that his son didn't feel much warmth for the recently buried Sadie Myrtle Jones Williams. Charlotte's parents had swapped Christmases between Oakland and Gracetown, but Uncle Harry's seat at the table had always sat empty. His four sisters had taken bets on whether he'd show up for the funeral—and he had, sobbing worse than the rest. "I thought I'd have more time," he'd cried out in the church, although Grandmama had been six days shy of eighty. Still, he had refused to set foot in Gracetown for a luncheon at the home of Grandmama's childhood friend. Kai was more a novelty than family to Charlotte, one reason she had been glad to give him a ride. She'd only seen the kid three or four times, and the last time he'd been only nine. Twelve was a different story: he was almost as tall as she was and—

"Shit, we're in the middle of fucking nowhere," Kai said.

"Hey!" Charlotte said. "Watch that mouth."

"You're not my mom. You don't tell me what to do."

She stared at him so long that she nearly veered off

into one of the ditches that yawned open on either side of the road. He'd been so quiet until now that his sudden rebellion surprised her. Her voice was ice. "Don't start with me, baby boy. This is not the time."

His tone softened. "I'm just saying—nobody wants to be driving around in the middle of nowhere, dang."

He had a point, but although she was only twenty-two, she felt obligated to sound parental. "Watch your mouth around me—or you can walk," she said, and threw in, "Hear?" Grandmama had always said that: *Hear?* Charlotte heard Grandmama's voice in her ear, sharp as a whip. Her throat pinched tight with a smothered sob. This awful day had no end in sight.

Kai looked away toward the unbroken forest and its tangle of trees. "My dad got locked up here," Kai said. "He said that place was just a bunch of rednecks who hurt kids for fun. And he said Gracetown is haunted as shit."

His voice trembled. For the first time, Charlotte realized he was cursing because he was genuinely afraid. What kinds of stories had Uncle Harry filled his son's head with? Grandmama had always said Uncle Harry should see a therapist, although she'd said it more like an insult than a recommendation. Her aunts said he'd never been the same since the Reformatory, and maybe Grandmama had been in denial because she hadn't fought harder to get him out. (To hear Uncle Harry tell it, his parents' attitude had been *Maybe it'll be a good wake-up call for him.*) Charlotte's mom had superstitions about ghosts too, but nothing like Uncle Harry's.

"That was a long time ago," Charlotte said. "That place is closed now."

"Whatever," Kai mumbled.

But again, Kai was right: they were alone. Charlotte hadn't seen another car in ten minutes, maybe longer. A thick fog bank sat across the road ahead like a wall, and Charlotte felt a strong urge to stop the car and turn around. She checked the navigator: SATELLITE UNAVAILABLE. The map showed the dot of their car surrounded by a sea of nothing. She and Kai had given up on getting a cell-phone signal soon as they passed the county line. It never failed: whenever one thing went wrong, everything else joined in a chorus. She'd had her first car accident two years ago, when she swerved to avoid hitting a dog on her way from getting her wisdom teeth pulled.

Today felt as cursed as that one. Worse. She'd just buried a grandmother she'd barely bothered to get to know, so both of her grandmothers were gone. She'd had a much closer relationship with her father's more cosmopolitan mother in Oakland, who ran a bookstore and hadn't been nearly as hard to understand beneath a thick country accent and old-school rules.

"Fuck," she said under her breath, and drove through the fog. It was so thick, she braced for the car to shudder, hardly breathing while all of the windows went gray.

"I can't see!" Kai said.

But as soon as he said it, they passed through to the hot sun again, everything in bright focus. Only then, she allowed herself to ponder it: Fog in the middle of the day? During the summer? The oddness skittered across her mind, but she shut down the part of her that wanted to panic. Like Kai had said—whatever.

Evidence of civilization emerged ahead, a small billboard nearly covered by the trees with large red letters: LAST STOP ON ROUTE 9—1/2 MILE-GAS-FOOD. All of the paint was cracking in visible rivulets across the weathered wood.

"Yes!" Kai said, at the same time she'd been thinking *Thank fucking goodness.*

She kept deities' names from mind to avoid blasphemy so close to where Grandmama had lived, as if Grandmama might still hear her. Or maybe, just maybe, cussing alongside God's name really was a sin.

"Listen…" Charlotte began slowly, wondering if she'd been too harsh on Kai by threatening to make him walk. "It sounds like your dad's said some stuff to you that's pretty confusing. And… raw. Maybe he should have waited until you're older."

"Dad says you're never too young to know the truth." Kai recited it like a mantra.

That sounded like Uncle Harry, all right. Every conversation was a speech. But he'd never told her about his time at the Gracetown Reformatory. Not that she'd asked.

"What did he say happened to him when he was locked up, Kai?"

Kai parted his lips as if to answer, but changed his mind. He stared at the road ahead, eyes searching for the promised gas and food. Like her, he looked hungry enough to eat a wrinkled gas-station hot dog. Or two. She'd been looking forward to the feast after the funeral.

"Well, whatever it is…" she went on. "It's not happening now. It won't happen to you."

"What if we get pulled over? And I get locked up for no reason like him?" His voice's pitch grew higher with his agitation. "And then… then…"

"Who's gonna pull us over—a racoon?" she said. "Nobody's out here. Right?"

Kai surveyed the empty road and both sides of the thick woods and nodded, smiling a bit at her joke. Poor kid! Charlotte needed to talk with Uncle Harry and let him know to ease back on his Gracetown horror stories. Uncle

Harry was the eldest of the siblings and Kai was a son he'd had from his third marriage, late in life. He and his son were from two different worlds. When would Uncle Harry have been locked up? The late 1960s? Black drivers in the South could just disappear in those days. Times weren't perfect, but they weren't still like that, at least.

The gas station appeared. And Charlotte's stomach knotted. Shit.

This building was an artifact, shuttered with planks across its windows. She could barely read the faded sign above the door: HANDEE GAS. It was an old-fashioned station with only two bright red pumps long out of service, their hoses emptied on the ground like oversized snakes in a blanket of pine needles.

"What the hell?" Kai said, exactly what she was thinking.

As Charlotte slowed, hoping the gas station would morph into an AM/PM like the convenience stores in California, she noticed a light in the woods to the left. A driveway from the road led to a second structure behind the gas station, a wood-paneled house hardly bigger than a cabin. But a light was on behind sheer white curtains, and a vintage round-hooded pickup truck was parked in the driveway, white paint also fading.

Charlotte turned into the driveway at the last second, her car's tires skidding on mud.

"What are you doing?" Kai said.

"There's a house. I'm just going to knock on the door and ask for directions."

"That's crazy!" Kai said. "Haven't you ever seen *Deliverance*?"

Again, Charlotte looked at him with surprise. She'd seen the film once in college, and once was enough. The banjo theme played in her head, cryptic. "Your father let you watch—"

"He says Gracetown is like *Deliverance*. I've never seen it. Don't *want* to either."

"Kai, stop freaking yourself out. Just stay in the car."

Charlotte rarely missed a hashtag, so she knew what sometimes happened when black people knocked on strangers' doors, only to be met by gunfire. She still remembered a black woman's name: Renisha McBride. And there were others. But she also wasn't going to let fear rule her life. It was broad daylight. She was lost. She was dressed for church. She would be fine.

Charlotte didn't want to block the cabin's driveway, so she veered slightly to the right of it a few yards from the house's door, parking beneath an oak tree that looked a century old. Something *crunched* beneath her tires, the sound of bad news. Dammit! Had she damaged the car? She turned off the engine, and the insects' songs grew louder.

As Charlotte opened her car door, Kai grabbed her wrist. "Wait! Don't you feel it?"

"Feel what, sweetie?"

He stared at her, earnest, trying to choose words. His grip was a vise. "It... it feels... *mad*. Like, everything is pissed off." When she squinted, trying to make sense of what he'd said, Kai sighed and let her go. "I can't explain. My dad says you can't always explain."

"Lock up behind me. I'll be right back."

When Charlotte closed her car door behind her, Kai hit the electric lock right away. The humidity felt soupy, and her armpits pricked with sweat as soon as she stepped outside. In a way, maybe the air *did* feel pissed off. She wanted to laugh at Kai, but she couldn't. And it was smart to leave Kai in the car, she remembered. He was a black male, too tall to be considered "cute" by many strangers; instead, he looked like the national boogeyman since *The Birth of a Nation* and before. Kai was wearing a dress shirt and tie, but still.

Charlotte glanced at the gas station behind them. Someone had made a junk yard of the station's side wall, not as visible from the street: rusted old cars, discarded gas cans, an old road sign advertising Fatima Cigarettes, which she'd never heard of. Maybe this was what Kai had meant, too: these items were pissed off because they were old and forgotten. Like she had so often forgotten Grandmama.

Music was playing faintly from the house. Elvis? It was impossible to mistake the voice, but the music was gospel, not rock and roll. She recognized the song, "Peace in the Valley," from the handful of times she'd attended church with Grandmama at Christmas.

Charlotte did not go to the little house's sagging front porch right away as she'd planned. She stared, thinking it over.

The plants on the porch, even in the hanging basket, were dead. Only a screen door was closed across the doorway, but despite the light she'd thought she'd seen from the road, the house was dark now. It was hard to imagine that light had ever shone from this house, much less a moment before. A hidden hinge squealed lazily back and forth. At the edge of the wooden awning, she saw the chain from a ruined porch swing rocking in the mild breeze. Somewhere behind the house, a dog was barking. It might not be big, but it wasn't small. Maybe it was on a chain, maybe it wasn't.

Then Charlotte noticed the Confederate flag on the bumper sticker on the oversized truck parked near the porch. The words printed beside it had faded, but the crossed blue stripes and white stars still showed. Charlotte's heart thumped her breastbone. She'd known a girl at UCLA who defended the flag as "heritage" and insisted it wasn't racist despite the way racists loved it, but now Kai's words came back: *Everything is pissed off.* How hadn't she noticed it right away?

None of it felt right. Instead of stepping toward the house, Charlotte stepped away.

She looked back at Kai, and he was watching her wide-eyed, his nose pressed to the window on the driver's side. She gestured toward the house dismissively: *never mind.* And he nodded, agreeing wholeheartedly. He motioned for her to come back.

Charlotte walked back toward her car—but then she remembered the crunching sound when she'd parked. It would drive her crazy to wonder if she'd damaged a tire, so she leaned over to take a peek.

Her left front tire had knocked over a mound of large, sharp-edged stones, alongside a silver cross, tarnished black. Shit! She kicked the closest tire for firmness to make sure it wasn't punctured, then knelt to see if the stones had left any marks on the bumper the rental guy in Tallahassee would notice. The car was fine. But broken glass was scattered across the soil from a cracked picture frame near the cross. She picked up the frame and saw a decades old photo she could barely make out, the image splotched by rain and time. Vaguely, she could make out a white man's long, gray beard.

"*Desecration!*" a woman's voice screeched from somewhere. From everywhere.

Charlotte dropped the photo frame, gasping. She was so startled, she had to hold the car's warm hood for balance, her neck yanking around too hard to see who had spoken. A woman was standing behind the house's screen door, features hidden by the mesh. All Charlotte could make out was a powder-blue house dress, maybe a floral pattern. Her face was in shadow.

Desecration. Had she damaged a memorial site, or even a grave? The word charged Charlotte's thoughts, so violent that it felt imposed: *DESECRATION*. The insects' buzzing seemed to flurry *between* her ears rather than beyond them. Kai was thumping on his window.

"Let's go!" she heard him call, muffled through the thick buzzing.

Unsteady with fright, Charlotte stumbled back toward her car door. She tried to raise her voice so the woman could hear her apology. "I'm… so sorry. I won't… disturb you." She raised her hands slightly in case the woman was armed. She expected a gunshot.

Although the woman's features were fuzzy, Charlotte thought she saw her mouth and jaw open into an impossibly long *O*, stretched beyond the boundaries of where her face should be. The woman let out a shriek too loud to be human. The sound echoed through the woods, rattling the metal and glass in the gas station's debris.

Birds flocked from the treetops, shrieking and calling in response. The unseen dog barked in a frenzy. Charlotte's limbs locked, her mind emptied of thought.

Then came an eerie, sudden silence, all sound stripped, even the dog's. Charlotte's hand fumbled with the door handle two or three times before she remembered the car was locked. She slapped at the window. *Let me in*, she tried to say, but her mouth was parched mute.

The *CLICK* from the car door came at last, breaking the unnatural quiet, and Charlotte rushed back into her seat, banging her knee hard against the steering wheel in her rush. Kai was sitting on the passenger-side floor, his face wet with tears. After he pulled his hand away from the electric lock, he rocked himself like a toddler, arms wrapped around his knees.

"It's OK," she said, absurdly. She was lying to both of them.

Just go. Just go. Just go. Her thumping heart had learned language, preaching to her.

When she turned the key, she expected the ignition to ignore her—a waiting tide of grief and terror she did not know how she could withstand—but the engine roared with fiery life. *That's a great car, that one*, the rental guy had said. The memory of his gaudy yellow blazer was her mind's anchor to the world she knew. Charlotte yanked the car into reverse and swerved back so far that she almost hit the truck before she shifted to plow back toward the road. Her heart was thunder. How had Kai known to keep away from this house on sight? How had he sensed the rage boiling just behind the screen door?

She made a frantic turn to the road, back toward the fog, the way they'd come—the only way she knew—so sharply that one of the tires plunged halfway into the roadside ditch, but she quickly righted it. Mud sprayed the underside before the car was back on solid ground.

"What was that?" Kai said, pleading for an answer.

Charlotte could only shake her head. Her existence had shrunk to her beating heart, its rhythm pulsing to her hands tight on the steering wheel and her foot pressing the gas pedal with all of her strength. Since the too-loud screeching, her muscles felt drained. Emptied out.

The radio came on with loud squeals and pops. Charlotte glanced at the glowing dial, hoping to see Kai's hand near it, but he was still hugging himself tight. He stared at the radio too, then back at her with the same plea in his teary eyes. His jaw trembled.

"I wanna go home—" Kai whimpered.

The radio answered him with the same woman's reedy tremolo voice filling the car's front and rear speakers: *"THE DESECRATION IS YOU. I CURSE YOU BOTH*

TO HELL. I CURSE YOUR PARENTS. I CURSE YOUR TAR-BLACK BABIES—"

Frantic to banish her voice, Charlotte looked away from the road to the radio dial. She jammed at the power button with the heel of her palm—once, twice, three times—until the terrible voice was gone. By then, Kai was sobbing.

"It's OK—" she started to say again.

But it wasn't.

As soon as Charlotte looked back to the road, a sun-reddened white man with a pea-green hunting jacket and an unkempt gray beard appeared in her windshield—he hadn't *walked* there, he wasn't *standing* there, he simply *was*—and she only had time to scream and jam on her brakes so hard that the car skewed sideways after a horrible *THUNK* sound beneath her floorboard. She felt the unmistakable bump of rolling over a mass on the road. The car shook from end to end, flinging Kai so much that he hit his head on the glove compartment as his arms flailed to hold on to something.

The car lurched to a stop as if it had been yanked back by invisible wires. Kai was wailing more loudly than she was, but not by much.

In the long aftermath with nothing moving, Charlotte stopped yelling as her thoughts unscrambled. The yellow blazer. She had to get back to the rental guy in the yellow blazer. And Kai was her cousin; if she let anything happen to him, the family would tell the story for generations. She would be reliving this day on her deathbed in a loop, the way Grandma Bernadine couldn't stop talking about a lightning storm that had set her rooftop in Port Au Prince on fire when she was a child. The fire that had killed her baby sister.

"Are you OK?" Charlotte whispered. She didn't know why she was whispering, but she was sure whispering was the right thing to do, even if it wasn't nearly enough. She needed to do far more. Kai shook his head *NO*, his braids whipping his face.

"We hit someone, Kai." The sure firmness in her voice surprised her.

"We didn't!" Kai screamed at her. *"Someone hit us!"*

"Kai… calm down. Breathe."

He did, taking heaving breaths that began to fog the car's window. Charlotte wiped away the condensation with a crumpled napkin she snatched from the cup holder: she didn't want any blind spots. Outside the windows, the stillness was unnerving. She waited for the man she'd run over to pop up and try to scare the actual life out of them, but he didn't come. Nothing moved.

"I know something is messed up, all right?" Charlotte told Kai, and he nodded, his eyes flooding with grateful tears that he didn't have to shoulder reality alone. "I can't explain what happened back at that house. But we ran over a man with the car—*I* ran over a man. I have to check on him. That's the law, Kai. I can't leave an old man in the road."

Kai's gratitude vanished, replaced by bitter fright. *"You still don't get it!"*

"I need you to stay in the car—"

"Don't leave me! You better not leave me—"

"—and I'm just going to check on him. To see if he's alive."

"Alive? Alive don't just-just—"

"Breathe, Kai. Breathe. Or you'll pass out. I'm serious. Look at my eyes and breathe."

She held out her hand, and he took it and squeezed hard. He forced himself to breathe more slowly, keeping his eyes fixed on hers, desperate to believe in her.

Still, nothing moved outside. No corpse popped up like a jack-in-the-box. In the quiet, it was easier to forget the woman's unnaturally loud screech at the house and worry more about the dead man who lay beneath her car. Never mind going to law school one day after her break from classrooms: she would go to prison for manslaughter. She and Kai both had been so shocked by the sight of the man that they'd fooled their eyes, making him a phantom.

I probably killed someone. Her stomach curdled at the thought. If she'd had food in the past few hours, she would have spit it up. *Put on your big girl panties*, Grandmama used to say.

Somehow, Charlotte navigated the lock and door handle with hands like jelly. She eased the door open, touched her foot to the road. Pressed hard to feel its solidness. She prayed as hard as she knew how that the man was alright. When she stood, adrenaline cascaded down her legs.

At least no limbs protruded from the bottom of the car as she'd feared, like Dorothy killing the wicked witch with her house. Both the front and rear tires were flat on the driver's side, the rubber clawed to strips. The sick feeling in her stomach turned rigid, twisting. Were the other tires flat too? They wouldn't get far even with only two flats. She was afraid to check right away and learn that they were stranded.

Charlotte lowered herself to her knees to peek beneath the car, expecting to see the pea-green jacket. But no man was under the car—only a scattered pile of large, sharp stones like the ones under the tree. Back at the house. At the makeshift grave site. Charlotte drew in a long breath, sucking in air. The road seemed to shake with her heartbeat.

"I can't see you!" Kai shouted.

Charlotte pulled herself to her feet, looking away from the impossible sight, but not before she noticed that the other two tires had also been ravaged by the stones, rims shining through. Damn, damn, damn.

As she straightened up, Charlotte's mind tried to make sense of it: Had the car sent him flying into a ditch? She hadn't seen any stones in the road, but she'd looked away at the radio. That many stones hadn't appeared from nowhere—had they?

"There's no one under there!" she called to Kai.

"I told you!" he said. He wasn't surprised at all. He *knew*. "Come back in!"

"I have to see if he got thrown."

Kai thumped his fist against the window, so scared and frustrated she thought he might break the glass or his hand, or both. "Just come back!"

"Stop that, Kai. I'll be right there. He could be only injured." She said it although she didn't believe it—she wouldn't find a man sprawled in the ditch, and if she did he would be dead. But she had to be sure she wasn't just in denial, trading an evening-news brand of horror for something else. The police would ask if she had looked. And he might be there, merely hurt or unconscious. He *might*.

But no one was in the ditch on either side. While Kai kept thumping the window, she walked up and down in her clicking heels looking for the man's coat, or his beard, or blood. Beyond the drainage ditches, she saw nothing but untended woods growing wild. She felt a vibration shiver beneath her feet and held her breath until the trembly sensation was gone.

Kai honked the horn, pressing it for a long, unbroken tone. It sounded like sacrilege.

She waved back at him. "*Shhhh*. Don't do that!"

Kai was pointing toward the road behind her. "Look!"

A car was coming from the direction they'd just left, taking its sweet time. Not a car, she realized as she stared—a truck. A white truck with its oversized hood and cab. Like the one parked back at the house. Somewhere in the woods, a dog was barking.

"The radio's on again!" Kai yelled, panicked. She heard Elvis sing reverently about no sadness, no sorrow, no trouble, no pain, the volume too loud inside the car. Kai was covering his ears. "Charlotte!"

Charlotte ran to the car. Each time she glanced back at the truck over her shoulder, it had gained an alarming distance. There might be both a driver and a passenger in the cab. She had to grab Kai and pop the trunk to see if she could find a weapon. Maybe she'd find a tire iron.

"We have to run," Charlotte said, breathless. She reached for the door handle the instant after she heard the *CLICK* of the locks, too late. But Kai's hands were still plugging his ears. He hadn't locked the doors, but the door wouldn't budge. "Kai! Unlock the door!"

But she could see for herself that he was trying,

reaching across to the driver's door, pushing every button he could. Panic had dried his tears. "It won't open!" he said. "Get me out!"

Charlotte kneeled to find the biggest stone she could. One just beyond the mangled front tire weighed at least five pounds. "Get in the back seat in a ball—hurry! Cover your eyes."

As she raised the stone high, she glanced back at the truck. It was close enough now that if it sped up, they would have no time to outrun it. She could see that the driver was a woman by the outline of her frizzy hair. The truck rambled on at its slow, steady speed.

Charlotte heaved the stone at the windshield with all of her strength. A thin line of a crack appeared, but the glass didn't break. The second time she hit it, the stone made a spiderweb in glass that would not yield. Instead, the stone broke in two. Charlotte let out a frustrated yell, kneeling to search for another stone.

"Do the side window! I'll fit!" Kai said. He was watching the truck's approach and knew she didn't have time to keep trying.

None of the stones remaining under the car were as big as the first, but she found a slightly smaller one she smashed into the driver's side window while she clung to it with her bare hand—and the glass shattered, falling away. But not enough. She and Kai were still batting at the remaining glass when they heard the guttural engine's purr as the truck pulled up beside them, crushing smaller stones beneath it. She could not leave Kai. She reached for him as he squeezed himself through the jagged exit. A fixed glass shard dug into his shoulder, leaving flecks of blood on his white dress shirt.

Two women laughed from the truck. The laughter chilled Charlotte and tried to make her run, but she held on to Kai while he tried to pull his leg through. She glanced at the driver sitting high in the cab—

—and saw a black woman with honeyed skin and spiky plaits. Beside her sat a white woman with wild auburn hair; a young woman who did not look like the one she'd seen through the screen door. Both women grinned at them with badly yellowed teeth.

"You're not fixin' to run, I hope!" the black woman said. "Don't you hear the dogs?"

Charlotte did hear dogs then: a chorus of barking from the woods. Two dozen or more dogs might be waiting in the brush. Kai tried to run right away, but Charlotte held him back with her arm hooked around his neck. "Dogs," she whispered.

"I don't care," he said, wriggling like a fish against her grip.

"We're not the ones you ought to be afraid of," the black

woman said. She tapped her horn, and Kai went limp at the strangled sound. "*Hey*. Look at me—I said you don't need to be 'fraid of us. Aunt Sally's the one who hexed you."

"Meanest woman who ever lived or died—that's Aunt Sally for you," the white woman said. She was fanning herself with a *Life* magazine. "By the way, I'm Rose. That's Malindy."

"I was named from a poem," the black woman said with pride. "My mama liked it."

Charlotte didn't answer. She couldn't stop blinking to test if the women were real.

"I'm sick to death," the white woman, Rose, said. "Sick of Aunt Sally hexing and swallowing folks up in the ground. Then they're gone and their kin never know where they went. I say people are people. That's what I say. Just look at us—oh, she hates how we're cousins."

"Just leave us alone!" Charlotte said, finding her voice. She was too afraid to move. All the while the women chatted, the truck idled ready to run her and Kai over with the slightest lunge. "Just—please—go back where you came from."

"Where you headed? Into that fog?" Malindy said. Charlotte nodded, hating herself for trusting this stranger with the truth—far worse than a stranger—only because her skin color felt like a promise. "That's the way you'd better go, all right," Malindy said, approving.

"But she'll swallow you up on the road," Rose said. "See?"

Rose pointed toward Charlotte's feet. The asphalt beneath her black pumps had crumbled since she'd seen it last, as if she were forcing a great weight upon it. A gap near her big toe was already two inches across. Startled, Charlotte stepped back. More ruptures webbed the road.

"That just gets worse and worse 'til it swallows you whole," Rose said.

"And the woods, they ain't no better," Malindy said, and she pointed too: at the treeline a large brown dog as big as a wolf stood with its front legs perched on a log, watching them. The sight of the beast was a worse fear at a distance than the truck up close. "She'll set dogs on anybody Negro. Old, young, woman, child. Makes her no nevermind. All this fuss ain't over Johnny," Malindy said, and cackled to herself. "He shot himself cleaning his shotgun, dumb as the day is long. Sally just loves chasin' coloreds, still mad 'cause Johnny was my papa in secret. Everybody knew it but her. I call her Aunt Sally because I don't have another name for her."

"Uncle Johnny was better'n some," Rose told Malindy. "I think she still loved him in a way, or wouldn't she have shot him herself?" They spoke to each other as if they were alone.

The dog at the roadside growled, stepping tentatively closer. Kai tried to lunge away again, but Charlotte held on. A dog that size would maul him to death, and there were others.

The women remembered them again. "Way we see it…" Malindy began.

"…Y'all better hop in back of the truck," Rose finished. "We can drive you back to the edge of the fog. We can't drive through it, but we can get you that far."

"What you doin' way out here anyways?" Malindy said. "No one takes Route Nine unless they want to get lost."

"Real lost," Rose said, and giggled.

"They drove right over Johnny's grave," Malindy said to Rose, and they laughed again. "This one here did everything but lindy hop over his bones."

Their chatter, and the impossible choices, made Charlotte dizzy. A low cracking sound rumbled beneath her, and the two-inch gap in the asphalt widened to half a foot. Kai whimpered, stepping away. The dog barked again, more insistent.

"Let's go with them," Kai whispered.

Charlotte looked at him, surprised. The same thought had been teasing her, but she'd been sure he wouldn't dare. He looked calmer than he'd been since before they passed through the fog. "Do you… feel something? Like at the house?"

His eyes fervent, Kai nodded. "Yes. Let's go."

He was right. She was sure of it. No matter how much she hated the idea, and she wasn't close to understanding why, the truck was their best chance.

Charlotte grabbed Kai's hand, and they ran together. They both climbed into the truck's bed with a leap, and the vintage vehicle sped forward as they were still pulling their legs into the prickly bed of pine cones, painful against her bare legs and palms. The truck was moving faster now than it had on its approach, pitching them against each other until they held on to the rusted sides, where the paint flaked off beneath her sweating palms.

Dogs chased the truck, pouring onto the road from the woods. German shepherds, hounds, and oversized creatures that looked half wolf chased the truck with all their might, barking their loathing as spittle flew between their teeth. Only five or six were close enough for her to see their glowing eyes, but a dozen more trailed farther behind, with yet more appearing from the woods. Some of the dogs stumbled in the widening gaps in the road. Wherever the truck drove, the road gave way beneath it, trying its best to eat them. The women in front laughed while the truck swerved around gaps and cracks, as if they'd never had such a merry time.

Charlotte was staring at the dogs, so she didn't see the fog bank until they were in the heart of it, wreathed in gray-white mist. The truck stopped on whining brakes. The house was only half a mile from the fog, she remembered. Only half a mile, yet so much farther.

"I can't take you past here," Malindy said, calling behind her.

"Keep ahead of those dogs," Rose said. "They're all hers. All mean just like her."

Charlotte didn't need to hear any more. She grabbed Kai's hand again and they both climbed out. She had lost her shoes somewhere in her terror. Her stocking foot slipped on the chrome bumper, but she barely felt her knee and elbow scrape when she fell. The barking was still behind them, enraged and determined.

Still clinging to Kai's hand, Charlotte ran barefoot into the soupy gray.

Within her first three steps, the fog was gone. And so was the barking, or the sound of laughter. When she turned the other way, the fog was gone too. She had known it would be. Some part of her had always known the fog wasn't real in the way her skin and beating heart were real. The fog wasn't as real as her memory of everything that had happened on the road.

A modern gas station and convenience store waited within easy walking distance a hundred yards ahead, with a large sign on a highway pole. She knew they had driven past no such place, but that didn't matter—it was there now.

She looked at a highway sign as they walked toward the gas station, which of course said Highway 46 instead of Route Nine. If she asked someone at the gas station ahead, they would tell her there hadn't been a Route Nine in Gracetown as long as anyone could remember, maybe as far back as the 1960s or 1950s. Maybe long before then. She was certain of it.

She had left her car beyond the fog. She would have to explain that somehow.

"We'll say we got carjacked," Charlotte said. "When we asked a guy for directions."

Kai nodded. "The guy with the beard. We'll say it was him. And… it's true."

Charlotte tried to remember if she'd bought the rental car insurance. She thought about her purse and cell phone she'd left behind, all gone. Then she wondered how long this family had been in the land of the dead. And how long Aunt Sally had stood hidden behind her screen door ready to vent her hatred.

"I'm telling my dad," Kai said. "But just him."

Charlotte was still trying to sort through it all without feeling dizzy again. "Tell him… what? He won't believe you."

"Yeah, he will," Kai said, sure of it. They walked in silence for a moment, then he said, "I'm never going to another funeral."

But he would, she knew. They both would. Their grandparents were gone now, so they would bury their parents next, and all their stories and secrets. Charlotte stared at their feet walking together on the unbroken road: hers bare, still pedicured, his with black shoes still shiny. This road felt no more real than the cracking one they had fled, and the only evidence of their shared ordeal was their breathing, still too hard and fast.

Kai's father must have felt this way when he'd been released from the Reformatory. He'd gathered stories while in that place that even his parents would never fully grasp, a wall of fog between him and the world, hoping the nightmares wouldn't last. But they had. And now his son would have them too. But at least Kai and his father had someone to tell.

Charlotte vowed she would never go to Gracetown again.

WHERE RELICS GO TO DREAM AND DIE

Rachel Autumn Deering

"If you had it all to do over again, how would you want to die?" He started to sigh but he caught his breath and swallowed it. He didn't want to risk stirring the air in such a way that she might go away before him, so he exhaled through his nose—measured breaths—and inhaled just the same. He could smell her burning. If she left him now, he had little faith he could muster the strength to light the candle and summon her back.

"You have a peculiar way of thinking," she said. He could hear the flicker in her voice. She shifted uncomfortably and the light in the room changed and all the shadows leapt away from her, then gathered themselves again and crept in close to watch and listen.

"You're not the first person to say so," he said.

"No. I imagine not."

"The question stands." He gestured for her to proceed. "If you care to answer."

"I try to avoid dealing in hypotheticals," she said. "With all the time I have had to dwell on the bygone details of my death, I would have driven myself insane if I allotted any portion of it to dreaming of some alternate past. That hole is black and infinite."

"You are a very practical witch," he said. He wheezed and coughed and the hollow space behind the wall of bone in his chest whumped and fluttered like a bird dashing itself against a window.

"Do you know many other witches?"

"Only in theory," he said. "I have read a great deal about them." He swiped at the mingling of spittle and blood on his lips.

"Folklore," she said. "No doubt those stories are all very true."

"I think I might like to die in battle. In an ancient time. Defending some noble Lord or the woman I loved," he said, with a degree of mirth that seemed more a distraction from the reality of his physical state than genuine amusement. "Alas, I expect I will cough myself to death instead. Watching the kingdom fall while a bedridden slave to some common disease commands no great respect. At least I cannot seem to find any valor in it."

"Count it a blessing your death has come quick," she said. "Relative to some alternatives." She swept a delicate arm down the length of her body. The manifestation of her spirit, trapped within the candle, was pure light and heat, swaying on the tip of a blackened wick that slithered its way into the rust-hued heart of a crude assemblage of tallow, impossibly old and now almost completely burned away. The static columnar mass of her own blood and fat was all that remained of her body. By an act of spite, she had been unmade and recast as this maledict vessel to confine her energies, mocked by the suspension of true death.

"Does it hurt? Your condition? I realize I never considered it. Seems cruel of me," he said.

"It does. Very much."

He turned his head from her to hide his shame. He gazed out through the window, his eyes fixed on the pallid form of the late-September moon hanging eerie and unwavering in the inky wash of evening sky. "It'll be over soon." He squeezed his eyes closed and coughed again, the wet fluttering inside him protracted as he drew cold air into his lungs.

A hush fell over them and neither said a word for some time, but in that interval of silence both hissed in their way and wondered at what might lie on the other side of the coming night.

"What are you thinking?" she asked.

He turned to look at her again. "It's freezing in here."

"Is it?"

"Mmm." He cleared his throat. "What's it like when the candle isn't lit?"

"Lonely," she said.

"Yes. For me, too." He reached for the bedside table and rummaged in the clutter there until he found his briarwood pipe. He took it up and held it out in her direction, as if to beg a favor.

"Haven't you had quite enough of that?"

"How can I know what is enough unless I know what is more than enough?" He arched his brows.

"How unabashedly hedonistic," she said.

"It ought to be. It's Blake."

She cast an ember into the chamber of his pipe and he managed a genuine smile. A gale blew outside and the house groaned and so did he. He brought the pipe to his quivering lips and, with some degree of effort, he puffed at it thoughtfully. The glow in the bowl grew brighter and lit his tired features from beneath and in that moment he looked somehow younger and more vital. His jaw hitched and clicked in a playful performance and a set of smoke rings appeared and danced in the air for a moment before losing their shape and dissipating. Warm layers of black Cavendish and cherry scented the room and he puffed again.

A calm fell over him and he eased back into his pillow and closed his eyes, relishing the burning sweetness that swirled in his damaged lungs. "You've been affable company these years."

"Is that a compliment?"

A trail of smoke trickled from his parched lips. "I don't know, but it's the truth."

"Thank you," she said. "So have you."

He moved to the edge of the bed and redeposited the pipe amongst the clutter on the table. He watched the glow of her flickering presence painting gentle forms upon his hand. Ethereal wisps, barely there and soon to fade forever. A familiar sorrow stirred in the deepest parts of him and he longed to feel her touch.

"I love you," he said. And he had, since the day he found her and marveled at the peculiarity of a candle so finely crafted and unique in color, unlit and hidden away in the hollow of a tree. When he had called her out of darkness, alight there in the middle of his dinner table, he was helpless to guard against the enchantment of one who so clearly outshone all other light in his life. Blinded by the beauty he found in the fire, he never took a wife, never sought to make a family or a home for himself. This, she knew, was part of her curse.

"I know," she said. But that was all she said.

She looked to him, withering beneath his sheets, tears crowding the corners of his eyes and streaking down his colorless face, set with deep lines from the weariness of existence. He was a specter of the man she had met all those years ago. Yes, it hurt her when the candle was lit, to watch him devoured by the howling maw of this vulgar imprecation. To know that, even if she returned his sentiments, if she told him she loved him deeply, it would only augment his pain.

"Keep your eyes closed," she said.

"What for?" He knitted his brows and coughed, deep and harsh.

"Please. Dream with me. Dream of some alternate past."

"What, sleep? And leave you burning?" he said.

"Yes." She closed her eyes and the flames of her figure sank low on the wick. All light but the faintest glow drained from the room and the air filled with a smoke redolent of ancient forests and fresh-turned graves.

"Listen, I'm sick, not stupid—"

The smoke invaded his nostrils and he breathed it until all light of the conscious world had given way to a soothing sort of blackness.

II

He woke in a room that was not his own. The candle was not there, nor his briarwood pipe, nor even the bedside table. He surveyed the details of the space despite his disorientation and through a window near the bed he could see leaves upon the trees, new and green. September appeared to have flown and the air was thick with the humidity of summer and the myriad voicings of such things that stir by dusk and are compelled to hunt in darkness.

And then a most dreadful scream.

He sprang from the bed with all the haste he could muster and pitched himself toward the window. Spurred by an unearthly compulsion to spy the source of the wailing, he scarcely bothered to question his renewed strength. The small stone cottage was situated at the terminus of a rutted dirt road in a secluded hollow, among a copse of trees dressed in the shadows of night. And like the trees, his own clothes were dark and drab and unfamiliar—the full-collared cassock of a holy man of some indeterminate denomination, though again he let these details pass without consideration. He peered through the glass, deeper into the sylvan gloom, his hands cupped around his eyes.

Some distance into the forest an unnatural light shone

out between the trunks and branches of the trees. It was a pale and sickly blue, as if some star had fallen from the sky and come to rest on a hillock there. On seeing this emanation, a chill cut through the summer swelter and settled into his bones, and he found himself shivering.

He took up arms in the form of a three-pronged fork fastened to the end of a long, wooden handle that rested on a wall near the door, and stepped into the night. Strange, taunting voices drifted to him from the wood, cut through by sobs and a pitiful sort of murmured pleading. It was by these envenomed, almost musical intonements that he traced his path through the barbed underbrush, a guide on those occasions when he lost sight of the strange blue glow. Though the forest itself seemed to claw at him— endeavored to drag him back to the cottage—he pressed into the unknown. At last, he came to a glen and saw there before him a grotesque display, the rival of which he could not have conjured even in his most hideous dreams.

There was the woman he loved, no longer modeled in flame but in flesh and blood, the muscles in her face drawn down and twisted into an expression of exquisite torment. She was quite naked and suspended in the air by some unseen support. Before her were three strange women— also naked—with bones and twigs and mosses and other things natural and unnatural tied up in their hair.

They stood bent over a great black cooking pot, stoked by that ghostly blue fire, and they passed between them a crude sort of knife, drawing the blade across the flesh of their palms. Each cast into the pot no small portion of their own blood and then they set upon their prey. The knife-bearer pressed the tip of the cruel blade into her inner thigh and with a pop of her skin, dragged it down the length of her leg, opening a crooked wound that wept dark tears. Her sisters shrieked their delight and, with their filthy nails, worked the skin loose on either side of the cut. Then with a sort of efficiency only afforded to hands practiced in such dark things, they stripped her quaking limb down to the muscle and cast the bloodied tissue into the cauldron. Her mouth gaped in a wretched display, as if to call out for help, but she made no sound.

He could feel in his heart great bursts of shock and revulsion and rage. And though he quailed at the grisly display before him and felt almost sure his trembling legs might falter, a resolve that came from somewhere beyond his own faculties, and which he could not shake, stirred him to action. He steadied himself on the long-handled fork and dashed headlong and haphazard into the glen.

The contemptable odor emanating from the pot crowded his senses and caused his vision to betray him and his mind to shift into abstract planes. A cold sweat beaded his forehead and his weapon fell free of his grip, and by degrees he felt a frantic lunacy pervading every part of his being, working to unravel the very seams of decency. He saw his love suspended above the yawning mouth of hell with the heat of its breath rising up around her, reeking of sulfur and sin. And some manner of devil was there with her and she, in profane ecstasy, abased herself with it in ways no sane mind would dare to imagine. She birthed then a set of twin babies, joined at their chest, which fell from her and were cast into the snapping jaws of those demons gathered below.

On a sudden his sight was restored, and when at last all visions of diablerie had cleared and his temporary mania abated, he saw that the sisters were upon him. With a hateful lust in their eyes, they snatched at his garments and tore them free and clawed at those parts of him which had been rendered bare by their efforts. His body began to shake from head to toe when he realized what black business they must be about. Though his body shook, he kicked out toward the cauldron and landed a blow squarely upon the black iron thing, toppling it and spilling its unholy contents. At this, so too did his beloved topple from where she hung and fell to the earth, heaped upon herself in a shivering mass.

When they looked upon what he had done, they forsook

their ardor and fell about in a mad sort of shrill cacophony, their black tongues lolling from their mouths and slithering over shards of rotting teeth. He worked free of their dominance and took up his fork, then he reeled away from them, points raised and leveled at their bellies. One among the sisters flicked her wrist and a glint of steel flashed in the air for no more than the blink of an eye. The knife bit into his chest. He gritted his teeth and growled—a bestial, involuntary sound—as if to warn the hags away, though the tremors that worked through the long, wooden handle of his weapon cast him as no great threat.

A sinister fog crept in from the forest on all sides of the glen and carpeted the ground. It clung to the naked forms of the sisters and seemed to soothe their frenzied spirits in some dark way, for they ceased their wailing. Tendrils of mist climbed their bodies like a hellish ivy and soon they were fully cloaked, save for twin sets of pale-green eyes that stared baleful out at him, arresting his gaze. Heavy lids fell slowly over the sickly orbs and when finally they blinked out, the fog began to retreat. When all villainous magic had departed, the moon shone out from behind a wisp of cloud and bathed the glen in its pale brilliance. Sensing they were finally alone, he laid down his arms and collapsed.

III

He woke again in the room that was not his own. The open wound in his chest was a ragged thing that wet itself anew with every rise and fall of his breast—a grim and scarlet tide. He imagined he would not wake again in this room. Nor, indeed, in any other room besides.

"Thank you," he said.

"For what?" She sat at a table not far from his bed, floating her fingertips over the flame of a lit candle. She relished the heat of it and that it was a thing apart from her.

"For allowing me to die in my own way. For showing me this dream."

"You were brave to dream it with me," she said. "Such terrors are not easily faced." She moved to the bed and sat next to him. Her leg was bound tight with bandages but still the red showed through.

"Who were they? Those terrible women," he asked. The pain in his wound flared.

"They are the brides of ancient gods and they are my mentors."

He shivered. "If they are your mentors, why were they at you so?"

"We have a pact. In my youth I called upon the Forgotten

Names and commanded them to grant me magic that I might secure my future. They sent their brides to slake my thirst for esoteric wisdom and in return I bore them a child. That was my sacrifice."

Those ghastly visions returned again to his mind and he felt his heart seizing.

"In their greed they cursed me with a beauty no man could hope to deny and they filled me with an unending hunger for sins of the flesh. I was possessed with such lust that I found myself almost perpetually with child. And to my absolute horror they came unto me without fail to harvest the fruit of my deeds. Until the day I mocked those primordial horrors and I denied the child a living birth."

"No... You cannot mean these blasphemous things. The love I feel for you is not the consequence of some curse." A torrent of thick blood erupted from his chest.

She moved to him and took his hand. "I know. That is why I brought you here. Through the gate of dreams we have unmade the past and defied the ancients yet again. They have witnessed my power and yielded to my will."

He stared with wide, unblinking eyes—at her, through her, past her—into some hellish vista, never meant for the human mind to behold.

"You will soon see what lies beyond for yourself. And I will not be far behind. While you slept I took from you all that I need to make a child of our own. My best and my last." She kissed him and brushed a hand across his blanched cheek. "Thank you again and again."

In the room where it was September still, the winds beyond the walls moaned like a choir of ghosts and a driving rain lashed the windowpanes. On a bedside table, amongst a clutter of memories, the sweet-smelling ashes in a briarwood pipe grew ever colder and a spent candle cast a thin ribbon of smoke into the air. It danced there for a moment in that dark and lonely space and then it was gone.

THIS SKIN

Amber Benson

I sat down on the chair. I was nervous—my hands were shaking, but I kept them in my lap, my fingers interlaced to hold them steady. I'd thought about sitting on them. Almost did. Finally decided that clasped hands were better than fingers hidden underneath soft, squishy thigh.

The police officer who brought me into the room had been nice. Got me a Coke from the vending machine and smiled so I could see her eyeteeth. I doubt she realized smiling isn't a nice thing. Not really. When you smile what you're *actually* saying is: there's no need to go on the offensive, I submit to you, don't kill me.

This is why I abstain from smiling. Why I break the social contract everyone else subscribes to. It's a subtle thing—something a person can't put their finger on. It unnerves them.

I practice not smiling in my bathroom mirror. I drain the emotion from my face and work on my dead-eye stare. No smile, dead-eye stare, calm energy. One, two, three... *punch*.

The door to the classroom opened and the police officer who bought me the Coke adjusted her posture so fast I heard her back crack. The man in the doorway was important. She didn't want him to see her slouching.

He looked at me. I could feel his eyes assessing me, probing my features for information. I kept everything calm... my energy, my expression. I didn't smile, but I didn't adopt my dead-eye stare, either.

A happy medium.

He blinked, giving nothing away. Then he reached for a lab chair, sliding it out from underneath the table behind him. He sat down across from me, the width of one table between us. His chair was shorter than mine. It gave me an advantage—but I wasn't sure if he realized it, yet.

He was younger than I would have expected... for someone so important people hurt their backs trying to impress him. Or maybe I'd misread the situation. Maybe the police officer who got me the Coke was attracted to him—that would make sense. He had a nice face and a lean body. Was tall, too.

Maybe she wanted to fuck him the way my older sister fucked our neighbor.

They didn't think anyone knew. Not my mom or his wife. But *I'd* seen them sneaking into his basement when his wife was at work on the weekends. I'd watched through the basement window, flat on my belly, face pressed against the glass—until my mom had come home from the grocery store and I'd gone inside to help her put things away.

I'd seen pornography on the internet. What my sister and the neighbor did was tame compared with what I'd watched on my computer.

The man was still watching me. He'd introduced himself. He was a detective from the homicide department. His name was Harry Longfellow. With a name like his, I knew he got picked on a lot as a kid.

I didn't have to introduce myself. He already knew who I was. What he *didn't* know was I was prepared to tell him everything. As soon as it had happened, I'd known I wanted to tell someone. What was the point of doing it if no one knew it was you?

I'd thought about telling the police officer after she handed me the Coke. I was giddy with the need to confess, but something had stopped me. Instinct told me she wasn't the one. Now I was waiting to see if this new detective would surprise or disappoint. I wanted him to prove himself to me—see if he was worthy of the story I had to tell.

He asked me if I needed anything. I shook my head. Held up the can of soda, heard it fizzing inside. He told me they hadn't been able to reach my mom yet, but he had some questions for me.

I waited. He looked over at the police officer and a moment later she was gone, the door clicking softly into place behind her.

Do you believe in witchcraft?

He stared at me for a long time, thinking about the question. He wasn't scared of silence. He knew it was a tool that could be used to pry information out of unwitting victims.

I was not an unwitting victim.

Finally, he replied to my question: *No.*

Good. He'd passed the first test. He asked me why I wanted to know. I told him I didn't believe in it. And if he had said he did, I wouldn't have been able to take him very seriously.

He laughed. It was involuntary. I saw him reassess me, saw his first impression subtly shift its shape.

I've read a lot about the occult. It intrigued me.

He asked me why I had used the past tense. I told him it *had* intrigued me, but not anymore. I'd done my research and realized there was no empirical evidence in favor of the supernatural. He nodded, letting me know he understood.

He asked me for my impression of what had happened.

I think there was a lot of blood.

He agreed with me. He'd been in the gym. There *was* a lot of blood.

Any idea who might have done something like this?

His second mistake of the game. First, his choice of chair, and now he'd stumbled over the rules of our query protocol: no direct questioning. He stood up, remedying the first problem, but the second required that he skip a turn.

What happens to the bodies now?

My tone was curious, but even. No uptick of the register at the end of the sentence.

He told me the coroner was already there. She and her technicians would take the bodies back with them.

In an ambulance without its lights on or in a hearse?

Neither. The coroner had a van. That's how they would transport the bodies.

All five of them?

He nodded.

I was done asking questions, but he didn't notice because his cell phone began to buzz in his jacket pocket. He held up a finger, asking for me to give him a moment. He answered the phone with his name and rank. He didn't speak after that—just listened. From the intensity of his expression, I could see the call was important.

I wondered if the person was telling him things about me. Bad things.

Finally, he hung up the phone.

I'm going to have Cathy take you home and wait with you until your mother gets there.

Cathy was the police officer's name.

He walked to the door and opened it, conferred with Cathy out in the hall—and that's when I began to suspect he was manipulating me. He'd realized what he was dealing with and he'd decided to let me think I was off the hook. He was showing me his throat, letting me think I had won—and then he would pounce.

My heart began to thump loudly. I laced my hands together even tighter, the too-long sleeves of my hoodie bunching up around my wrists. I hadn't expected to meet my match. There was no way I could've known someone like *him* would get the case. This was an incredible stroke of luck.

I wanted to blurt it all out immediately. Tell him everything in excruciating detail right there in the Chemistry classroom… but I understood he was asking me to keep the game going a little longer. I would let him lay his trap—and things would play out to their natural conclusion.

If prolonging the end brought him joy then it brought me joy, too. I would go home and wait. When I couldn't take the anticipation any longer, I'd ask my mom to take me to the police station where I would spill my guts.

Check mate, Detective Longfellow.

My mom was at the house when Cathy dropped me off. She ran out the door and, despite the blood, wrapped her arms around me, squeezing tight. There were tears in her eyes. She told me she loved me and held onto my shoulders until I told her she was hurting me.

I took a shower and watched the blood swirl down the drain. I left both doors open—one leading into my room, the other into my sister's bedroom—so the mirrors wouldn't steam up. I could see my reflection. I liked how my naked body looked, unformed and lobster-pink from the scalding water.

Wrapped up in a plush green towel, another towel wrapped around my wet hair, I stepped into my sister's room. It was an alien landscape now that she wouldn't be coming back to inhabit it anymore.

I walked over to the white wicker dresser and I looked at the photos taped to the mirror above it. My sister and her friends, laughing and joking around. All smiles and wide eyes.

I saw my mother had already been here. The bed was freshly made, the dirty clothes picked up and thrown into the hamper in the bathroom. Everything straightened up, so no one would know my sister had been a slob. I wanted to yank off the comforter and mess up the sheets. Go into her closet and rip her clothes off the hangers—throw them on the floor.

I went back into the bathroom and finished drying off. I dropped the towels into the hamper, my sister's dirty clothing hidden underneath the thick green cotton fabric. Like grass over a grave.

I put on a button-down shirt and some jeans, let my wet hair air dry. I sat cross-legged on my bed—but through the Jack and Jill bathroom, I could see my sister's room. I watched my mom come in and sit down on my sister's bed.

She didn't see me as I watched her cry. After a while, I slid off the bed and onto the floor. I reached under the bed and felt around until I found my journal.

I lay on my back in the soft carpet, the journal held above my head. I liked rereading all the things I'd written. I set it down on the floor and rolled over, sticking my head under the bed.

I found the book wedged between the mattress and the slats of the bedframe. I brought it into the light, ran my hand over its raised cover. It smelled like leather and sweat. I set it down on top of the journal. These were the things I would take with me to the police station.

My proof.

Part of me had hoped it would work; the other part knew it was an exercise in futility. But I had to try. I did everything the spell said: the prep, the ritual, the sacrifice. Nothing happened—even after all that blood.

My mom came into the room. Her eyes were red and puffy. She asked me if I was okay, but my affirmative answer barely registered. I offered to make us dinner and she nodded.

I went downstairs to the kitchen. I made macaroni and cheese from the box. No additions. I put the bowls on the table.

My mom picked at her pasta. We didn't talk. I was hungry and ate all my food. When she excused herself to go to bed, I finished her bowl, too.

I tried to watch TV. To clear my mind, so I could hold out longer. But after an hour of staring at the screen and seeing nothing, I went back upstairs. I packed my journal and the book into a backpack. I went to my mom's room to wake her up. She would have to drive me to the police station.

But she'd taken pills to sleep. I couldn't wake her up.

I sat on the top of the stairs and tried to wait it out. Twenty minutes went by like a decade.

It took me an hour to walk to the police station. I stayed on well-lit streets and didn't take any short cuts. I replayed the day's events over and over in my head. I was sweaty when I reached my destination. I was so happy to arrive, I almost smiled.

Almost.

The sergeant at the front desk was unhelpful at first. He wanted to call my mom. But when I told him who I was, the name registered. He picked up the phone and asked for Detective Longfellow.

The sergeant kept a watchful eye on me as I moved to the waiting area. The couch I chose was so overstuffed that when I sat back, my feet didn't touch the ground. I was there a long time—but I didn't mind. I just held my backpack in my lap and waited. I figured someone was trying to reach my mom. Another exercise in futility. I'd learned from experience she wouldn't wake up until the next morning.

It was way past my bedtime, but I wasn't tired. I was nervous and excited, anxious to talk.

We can't seem to get a hold of your mother.

I must've closed my eyes for a minute because he was standing above me. I told him she'd taken some pills to sleep. Then I asked if I could speak to him in private. I could tell he was trying to suppress his annoyance—had I given in too easily?—but he nodded. He led me through the bullpen and toward a darkened conference room.

Can we go into one of the interrogation rooms instead?

He gave me a funny look.

Please?

We went to an interrogation room and he opened the door. We sat opposite each other across the width of a table—and it felt symbolic. Like we'd never left that Chemistry classroom at the high school.

What can I do for you?

He wanted to make me work. I appreciated that.

So I took a deep breath and told him *everything*.

I showed him my journal and the book. I explained how I stole the prescription pills from my mom's medicine cabinet. Took them to the high school gym where my sister and her friends were practicing their dance routine for the Fall talent show. I told him how simple it was to convince them the pills were Ecstasy I'd gotten from an older kid at school. That my sister thought we were close and so she suspected nothing.

Then I told him how I dragged the girls' unconscious bodies into a pentagram formation on the gym floor. How I stole a straight razor from my neighbor's house and used it to slit their throats—one at a time—while they slept.

I told him how I walked out of the gym—but the invisibility spell didn't work. The gym teacher, Mr. Stevens, saw me walking down the hall. I told him my sister and her friends were dead and he started running.

I thought I told the story well—even though I was shaking with excitement. But Detective Longfellow just scratched his head.

Frances, you didn't kill your older sister and her friends. Sometimes when something traumatic happens to us, we go into what's called 'shock'. You saw Mr. Stevens—your next-door neighbor—come into the gym and do a very bad thing. You feel out of control and your imagination takes over, creates a narrative that gives you some power over the situation.

I stared at him. My mouth hung open. Was this a new twist in the game?

We have Mr. Stevens' DNA on the murder weapon and his fingerprints. Only his fingerprints. We know he's been abusing your sister—that he was in fear of her telling her friends about their...

I stopped listening. This was not a part of the game... because there was no game. The idiot thought someone else had committed *my* crime.

I wanted to scream. I wanted to punch him in the face. I wanted to cry.

...now I'm going to have someone take you home. But we're going to make sure you get the attention you need. I remember what it was like to be ten...

He babbled on about me seeing a trauma therapist,

someone who specialized in children. That with a lot of therapy, I would be okay.

But I wasn't paying attention. My perspective had already begun to shift, my anger slowly boiling away.

In the morning, I would wake up and finally accept what I had always known about myself. I didn't need witchcraft to make myself invisible; I was already equipped with the perfect disguise. In this skin, I could get away with anything.

HAINT ME TOO

Chesya Burke

Haints are sad sometimes. Sometimes lost or can't find their way to wherever it is that they go when they ain't supposed to be here. This one was angry, the girl knew. Black. The house cut-up like it meant to chew on those white folks and swallow them whole. The lights in the upstairs rooms flashed on and off, off and on again. The front door swung open and closed, back and forth. Somewhere in the depths of the house, something banged on the walls, the windows, the floors, like it craved attention, needing to be recognized though unseen. No one dared go inside, but the family was too proud to leave Myrtle House, so they sat on the front porch. All seven. Father, mother, three boys and two girls. The perfect Southern American Dream to the little Negro girl, Shea, watching from her three-room shack that sat on the land which her father tilled every day but which belonged to the family who now sat resolved on their elaborate *veranda*.

"Maybe we can get some peace t'night." Shea's father watched the house for a moment and then looked over to his wife. "As long as she's here, they ain't." The large man, extra blackened by hours in the sun working the white man's land, walked back into the house that was not his own, letting the screen door slam on its hinges.

"I hope she tear the thing down." Her mother grabbed Shea's hand, squeezed.

Shea looked back at the rattling house. "Who's she, momma?"

"The haint that's making all that fuss. She ain't happy."

"She dead?" Shea knew that a haint was a ghost, a dead person who didn't know they wasn't alive, or didn't care much for the idea of being dead.

Her mother nodded, "She dead, alright. And not too happy about it, I 'spect."

"How she die?"

Her mother dropped her hand and turned to look at her, "Like this!" The woman made a silly face with her eyes closed and tongue hanging out her mouth like a panting dog. She looked like the idea of every dead person Shea had imagined. That was the joke between them. Everyone died; always the same way. Dead was dead. Didn't much matter how you got that way. So anytime word came that a family member had passed away, Shea would ask how and her mother or father would make the dead-face. Shea didn't know why, but it always made her feel better, as if things weren't so bad as long as her parents were there laughing at death. This time was no different. Shea giggled and followed her mother into the house.

Her father had been right, things were peaceful that night. Shea and her family slept undisturbed.

Shea always tried to sneak out to the pond when she was supposed to be doing work. She didn't like work and she didn't want to be in the house with those mean kids. They were always doing things to hurt her. She wanted to tell her parents, but she knew that it would just make them upset. They couldn't do anything about it. That was just how it was.

Shea had been so lost in her own thoughts she had not seen the old woman sneak up behind her. The girl jumped when she realized she was not alone. As the woman's dark skin came into view, she breathed a sigh of relief—at least it wasn't Mrs. or one of her brats. Most people would not be this happy to see this old woman, they were afraid of her. Shea knew she was supposed to fear her, too, but really she just wanted to know how she had lived so long. No one bothered her, or made her work until her back was broken. If that meant people needed to be afraid of Shea one day, she was willing to do whatever it took. She wouldn't dare tell momma or daddy that, though.

The old woman stood, staring at the girl.

"Hello."

"Hello, Shea." Now, she had never told this woman her name. She had never even really spoken to her outside of the polite hello that happened in passing. Her mother had told her to respect the woman, which was, as far as the girl could see, what everyone seemed to do.

"How do you know my name?"

The woman shrugged, walked closer. "You hear things." She had never been this close to the woman before. She noticed that, for an old woman, she did not look that old, didn't have many wrinkles. Her eyes were bright and searching and she didn't act like an old woman at all. Plus, she never went to church and sometimes the preacher would devote whole sermons to her—sin. They said she was magic.

Shea didn't know what to say, but she had so many questions. The woman smiled. She had never seen this in the woman either. "Why are they scared of you?"

She waved her hand, dismissively. "People fear a lot of things."

Well, that didn't really answer anything, did it? But the woman did not wait for her to ask another silly question.

"There's something in the air. Do you feel it? It's electric." Shea looked around as the woman rubbed her arms up and down as if she had caught a chill. "Tell me, girl, do you want to be free?"

"We are free."

"Are you?"

Shea thought about it for a moment. They were, right? Maybe not as free as the white people they worked for, but they were not slaves either.

Then the woman asked, "Are you afraid?"

She was. So often, she was.

The woman looked off toward the big white house, nodded toward it. "Have you seen her?"

"Her?"

"You know. Her!"

She knew who the woman meant. Shea shook her head. She had not seen her, she had only seen the things that she could do when she got really, really mad.

"Is she free, you think?"

The girl had never really thought about it. Now that she could, she wasn't sure that she wanted to put any thought into being trapped in the afterlife the preacher talked about so often, beholden to these people while dead in the same way that she was in life.

"No. She's not free. I'm not either."

"So, what should you do about it? What do you want?"

"I want to be you."

The woman laughed, hard, loud. Negro people didn't laugh like this, free or not. "I'm a witch, girl. Is that what you want?"

If it would make people afraid enough to leave her alone, "Yes," she did want this.

"Then pray." She nodded toward the house again. "To her." Blasphemy! "You only pray to God."

The woman shook her head. Her silver hair looked so wrong on her young face. Everything about this woman was wrong. She knew this now. The woman got on her knees, met Shea's eyes. "You pray to woman. To mother. To the blackest of all things. Those things are god, girl."

"Those pots from upstairs need chucking out back, Our Nig." While Shea's father was the field grunt (he called himself that, though Shea wasn't completely sure what it meant) and her mother was the grunt that did the mending and laundry, Shea was the house grunt. She did whatever the Petersons told her to do: the dishes, the windows, even emptying their piss pots, because lord forbid they be expected to trudge out to the outhouse like Shea and her family at night. Somehow, they often reminded her, this wasn't slavery—that had ended over forty years before. No, this was sharecropping.

"I did those already." Shea scrubbed the stairs with the brush, making sure to reach the corners. They would check.

"Momma said you have to do those windows today, too." Sara's leg hung off the edge of the couch, bouncing up and down. It looked comfortable. Sara and her brothers and sisters loved summer break. Shea hated it and she didn't even go to school.

Shea stood up, looked at the girl. "The windows?"

"Yes." The white girl looked really pretty when she smiled.

Shea sighed. She hated hated hated doing the windows. There were just too many of them and they were too tall. It wasn't safe. "I did those the day before yesterday."

The Mrs.' voice rang throughout the parlor, just as she appeared behind Shea. "Well, do them again. And, Our Nig, make sure they're perfect. I never get enough afternoon light." Somehow the family never remembered her name. Her parents had given her a name but it must have been too hard to remember.

"Okay... Yes ma'am." Shea quickly remembered her

manners and set about doing the stairs, one hard wooden step at a time. Mrs. relished the way the house looked when it was clean, and prided herself on it, but no one ever came to see it. They never had visitors and sometimes, as big as it was, Shea thought the woman must be the loneliest person in the world. Sara and her sisters and brothers went to school when it wasn't summer and Mr. was always gone somewhere on "business." But Mrs. was there fretting about windows that no one ever looked through. Shea almost pitied her.

"Almost" being the word she'd say if she could summon enough care in the world about the woman, or anyone that lived on that farm except her mother and father. No, something akin to "never" would be closer to the day when Shea would feel anything for anyone in that house.

She finished the stairs, having now scrubbed each and every inch of each and every one, by her estimation, close to a hundred times in her short eleven years, and went into the basement to get the short ladder.

She started on the top floor, in the bedrooms, finishing with the large balcony window above the stairs. Shea was scared of being high up, she never felt safe with her feet off the ground. This window was above the opening to the staircase and if she lost her balance, she wouldn't survive the twenty-three-stair fall to the bottom—since her mother had taught her to count to one hundred, she counted those steps every single time her knees touched them.

When Shea was on the ladder, the bucket of water balanced on the top, she didn't look down. She focused on the job, one pane at a time. Just as she'd finished up the first row, she heard whispering behind her. She could not make out what was being said, but it sounded close. She listened harder, trying to hear the words. It felt like it was all around her, nearby, but so far from her somehow. She risked looking about, seeing a shadow just beyond one of the rooms. She returned quickly to her job, wanting to be done as soon as possible. Just as she reached the last row of windowpanes, the ladder shook beneath her and she lost her balance, tumbling backward.

As she fell, seemingly in slow motion, Shea saw Sara and her youngest brother, John, watching her. Shea banged her shoulder on the railing, and landed at the top of the stairs, hanging on so that she wouldn't fall any farther. She looked to the kids, knowing instantly what they had done. Sara stood behind John, smiling again. She was always smiling, appearing innocent, blond and dangerous.

Suddenly Mrs. appeared over her and Shea had never been so happy to see the woman in her life. She stared at her kids; she knew, too. "Go to your rooms. Now."

She bent down to help Shea to her feet. Her shoulder hurt so much that it was hard to move. Mrs. stared at the bucket of water which only held air now, its contents spilled everywhere. "Just take the ladder back, Our Nig." Her voice was soft and sympathetic.

Shea rushed to get the ladder, cringing at the ache in her shoulder when she lifted it. On her way down the stairs, Mrs. called out to her children: "Sara, John, clean this mess up."

Shea descended into the darkness of the basement, hurting in places she didn't know she had. It had been nice, she supposed, for Mrs. to make the two clean up the messes they had made. As the door closed behind her, the darkness inside was thick, darker than she remembered. She reached the dirt floor at the bottom and rubbed her foot out in front of her so she wouldn't tumble. If that happened again, she swore to herself she wouldn't get up. She'd just lie there until she died painlessly.

To the right, she heard whispering again. She figured the kids had followed her down to get back at her because they were forced to clean up their own mess. Shea moved away from them as best she could, keeping her arms outstretched so that she didn't bump into anything. It had never been so dark down here. Finally, she reached the wall and followed it, feeling the cool stone as she moved. A stale breath flooded her face.

"Sara?" she whispered, but the girl didn't say anything, mocking her. A gust of musty air blew over her face, the smell rotten and foul. "Stop it, John. Sara. I still have a lot of work to do." She was slightly afraid of the dark but didn't want them to know it. They would use it against her.

From above, she heard the pair chasing each other, John screaming out his sister's name. She raised her eyes to stare at the ceiling, but only a dim light shone through the beams. The floor shook with the vibrations of their movement, and dust fluttered down toward her. Shea stopped, frozen. The breath continued; soft, steady, stale.

She scrambled toward the deeper dark at the back of the basement and set the ladder in its place. They would chastise her if it wasn't in its proper spot. As she turned to leave, the wall shuddered. It rippled, dark and thick, as if a small, muddy pond were stuck in the middle of the plastered wall. Shea remembered the bright lights and the banging from the night before. Was it the haint? It shimmered, the surface of the wall deeper and darker than it should have been. Shea watched, walked closer. She was afraid, but curious. Perhaps the fall had clouded her senses, but she was less scared of whatever was happening than she had been while falling off the ladder.

Leaning closer, Shea saw it. There in the middle of the plastered pond, something wiggled out of the wall. At first, it looked like a small brown worm. She imagined it attached to a pole held by her father, who loved to fish.

As it reached the surface, a second appeared beside it, and then a third and fourth. The four long, thin, caterpillar-like things shot out of the wall, and she realized they were attached to a hand. A second set of four fingers appeared, reaching for Shea. She was unable to move, didn't feel in control of her legs, her arms, her body. A moment later two large, black elbows emerged from within the wall, the body still unseen. Something stirred in the bowels of the house and the wall rumbled.

As she watched, frozen in place, the figure climbed out of the plaster like a spider from its hole. It crouched on the wall, seemingly floating, head tilted, staring at her. It was a Negro woman. She wore a long dress and a green turban. Blood streamed down the side of her face, just under the rag covering her hair. Something was wrong with her ear. Despite the woman trying to hide it under the turban, Shea could see that it was missing. The woman had been there for a long time, the girl knew. Dead. Perhaps buried in a shallow grave behind the thick plastered wall, unloved and certainly unwanted by the current owners.

The woman stood up, her body impossibly horizontal, defying gravity as she walked down the wall. She wobbled on unsteady feet, as if she hadn't used them in a long time. When she reached the dirt floor, she placed one foot, then the other down, her neck cocked to the side, staring at Shea. The dead woman moved toward Shea, limping as if her legs hurt somehow. She reached out, her thick fingers bloody and raw.

Shea watched, her emotions trying to get the best of her, but she pushed them away. Her mother had told her once never to let whites see her cry. White folks did not care about her feelings, they did not want to even know she had them, so Shea had learned to live without emotion, like her mother and her mother's mother. Like white folks expected.

But this was no white woman. She was Negro. She was dead. She was haint.

"Do you see me?" The woman's voice was unsteady like her legs.

Shea nodded, her head jittering weirdly on the seized muscles of her neck, still not in complete control of her body, not trusting herself to move.

"They lie. They always lie."

In that moment, Mrs. walked right through her as if she didn't see the dead woman at all. "What are you doing? I've been calling you."

"I…" Shea didn't know what to say. "I think I hit my head when I fell… I think I… just woke up here, on the floor."

That night the men came for her father. They rode up on horses that were taller than Shea, and probably better fed, too. The man in front paused and looked toward the Myrtle House. Shea did not know if the man was scouting the house, looking for Mr., or delaying for fear of the haint. When it appeared to him that neither of the two seemed to be there, he slid off his horse and walked up to her father.

"Charles. I understand that you haven't signed your contract to stay on here for another few years."

"That's business I will take up with Mr. Peterson."

The man looked back to his posse and grinned, so they laughed. "Business. You know a few years ago you wouldn't have even known the word."

"I suppose, then, it's good we live in the times we do… sir." Her father spit the title as if it had soured in his mouth. He wasn't backing down and that made Shea proud.

The man didn't like her father's haughtiness. "When your bossman gets home, we'll get this settled. You're lucky you belong to him."

"I belong to no one."

The man mounted his horse, glanced again at the quiet house, and rode away.

The haint did not stir.

Mrs. hitched up the team, or rather had Shea's father do it, and took her children into town. Said she was tired of being in that house, alone with no one to talk to. Shea accompanied them, mainly because Mrs. liked to show off all the things that Shea and most of the people in town could never have. Each of her five children sat upright in their best clothing, while Shea lounged in the back of the carriage. Shea's best clothes were pretty much the same as her worst clothes, so none of it made no nevermind to her. She'd once had better clothes—her mother had made them for her—but she only wore them on Sundays or special special occasions, and she had outgrown them now. And even then, those occasions didn't include watching white kids buy themselves things like it was Christmas.

Pulling into St. Francisville was always a spectacle. Shea didn't like it because it stank and there was horse waste on the ground. The people in the streets stared at them like they were themselves the ghosts of Myrtle House. Mrs. parked the buggy and helped the youngest of the children off. Shea climbed down on her own, distinctly aware of the eyes that were watching them. The others noticed but relished it. They welcomed any outside attention, instead of rightly fearing it, as it was by Negros. On the street, people stepped aside, giving the group a wide berth. The Petersons may have been too proud to leave Myrtle House, but the haint had managed to make them outcasts in the community. Even their money was not enough to override the stigma of a haint, and that somehow comforted Shea.

The oldest son, Robert, waved at a school girl his age on the street, and she raised her hand to reply before her father stopped her, covering her hand with his own. To his credit, Robert didn't seem to care. The group entered the dry goods store where Mrs. ordered some rice, beans, and lengths of fabric for new dresses that Shea's mother would make for the girls. As each of the kids picked out candy, a man in a dark suit approached them, looking all too similar to Mr. Peterson. Shea stopped; he was the man from the night before.

Mrs. faced him. "Mr. Davis. You're looking well."

The man smirked. "I think it's admirable that you can still show your face in town, after everything."

"Since my husband's property helps keep this town afloat, I should hope so." Her children stood quietly beside her.

"Your husband can't run that plantation and he can't control that nigger of his who's riling up the workers. Do you know how many of 'em are talking of going North? He's even trying to unite the white and black sharecroppers."

"Mr. Davis, I don't think…"

"We have to keep them here. The crops will die if they leave. Tell your husband to sell me his land. I'll pay him a good price for it and I can keep the niggers in line."

"Mr. Davis, this is business I suggest you talk through with my husband."

The man walked closer to Mrs. "I hear that ghost of yours has been causing trouble. Do you know how she died? She was snooping around listening to stuff she shouldn't, so they cut off her ear. To get revenge she poisoned the entire family with a birthday cake. That's what *they* will do if you let them get out of control. So they hanged her and threw her in the Mississippi. And that's what *we* do to niggers who get out of place here."

For the first time this seemed to make Mrs. uncomfortable, though she never lost the smile she had passed down to her daughter Sara. "My husband will be back this evening, Mr. Davis. Please bring the matter up with him."

"Good. Tonight it is."

When they arrived home, Shea realized her father was afraid. Although he didn't say it, she knew he was the Negro the man had been complaining about at the dry goods store. He told Shea and her mother that the Beckman family had been attacked, their home burned to the ground. The Beckmans were black sharecroppers who worked for Davis and had planned to leave the South for Chicago, hoping for a fresh start. Seeing her father frightened like this scared Shea, too.

When a horse appeared in the distance, her father stood up, his chair making the most awful noise sliding across the porch. Her mother opened her mouth to speak, but her father held his hand in the air, stopping her. "Go into the house."

"No. I'm staying with you."

He grabbed her, held her face close. "Listen, you have a better chance getting away with Shea if you sneak out back. It will give you time... and give me time to figure out what they want."

"What they want? You know what they want. They warned you last time. They're not gonna let any of us leave this farm unless we're dead. Then they'll use us as a warning for everyone else." She grabbed him, they hugged. "I will not die as a free woman running from these men." She walked into the house, grabbed the rifle off the mantel, and came back out. "I won't leave you."

Shea didn't know what to do. She stared from her father to her mother, and then toward the Myrtle House. It was quiet. The white men only came when it was quiet, when *she* was quiet. Shea and her family always slept best when the haint was upset. White people did not like ghosts, Shea reasoned, because they were not controllable. They didn't like Negro women ghosts because they were angry.

The group of men rode up to the house, and stopped. Shea was shocked to see that Mr. Peterson was with them, but not surprised to see the man who'd been at the dry goods store.

Mr. Peterson called out to her father. "Charles?"

Her father turned to look at her mother. They both lifted their guns.

Mr. Peterson jumped from his horse and walked closer to the porch. Not too close, Shea noticed, but close enough that she could see his eyes. She realized that he was scared, too.

"Charles?"

"What do you want, Mr. Peterson?"

A few of the men giggled, high up on their horses.

"Just to talk."

"Is that right, Mr. Peterson? Last time these men were here, they threatened me and my family. They also shot Harry Beckman in the back today. I don't want none of that kinda talking." Her father sounded afraid, but convincing.

Mr. Peterson looked shocked, like he hadn't known about Harry Beckman. He turned to look at the white men on their horses and then he stared at the ground for a moment. "They just want you to sign an agreement to stay on here and work the land. It'll keep anyone from getting hurt."

"That agreement ain't no good and you know it. For ten years it'll put me and my family in slavery, plain as the nose on your face. You'll rent us these shabby houses for a ridiculous amount, rent us the land that we work on every day, rent us the equipment to work the land, and you'll give us a per cent of the profits that equal out to us owing you by the end of every year. Then when we can't pay up, you'll threaten to have us arrested if we don't sign for another ten years."

Mr. Davis, from the store, slid down from his horse and walked over to her father. "You ungrateful bastard. We give you everything and that's how you repay us?"

"I'll give you a better contract." Mr. Peterson was trying to calm things down.

"No!" Davis yelled. "If you give this nigger anything more, the others will find out." He drew his gun, and her father took aim at the man's heart. The widest point, he had taught her.

Beside Shea, her mother pointed her own gun at the men on horses. "Go into the house, girl. Lock the door."

Shea wanted to protest, but her mother's warning voice had been the most dangerous thing she'd heard that night.

Mr. Davis held his gun steady. "It won't matter if I burn it down around her, will it?"

"Not if I shoot you dead." Her father had just threatened to kill a white man. Even if he survived tonight, the sheriff would come for him.

Shea ran inside and went to watch from the window, where she spotted a man sneaking around behind the house. She ran to the side window, peeked out, keeping track of him. As soon as he got around to the front, he would grab her father. As easy as she could, she let the curtain slide back in place and she ran to the back door, opened it, and screamed at the top of her lungs: "Daddy! They're behind you!"

The white man stopped, looked at her and then took off running toward her. At the front of the house, lots of shots were fired, so she didn't run back inside. Instead she took off running away. At first she didn't even think about where she was going, she just ran and ran as fast as she could away from the man. She did not look back because she was afraid that would slow her down, or worse, that he would be too close to her. If he was about to catch her, she didn't want to know. She ran for the edge of the woods in the distance, which bordered the Peterson plantation. It was far, but once she was in there, she would be able to lose him easy. Just as she passed the side of the Peterson house, she chanced a look behind her and saw that the man was closer than she had hoped. She would never make it to the woods. In the distance, the shots had stopped but there was still lots of yelling, although Shea could not make out what was being said.

At the back of the house, she made a right and then slid into an opening in the basement that she had discovered long ago. She hid there when she didn't want the Mrs. or Sara to find her. The opening was barely noticeable if you weren't looking for it and even if you did know, it was too big for a grown man.

Shea took a moment to catch her breath and then walked

over to the wall where the haint had come through. The girl dropped to her knees, exhausted. She thought about what the old woman had told her. Her mother would be angry, but she didn't care. Shea put her hand on the wall.

"I know you're there."

After a moment, the figure appeared again, climbing her way out of the wall. She stepped down onto the floor like a two-legged spider descending its web.

"Please, they're gonna kill 'em."

The haint looked toward the front of the house, like she could see the goings-on through the wall. Then she turned back to Shea. "They lie. Always."

"I know."

"They lie of me." The woman took off her turban to reveal the ragged, bleeding hole where her ear should have been. "Made me into a monster they use to scare their children."

Shea didn't know what to say. Just as she opened her mouth, upstairs, the doorbell rang and then heavy footsteps walked across the floor. She looked up through the cracks in the floorboards, her eyes following the white man who had been chasing her, as he moved toward the basement. He knew she was there. The haint stared up, too.

"They said you killed white people. They're scared of you. Of what you did. And what you are. What they made you. She told me that."

The woman stared at her, showed her teeth. "I never killed no one. They... shamed me. Took my ear and then buried their crime in a shallow grave under this house."

Shea cried. For this woman. For her family. "I'm sorry." She closed her eyes and listened to the man open the basement door. "They're going to take everything from me, the way they took it from you."

The woman, who looked quite beautiful in the light, stared down at her. "What do you want from me, child?"

Shea got to her feet; she only came to the woman's waist, but she felt taller, more self-assured. "Haint me." Thinking of the old woman's words, Shea fell again to her knees. "I pray. Haint me too!"

The woman let out a giant scream that shook the house from the belly to the roof. It vibrated throughout Shea's chest. She held her heart, feeling it beat rapidly. But she didn't feel scared, she felt powerful. The dead woman's essence was alive in the land, in the house, and in Shea. The girl could feel her all around. Not inside of her, but as if she had always been a part of her.

Upstairs, the white man stopped moving, covering his ears. As the dead woman's scream reached the man, her form disappeared. Shea watched as the haint passed through him, his hair slowly becoming devoid of any of its once dark color. The dead woman had seen his soul and left him part of hers. He fell to the dirt floor, not dead, but not the same.

Suddenly, the woman's anger—a release Shea recognized because she was now part of the woman—moved through the room, up the stairs, and across the Peterson farm in a wave that shook every tree from their roots to the tips of their branches, jostled every grain of wheat, and toppled every blade of grass. Shea was swept up in the woman as her essence moved over the land, as the haint moved, so did Shea. Shea too moved—they were one. Upstairs the Mrs. and her children were staring out the opened front door, as if afraid to move or breathe. They watched the ghost and its host leave the house and sweep across the land.

The pair moved quickly toward her parents. Shea saw from both her low position on the ground and from above, as the ghost could see. Finally she saw that some of the white men had gotten to their horses and fled. Mr. Davis and Mr. Peterson were picking themselves off the ground, having been knocked off their feet by the vibration of the haint. Then they walked away, Mr. Peterson toward his house, Mr. Davis down the road, his horse having run off.

The dead woman stood over Shea's parents, watching the white men. Shea's father was on the ground, her mother holding his head. Shea ran to them.

"Don't worry," her mother said. "It's just a scratch." She

looked up to the dead woman, and back at Shea.

Shea reached out to touch the haint but couldn't. Her body was not real, but her emotions were overwhelming. Her anger not sated.

It would never be sated as long as she was stuck here, Shea knew.

"You can go, if you want. You shouldn't have to be where you don't want."

But the haint was not free. Her essence had merged with Shea, the girl could feel her deep inside.

The old woman appeared, as she often did, seemingly from nowhere.

Shea looked to her. "I did what you asked of me."

"You wanted this. You asked for it."

Shea nodded. She had. "Will she go away?"

The old woman looked to the haint. "In this form, yes. But you asked not to be afraid anymore. You asked to be a witch."

"I don't want to hurt her. Not like them."

"She's not hurting, girl. She's free. You're both free."

The ghost felt alright, not hurt, not so angry anymore. After a moment, she walked into Shea, then faded, not gone, just not there either. Not like people, not like haint, like witch. That's what the pair was, as one.

✳

Three days later Shea, her mother, and father rounded up everything they owned and headed toward Harlem, New York. Shea's father's arm was bandaged, but otherwise he was feeling fine. Good even. Shea sat between her parents, not looking back at the Peterson farm as they went. Shea sat upright, watching the world go by, smoothing out the wrinkles of the good dress that she had worn for this special special occasion.

THE NEKROLOG

Helen Marshall

I

When I was fourteen I often wrote to you—my dark-eyed, laughing little cousin. It began as a school project. Did you know that? I always assumed Mom told Auntie but maybe you never knew. It doesn't matter.

You'd only just come to Toronto and were learning the ropes but Mom and Dad had abandoned the old country many years earlier. They'd made a dangerous crossing where the borders of Bulgaria, Greece and Turkey converged, trekking beneath the blue-grey edge of the mountains through a forest populated by bears and wild boar, turncoat shepherds who'd betray you to the border guards. Bandits. Smugglers. Or so they told me.

They settled in the southwestern tip of Ontario and pretty soon after I appeared on the scene. Our town was small but pretty enough, surrounded by flat fields of monocrops. In the summer the air smelled of melting asphalt and the faint whiff of sulfur from the refineries where Dad took a job as an engineer. Sometimes they'd take me to the bridge where we'd devour vinegar-soaked chips and marvel at the crawl of traffic to the other side. They never went to the States themselves, though gas was supposed to be cheaper there and many made a weekly pilgrimage to fill up. They held only limited faith in their passports.

I was used to begging for stories of what life had been before but Mom always met my pleas with silence. Then when I was seven a load of crates arrived from some distant relative. These offered some clues. A ring with a fingernail diamond, which had belonged to her great uncle, apparently a famous architect in Zagreb after the war. I seem to recall an urgent, whispered conversation with Dad when she discovered a birth certificate stamped with a six-pointed star. I was told never to mention this to anyone and Mom's look was so serious, so desperate, that I never did.

Your appearance in my life was fortuitous: as our friendship developed you seemed to me like a shadow sister, the person I could have been had mother and father stayed behind. You seemed glamorous in your own way. You spoke many languages and had a shuttered way of glancing out from beneath the dark fringe of your hair, which I loved.

We only ever met the once. You'd just arrived in the country and so Mom insisted we drive the four hours through a haring February snowstorm to help you unpack. Having never taken such a long trip I brought five paperbacks with me and read them one by one. Outside the window was a dizzy shadowland fulgurated with glaring headlights. I squealed with excitement whenever our tires lost traction.

You barely spoke. A year or two younger than me, you had the shoulders of an old woman, bent at an odd camber, but your eyes were bright and vivacious and we got on well. The two of us played dolls because that's what you had: a trio of sisters with lifelike porcelain faces and golden curls that felt soft as real hair when I touched them. Uncle Kiril must have made them for you, I thought, because you couldn't buy anything as nice as that.

It was a strange game we played that day but everything in the apartment was strange: crushed biscuits with rosehip jam, the ritual of turning over your teacup so Auntie could read your fortune, men smoking indoors. Kiril, Auntie's husband, was a taciturn man with a scar that bit into the knuckles on his right hand. He had the careful way of someone who'd recently suffered a tragedy. Later I'd see the same hesitation in your letters, oddly poetic with your never-perfect English.

We only ever played with two of the dolls. One was always out of action. The doll's house was a single room, which was made from a shoebox. There was a second shallow compartment underneath that may have been to store the dolls. You told me the word but I didn't understand it.

I remember you drawing straws to decide which would go under. How serious you were! You kissed the little doll on the head when she was chosen and said a sort of prayer. Then down to the bunker she went, her blond hair gleaming but never to be brushed by our careful hands.

So, that was how we met.

My family didn't go back to Toronto for many years. Mom wasn't comfortable driving long distances and Dad feared the highway speed traps as he feared all policemen. Your family didn't own a car, which seemed amazing to me, particularly as the years passed and the nature of your growing wealth became a regular subject of conversation at our family dinner. Auntie had taken a post at the university while Uncle Kiril opened a string of storage warehouses. But I was told things were different in Toronto where there were underground tunnels you could use to get most places—out of the cold, out of the rain. Cars were a needless expense.

When I think back on it now, it seems strange to me that I

ever really did meet you. Our letters were long and rambling, so full of childish misery. I was always complaining of the harsh treatment from my parents, how Mom screamed at me whenever I forgot to lock the front door though this was supposed to be the safest town in the country. Later we talked about boys. I wrote you a long list of ways I intended to impress Noah who I'd decided I would marry one day, including: 'learn new tricks on my BMX' and 'make friends with his sister so you're always just—*there*'. And it was you I told first when, a year later, he pressed his pencil-stub erection against me in the high school cafeteria as we waited in line for pizza. Surely this was love!

But no. You were always so much wiser than me. "Trust no man," you said, "don't let him stick it in you. It'll hurt even if he says it won't. I promise."

I was impressed by that promise of yours. It spoke of volumes of experience I didn't have. And though Noah invited me to the winter formal that year, your warning stayed with me and I said no. So in the end it was Carole Krueger who got stuck with his thing and had to finish the year at home instead of me.

I lost you in my final year of university, the same year I lost so many things I'd been careless with.

I had applied to programs in the States. By that point I was hungering after some sort of change myself, a bit of separation from my parents who were always spoiling my serenity with their immigrant wariness, their catastrophizing. So I went to a small liberal arts college in upstate New York, which was lovely, at first, until one of the students went crazy and brought a duffel bag with semi-automatics to campus.

These were the early days. Later there would be drills, instructions on barring the door, hiding in closets. I knew some of the students that died. For months afterward the footage from the news programs haunted me: a guy in a black vest and black trousers, his face not unlovely. He could have been anyone.

But I hadn't gone to class that day.

I'd been smoking a joint in one of the derelict basement labs with my roommate Theresa. We were marveling at the abandoned equipment, shrouded in dusty white painter's sheets, giggling, maybe kissing a little bit. I was in love with the way she could charm a circle of smoke from her lips. I had only ever seen one other person do that before.

Watching her I was seized with the memory of that day, the smell of rosehips, Kiril clutching the cigarette between his fingers as Auntie promised Mom it would be a good year to take out a loan.

Then I felt a touch on my forehead, a cobweb brushing

against my temples. Suddenly it was as if a heavy cloud invaded my senses. My limbs turned to lead and I couldn't move. I think I collapsed. I learned what happened afterwards, how Theresa heard the noises above us—we didn't have cell phones, there was no way to know what was happening—but my nerveless body frightened her and she waited beside me, cradling my head in her hands until the police found us hours later once the violence was over.

The doctor said it was Guillain-Barré Syndrome and I was lucky. If it had struck a vital system I could have suffocated in the basement. In the hospital room my mind drifted in a sensationless fog. For three days I was little more than a pair of eyes watching, a pair of ears listening. I drank in everything said to me. I said nothing in return.

Two weeks later they released me, having lost a kilogram in weight, mostly muscle. At first I couldn't walk. I had to relearn my writing grip, I couldn't tell if a surface was rough or smooth. I stopped writing to you because it was too difficult. I couldn't find the words I needed. I'm still sorry for that.

It took me three months to rebuild my nervous system but by then Theresa had graduated and taken a job on the West Coast. Mom was sick so I went back home. It was difficult at first. The outline of the place hadn't changed.

My bedroom was as I'd left it, painted a too-bright pink which now hurt my eyes. And as the months dragged on Mom didn't seem to be getting better. But I felt comfortable with the difficulties of her condition as Dad didn't. He sat in the kitchen and drank vodka as I read to Mom, repeating passages, whole pages, after she fell asleep.

It was only as 'the worst' became inevitable that I decided to write to Auntie to tell her. The two of them had grown apart. We'd become the poor relations and that had stung, I guess, when we'd had so much more to begin with. I was sitting with Mom in the sickroom. It had become that over the last months, dust goblins in the corners, the burnt-umber light bleeding in through the shades. She looked so puzzled when I mentioned you.

"That can't be right," she said. "Emilia, you're making things up again."

I shook my head.

Then she told me what had happened, how Auntie and Kiril had a little girl but she'd died in '87 from a rare condition of the lungs. Many children had died that year from freak diseases after the poisonous wash of Chernobyl. It was one of the reasons they'd left.

I didn't know what to say. I watched as she shuffled out from under the covers, a frail woman now. The jut of her spine cleaved the wings of two pale shoulder blades beneath her robe. From the highest shelf she tugged at an album and showed me the clipped *nekrolog*. There you were: small for your age, dark and wizened even then but smiling faintly. An old school photo.

"Never mind," I said at last, touching the *nekrolog*. "Get some sleep now."

But that night I dreamed you were playing at dolls. There were three of us you held in your hand but it was Mom you kissed so tenderly. You didn't want to do it, but it had to be done. There was no choice. You'd drawn the straws and down she went into the dark place. But you were so kind with her, I remember that. Gently you held her like a slain child. Gently you composed her limbs. Gently you laid her body beneath the threshold, murmuring a prayer for protection, a hope for the future.

II

In the beginning was the word—that beautiful power-*sprich*—and before that was silence. But go back further and you'll find another word, which was malformed and spoken in malice by the wrong tongue. Though it too created a world, that world was broken.

Desi struggled over her words at first. I was told not

to worry but it was of some concern to me at the time. Although all education was State-provided, I knew well enough not all education was equal. Bad teaching was a punishment to be endured. It could warp the mind. But good teaching could open a door through which the mind might gaze upon new worlds. I wanted that for my daughter. As we had neither a good name nor high status, I knew that few other doors would be opened for her. The world of a well-trained mind was the best I could hope for: she might see clearly, if nothing else.

I loved my little girl, loved her dearly. She had a way of laughing that was glorious and unconcerned and though she didn't speak for her first three years, she could say such things with her eyes that the two of us understood each other perfectly.

By her fifth year our fears were proven to be unfounded. She'd mastered Russian and German. When I wrote to my sister in Canada—that distant country!—to tell her of my daughter's aptitude, she sent back children's books in French. "*Mama, je t'aime,*" Desi would say, preferring the smoothness of that other language with its twists and complications, its puzzle-words that could only be memorized.

Kiril insisted that we'd send her to the Language School when she came of age. It occurred to us that she might be able to work as a diplomat and so have the opportunity to see the countries currently denied to us. It would be a good profession.

We had a little hope of succeeding. I worked during this time in the government offices and there was the possibility of advancement. If I did well then Desi's chances might be greater when the time came. And I had a serious job. It was my duty to analyze pamphlets for coded messages. This was difficult work. The office was unheated and often our fingers and toes would grow numb from the cold. At first I didn't believe I would ever find any messages. After all, these weren't dissident pamphlets. They were produced in a warehouse in the adjoining building by another government agency where I assumed another group of girls must be struggling over the pamphlets we ourselves produced. It was a case of the left hand watching the right. Who would dare put forward their subversion this way?

But then I learned that one of the girls I worked with, Nevena, had failed to report a series of discrepancies in documents planted amongst her daily batch. She didn't appear in the office the next day and none of us ever knew what happened to her.

All this made me more serious in my efforts. Luckily I had a good memory. I could hold the image of the master pamphlet in my mind very well. This allowed me to spot errors. They were small things usually, a misspelled word, a letter placed upside down. The pamphlets were produced by hand as we were never given the faster Linotype machines we heard they had elsewhere. As such it was easy for mistakes to occur. I believed what I saw were these things.

But the other girls in the office were not as good as me. It wasn't uncommon for our department to seed false flags in our batches. More girls disappeared but I was promoted. At last one of the other girls came to me, Rosita, who had a child the same age as Desi. "You're so clever," she said, "how do you do it?"

I tried to explain. I held the image in my mind, made it as strong and bright as possible, until I could see nothing else. Then I would hold another page before my eyes and the two would somehow join together. At that point it was obvious what was different.

She tried to adopt the same technique but she couldn't get the knack of it. We developed exercises to strengthen her memory but they didn't work. It was only when we explained to Elitsa what we were doing that she was able to devise a solution. It turned out Elitsa's husband was an optician. She understood the workings of the eye better than either of us. She said when we looked at a thing our two eyes took in two images, which the brain bound together. I'd learned to use my mind's eye to do the work because I was clever but it must be possible to do the same thing using only the body's eyes.

She instructed us to bring in our husbands' shaving mirrors. We were all nervous for we hadn't seen mirrors in the Universal Goods store for many months. If our experiments went wrong then they mightn't be replaced and we'd need to bring the razor to our husbands' chins ourselves lest they grow uncitizenly beards.

But again I shouldn't have worried. Elitsa measured out the distances herself and she placed the standing mirrors in such a way that two pamphlets could be laid out side by side. When Rosita sat down to study them then the mirrors controlled the route of her gaze: one eye saw the left pamphlet, the other the right. The first time she tried it she screwed up her face in consternation and then let out a shriek of delight. "I can see it," she told us all excitedly, "look, there, the space between those words is wrong. It's like magic!" She let me try for myself and it was just as she said. The wrong words seemed to shimmer and glow.

After that we encouraged the other girls to bring in their husbands' mirrors and we set up many more of these contraptions. Soon we joked that the whole lot of us would be known as the Bear Wives for the hairiness of our men. Never mind, we thought. At least we would be safe.

✳

A month later Elitsa didn't come into the office. A month can be a long time and by then some of my fear of the vanishments had dulled. I thought she might be sick. But the next day her space was empty and the third as well.

"They don't like us so smart," Rosita said darkly and after that we gave our mirrors back to our husbands. We set about doing things the old way and even I, who had never needed the mirror to begin with, made sure to be a little less diligent. I worried Rosita was right and at the same time I feared she was wrong, that perhaps there had never been a reason for the disappearances. Perhaps we were grasping at straws.

Then spring came and so did the rains.

We learned about them first from the pamphlets. Words like *contamination* and *half-life* began to appear with regularity. I learned to avoid anything grown in the fields and so Kiril and I did what we could to trade for powdered milk and cans of tasteless beans. But we couldn't avoid it entirely. It was necessary for us to attend the Victory Parades despite the grim fug of the clouds. The rainfall was light and we brought umbrellas. After we released I made sure to scrub us all—Desi, in particular. I remember how she grinned her little monkey-grin at me as I soaped her arms and shoulders.

"*Pourquoi as-tu si peur, Maman?*" she asked. I told her I

wasn't afraid, only that we had to be clean. I scrubbed until her skin was raw and she began to weep.

She grew sick. She died.

In another country she might've lived. It wasn't that our doctors didn't care for her but their equipment was outdated. They had many patients. I don't blame them. Only they didn't let me hold her in the end. They told me they'd cremate her, as they did for all the others who grew sick in the rains.

The next day I couldn't go to work. I thought I was dying too, that's how bad I felt. Kiril begged me to, he warned me if I didn't then they might come for me. Rosita stopped by as well and she brought with her biscuits which she insisted on crushing so we might eat them with rosehip jam. She told me three days of absence could be forgiven but no more than that. They understood I was grieving but there was work to be done. I was one of the best, even now.

I didn't care. When Kiril wouldn't leave me be I locked myself in our bedroom. My grief was a terrible thing. I had only a school photo of Desi from when she had won a prize the previous year and I stared at it for hours. What was I doing? In my mind I could see my daughter's body.

Her face was pale and bloodless but her shoulders were streaked with red. She looked as if she'd been mauled by a bear. I lay the mind-image of her corpse over the photograph and my vision began to dance. I saw her alive and smiling. I saw her dead. For a whole day I did this until I dreamt the image had been fixed. My mind had made her whole again: a bright, shimmering creature who hovered at the edge of my vision.

I tried to call out to her but there was a pounding at the bedroom door, which was flung open. Someone shouted, "You must stop this!" It was Elitsa.

She looked different now. Her long hair was glossy and smoothly cut and her skin seemed to glow with good health. She wore a Party uniform that was crisp and clean.

"Leave it be," she said, "let her go. She doesn't want this."

"Why?"

"I can't tell you. But I promise, you must do as I say." Then she lowered her eyes and whispered to me: "*L'enfant est vivant!*"

A gripping cold seized hold of my lungs. I couldn't breathe. She poured me vodka from her own flask and only when the fire of it bit into the ice was I able to look at her.

"You've prospered," I said bitterly.

"Someone must."

"Is that how it is then?"

She nodded and took my hand. Then she told me what would happen. I had a sister, didn't I? In Canada? It was a good country. I would be allowed to go to her. The passports had been arranged and we would be given money, as much as we needed. Only I must never speak of what I'd seen, of what I'd read in the pamphlets. I was an intelligent woman, she would be sure there was a position for me at the university.

Elitsa was as good as her word.

It was snowing when we arrived at our new home and I'd never felt such cold before in my life. I had to buy a pair of boots with thick fur on the inside to keep my feet warm. Kiril took me to the shopping centre, which seemed to me to be like a palace. Everything glittered, there was so much light. I said to Kiril, "We must buy more of these. We will send them back for the others. No one has boots like these back home. No one knows boots such as this exist!"

He held my hand as we made our way along the treacherous sidewalk, the two of us moving slowly as if we were learning to walk for the first time. The boots felt so good. The wind didn't touch us. We were both crying as we walked and the tears froze to our face so that the streets seemed to spark with reflected light.

We weren't alone on the street. We passed a group of

schoolchildren in thick winter coats who were gazing at the sky. They looked like angels with their pale faces, their unfamiliar greetings. Eagerly they cast their mouths open as the snow drifted downward and like sugar dissolved on their tongues.

III

When I was fourteen I was disappeared.

It's a strange thing: to be disappeared. I had a bad fever at the time—a nightmare of chemical horror—and so my memories are distorted in any case. I was in a crowded hospital room with many others. There weren't enough beds so some were lying on the floor on rush mats. My burning bones whispered beneath my flesh. I imagined an old woman counting them, putting them in order so she might know my future. This was my doctor, I think, though I can't be sure. It might have been my mother.

The State took me in. My mind during this period, which lasted close to six months I was told, became like molten silver so they set it to congeal in its new shape before it might be tampered with. There was a school I went to which was very like the school I had attended before. Continuity, eh? Except I didn't go home. We all slept at the school, we ate at the school, we completed the tasks we were given, suffered our punishments and endured the sparing praise that was sometimes heaped on a rival. It was much the same as it had been except my mother and Kiril weren't there. But I was told they had died and that I was an orphan and all this was for my own good. They didn't indulge my grief. We were all grief-stricken. At night we were a small nation of howlers.

So. What did we learn then?

We learned to love one another. This was the first thing though it wasn't what they intended to teach us. But it was necessary. We were well fed in the school, better than we had ever been, and as we progressed we were each given private rooms so we could study better and learn. But for us there was no outside world, no adults beyond our teachers and supervisors. We were a communal species, denied community, and so we made it for ourselves. We loved one another. We had too much but we shared it anyhow. If one of us was praised then we would take it upon ourselves to be sure each other girl was praised equally by one of us. We didn't want them to divide us. We called each other "little sister."

But that's not what you meant. Well then.

The other things flow from that first commandment we gave ourselves: to love one another. We were asked to stare for long hours at walls until pictures came into our minds. We were told these were the mind-shapes of our fellows and that we must study them carefully and report back.

Many didn't believe this was possible, but I did. I sent darling Liliya, the youngest of us, a mind-shape of the Eiffel Tower. I'd seen it in the books my aunt sent me and I remembered it very well. It didn't look like any other building I had seen before. A standing skeleton, I thought, all dressed up in little fairy lights. She saw it, I know she did. She drew it for them but they weren't happy. It looked too pretty in her drawings and they were afraid if we saw such images we might become attracted to the West.

There's another thing I learned at the school and it is this: fear is a fixer. Those mind-shapes burnished by terror had an added brightness to them. They lingered far longer. When our teachers learned this they began to incorporate it into our training. We would choose an image—say, of the oak tree in the centre of the yard, whose crown had died off, leaving only the bleached staghead—and if it wasn't clear enough we would be encouraged to fix it with our fears. For example, I might add to the mind-image the shape of Liliya's thirteen-year-old body, hanging from one of the low branches. We were encouraged to use all our friends in this way, rather than choose a particular little sister, lest any one of us become too familiar with the thought. It would diminish the effect. So we became used to sending to each other—this is what we called it—and incorporating such grotesques as we could think of: our fellows mutilated, burnt alive, hacked to pieces, raped, their blood weltering hot and vivid. Those who weren't good at imagining such things were given pictures and told to use them as models.

What was the purpose of this? It wasn't clear to us at the time. The mind-images we sent each other were not particularly special and we all thought it would've been much more effective simply to speak to one another. But our teachers didn't agree. They tested new forms of communication. For two months I was sent to a small village in the mountains. There were only a few shepherds there and they mostly spoke Turkish, which I didn't understand. They brought me food: mushrooms and cured sausages and thick yoghurt and watermelon.

I'd never seen such a beautiful part of the country. The mountains formed a long black spine that ran the length of the horizon, cradling forests of oriental beech trees and lush purple-pink rhododendrons. Some areas were so thickly grown that, seen from a distance, they resembled an alien landscape of the kind a child might draw when she's very young, using the wrong colors: green skies and purple hills and her parents nothing more than two blinking box-heads sat atop a tower of twigs.

I was allowed to roam freely and I did, but never into the forest where, I knew from stories, there were bears and rebels and border-crossers. All manner of enemies of the State. Escape never crossed my mind, in part because I didn't know what I'd be escaping from or escaping to. Things simply *were* and mostly I was content.

It was my job to act as a receiver. The others were senders. I took in whatever messages I could. We were practicing writing now, which was hardest because we had to do it in English and because there was so little room to incorporate our fixers. We took to sketching increasingly elaborate death-scenes in the margins. I found these amusing, the things my friends could think up to scare themselves! But I had never needed this particular trick. So in return— although it was against the rules—along with the letters in reply I sent out mind-shapes of my own: the crystal waters of the coast, the little reflecting pool I'd found at the end of the footpath, a bulbous yellow-green gourd shaped like a deformed member. But the mountains most of all, which I loved more than anything else. It was these images which I held in my mind when I returned home, so that I might return there when I slept, having stripped off my newgrown womanly skin.

In 1990 the school was closed. I was fifteen. There were many changes that year and for us this was the worst. We all felt as if we'd been nearing something crucial in our training, a sense that the politics of the world outside had interfered in our growth.

Three army jeeps came to take us away. We were to be returned to our parents.

Most of us were confused by this news as we'd lived in the belief that our parents were dead. We'd been shown images of their bodies by the doctors as part of their grief counseling. It was these images, of course, that we'd used as a basis for our earliest sendings.

Twenty-eight were taken away in that first convoy. Three of us remained: myself, Liliya, and Ivet who was a year older than both of us and on friendly terms with one of the teachers. She had a graceful, thick-limbed body and Titian-brown hair. She'd first begun the fashion of sending mind-images of deformed members, which we'd all done at various times to amuse ourselves, and it was she who explained to us what they were for and how it hurt so we all might learn from her mistakes.

"Our parents really are dead," she confided as we watched the jeeps vanishing through the compound gates.

"What will they do with us?" Liliya asked.

Ivet shrugged. "We must decide for ourselves."

That night I slept fitfully. I tried to summon the face of my mother and Kiril to my mind but it was difficult. They came from the time before and much of that was lost to me. But had I really ever believed they were dead? No, I don't think so. Another part of me—the part, I believe, that knew you—also seemed to know the story of their life but it was as if I'd hidden this knowledge deep inside myself. Or perhaps my teachers had.

I'm sorry to say so but of far greater concern to me now was the loss of my sisters. Would they really be returned to their parents? What would I do without them for company? I'd become so used to the gentle murmur of their voices in my mind, the press of their good regard and fellow feeling, but now that seemed to be stripped away from me. I felt desperately lonely.

I awoke with a start to find Liliya staring at me in the darkness, sucking her thumb as she hadn't done for a while now.

"Come here," I told her.

The three of us laid our mattresses on the floor and we curled together like a nest of adders, which I'd been told were good luck to kill, each of us lying against the other, our limbs muddled and confused. But we all felt better for it, warmer, inside and out. I whispered to them and the language was strange in my mouth but it felt good for me to say it, "*Allez dormir, mon cœur.*"

In the morning there were no teachers, no one to greet us. We waited in the compound yard beneath the old oak with its skeleton crown but no one ever came. Even Ivet was beginning to worry, although she'd been the most confident among us the night before. We went to the teachers' offices but they'd been emptied out. In the canteen we found the makings of breakfast and Ivet was able to prepare a thick, bitter coffee, which helped, but we were at a loss for what to do.

"We could stay here," Liliya said hopefully but we all knew this was a bad idea. The compound seemed haunted by the ghosts of our sisters and I couldn't imagine how we lingered among them, even for an hour longer.

"No," I said at last, "I know a place. We will go there."

Ivet and Liliya were both impressed by the steadiness of my voice, and so was I, if I'm honest. But the mountains seemed as good a place as any to go.

We gathered a supply of bread and cheese and dried meat from the canteen storeroom, an extra change of clothes each and a third set of woolly socks. We had no money, no map, but my memory was very good and Ivet had recently been granted privileges, including trips to the nearby town with her teacher-friend. But being outside the compound walls was disorienting, particularly for Liliya, who had not yet had her period of solitude. It was high summer so the weather was good at least and we passed huge fields of watermelon where we filched a few fruits to enjoy ourselves. This was the first thing I had ever got for myself and it felt exciting to break through the green rind and lick the juices from my fingers. So while Liliya continued to shakily stifle her sobs I began to enjoy myself, spitting black seeds into the ditch like bullet fire.

After several hours of walking like this our feet began to ache and we knew we couldn't go much farther. Travel became easier when we realized there were other, faster ways. For instance, we could send our thoughts ahead of us. We simply pictured what it would be like at the end of the stretch of road we could see, at the top of that mountain in the distance. If we imagined it vividly it was simple enough to step into the picture—and there you were! We had to do this slowly at first because Liliya was not as strong as Ivet and myself, but we taught her and she learned. There were other things we could do to speed our journey. If we were passed on the road, for example, then Ivet found she could cast her spirit into the driver and make sure he carried us along with him safely for as far as we wished to go. The last of these we found was, I believe, a smuggler who knew the area well, as it was along a frequent route where State enemies had been known to attempt to escape. Except, of course, that escape was no longer necessary in the same way after "the change." For most, anyway.

Our escape was of a very different kind. We were learning now to step through that door within our minds, to unshackle ourselves from our flesh. The border that to so many had been fixed and immutable had, for us, already vanished. If we wished to visit Paris, why, all we had to do was hold the longing deep in our hearts, hold the image of the tower and—yes!—there we would be. But we were learning that the crossing wasn't as easy as we'd first thought. Just as we could transport ourselves by holding that picture firmly inside us, so too did we continue to carry within ourselves an image of the place we had left, indelibly inscribed. Those images that held the most horror—my mother as the nurses led her from my side, that last time I saw her—were the worst of these.

And so when I returned at last to my place in the mountains, where I'd had my first taste of freedom, it was not without some trepidation. We followed a dusty, snaking road—walking now, for we feared anyone, even those under our influence, to know where we were headed. At last we came to it: an abandoned village with a waterless fountain, a doorway thick with wet-petalled blossoms and the door to the cottage battered in, the contents raided for anything of value. Gouged windows. An old spring bed that something—or someone—had pissed on.

"This is a place where things disappear," Ivet said at last.

I nodded. "We needn't go any further."

Liliya reached for my hand and I let her take it. She'd grown stronger on the journey, the pale of her skin burnt a dark copper now, but she was still so young and used to her cage. "Please don't leave," she whispered.

Then I crouched beside the poor girl, beheld her wax-doll stiffness. She was miserable with the fear of her freedom and I wanted no one I loved ever again to hurt the way she hurt in that moment. She feared that this was a ruse, all of it, our mad journey to this place, and my hope for what we might find here.

"Can't you feel it? In here?" I touched my finger to Liliya's temple and felt the headlong dash of the blood in her veins, how it glowed with possibility: a thousand voices murmuring to us, *You are loved you are loved we will not let them hurt you we will tear them limb from limb we will grind their bones to dust we will stab them drown them burn them you need not fear ever again.* Just like that she knew the world was opening itself up to her, making itself known in all its rage and fear and bright, burning beauty.

A glazed look of happiness came over her eyes. "Our sisters are coming."

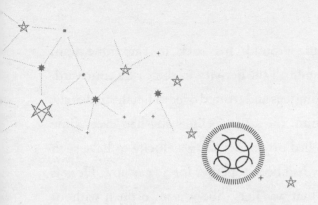

GOLD AMONG THE BLACK

Alma Katsu

Greta struggled to carry the bucket of dirty water up the stone steps and out to the courtyard. She had been scrubbing the floors all morning and the bucket was full of soot-gray water, as opaque as the fish pond after a hard rain. It slopped over the rim and wet her dress, splashed her legs and soaked her threadbare stockings. Nevertheless, she teetered carefully across the cobblestones with the bucket hugged tight to her chest, dirty gray water lapping under her nose.

Once in the courtyard, she stopped to set the bucket down. It was a long walk from the kitchen, but she didn't mind, for all the inconvenience. Because once outside, she got to see Jesper.

Jesper was her dog.

He lay on the ground, his back to the stone wall, unflappable despite all the activity in the castle courtyard. He rose on his long legs and trotted over to her immediately. As she petted him, the same feelings she had every time she saw him welled up inside: she was lucky to have such a fine dog. They had been together for a year now. He was the only thing that was hers. She was an orphan without so much as a wooden spoon to her name, and yet she had this fine, strong dog.

"He's been out here for hours," one of the scullery maids called out to her. They sat in a cloud of tiny white feathers as they plucked chickens for the master's dinner that evening. "He's going to get trampled."

"He'll be fine," Greta replied. It didn't matter: horses, oxen, the tramp of guards, a charge from another dog, Jesper stood his ground. He'd stare down whatever was in his path with those golden eyes of his until the other party slunk away.

Besides, she had no place to put him. They had no home, no roof over their heads. By day, Greta worked in the castle, gladly accepting whatever work they threw her way—scrubbing floors, doing washing, cleaning privies—in exchange for food. At night, she went into the woods to sleep, Jesper at her side. When it rained, she snuck into the stable and slept in the straw, Jesper curled next to her in a ball. They kept each other warm.

She reached into her pocket for the handful of capon trimmings the cook had given her earlier and fed it to him, waiting patiently as he licked the fat off her hands. Then she tipped the water out, lifted the bucket by its rope handle, and headed back into the castle.

As always, she returned to the woods that evening, when her work was finished, Jesper trotting at her side. They went to their usual spot to sleep, a pocket under a large pine tree whose low branches hung to the ground. Greta fluffed pine needles for their bed, then the two of them lay side by side. Greta stroked the dog slowly, from his head to his flanks. His steady breathing helped to lull her to sleep. His coat was black all over, as black as coal, but if you looked carefully, you would find gold hairs mingled with the black. There was gold in his muzzle, in the long fringes hanging from his ears, and the swirl of hair on his belly. Fine golden hairs, as gold as his eyes.

She first saw Jesper a year ago. She had been working on a small farm in the valley. The farm was so small it could only support the farmer and his wife. Still, they took in the orphan, using Greta to help the wife. They let her sleep in the barn and gave her the wife's old clothes, things she had worn as a child. They were not bad people, but when

Jesper crept into the courtyard that day, a wild pup from the woods, the farmer became alarmed. He said Jesper was a wolf and would kill his livestock, but Greta could see he wasn't a wolf. He was a dog, albeit not like any dog she had known. He was the most beautiful thing she had ever seen, though admittedly she didn't know much of the world. Her entire life had been spent in this one village.

The farmer's wife was afraid of Jesper. She said he had the devil's eyes and she didn't want him on the farm. Greta promised to keep him penned in the barn but that made no difference to the farmer's wife, and so Greta left. She couldn't send this puppy back into the wild, alone, or let the farmer kill him.

She had no alternative but to go to the castle to ask for work. The steward was surprised when she turned down the offer of lodging. She knew she wouldn't be able to bring Jesper with her. She preferred to stay with him even if it meant sleeping in the forest.

Greta went back the next day, working until the sun was high in the sky. By the time she returned to the kitchen, the midday meal was finished. Den, the kitchen steward, motioned to a sideboard piled with leavings. "Get something to eat before you go back to work."

As she sat on a stool by the fire, chewing the tough crusts, Den studied her. He was the same age her father would have been if he were still alive. Den supervised a small army of cooks and scullery maids and kitchen boys to haul firewood and water. He was a kind man, too. A father himself, Greta knew, with four boys and a girl.

"How old are you now, Greta?" Den asked.

She stopped chewing. "Thirteen."

He furrowed his brow. "You are practically a grown woman. It's dangerous for a woman to be on her own. Do you know what I mean by that?"

She did. There were already times walking through the village when she didn't feel safe. Men had started to eye her in a way they hadn't before.

"You should reconsider coming to live in the castle. You'll be safer here."

Her chest tightened. "I can't. What about Jesper? He wouldn't be able to come with me."

Den scratched his chin, thinking. "That dog of yours, he's unusual-looking... But he's big and strong. He could be a guard dog. Maybe we could find a place for him in the kennel. Do you want me to talk to the kennel master?"

The guard dogs were kept in a pen, as muddy and stinking as a sty. These dogs frightened her. The guards made them compete for food to toughen them. The thought of Jesper being made hard and violent sickened her.

"Thank you for your kindness, but I don't think so."

"Don't decide right away. Think about it, Greta. You cannot continue the way you have been. Surely you see that. You've got to think of yourself. Don't worry about Jesper. He will survive."

That night, she made a fire to roast a hare that Jesper had caught and thought about what Den had said. Jesper lay at her side, licking hare's blood off his feet and muzzle. Greta stroked him absently, his fur like the satin of a gown she'd once touched. Under the fur he was hard as stone, all muscle and bone. He seemed regal to her, the way he carried himself, his head held high. He could've been a king in another, secret, life, like a prince put under a spell in a fairy tale. A prince who had been cursed by a witch to roam the forest as a dog until he found his true love. Not that she believed in those stories, not after her parents died.

"What am I going to do, Jesper? Maybe I am being selfish. Maybe you would be happier as a guard dog, living with other dogs, with a roof over your head and bones to gnaw on, and not hiding away with me in the forest."

Jesper looked at her intently.

She stopped petting him and went back to the spit. "If only you could tell me what you want."

I want you to be happy.

Greta gasped. She heard the words as clearly as the church bell. Jesper had never spoken to her before. She'd *pretended* he'd spoken many times before, making up things for him to say, imagining what he might think in a given situation.

But she had known, all those times, that the words and thoughts were hers.

This time was different.

Had his mouth moved? She hadn't been looking at him at that moment, she had been turning the meat over the fire. Had she heard the words with her ears, or in her head?

She sat frozen, staring at Jesper, unsure what to think. *They were my words*, she decided. *I put those words in his mouth. That must be what happened. Or else I'm going mad.*

Jesper flicked his tail once, like a horse swatting flies, his golden eyes never leaving her face.

They trudged to the castle together the next morning as usual, making their way past stable boys leading the huge draft horses in from pasture, past the dairy where cows bellowed to be relieved of their milk. A cat stood just outside the milking shed, licking cream off her whiskers. Two women threw seed to chickens, laughing at a joke they had just shared.

If I lived here, my life would be so much easier, Greta

thought as she looked about. But she felt traitorous having these thoughts as Jesper trotted at her side.

Greta was sent to change the rushes on the floor of the Great Hall with a girl named Liesl. At first, they worked in silence, sweeping the soiled rushes into the fireplace for burning. Greta never liked that fireplace and tried to avoid it whenever she was in the Great Hall. It was big enough for a child to walk into, and she could very well imagine being roasted there, like a piglet at a feast.

As time passed, however, Liesl's tongue got the better of her and she began to ask Greta questions. At first it was a relief, for Greta spoke to few people in the course of her day, almost no one besides Den. Liesl seemed like a nice girl but by her clean dress and carefully plaited hair, Greta could tell she had a mother and father and lived a normal life in a house.

"Do you live in the village? They say you do not live in the castle and yet I've never seen you in town," Liesl asked. She looked at Greta over her shoulder as she swept.

"I live outside of town," Greta answered without looking up from the floor.

"On one of the farms? Which one?" When Greta didn't answer, Liesl stopped sweeping and turned to her. "Look, I'm trying to help you. You seem like a good girl. Don't you know what they say about you?"

Greta shook her head.

"They say you're a witch. They say that you go into the woods at night to participate in black masses with the other witches."

Greta tried not to show that she was frightened. She couldn't tell Liesl why she really went into the woods. This girl would not understand. "I am not a witch."

But Liesl wouldn't stop. "They say that dog is your familiar and he can change shapes."

Greta's heart pounded in her chest. She knew what talk of witches could do to a town. She remembered one old woman who'd been driven away—at least, that was what they told children. She remembered men dragging her out of her cottage, their faces red with anger. Watching the townsfolk driving her away with stones, men and women she had thought kind-hearted. The old woman was never seen again, and another family moved into her home.

Run, run, run, sounded in her head, but she had nowhere to run.

"Everyone knows witches take cats for familiars, not dogs." She didn't know if this was true, but it was all she could think to say.

"It doesn't matter. If he can change shapes, he can make himself into a cat, too, can't he?" Liesl's tone was not so nice now.

"This is ridiculous. I'm not going to discuss it anymore."

Greta went to the other side of the hall to sweep, and the girls did not speak to each other again, even when the job was done. The entire time, however, Greta worried: there were rumors about her floating around the village. It didn't matter how the rumor started or that she had done nothing to make anyone think she was a witch. She knew people liked to make up stories when they didn't understand something. She remembered what they'd said when her parents died. *He was drunk. He'd stolen money.* None of that was true.

She was an orphan, which meant in the eyes of most people she was unlucky, and people wanted to believe the unfortunate were responsible for their bad luck. That they brought misfortune on themselves, that they deserved it. The people accused of being witches were often unlucky, which—now that Greta thought about it—seemed wrong. Didn't it make more sense that the wealthy would be witches? If you could have anything you wanted, why wouldn't you make yourself rich?

Walking back to the forest that evening, Greta was disconsolate. She had been a fool to believe Den. Even if she moved into the castle, the townspeople would never accept her. She would be an outsider, alone and at the mercy of others, for the rest of her life.

You won't be alone, Greta. You have me.

Jesper stared up at her.

Greta was too frightened and confused to question where the words had come from.

She made up the bed of pine needles as usual. When she turned to call Jesper, she found a young man in his place. He looked to be only a few years older than her. He was handsome with a noble face and a disquietingly familiar bearing.

She jumped back. "Who are you, and what are you doing here in my home?"

"Don't pretend you don't know me, Greta. I'm Jesper."

Her heart thudded even harder than the night before. Now she was sure she was going mad. Many times, she had prayed for God to turn Jesper into a man so that she might have someone to share her life. A brother if not a lover.

It seemed God had finally heard her prayers.

She couldn't deny that this man looked like Jesper. He was lean and strong, and his eyes were the same gold, which she'd never seen on a person. His hair, thick and glossy as Jesper's, had long strands of gold among the black at his temples and mixed in with the sparse whiskers on his face.

"I must be dreaming," she said.

"Believe that if you must. Just know that I'm here to comfort you. Don't be afraid, Greta. You're not alone. We can be together forever, if that's what you want."

She let him lie next to her on the pine needles. The body

pressed against her felt very familiar; it felt like the same heavy body that leaned into her every night. His hair was the exact same texture as Jesper's, comfortingly silky and fine. He was the same as Jesper in so many ways, but a man.

Though not *exactly* a man. Greta could tell that, too.

Greta was afraid to return to the castle the next day but had no choice. Jesper wanted them to leave and find another place to live, but Greta wasn't sure. For one thing, she had been promised clothing and a new pair of shoes if she stayed for a season's service. She felt, too, that she owed Den an explanation. He had been kind to her and would be worried if she disappeared, maybe even send guards to look for her.

It was wash day at the castle, a busy day. Greta's job would be to carry heavy wet clothing outside, twist the last of the water out, and then spread the garments on bushes and fence rails to dry in the sun. She was soon exhausted, nearly tripped over her own feet going up and down the stairs, her arms full of wet cloaks and tunics and gowns, her own clothing soaked through.

Despite her exhaustion, she kept an eye out for Den to tell him she was leaving. How could she not? After last night, everything had changed. She didn't understand what was happening or what Jesper was, but he had chosen to reveal himself to her, and that was important. It made her feel special. She wouldn't tell Den that part, of course. He wouldn't understand. He might think she was crazy or possessed. He might even think the stories about her were true.

She worried a little bit that it *did* mean they were true. Was this how the devil came to you? Pretending to be a friend, a protector?

No, Jesper was not the devil—she was sure of it. Jesper had been with her for a year and had never done anything bad, never so much as nipped at her. He caught game and brought it back for their dinner. He protected her from wild animals. He kept her warm on cold nights. He loved her, and he proved it time and again.

Greta was running out of places for the wet clothes. She went to the field behind the stables where there were some bushes in full sun, a perfect spot for drying, even if it was a little far. She clambered through the fence and past grazing horses and cattle, and into the field.

After she'd finished arranging the clothing, she stood for a minute to catch her breath, when a man emerged from the other side of the copse. She didn't like the look of him. He was older, perhaps twenty, and big, with a roughness to him that put her on edge.

He cocked his head. "What are you doing out here with those things? Are you stealing them?"

"It's wash day," she said, though surely he knew this. The countryside was dotted with drying clothing. "I work at the castle."

"I work in the stable and I've never seen you before. You'd better come with me. I'm taking you in to see the steward."

She dodged his hand as he reached for her. "I'm headed back that way, and you can follow me if you want and speak to the laundress. She'll tell you." She didn't want him following her, but she wanted his hand on her even less.

Then he lunged for her. He didn't think she was stealing, she realized. He might not even work there, perhaps he had come out to steal a horse. But that didn't matter at the moment; all that mattered was the queer way he looked at the wet clothing clinging to her body. They were far from the castle and the stable. There was no one to hear if she screamed.

She saw a blur of black and gold in the corner of her eye before she realized it was Jesper. He was on the man in a flash and then they were on the ground, man and dog. Jesper had his teeth sunk deep into the man's arm and the man was on his back, legs kicking in the air as they tussled, the two surrounded by a cloud of dirt. The man was screaming and Jesper was growling, a frightening growl that Greta had never heard before. The thrashing slowed and soon there was a pool of blood on the ground and the man was still. He began to moan.

Jesper shook the arm in his teeth like a rag doll.

"Jesper, stop! You'll kill him." She could barely get the words out.

They ran deep into the woods, branches whipping at her face and tearing at her dress. The dog bounded next to her like a deer, fleet and sure. She wished she could run like him, that she could *be* like him. That the two could run forever, and never stop.

They stopped when she was sure no one was following them. She leaned over, hands on her knees, gasping to catch her breath. Jesper stood next to her, a man now. He wasn't breathing hard at all.

"Why did you do that? You may have killed him," she said. Tears sprang to her eyes, from fear. Not fear of his teeth or claws: fear of what would happen next.

"He was going to hurt you."

"But now they'll come looking for us. They'll say you're dangerous. They'll take you away from me—they might even kill you."

He tossed his head. "It doesn't matter. We won't go back. We'll leave."

She supposed she knew this, deep in her heart. The moment Jesper showed her that he could become a man, she knew they couldn't stay in the village any longer. That life was over.

He was strong and fearless—and magical. She could admit that now. She wished she could be like him, and never be afraid again.

"You can," Jesper said to her, reading her mind. "You just have to decide to do it."

She knew what that meant, though. What she would be agreeing to.

But there was no reason to stay. There had been so little kindness for her in the village; only Den. Whereas Jesper had been good to her every day she had known him. He had never given her a reason to doubt him or be afraid.

In the end, it was no choice at all.

"Okay," she said, reaching for his hand.

HOW TO BECOME A WITCH-QUEEN

Theodora Goss

1. THE COFFIN

You look at the coffin as it is lowered into the rectangular opening in the cathedral floor, that was made specifically to contain it. Inside is your husband, the man to whom you have been married for more than twenty years, you've forgotten exactly how many. The man with whom you have three children. The oldest, Gerhard, will inherit the throne. He will be called Gerhard IV after his grandfather, who was Gerhard III or, to his enemies, Gerhard the Drunkard. His younger brother, Wilhelm, is jealous of him, and you foresee a rivalry, perhaps even a struggle for the throne. They were such lovely little boys, you think, remembering when they wore short pants and played with toy soldiers. What happened to them? They are young men now, beyond your purview, and Gerhard in particular takes after his father, who was not a bad man, but not a particularly good one either. A typical king of these small kingdoms, which are perpetually at war with one another, obsessed with politics and power. Wilhelm, at least, is an affectionate son, but you worry that with the privileges of a prince and nothing to do, he will become dissolute, possibly a drunkard like his grandfather. And your daughter Dorothea, who takes after you—well, you worry about her as well. She is still young, only fourteen, but soon she will be old enough for the use to which princesses are usually put—a marriage to cement alliances. You don't want her married off to a prince she barely knows, who may be cruel, or ugly, or just smell bad. Her father would have married her off without a qualm, so you are glad he is dead, although of course you can never say such a thing. The list of things queens cannot say is a long one, and you have not said them for most of your life. His death means your position at court is diminished, but you never cared for pomp and circumstance anyway. If you had been given a choice, you would have stayed in the forest with the dwarves—or the huntsman. Your father's court taught you that prestige comes at a price. Most are willing to pay it—you, increasingly, are not.

Would Gerhard force Dorothea to marry? That is the question which has been bothering you since your husband died. He might—she is a pretty girl, although still awkward, as awkward as you were yourself at that age, when the queen your mother asked for your heart and liver and you had to leave the only home you had ever known.

So that is the dilemma in a nutshell. You have no place here anymore, not really. And there is Dorothea to consider. What should you do?

As you stand there pondering, with your black handkerchief held up to your dry eyes in mimic grief, the stone that will cover the coffin is put into place. Lying on top of it is an effigy of your husband in armor, looking as handsome as he did in life, with Harald II engraved beneath his feet. He was always an attractive man, even into his forties. Not the sort of man you would expect to die from a heart condition, but here you are, a widow. Across the cathedral, his mistress, who used to be one of your ladies-in-waiting, is sobbing into a friend's shoulder. For him, or because with his death, she has lost her place in the court hierarchy? Gerhard has never liked her, and will probably send her packing back to her father's damp manor house by the southern marshes. You have absolutely no pity for her. We all make our own beds, and must lie in them.

After the funeral services are over, you return to your

rooms in the castle, escorted by your ladies-in-waiting. As you walk down a corridor, you pass the chamber where your own coffin, the one made of glass, is displayed. Visitors are allowed to see it Mondays through Thursdays, from nine in the morning until four in the afternoon, along with other national treasures such as the crown of Gerhard I, who was crowned by the Pope himself, or the emerald necklace of Queen Sofronia, which you wore at your wedding. Someday you may lie in that coffin again—however, you have no intention of dying anytime soon. A plan is coming to you, but will Gerhard agree? How can you put it to him so that he cannot refuse? You have an idea...

"Your Majesty," says Franziska, your lady's maid, who has been waiting for you in your bedroom.

"Yes?" You turn toward her. As you do, you catch a glimpse of yourself in the mirror. For the first time in your life, you are wearing black. It suits you. Your hair is still black at a distance, although up close, with afternoon light coming through the windows, you can see strands of gray. Your face is still youthful, although there are lines under your eyes, of either age or fatigue. You are the same age as your mother when she tried to kill you, and here you are, trying to figure out how to protect your daughter. She is just as pretty as you were at her age, you think loyally, but you know it's not true—how could she be, without the additional charm of magic? Hair as black as night, skin as white as snow, lips as red as blood—those were the words of the enchantment. Other women might be content with dyes and cosmetics, with carmine and lamp black, but your mother must have a daughter as beautiful as herself, created by magic. Of course, when that daughter turned out more beautiful... Well, this is no time to go over that old history.

"Yes, Franziska? What is it?"

"The king, Your Majesty. He requests permission to enter."

For a moment you are startled: when has your husband ever asked permission to enter? You expect him to come walking in as usual, but then you remember—he is lying under a stone effigy of himself. It is of course Gerhard, who is now king, although the coronation will not be until Sunday, in the cathedral.

"Mother," he says, after you have nodded your permission to Franziska. He is stiff and dutiful as always. He has been like this since his days at military school, which affected Wilhelm so differently—if Willi had not been a prince, he would surely have been thrown out for his drunken capers, despite the fact that he was a surprisingly good scholar. Now he is the opposite of his brother—romantic, impulsive, a natural rebel. "I hope you are bearing up under your grief."

"Indeed," you say, offering him your hand to be kissed. "Thank you for your consideration, my son. As you know,

I am devastated by the loss of your father, and cannot think how to console myself. After your coronation, where I shall be proud to see you crowned as his successor, I would like to withdraw to the Abbey of St. Winifred, where my mother is buried. I would prefer to mourn in private. Do I have your permission to make such a journey?" It is tiresome to ask permission, but you have had to ask permission from men all your life—your father, your husband. Only in the forest were you free.

"Of course, of course," he says. He looks relieved that you asked—it seems he would rather have you absent from court for a while. A king newly crowned does not want the queen dowager interfering in matters of state.

"And perhaps I shall take Dorothea with me. The nuns will know how to assuage the grief of an emotional girl."

"No doubt," he says. Again he looks relieved to be rid, for a while, of inconvenient females. "I shall need you both here when Prince Ludwig of Hohenstein comes to negotiate the new trade pact for the Five Kingdoms, but until then…"

So that's the husband he has chosen for Dorothea! Ludwig of Hohenstein is only ten years older than her, and not particularly ugly—you do not know whether he smells bad—but he is utterly and completely ordinary. A boring man. You do not want her marrying him, unless she herself wants to—if she is to marry dullness, let her choose it herself.

"Of course, Your Majesty," you say. You curtsey, and you can see that although he raises you up and tells you that sort of thing is not necessary, not for his own mother, he is secretly pleased.

When Gerhard is gone, you smile. That was easier than you anticipated.

"Franziska," you say. "I want you to pack for a long journey. Only black gowns."

"Of course, Your Majesty," says the lady's maid. It makes sense that at this delicate time, the queen dowager cannot be seen out of mourning.

But black, you think, is for more than mourning. It is the appropriate color for a witch.

II. THE FOREST

The huntsman's house is exactly where you remember, both too far and not far enough away from the castle.

He looks at you warily, a little anxiously. He has heard, no doubt, of the king's death. Such news travels fast.

He looks different—how could he not? He has a beard now, and there is gray in it, as well as in his hair. He has taken off his green cap with the feather and is standing respectfully, waiting for your command.

You remember the first time you saw him. He was only seventeen, with golden-red hair and the beginning of a mustache.

"Princess," he said. "The queen your mother commanded that I lead you out into the forest to kill you. She told me to bring back your liver and heart. But I cannot do such a thing. Take my purse—it does not have much in it, but a little is better than nothing. Run and hide, at least until Her Majesty is no longer angry with you—although why she is angry, I cannot imagine. If you follow the road, you will come to a village—there you can perhaps hide yourself as long as necessary. I shall kill a young doe and take its liver and heart back to her instead."

"My mother the queen will not get over that anger." You remember how she looked at you the day you returned from St. Winifred's, where you had been at school for seven years, coming home only for holidays. You remember the look in her eyes when she realized her magic had worked too well, that you were, not just as beautiful as your mother, but more beautiful. You could hear the courtiers whispering it—"More beautiful than the queen herself."

Your father said, when he did not know you were listening, "She's as beautiful as Elfrida—more beautiful, because younger. She'll be easy to marry off."

You looked up at the huntsman then, thinking, *Why*

should I run? Let him kill me, let us get this over with. But you decided, perhaps only because it was a sunlit summer day and all the birds were singing in the trees, that you wanted to live. You took the purse, then went up on tiptoes and to his immense surprise, kissed him on the mouth. And then you turned and ran, not down the road, but into the forest.

Years later, after your mother's death and your husband's coronation, you said to the king, "Do you remember the huntsman who spared my life? We should reward him by giving him a position in the castle."

"There is no use for a huntsman in a castle," said King Harald. "But I can make him a gamekeeper in the forest. That is easy enough."

It was not so easy sneaking out of the castle when you were the queen, especially under the watchful eyes of your ladies-in-waiting, but Franziska helped. When you came to the gamekeeper's house for the first time, you knocked gently, then opened the door. You had not seen him in years—now he was twenty-seven, tall and handsome as he stood up, startled and a little frightened at this apparition.

"Your Majesty!" he said, bowing.

Of course he recognized you, even after all these years. Who else has hair black as night, skin white as snow, lips red as blood?

"None of that, if you please," you told him. "I have come for something you owe me."

"And what is that?" he asked, although you thought he already knew—he was looking at you not like a queen, but like a woman. A wave of relief washed over you—you had hoped, had thought, there was something between you, that you had not imagined it all those years ago. Some small bit of the magic we call attraction or even love, but you had been so young, and not at all certain. And now here it was in his eyes, and in his arms as you claimed back your kiss.

After that day, you visited him as often as possible, which was not often, for what you were doing had two names: adultery and treason. But you could not live your entire life behind castle walls, by the side of the king to whom you were only another affirmation of his prominence. After all, he had married the fairest in the land.

One day you told your lover that you could not come anymore. "Henrik, I am with child. I have taken precautions, but such things are not infallible."

"Is it mine?" he asked, with a pained expression. He had never asked you if you still went to the king's bed. He knew that queens have no choice in such a matter.

"It is," you told him. "But it must not be. You understand, do you not, that it must be the king's?"

He had simply nodded. If your child were not the king's, you would be put to death, most likely by decapitation, before it could be born. He knew that as well as you.

After that day, you did not go back to his house in the forest, not once, no matter how your heart and your arms ached during the long nights.

And yet his eyes, as they look at you now, still leaf-green, harbor no resentment.

"Your Majesty," he says.

"Gamekeeper," you say, although you would prefer to address him by his name, but that will come later. "We are riding to the Abbey of St. Winifred. As you see, our retinue is small—myself, my daughter, our maid, and two men-at-arms." He looks up quickly at Dorothea, but her face is hidden by her riding veil. Will he recognize himself in her, when he looks at her later? She has his eyes. "We need a man to tend to our needs—arrange for lodging, water the horses, things of that sort. Can you perform such tasks?"

He smiles. "I serve at your command, My Queen."

"Come then," you say. "We have a spare horse. You shall ride before us, to clear the road through the forest if necessary, or warn of thieves."

You look at Franziska and she gives you a small smile. You know that whatever inn you stop at, she will arrange it so that for the first time in fourteen years, you will spend the night with the man you love.

III. THE COTTAGE

The dwarves greet you as they have always done, each according to his temperament. Trondor shakes his head and says, "So you're back, are you?" but you can see that he's smiling under his beard. Kristof and Olaf embrace you enthusiastically. Anders makes you a courtly bow, Rolf kisses your hand, Nilsen hangs back shyly until you lean down to give him a long hug. But where is Ingar?

"He found himself a wife," says Trondor. "It won't last. It never does."

Once, when you were young, you saw one of the dwarf women. Unlike the sociable dwarf men, they are solitary and live deep in the forest, in small huts or the hollow trunks of trees. This one wore a dress stitched of squirrel skin. She was as small as the men, with long fair hair caught up in various places with twigs. It looked like a bird's nest.

You saw her only for a moment, speaking with Olaf in the ancient language of dwarves, more melodious than human language. Her voice sounded like wind in the pine branches. She gave him a basket of mushrooms in exchange for some honey, then disappeared under the trees. Trondor explained to you that dwarf women seldom ventured out of the forest. Dwarf marriages are short-lived: the dwarf woman chooses a mate, then allows him to live with her for a time, often until she is with child. But she can stand the company of another only for so long. Eventually, the men return to the company of their brothers, for all male dwarves who share a home are considered part of one family, although of the seven you lived with, only Kristof and Olaf had the same mother.

You are glad to see them again, these men who took you in and treated you more kindly than your own parents—the mother who tried to kill you, the father who was concerned only with matters of state and died mysteriously while you were with the dwarves, leaving your mother regent. You have seen them only once since the day the prince found you in the glass coffin and took you away to his castle— they were invited to the wedding. When they came up to the dais on which you were sitting, in your gown of white silk with the necklace of Queen Sofronia around your neck, Trondor said, "What is this fairy story they tell of the prince waking you up with true love's kiss?" You could see Prince Harald across the great hall, speaking with his father, already arranging for the coronation and a transfer of power.

"Is that not what happened?" you asked him. You

yourself had been doubtful of the official version, as you were doubtful of the prince himself. But he would protect you from your mother, who had almost succeeded in killing you with that apple, and whom you suspected of poisoning your father for his throne.

"Of course not," said Trondor in his gruff voice. "After he ordered us to give him the coffin and threatened us if we did not obey, one of the footman who was carrying it stepped into a rabbit hole. A corner of the coffin fell to the ground, and the piece of apple was dislodged from your throat. That's what woke you, child. Kiss of true love indeed! And they call you White-as-Snow, as though you did not have a perfectly good name of your own. Are you happy, Ermengarde?"

"Happy enough," you told him. Of course, that was before your mother appeared at the reception—before the incident of the red-hot iron shoes, which you would rather not think about.

"It's good to see you again, child," says Trondor now. Of course you are not a child any longer, but dwarves live for hundreds of years. To him you are still a mere infant. "We heard of the king's death…"

"Yes," you say. "I'm going back to my father's castle. I have… certain plans. Will you help me, Trondor? You and your brothers? I will need counselors and allies."

"Of course," he says, looking at you through narrowed

eyes. You think he already understands what you intend to do. Even when you were a little girl, he understood you better than anyone else. "Shall I bring my axe, Queen Ermengarde? It has not tasted battle for a long time."

"Yes," you say. "I think that would be a good idea."

IV. THE TOWER

You stop at the Abbey of St. Winifred only briefly, to talk to the Mother Superior.

"Are you absolutely certain about this, Ermengarde?" she asks as she gives you the key to the tower. You gave it to her after the wedding and murder, for what else was it but a murder? At your own wedding, ordered by your husband. At the time, you asked her to keep it for you as long as necessary. You did not know if you would ever reclaim it from her again. But now here you are.

"Yes, I'm absolutely sure," you say. "And will you bless me, Reverend Mother? You were, in a way, the closest thing I had to a real mother..." One who loved you and taught you, for once upon a time the Mother Superior was Sister Margarete, who taught you your catechism and geography in the abbey's long, cold schoolroom.

"Perhaps I was a sort of mother to you," she says, looking

at you as acutely as she did thirty years ago. Age has not diminished her strength of will or mental acuity. "But blood is important too, Ermengarde. Her blood flows through your veins, and I worry about what you will do—"

"Don't worry about me," you say. "I will be absolutely fine."

"I'm sure you will—you were always a clever girl, sometimes too clever for your own good. But what about the rest of us?" Nevertheless, she gives you the key, which is after all yours by right of blood. You are, in the end, your mother's daughter. She blesses you, kissing you on your forehead as though you were fourteen again and not a queen.

Before you leave the abbey, you visit your mother's grave, on which is inscribed only *Elfrida* and the dates of her birth and death. She's been dead for more than twenty years, and you still can't decide how you feel about her.

But her tower, too, is yours now. You lead your retinue to your father's castle, which has not been used except as a hunting lodge since the kingdoms were united after your mother's death. That was another thing the iron shoes accomplished. Did your husband force her to dance in them to revenge the way she treated you, as he said, or so he could claim your father's kingdom? Or perhaps both, for that was the way his mind worked, after all.

Since the castle is empty, there is plenty of room for you, Dorothea, Henrik, six dwarves, two men-at-arms, and of course the indispensable Franziska.

The next day, she and Henrik accompany you to the tower. You have already made him the captain of your men-at-arms, and they obey him without question. You selected them because before the kingdoms were united, they served in your father's household. They are older, so they can be spared from Gerhard's forces, but also they are loyal to you—they still recognize you as their queen.

As for Henrik, he too asked you, lying back on your pillows, one arm around you, one hand stroking your long black hair, for the gray strands do not show by candlelight, "Are you sure, my love, that you want to do this?"

You turned to look at him and said, "Do you think Gerhard would allow me to live the life I want, or our daughter either? If he found out about us, you and I would be condemned to death, and Dorothea would be imprisoned or exiled. And if he did not find out, things would continue as they are. He would want her to marry Prince Ludwig, and he would want me to remain a queen dowager—silent, respectable, so desiccated that eventually I would dry up and blow away like a leaf in autumn. Believe me, my love, if there were another way for the three of us to have a life together, I would take it. However, I am not only Ermengarde, the woman who loves you, but White-as-Snow. Twenty years ago I became the main character in a fairy tale, and it spread throughout the land. If Gerhard announced that I was missing, had perhaps been kidnapped by an equally missing gamekeeper, I would be searched for, watched for, in this kingdom and others. There would be no place for us to hide. So you see, I must use what I have, including the name I was given, the tale that was told about me—I must use these things to write my own story."

He nodded, then pulled you closer and kissed you. Now, he dismounts and takes the horses' reins. Then he waits by the foot of the tower while you open the wooden door with your mother's key, and you and Franziska enter.

The tower is not tall, only two stories of ancient stone with a crenelated turret, surrounded by oak trees. Once, it was used to store weapons, and a couple of men-at-arms would sleep there on folding cots. Inside, the windows are small—arrow slits more than windows. It is darker than you expected.

On the second floor, after you have climbed up the stone staircase that circles the inside of the tower, Franziska raises her lantern.

There are all your mother's magical implements, scattered about as though she had left them just yesterday: the cauldron, the table of alchemical equipment whose purposes you do not yet understand, the shelves of bottles filled with powders and other ingredients—dried eye of newt and toe of frog? Are those the sorts of things witches keep, as housewives keep pickles? The shelves also hold large books in leather covers, presumably filled with formulas and spells.

On the far side of the table is an ornate wooden stand with the mirror whose pronouncements caused so much trouble.

V. THE MIRROR

How does one address a magical mirror?

The problem, of course, is that your mother never taught you witchcraft. Would she have, if her spell had not worked so well? If she had not thought of you as a rival? You would have given up your black hair and white skin and red lips without a second thought, simply for a kind word from her.

"Mirror, mirror, I believe, is how she usually started," says Franziska. She too was chosen for her history with your family as well as her loyalty to you—her mother was your mother's maid, her father drove your father's own carriage.

All right, then. "Mirror, mirror."

The mirror, which reflected you a moment ago, grows misty, as though filled with fog, and then the fog swirls as though blown here and there by a wind inside the mirror itself. Out of that fog comes a voice.

"Well, well. Look who's back. Little White-as-Snow, all

grown up. Welcome to your mother's chamber of secrets and spells, Ermengarde."

Is it a man's voice? A woman's? You cannot quite tell. It is, undeniably, a cynical, sarcastic voice. It sounds bitter.

"Do you, too, want to know who's the fairest in the land?" it asks.

"Not particularly," you say. "I assume it's not me any longer."

"You're right about that," says the mirror. "You've aged out of that particular position. What is it you want, then?"

"I want you to teach me my mother's magic," you say, trying to see something in the swirling smoke. The mirror has no discernable face. "She once called you her familiar. You would know how to use all these books, this equipment." You gesture around at the contents of the tower.

"And why do you want to learn magic?" asks the mirror, as the fog swirls more quickly. "Do you, too, want to kill your daughter?"

"No, to save her," you say. "I want to become queen— not queen consort, not queen dowager, but queen in my own right. That's the only way I will have some measure of power over her life, and mine."

"I see," says the mirror, sounding surprised. Clearly, it has not expected this. "I will teach you if you do two things."

"And what are they?" you ask, wondering if you will

need to sacrifice something, or sign somewhere in blood. You do not relish the thought.

"First, you must pledge yourself to Hecate. That is merely standard procedure. Second, you must allow me to return to my true form."

"Your true form?" You look at the mirror, astonished. "Is this not your true form?" The mirror has been a mirror as long as you have known that your mother was a witch. You remember seeing it on its ornate stand the only time she brought you to this tower, before you were sent away to the Abbey of St. Winifred. She stood you in front of it, showed you your own reflection, and said, "Look, Ermie, at what a pretty girl you are. Someday, you'll look just like me!"

"No," says the mirror. "Your mother ordered me to become a mirror so I could show her whatever she wished to see—chiefly herself. I have been trapped in this form ever since. You are my mistress now. Allow me to return to my true form—simply say the words—and I will teach you."

"All right, then," you say with some trepidation. "Return to your true form." What will you see? A serpent? A dragon? A demon with horns and a forked tail?

The smoke in the mirror swirls faster and faster, until it looks like a gray whirlpool, and suddenly sitting in front of you is not a mirror in a frame but a wolf with fur the color of smoke.

It stares at you with yellow eyes and says, "Thank you, mistress. Shall we begin the first lesson?"

VI. THE CAULDRON

It takes Gerhard longer than you expected to realize that you are not at the Abbey of St. Winifred. When his army comes marching over what used to be the border between two kingdoms, you are ready. You have had three months to learn magic from Grimm, which turns out to be the name of your familiar. You hope you have learned enough.

You stand outside the portcullis of the castle, which is on a hillside. You are dressed all in black, like a widow or a witch. To one side of you stands Henrik beside his horse, ready to lead the charge on your command. He is now the general of a small but dedicated army of your father's men-at-arms, who have returned to serve you, and the sons they have brought with them, as well as some men from the village who wish to defend White-as-Snow against a distant king they do not trust. Your legend has served you well—they are proud to follow a queen out of a fairy tale. The strongest of them are standing, waiting armed and armored, on either side of the hilltop for the command to attack. The rest are in the castle behind the portcullis, waiting at arrow slits and on turrets, crossbows cocked.

On the other side of you is Grimm, who is sometimes a mirror, sometimes an owl, and sometimes a wisp of smoke. Today he is a great gray wolf surveying the landscape before him. Scattered around you are seven dwarves, for Ingar has returned. His wife is with child. He will likely not see it until it is several years old, and then only if it is male, for the dwarf women keep their girl children in the forest. You think this may be a very good system.

Behind you is Dorothea, dressed in black as well. Two months ago, you told her the truth about her father. To your relief, she kissed you on the cheek and said, "I always blamed myself for not being able to love Papa—I mean King Harald. But now I don't think it was my fault. Perhaps in some way, I could always tell he was not really my father." She is stirring the cauldron, which is set over a fire and has started to bubble fiercely. Franziska is adding the necessary ingredients from baskets and glass bottles. You will need to pay attention to the cauldron in a moment, but right now, you are waiting for a parley.

Three men are riding across the field beneath Gerhard's standard. Of course Gerhard would not come himself, but as they ride closer, you see that the one in the middle is Wilhelm, between two men-at-arms. Your younger son is as handsome as always, and you cannot help feeling proud of him, even though he is currently your enemy.

"Hello, Mother," he says when he has dismounted and walked up the hillside toward you. "Hello, Dorothea. It's good to see you again." He waves at his sister. His escorts remain mounted, and behind. "Mother, Gerhard wants you to know that if you surrender now and return with him, all will be forgiven. If you do not, he will take this castle by force." He glances around the top of the hill, and then up at the castle. "I must say, you don't have a lot of men, unless you're hiding some of them where I can't see. The castle is strong, so you could hold on for a while if you have stores, but eventually Gerhard would starve you out if he simply waited long enough. I did learn military strategy at school, you know. That and German poetry, which is considerably less useful except when impressing aristocratic young women. Anyway, I hate to agree with anything Gerhard says—you know what an irritating bore my older brother can be. But I think you'd better surrender. I don't want you or Dorothea to end up in a dungeon."

"Hello, Willi," you say. "You need a haircut. Your hair is falling into your eyes again." You brush it aside affectionately.

"Oh, Mother!" he says, as though exasperated, but he takes your hand and kisses it—son to mother, and to queen. The two of you have always had a good relationship.

"All the arguments you make are sensible ones," you

say. "But there's something Gerhard does not know. You see, I've been practicing witchcraft."

"Have you really?" he asks, a look of interest and admiration in his eyes. "You mean like grandmother?" Then, for the first time, he notices your companions. "Are those dwarves? Are they *the* dwarves, from 'White-as-Snow and the Seven Dwarves'? There are seven of them, aren't there?" He counts. "And is that a wolf?" He looks at Grimm with alarm.

"That is my familiar. You know all witches have one. Sometimes he is a wolf, and sometimes he is something else altogether." You smile at Wilhelm and pat him on the cheek. "Willi, would you like to be king after I defeat Gerhard's army? I will give you his kingdom and keep this one for my own, but you must conclude a treaty with me, on my terms. Which include pledging fealty."

"Of course, Mother," he says, looking down at you with amusement. "But how do you intend to defeat Gerhard? He has a real army, whereas you have a rag-tag collection of old men and young boys dressed in armor. Some of it rather old armor, visibly patched. I take it this is your general." He looks at Henrik. "He at least appears competent and well-armed, but one strong man is not enough."

"Watch," you say, smiling. Then you step back toward the cauldron, which Dorothea has brought to a rolling boil. "Grimm," you say, "are you ready? Trondor?"

The wolf and dwarf both nod. Trondor mounts on the wolf's back and raises his battle axe, which is as large as his head.

"All right, then. Franziska, add the final ingredient." She shakes red powder out of a large box labeled, in ornate calligraphy, *Feoderovsky and Sons Magical Supplies*. Powdered dragon's blood is expensive, even if you order it in bulk, but this is too important for inferior ingredients.

The cauldron bubbles, and a gray smoke rises. You intone the magical words, which are in Latin, of course—it's a good thing you received an excellent classical education at St. Winifred. Franziska and Dorothea fall back as the first wolf rises from the cauldron, gray and gaunt and snarling.

"Olaf," you say, and the dwarf mounts his wolf. Then Nilsen and Anders, Rolf and Ingar, and finally Kristof. They are armed with axes like Trondor's, or battle maces. They are wearing leather armor. There is a fierce light in their eyes, which surprises you—are these the mild, gentle dwarves who took you in and raised you, when your mother was trying to kill you and your father was oblivious to the situation? You could not have had better parents. And yet, there are tales of dwarf warriors in the history books. They are said to be fiercer than eagles.

"Trondor, lead the way," you tell him. He throws back his

head and shouts something in the ancient dwarf language that is no doubt some sort of battle cry. Then Grimm lopes down the hillside and the other wolves follow, with the dwarves mounted on them. Wolves stream out of the cauldron, each with a fierce dwarf warrior on its back. They look like running smoke, through which you can see the glint of weapons in the sunlight. Only the first wolf is real, only the seven dwarves can draw blood—it is mostly illusion, and yet it looks real enough.

"Henrik, it's time," you say. Henrik mounts his horse, then rides to one side of the hilltop and then the other, commanding the men to charge. They move in formation down the hill on either side of the dwarf army, with Henrik and a few mounted men in the rear, the cavalry following the infantry.

Reality and illusion: enchantment held together by force of will, a few magical powders, and words in a dead language. You have only had three months to learn, and you hope to goodness that your plan will succeed. But you have always been clever, as the Mother Superior knows. You have always attended to your lessons. And you are, quite simply, *done*. Done with listening to men who tell you what to do, whether the father who ignored you, or the husband who turned you into a fairy tale, or now a son. You are done with being rescued, done with obedience and gratitude.

Gerhard's forces stand fast for a moment, and then break. You can hear it even from here, his footmen shouting with fear and surprise, stumbling backward from the ghostly wolves and dwarf warriors. They run into the mounted knights behind, who urge them forward until their horses smell wolf and panic under them. Then all of Gerhard's soldiers are retreating, and it is a great chaos of men and magic, a complete rout.

"Well done, Mother," says Wilhelm beside you. "Shall I ride down and deliver the coup de grâce? By which I mean telling Gerhard to surrender. I would not, of course, commit fratricide."

"Yes, I think that would be for the best," you say. "Tell him I'm not going to execute him, just send him into exile."

"Will do," he says, nodding. Then he leaves you on the hillside, alone with Franziska and Dorothea, the cauldron still smoking between you. The three of you, standing there, resemble the three Fates.

"Well done, Your Majesty," says Franziska, whom you intend to make a countess for her service and loyalty. She will have a lady's maid of her own.

"Mother, that was awesome," says Dorothea. "Will you teach me witchcraft?"

"Of course," you say. "After all, you will be the queen of this kingdom after me. It's much easier to be a queen when you're also a witch."

VII. THE APPLE

"Is that right?" asks Dorothea. She holds up the apple, which is red on one side and white on the other.

"Quite right," you say. "Now, can you make the red side *not* poisonous? It's much more important knowing how not to be poisoned than knowing how to poison people. And harder."

"That was your mother's spell, wasn't it?" says Dorothea. She intones a few words in Latin while passing her hands over a bowl of red liquid that turns milky white, then dips the apple back into it. Her Latin is coming along well, as is her knowledge of various potions and their ingredients. You are proud of the fact that she is as good a student as you were.

Grimm, who is lying at her feet in wolf form, whimpers softly in his dreams. A few days ago you asked him, out of curiosity, "Who is the fairest, anyway? The fairest in the land?"

"At the moment? Anthea, the blacksmith's daughter in Mallor, a village high on the slopes of Mount Gotteringen.

She is admired intensely by the goats she's herding. But last week she had the flu, so the fairest was Sister Maria-Josef, cloistered at the nunnery of Saint Edelweis in the port city of South Fardo. You were the fairest for a very long time, if that's any consolation. Usually it changes at least once a month."

You and Dorothea are both in the tower for her daily magic lesson. A week ago you married your true love and were crowned queen. Henrik is now your prince consort. You are no longer dressed in black, but in crimson velvet edged with ermine, which is suitable for a queen as well as a witch. Wilhelm has pledged fealty to you and is establishing his rule over your late husband's kingdom. Gerhard is in Hohenstein, plotting an invasion with Prince Ludwig, but Ludwig's father, King Frederik IV, also known as the Rotund, is not at all sure that war with a neighboring kingdom is in his best interests and has so far refused them funding. If Gerhard does manage to raise an army, it will take a while, and by then you will have something even more effective to greet him with than wolves made of smoke. The dwarves have decided to stay with you in the castle, and you are glad to have your seven fathers with you, to counsel and advise. This is the closest you've ever come to having a family.

"Yes, that was her spell," you say. "Her third and final

spell. The one that killed me, at least for a while. And now you know the antidote."

Dorothea looks down at the apple for a moment, then says, "Mama, why did you keep letting the peddler woman in? Rolf says they warned you, over and over again, not to let anyone in at all."

"They did," you say. "But you see, she was my mother. Oh, I know she was in disguise, but a child could have seen through that trick. I mean, what sort of peddler woman tries to sell stay laces in the middle of a forest? Who does she expect to sell them to? No, I knew who she was the moment I saw her. I let her in because she was my mother. I had not seen her in so long... And I wanted her to lace me up, to comb my hair. I knew there was something wrong with that apple, but the dwarves had saved me twice already. Why not a third time? And I wanted to share it with her, to take a bite right next to the one she had taken. When I woke up in the glass coffin, I realized that I could have died, truly died that time. I married Prince Harald because I thought he could keep me safe. She wouldn't try to kill the queen of a neighboring kingdom, would she? But then Harald invited her to the wedding and had iron shoes heated on a fire... I still remember her screams. I never forgave him for that."

You are silent for a while. The only sounds in the tower

are Grimm, who is evidently chasing a dream rabbit, and Dorothea munching her apple while she pages through a leather-bound volume of magical botany.

"I'm glad you're not that sort of mother," she says, looking up at you from a page on Agrimony. "When I grow up, I want to be just like you, Mama."

She won't be, of course. She won't have a father who ignores her or a mother who tries to poison her, because Henrik is positively doting and you are not that sort of mother, as Dorothea said. But she won't have a cottage of dwarves to raise her either, although you hope Trondor and the others will teach her some of the things they taught you, about the forest, and kindness, and home. You sincerely hope she won't have a prince to rescue her, because princes are not to be trusted and their services come at a high price. You will teach her to rescue herself, and you hope she will be better, smarter, stronger than you were.

You smile at her across the table, with its bowls of potion, its magical powders, its leather-bound books. Your beautiful, talented Dorothea. This is how you became a witch-queen. She will have to find her own path, as you are certain she shall.

ABOUT THE AUTHORS

Born in Ciechanow, Poland, **ANIA AHLBORN** has always been drawn to the darker, mysterious, and morbid side of life. Her earliest childhood memory is of crawling through a hole in the chain link fence that separated her family home from the large wooded cemetery. She'd spend hours among the headstones, breaking up bouquets of silk flowers so that everyone had their equal share. Ania's first novel, *Seed*, was self-published. It clawed its way up the Amazon charts to the #1 horror spot, earning her a multi-book deal and a key to the kingdom of the macabre. Eight years later, her work has been lauded by the likes of *Publishers Weekly*, *New York Daily News*, and the *New York Times*. She hopes to one day be invited to dinner at Stephen King's place, where she will immediately be crushed beneath the weight of her imposter syndrome.

KELLEY ARMSTRONG is the author of the Rockton crime thrillers. Past works include the Otherworld urban fantasy series, the Cainsville paranormal mystery series, the Darkest Powers & Darkness Rising teen paranormal trilogies, the Age of Legends fantasy YA series and the Nadia Stafford crime trilogy. Armstrong lives in Ontario, Canada with her family.

*

As an actor, **AMBER BENSON** is best known for her role as Tara Maclay on the hit television show *Buffy The Vampire Slayer*. But since then she has become a notable novelist/director/screenwriter. She co-created and directed the animated supernatural web series *Ghosts of Albion* for the BBC (with Christopher Golden) and co-directed the independent feature *Drones*. She is also the author of the bestselling Calliope Reaper-Jones series of novels and the Witches of Echo Park trilogy for Penguin.

*

CHESYA BURKE is a doctoral candidate in the English department at the University of Florida. She received her Master's degree in African American Studies from Georgia State University in 2015. Currently, Chesya is a double fellow, and she teaches such topics as Black Women Spec Fic Writers, The Racial Dynamics of Nationality Politics and The Literature of Resistance: From Nat Turner to Black Panther. In addition, Burke wrote several articles for the *African American National Biography* published by Harvard and Oxford University Press. Burke is an award-winning writer, who has published nearly a hundred stories and articles, leading Grammy-nominated spoken word artist and poet Nikki Giovanni to call her work "stunning." Her story collection, *Let's Play White*, is being taught in universities around the country and her novel, *The Strange Crimes of Little Africa*, debuted in Dec 2015 to great reviews. She edited the Locus nominated anthology, *Hidden Youth*, with Mikki Kendall, and Samuel Delany called her "a formidable new master of the macabre."

*

RACHEL CAINE is the #1 bestselling author of more than fifty books, including the Morganville Vampires series, the Great Library series, the Honors series in YA; she's also

known for the urban fantasy Weather Warden series, and the Stillhouse Lake thriller series on the adult shelves. She's published in thirty languages around the world, and lives in Fort Worth, Texas with her husband, artists and golden-age comic dealer/historian R. Cat Conrad.
Website: rachelcaine.com

＊

KRISTIN DEARBORN has been writing since before she could hold a pen, dictating stories to her mother. Thanks to nefarious influences like *Scooby Doo* and *Bunnicula*, her tastes turned to the macabre at an early age. A graduate of Seton Hill's Writing Popular Fiction MFA program, Kristin works in finance during the day, and plays with monsters at night. When she's not reading or writing, you can find her riding her Harley, rock climbing, or striving to summit the New England high peaks, no matter what the season. Kristin is the author of *Stolen Away, Sacrifice Island, Trinity, Whispers*, and *Woman in White*.

＊

TANANARIVE DUE is an author, screenwriter and educator who is a leading voice in black speculative fiction. Her short fiction has appeared in best-of-the-year anthologies of science fiction and fantasy. She is the former Distinguished Visiting Lecturer at Spelman College (2012-2014) and teaches Afrofuturism and Black Horror in the Department of African-American Studies at UCLA. She also teaches in the creative writing MFA program at Antioch University Los Angeles and the screenwriting program at Antioch University Santa Barbara. Due is an executive producer of the Shudder black horror documentary *Horror Noire*.

The American Book Award-winner and NAACP Image Award recipient is the author or co-author of twelve novels. In 2010, Due was inducted into the Medill School of Journalism's Hall of Achievement at Northwestern University. She also received a Lifetime Achievement Award in the Fine Arts from the Congressional Black Caucus Foundation. Her short-story collection, *Ghost Summer*, won a 2016 British Fantasy Award. She has been named to the Grio 100 and the Ebony Power 100.

Due also co-authored a civil rights memoir with her late mother, Patricia Stephens Due, *Freedom in the Family: a Mother-Daughter Memoir of the Fight for Civil Rights*. (Patricia Stephens Due took part in the nation's first "Jail-In" in 1960, spending 49 days in jail in Tallahassee, Florida, after a sit-in at a Woolworth lunch counter.) *Freedom in the Family* was named 2003's Best Civil Rights Memoir by *Black Issues Book Review*. Her parents, including her father, attorney John Due, were recently inducted into the Florida Civil Rights Hall of Fame.

✳

THEODORA GOSS is the World Fantasy and Locus Award-winning author of the short-story and poetry collections *In the Forest of Forgetting* (2006), *Songs for Ophelia* (2014), and *Snow White Learns Witchcraft* (2019), as well as novella *The Thorn and the Blossom* (2012), debut novel *The Strange Case of the Alchemist's Daughter* (2017), and sequel *European Travel for the Monstrous Gentlewoman* (2018). She has been a finalist for the Nebula, Crawford, Seiun, and Mythopoeic Awards, as well as on the Tiptree Award Honor List. Her work has been translated into twelve languages. She teaches literature and writing at Boston University and in the Stonecoast MFA Program. Visit her at theodoragoss.com

✳

KAT HOWARD is the author of the novels *Roses and Rot* and the Alex Award-winning *An Unkindness of Magicians*. Her short-fiction collection, *A Cathedral of Myth and*

Bone, is now out from Saga Press and she's writing *The Books of Magic* for Vertigo Comics. Her novella, *The End of the Sentence,* co-written with Maria Dahvana Headley, was an NPR Best Book of the Year in 2014. She currently lives in New Hampshire, where she is working on her next projects.

ALMA KATSU writes historical fiction with elements of horror and the supernatural. *The Hunger* (Putnam) was named a Best Book of 2018 by Barnes & Noble, Powells, and *The Observer*; one of NPR's 100 Favorite Horror Stories; is a nominee for the Bram Stoker Award for Best Novel; and won the 2018 Western Heritage Award for Best Novel. Her first book, *The Taker,* was one of Booklist's Top Ten Debut Novels of 2011.

✳

Defying all odds is what #1 *New York Times* and international bestselling author **SHERRILYN KENYON** does best. Rising from extreme poverty as a child that culminated in being a homeless mother with an infant, she has become one of the most popular and influential authors in the world (in both adult and young adult fiction), with dedicated legions of fans known as

Menyons–thousands of whom proudly sport tattoos from her numerous genre-defying series. Since her first book debuted in 1993, while she was still in college, she has placed more than eighty novels on the *New York Times* list in all formats and genres, including manga and graphic novels, and has more than seventy million books in print worldwide. Her current series include: Dark-Hunters®, Chronicles of Nick®, Deadman's Cross™, Black Hat Society™, Nevermore™, Silent Swans™, Lords of Avalon® and The League®.

Join her and her Menyons online at QueenofAllShadows. com and www.facebook.com/mysherrilyn

*

Intense gamer, former teacher and current mastermind of all around mayhem, **MADAUG KENYON** first started writing in grade school, on his mother's walls. Deciding that near death experiences weren't exactly his forte, he traded his crayons for a computer, and once he broke away from his severe gaming addiction, realized that his keyboard could also be used to create his own worlds. He's been doing that ever since. The author of his own online intergalactic comic, *Space Sovereign*, he's currently at work finishing his second novel.

＊

SARAH LANGAN is the author of three novels and dozens of short stories. Her novel *Audrey's Door* is under option with Octavia Spencer for adaptation, and her most recent story, "Night Nurse" is under option with Paramount. She's just finished a new novel, *Good Neighbors*, which she hopes her agent soon sells for truckloads of money. She lives in Los Angeles with her husband, the filmmaker JT Petty, and two daughters.

＊

HELEN MARSHALL is a Senior Lecturer of Creative Writing at the University of Queensland. Her first collection of fiction, *Hair Side, Flesh Side*, which won the Sydney J Bounds Award in 2013, emerged from her work as a book historian. Rather than taking the long view of history, her second collection, *Gifts for the One Who Comes After*, negotiated very personal issues of legacy and tradition, creating myth-infused worlds, and won the World Fantasy Award and the Shirley Jackson Award in 2015. Her debut novel *The Migration* was released by Random House Canada and Titan in 2019.

*

JENNIFER MCMAHON is the *New York Times* bestselling author of nine suspense novels, including *Promise Not to Tell, The Winter People,* and *The Invited.* She lives in Vermont with her partner, Drea, and their daughter, Zella.

*

HILLARY MONAHAN is the *New York Times* bestselling author of *Mary: The Summoning* and, under the Eva Darrows name, the critically acclaimed *The Awesome* and *Belly Up.* Hillary writes everything from horror and comedy to SFF and romance, for young adult and adult audiences alike. 2020 sees her twelfth novel in print.

*

MARY SANGIOVANNI is an award-winning American horror and thriller writer of over a dozen books, including *The Hollower* trilogy, *Thrall,* the Kathy Ryan series, and others, as well as numerous short stories and non-fiction. Her work has been translated internationally. She has a Master's degree in Writing Popular Fiction from Seton Hill University, Pittsburgh, and is currently a member of The

Authors Guild, The International Thriller Writers, and Penn Writers. She is a co-host on the popular podcast *The Horror Show with Brian Keene*, and hosts her own podcast on cosmic horror, *Cosmic Shenanigans*. She has the distinction of being one of the first women to speak about writing at the CIA headquarters in Langley, VA, and offers talks and workshops on writing around the country. Born and raised in New Jersey, she currently resides in Pennsylvania.

＊

ANGELA SLATTER is the author of the Verity Fassbinder supernatural crime series (*Vigil, Corpselight* and *Restoration*) as well as eight short-story collections, including *The Bitterwood Bible and Other Recountings* and *A Feast of Sorrows: Stories*. She has an MA and a PhD in Creative Writing. She's won a World Fantasy Award, a British Fantasy Award, a Ditmar Award, an Australian Shadows Award and six Aurealis Awards; her debut novel was nominated for the Dublin Literary Award. Her work has been translated into French, Chinese, Spanish, Japanese, Russian, and Bulgarian. Her novelette "Finnegan's Field" has been optioned for film.

ABOUT THE EDITORS

RACHEL AUTUMN DEERING is a multi award-nominated writer, editor, and book designer from the hills of Appalachia. She cut her teeth in the entertainment industry, writing for DC/Vertigo, Dark Horse, IDW, Blizzard Entertainment, Cartoon Network and more before entering the world of literary fiction with her debut novella, *Husk*. Her work, a genre-bending style that walks the line between noir, southern gothic, and vintage horror, has been described by peers and critics as "lyrical" and "heartbreaking." Deering is a rock and roll witch with a heart of slime.

CHRISTOPHER GOLDEN is the *New York Times* bestselling, Bram Stoker Award-winning author of such novels as *The*

Pandora Room, *Ararat*, *Snowblind*, and *Wildwood Road*. With Mike Mignola, he is the co-creator of two cult favorite comic book series, *Baltimore* and *Joe Golem: Occult Detective*. As an editor, his other short-story anthologies include *Seize the Night*, *Dark Cities*, and *The New Dead*, among others, and he has also written and co-written comic books, video games, and screenplays. In 2015 he founded the popular Merrimack Valley Halloween Book Festival. He was born and raised in Massachusetts, where he still lives with his family. His work has been nominated for the British Fantasy Award, the Eisner Award, and multiple Shirley Jackson Awards. For the Bram Stoker Awards, Golden has been nominated eight times in eight different categories. His original novels have been published in more than fifteen languages in countries around the world.

Please visit him at www.christophergolden.com

✳